William Gammell

William Gammell, LL. D.

A biographical sketch, with selections from his writings

William Gammell

William Gammell, LL. D.
A biographical sketch, with selections from his writings

ISBN/EAN: 9783337011659

Printed in Europe, USA, Canada, Australia, Japan

Cover: Foto ©Raphael Reischuk / pixelio.de

More available books at **www.hansebooks.com**

WILLIAM GAMMELL, LL.D.

A BIOGRAPHICAL SKETCH

WITH

SELECTIONS FROM HIS WRITINGS

EDITED BY

JAMES O. MURRAY, D.D., LL.D.

DEAN AND PROFESSOR OF ENGLISH LITERATURE IN PRINCETON COLLEGE

CAMBRIDGE

𝔓rinted at the 𝔑iverside 𝔓ress

1890

"*If love lives through all life; and survives through all sorrow; and remains steadfast with us through all changes; and in all darkness of spirit burns brightly; and, if we die, deplores us forever, and loves still equally; and exists with the very last gasp and throb of the faithful bosom whence it passes with the pure soul, beyond death; surely it shall be immortal! Though we who remain are separated from it, is it not ours in Heaven? If we love those we lose, can we altogether lose those we love?*" — THACKERAY.

CONTENTS

WILLIAM GAMMELL.

THE aim of this memorial volume is to preserve
for the pupils and friends of its subject some permanent record of an accomplished Christian scholar.
The scholarship which characterized and controlled
his career was not that of a recluse, apart from the
world, breathing only the "still air of delightful
studies." It recognized the claims of society on the
student, mingled freely with men, and, while drawing its life largely from books, brought that life to
bear on the welfare of the community at many different points and for more than fifty years. It was
eminently an academic life, yet it kept a steady and
observant eye on the course of human affairs, and,
after completing a long and distinguished service
in high academic positions, entered on a closing
period of general but no less efficient usefulness.
Though no striking incidents are to be narrated in
the biographical sketch, yet the absence of these is
more than compensated by the presence of noble
endeavors that

> . . . "Wrought
> All kind of service with a noble ease
> That graced the lowliest act in doing it."

The world is now grown too wise not to recognize

the sphere and the worth of such lives. Men of high endowments and contemplative habits, who use their scholarly attainments for good ends, either of education or of practical beneficence, are sure not only of a kindly but a long remembrance. The work of the teacher has assumed the greater importance as our civilization has grown more advanced and complex. Higher education is in the forefront of the best thought and work to-day, and the teacher who has given his life to its promotion may be sure that a circle far wider than that of kindred and friends stands ready to accord a just and also a grateful estimate of the ended toils, of the aspirations which have passed into achievement, of the influence which survives when memory has become dim or fragmentary.

William Gammell was the son of the Rev. William and Mary (Slocomb) Gammell, and was born in Medfield, Mass., February 10, 1812. His grandparents, John and Margaret (Uran) Gammell, were of English descent, natives of Boston, Mass., and members of the Federal Street Congregational Church. John Gammell was an ardent patriot, early devoted to the cause of American independence, and as one of the "Boston Tea Party" aided in the destruction of tea in Boston Harbor, 1773. His son, who seems early in life to have embraced Baptist tenets, was educated for the ministry. His theological training was pursued under the Rev. William Williams, of Wrentham, Mass., a somewhat noted teacher of theology in days when there were

no theological seminaries; when the "schools of
the prophets" gathered in the study of a clergyman
learned in the sacred tongues and in divinity. After
spending some time under the care of Mr. Williams,
William Gammell, the father of Professor Gammell,
was ordained to the Christian ministry in 1809, and
for a time preached to the Baptist congregation in
Bellingham, Mass. In 1810 he became the settled
pastor of the Baptist Church in Medfield, preaching
on alternate Sundays in Medfield and West Dedham,
Mass., having the pastoral care of both churches.
Here (Medfield) Professor Gammell was born, and
here his early boyhood was passed. In this double
pastorate his father labored till 1823, when he removed to Newport, R. I., and became pastor of the
Second Baptist Church. All accounts agree in
representing him as a man of decided mark. He
had rare gifts as a preacher, a commanding presence, a voice of unusual flexibility and power, an
eloquent manner. His discourses were always well
wrought and impressive, so that he soon rose to
eminence in his denomination. In 1817 he was
given the honorary degree of A. M. by the Corporation of Brown University, and was subsequently,
in 1820, chosen a member of that body, as a trustee. Independent in forming his judgments, he was
fearless in avowing them. He had an aristocratic
bearing, long remembered in the scenes of his early
ministry, which, however, did not prevent his gaining
a strong hold upon the hearts of his parishioners.
Besides his parish labors he interested himself in

matters of education, was engaged in the movement to establish the first public school in Newport, and was also a frequent contributor on topics of public interest to both secular and religious journals of the day.

For four years he remained the pastor of the Second Baptist Church in Newport, and died suddenly of an apoplexy, May 30, 1827. From the Newport "Mercury" of June 2 we learn that "the funeral services were attended on the afternoon of June 1, at the Second Baptist Church, when an impressive and discriminating discourse was delivered by the Rev. President Wayland, of Brown University."

It is evident that Professor Gammell inherited many of his qualities and tastes from his father, whom he resembled in person and in bearing. The interest in all public affairs, which in later life characterized him so strongly, had been stimulated and educated by the habit of conversation with his father on public questions. The independence with which he formed his opinions and the courage with which he maintained them were inherited gifts. From a very early period all his tastes were scholarly. His love of books, his fondness for study, rendered him indifferent to sports in which boyhood generally delights. It was a foregone conclusion that he should be liberally educated. He was prepared for college at the classical school in Newport, then under the care of the Hon. Joseph Joslin and Mr. John Frazer, and was entered at Brown University, a member of the Freshman class, in September,

1827. It is said that, while attending the funeral of his father, President Wayland noticed him, a young lad sitting in the pew beside his widowed mother. After the service was over, and as he passed down the aisle, Dr. Wayland put his hand on his head, saying, " My son, you shall never want a friend while I live." The years that followed Professor Gammell's entrance at college furnish abundant proof that the promise was never forgotten, and its fulfillment was indeed repaid by life-long gratitude and devotion on the part of Professor Gammell.

His record as a student in the four years' course of study is that of an uncommonly faithful and earnest scholar, making the most of his opportunities, and winning the respect of his instructors as well as of his fellow-students. One of his class-mates, the Hon. Francis W. Bird, between whom and Professor Gammell, though differing very widely in their pursuits and mental habits, the relations of a college friendship were cordially maintained to the last, says of him that "he was a close student, quiet, unassuming, 'walking his round of duty' serenely day by day." Among his college friends, none stood nearer to him than Mr. John M. Mackie, now of Great Barrington, Mass., and the late Professor Chace. The friendship between Professors Chace and Gammell was an ideal one, interrupted only by the death of the former, after fifty-eight years of unbroken, almost daily communion. The letter of Mr. Mackie, of the class of 1832, subjoined, gives an interesting view of the student-life and accomplishments of Professor Gammell : —

GREAT BARRINGTON, MASS., *February* 12, 1890.

In reply to your request for my recollections of William Gammell in college, I can say in a word that I remember him as a model student. He appeared to have come to college for the sole purpose of getting an education, and he made the most of his privileges. As scholar he was so *totus, teres atque rotundus* that it is difficult to lay hold of any specially salient points of description, — all being evenly and well developed. Like an athlete oiled, he was hard to be tripped up or taken at fault. He was scrupulously faithful in the performance of all collegiate tasks and duties ; always punctual, always ready, always did his best. Ambitious of success and rank in scholarship, he rarely tripped, and never failed.

I remember that, having resolved to perfect himself in extemporaneous declamation, he made it a rule never to allow any opportunity of speaking in the debating society, of which he was a member, to pass unimproved. His speeches, never too lengthy, and apparently not unduly labored, were uniformly interesting and effective. They held closely to the point in debate, were weighted with good sense, and were adorned with a chaste flow of rhetoric which never degenerated into youthful rant nor bombast. Indeed, his early style of speaking and of writing was characterized by the same clearness of insight and purity of ornament, the same self-restraining fervor, the same choice selection of words and classical allusions, which afterwards threw so graceful a charm of fitness and propriety over all the compositions of his pen.

Gammell in college was emphatically a worker. He was a steady, well-regulated worker, — not putting off the stated labor of one hour to the next, not trusting to the chances of sudden inspiration, not putting his powers to an unnatural strain at the home-stretch of the heat. It was by a steady pace that he reached first the goal. Curbing the sallies of youthful imagination and sentiment, he kept all the faculties of his mind well in hand, and made them coöperate harmoniously in the tasks to be accomplished. He kept regular hours; for relaxation took daily walks in the country lying between the two fair rivers that now embrace the city of Providence; was not devoted particularly to games of any kind, but preferred the pleasures of conversation with cheerful and intelligent companions. He was himself always cheerful and freely communicative, — a genial comrade, a sensible counselor in time of need, a friend so fast and faithful that most of the intimacies contracted by him before graduation were subsequently kept up by correspondence, and lasted to life's end.

It is a pleasure to keep in memory a college associate of a character so built up throughout of seasoned timber, not a false-hearted stick in it, and which completely fulfilled the requirement of Cicero, that a young man should have in him something of mature manhood, as old age also should retain something of youth.

JOHN MILTON MACKIE.

Professor Gammell was graduated from the college, September, 1831, with the first honors of the class, and was assigned the valedictory oration. The theme on which he spoke at Commencement was "The Cause of a Diseased Imagination."

Immediately after his graduation, he sought and obtained employment as a teacher. No calling in life seems to have been specially before him during his college career. It is evident, however, that

from the first the vocation of the teacher attracted
him. He always reverenced this calling. It held,
in his view, equal rank with what are called the
learned professions. He had been inspired by President Wayland with such views, and turned to it
naturally therefore, when at graduation, he was
thrown upon his own resources. He accepted the
position of principal in the Academy at South
Kingston, R. I. The eye of President Wayland
was upon him, and he was called, in 1832, to a
tutorship in Brown University. The catalogue of
1834 styles him "Tutor and Lecturer in the Latin
Language and Literature." It seems evident from
this that he sought to make his classical teaching
something more than a mere grammatical drill. No
report of what his lectures were survives ; but it is
quite safe to infer, from what he was in other departments, that he sought to unfold the literary
power of Latin authors read in his classes. Professor Gammell had a stronger bent than that for
classical study in the direction of the English language and its literature. That he was successful in
his tutorship is evident from the fact that it led to
his subsequent advancement upon lines more congenial to his tastes. In 1835 he was promoted to
the Assistant Professorship of Belles-Lettres. This
chair of oratory and belles-lettres had been filled
by very distinguished men. The Hon. Tristam
Burges, LL. D., whose eloquence in Congress made
even John Randolph of Roanoke sometimes quail,
had held the chair from 1815 to 1828. Then

Professor William G. Goddard, formerly Professor of Philosophy and Metaphysics, became its incumbent in 1834, — holding it till 1842. His high literary abilities, his finished style, his large knowledge of literature, his unerring literary tastes, were the admiration of Professor Gammell. More than any other man, Professor Goddard may be said to have moulded Professor Gammell's literary culture. Through life he was wont to refer to Professor Goddard as the model of what a literary man should be. With him he was associated as Assistant Professor of Belles-Lettres in 1835. In 1837 he was made Professor of Rhetoric, and on him thenceforward, owing to Professor Goddard's feeble health, devolved the chief labor of this department.

Five years had now elapsed since he had entered on his work as tutor in the University. Academic life was for him the ideal life. It drew out his best powers. These were years of hard labor and of gratifying successes. Along with his associates, Professors Caswell and Chace, he was giving his best efforts not only to make his own department of instruction successful, but to build up the college on the lines of development marked out by Dr. Wayland. The following letter to Professor Chace, then absent on scientific explorations for the college, gives us a glimpse into his life, and discloses also the friendship which had been cemented between them. Both, it may be premised, were then occupying rooms in University Hall.

PROVIDENCE, *July* 13, 1836.

MY DEAR PROFESSOR, — We have at length reached
the middle of the last week of the term. It has gone
like a dream. I expected a long and lingering summer
term, but never since I have lived here have the hours of
study flown on so rapid wings as this season.

You have been away among new scenes and unaccus-
tomed companions, and I doubt not days have sometimes
rolled heavily; but with us all, who have been at home,
I believe the summer has been uncommonly short. We
were conscious of its beginning, and now know that it is
closing, and this seems to us to be nearly its entire history.
I have become accustomed to the loneliness which for a
few days after you left us seemed so strange and oppressive, and have learned rather to exult in the undivided
empire of this old hall, for after nine in the evening I am
"monarch of all I survey," with no rival prince to set
limits to my authority; and though I have often had my
royal authority less respected than it deserved to be, yet
I owe it to myself to say that I have swayed the sceptre
with great mercy and forbearance. . . . We are to have
the Junior exhibition next Saturday, and I am now in the
midst of rehearsals and all the various preparations for
the occasion. The speakers are selected from the first
half of the Junior class, — eleven in number. What will
be the character of the performance I hardly dare venture
to predict. You know it is the first appearance of my
Rhetoric; and were I to exhibit it myself, I verily believe
I should care less than I do now in prospect of the approaching Saturday. The arrangements for Commencement are all made, the honors assigned, and the class
dismissed and gone. It is thought we are to have an
uncommonly good Commencement. The conscientiousness
that so distrusted us last year has, I believe, wholly died
away, and the class seemed to feel somewhat as classes

were wont to feel in olden time, before the modern improvements in the moral sense had become so common. Eight of the Seniors have been elected and initiated into the Phi Beta Kappa, and five of the Junior class; among them is your fellow-townsman, Harris. We are going for the future to have an undergraduate organization. The society have been again unable to procure an orator from abroad, and Professor Goddard has kindly consented, as he says, " to stand in the gap." But seven of the Seniors, I ought to have said, have been initiated; the eighth is with you.

. . . Your room has been the greater part of the time the dwelling-place of silence, — sometimes, though seldom, sharing her domain for a few hours in the day with Professor Goddard. The moonlight and the sunlight, though often flying to the closed blinds, have rarely been permitted to enter. Silence has made it her chosen home, and has reigned almost unmolested throughout all your apartments.

The only occasion which is at all prominent in the future before our Commencement is the approaching celebration of the two hundredth anniversary of this city's settlement. It will occur on the 5th of August, and be filled with the best ceremonies and the most impressive pageantry our ancient city can furnish. Judge Pitman is to be the orator. We may expect the whole story of Rhode Island history. Though the oration will hardly be eloquent, it doubtless will be interesting and patriotic, and I hope calculated to wake the almost sleeping attachments and pride that ought to swell and be ever active in the bosom of every citizen of a State whose origin and history have been so illustrious. . . .

Farewell, my dear Professor. I hope you will have gathered before you get home not only stones enough for all the purposes of your science, but the materials for a good long epic poem, which may be rehearsed through the long evenings of next winter.   Faculty are all well.

Yours truly,   W. G.

Mr. George I. Chace,
   Niagara Falls.

Professor Gammell's success as a teacher in the college was gained early.   In three years after assuming the duties of his Professorship of Belles-Lettres, he had made his reputation as a finished and well-read English scholar, and also as an efficient and esteemed professor.   He was also a favorite in the social circle which then gathered round the college. Life was opening brightly before him.

In October, 1838, he was married to Elizabeth Amory, daughter of the Hon. John Whipple.   The union was but for one short year.   Her death, November 25, 1839, followed quickly by that of their little child, plunged him into a grief which for a time seriously threatened his health.   He was sinking into what seemed a settled gloom under the pressure of his bereavement, when his friends insisted upon change of scene with relaxation from incessant work, and readily secured for him six months' leave of absence from college duties.   He was offered the post of private secretary to Commodore Morris, a friend of the family, who at that time was expecting to be sent to the Mediterranean.   The letter informing him of the appointment bears date of June 1, 1841, and he was directed, in case of acceptance, to report at once at Washington.   He accepted the appointment in the expectation of the voyage to the Mediterranean. For some reason, however, the original plan was not carried out. In the autumn Commodore Morris was ordered to Brazil. Professor Gammell, not caring to take the latter voyage, resigned his appointment, and returned to his college duties. For several months, probably from June to October, he was on the vessel with Commodore Morris, and served him as private secretary. They were, indeed, months full of interest to him. He was fond of dwelling on the new experiences of life they gave him. He saw much of Washington society, and though deeply regretting the change of destination for the ship of Commodore Morris which frustrated his plans of travel, always remembered this episode in his life with keen enjoyment.

He took up at once his round of college work, and continued his teaching in the chair of rhetoric. In the catalogue of 1843, the course of study in the Junior year mentions also instruction in modern history, during the third term, by him. At what time these new duties were added is not precisely known. Probably they had not been assigned him at any earlier date. President Wayland was always ready to welcome expansion of the curriculum along lines of modern thought. Whoever proposed the new department, we may be sure it had Dr. Wayland's earnest sanction, and was an inviting field of labor to Professor Gammell. His early tastes were strongly historical. They had been carefully nurtured by his father. They had been indulged and cultivated by himself along with his collegiate and professional work. Admirable as were his rhetorical teachings, it is a question whether from the beginning his aptitudes were not for historical studies as much as for belles-lettres. His fondness for them grew stronger and stronger to the end. Of what he accomplished in this department, while it was still incidental to his main work, President Angell, of Michigan University, and Dr. Fisher, of Yale University, speak in their letters published in this Memorial. The chair of rhetoric, for fifteen years, from 1835 to 1850, absorbed most of his time and strength. His duties were manifold and exacting. They demanded from him instruction in the principles of rhetoric and logic, Campbell and Whately being used as text-books. They began with the Sophomore class, and did not end till the Commencement oration was written and fully rehearsed. Added thus to the work of the class-room, was the supervision of all the writing of the college. This began in the Sophomore and extended through the Senior year. Essays were required from the three upper classes at frequent intervals. Beside these, orations from Juniors and Seniors were submitted to his inspection and delivered before him. In the class-room, his prompt, incisive manner kept the class closely attentive. He was always dignified, but courteous, and his somewhat formal manner had no trace of pedantry about it. He brought to the chair of belles-lettres a large acquaintance with the best English writers. Mere "curiosities of literature," writers of the second rank, had little interest for him. He had been brought up in the school of Addisonian English. He taught his classes in the spirit of that school. That it may have tended somewhat too strongly in the direction of the coldly elegant, and have developed too little flexibility and naturalness of expression, may be true. But it is safe to say that a school of rhetorical training which inculcates reverence for pure, racy English idioms, for high and just literary taste, which abhors coarseness and vulgarity in style, which discriminates between roughness mistaken for strength and the real strength of simplicity and purity, has not much to lament by way of deficiency, and has much to praise by way of attainment. As a critic of college writing, he was altogether admirable. He was ever ready to praise good work. None knew better than himself that the true critic is first appreciative, and then corrective. He was quick to detect faults of idiom. He could not endure flashy nor meretricious ornament. Above all, he disliked obscurity, fustian, and affectation of every sort. Minor as well as major blemishes were carefully noted. Nothing seemed to escape that vigilant, penetrating eye. He was kindly in his criticisms. Only when a student was restive and disposed to defend his blunders was he at all severe. The sting of these criticisms lay in their accuracy and justice. He could be sharp on occasion. His favorite students felt the knife, as it pruned away some of the darlings of their hearts in a mixed figure or overstrained expression. But it is his high praise that he moulded the writing of the college after high ideals. He impressed himself on his students to a degree reached by few professors of rhetoric.

In his day the modern professor of elocution was unknown in most of our colleges. What training the students of Brown University got in this line from 1835 to 1850, they obtained from Professor Gammell. He never pretended to play the orator himself. He believed in certain cardinal principles of good speaking, clear enunciation, sparing but appropriate gesticulation, and an earnestness strictly proportionate to the style of thought presented. His training, therefore, was mainly the correction of glaring faults of manner or intonation. His patience here seemed untiring. It was the training of common sense, aiming at no niceties of oratorical effect. His labors in preparing the students for Junior and Senior exhibitions and for the Commencement exercises were unremitting. Nothing slipshod ever passed his scrutiny. If the speech was not well planned, if it was lacking in careful finish, if the subject needed different treatment, it must be rewritten, and sometimes he insisted on this to a third revision. But his pupils generally had the good sense to remember that if this involved labor on their part, so it did on his. They bowed to his decision, and went back to their work with the conviction that not a captious but a discerning criticism was working in their interests. There is the less need to dwell longer on this part of Professor Gam-

mell's work as two of his distinguished pupils have
testified to its value as well as to his general worth.
The Rev. George P. Fisher, D. D., Professor of
Church History in Yale University, a graduate of
the class of 1847, thus characterizes Professor Gammell's career : —

NEW HAVEN, *March* 8, 1890.

During the period when I was a student in Brown
University the Faculty was composed of excellent and
faithful men, to each of whom belonged a marked individuality. Professor Chace and Professor Gammell were
socially intimate, and their names were habitually coupled
together in the talk of students. Yet they were quite unlike in their intellectual traits and their types of character. Both were dissimilar, each in his own way, from the
beloved Caswell, as all differed widely in personal characteristics from President Wayland, whose dominant per-
sonality caused him to be held in universal respect. That
admirable scholar, the now venerable Professor Lincoln,
entered the Faculty as professor a year after our class was
admitted to college. Professor Boise, who has not for
many years past been connected with Brown, then had
charge of the instruction in Greek. The late Professor
Frieze, of the University of Michigan, was our tutor in
Latin during the Freshman year. In this body of teachers, all of whom were deserving of honor and esteem, Professor Gammell had a distinctive place, and manifested
qualities altogether peculiar to himself. He' struck the
students at once as a man of refined manners and elegant culture. It was obvious that he set a high value
on good manners, and was impatient of all sorts of coarseness and vulgarity. He expected his pupils to be gentlemen in their deportment and language, and — although

he said nothing about it — they tacitly felt that he did
not like to see them slovenly in dress.   There were traditional sayings to the effect that his estimate of a student
was modified by the degree of his carefulness in this particular.   A keen and caustic critic, he was not solicitous
to conceal his disapproval of any violations of decorum or
offenses against good taste, whether they consisted in a
neglect of the canons of polite intercourse or of the rules
of literary expression.   He was the Professor of Rhetoric,
and everybody felt that he meant to discharge his function
resolutely, whether men would bear or forbear.   His criticisms were fair and just, but the arrow generally hit the
mark, and his reputation as a censor of rhetorical faults
and follies caused his utterances to be awaited by some
of the young authors with a degree of apprehension.   No
sort of affectation, or bombast, or cant in the choice of
phraseology flourished in his presence.   It was evident
to all that Professor Gammell's standards were high.   He
demanded an easy naturalness in style, free on the one
hand from everything tumid, and on the other from everything careless or coarse.   He labored perseveringly to
train his pupils in the art of writing, sparing no pains in
the correction of their juvenile essays, and in giving to
them personal suggestions and advice.   In the department of rhetoric and English literature, his influence
was great upon the generations of students who were
trained by him.   On the select number who were drawn
into close personal relations with him the effect of his instruction and guidance was of course especially marked.
The acknowledged literary excellence which distinguished
the students at Brown as a class is the best possible
proof of the capacity and fidelity of their instructor.   It
should be added that in the daily routine of college work
Professor Gammell was strictly conscientious.   He required his pupils to do their work faithfully, and never

failed to exact of them, in recitations and examinations, suitable proofs that they had rightly spent their time. In my day, it was customary for the instructors to make domiciliary visits to the students' rooms, — if visits can be called domiciliary which began and ended with a bow at the door. The design was to find out if we were at home in the prescribed study-hours. In my Freshman year, I was in Professor Gammell's division. He made his calls with much regularity, — no officer, I believe, except Professor Chace, being more exact in his adherence to this ancient law.

Professor Gammell, in addition to his duties as Professor of Rhetoric, took up the work of an instructor in history. The amount of time given at first to the study was not very large. We attended mainly to English history, and gave special attention to the period of the Rebellion and the Commonwealth. In this department, the influence of Professor Gammell was very quickening and serviceable. He led us into paths of investigation and reflection of the highest interest and importance. I have special occasion to express an indebtedness to his kind, thoughtful assistance in initiating me into historical studies. One day he invited me to his room, and showed to me several volumes of manuscript correspondence of Roger Williams, which had just been added to the collections of the Rhode Island Historical Society. He gave to me this correspondence as a theme for a composition, and let me come to his room, from time to time, to examine it, and prepare for my task. This incident will illustrate the disposition to aid his pupils whenever he found them receptive.

I shall not venture to speak at length of Professor Gammell's personal qualities, beyond what has been already implied. His conversation was entertaining, and seasoned in some degree with a certain caustic wit, not inconsistent with genuine good-will and kindness. He never forgot his pupils. He followed them after they left college, and took an almost parental satisfaction in whatever successes they achieved. Those who have been entertained under his roof will never cease to remember his hospitality, and to recall the proofs of his interest in them and of his continued solicitude for the welfare of his former pupils generally. For myself, I cannot think of Professor Gammell without sincere respect and tender recollections of his kindness, and gratitude for what I owe to him.

Yours faithfully, GEORGE P. FISHER.

The following estimate of Professor Gammell from President James B. Angell, LL. D., of Michigan University, and who was graduated at Brown University in the class of 1849, bears testimony similar to that of Professor Fisher. Both these gentlemen were favorite pupils of Professor Gammell. He had the deepest pride in their highly successful careers, and none of his students stood in closer relations to him.

I pursued studies under Professor Gammell from the beginning of my Sophomore year to the end of my college course. Two years later I traveled in company with him through Italy. I was afterwards associated with him in the Faculty of Brown University. Since I left Providence I have maintained an intimate acquaintance with him through annual visits to Rhode Island, and through a somewhat regular correspondence with him extending down to the date of his last illness. My appreciation of the value of his friendship is measured only by the depth of my sorrow at his death.

In my college days he taught rhetoric, logic, and history, and trained the students in writing and speaking. He was an efficient instructor in all these branches, though, in accordance with the usage then prevalent in Brown University, he held us more closely to the recitation *verbatim* of the text-book or the lecture than we should now deem wise. His drill in writing was excellent. He insisted that the essay of his pupil should have a distinct plan, a beginning, a middle, and an end, a simple and natural introduction, and — old students will recall his expression — "a free, easy, and appropriate conclusion." If we sometimes thought that he emphasized the importance of the style rather than of the thought, in our compositions, possibly we see now that what we then most needed to learn was the art of accurate, chaste, and graceful expression. He was a nice verbal critic. If necessary, he could embody his criticism in a pointed, perhaps caustic expression, which was likely to be remembered. The style which he desired us to cultivate was like that of most writers half a century ago, — less incisive and direct, more stately and artificial, than that which is commended at the present time. But it was graceful and dignified.

He inspired his classes with high aspirations for excellence in writing, and with zeal for the study of the classic English authors. His students took sides as lovers of this author or that, and discussed with ardor literary questions. Most of them learned under him to appreciate and to cultivate style in writing, and to become familiar with the great masters of English thought. I have heard many of his pupils, even those who had felt most keenly the wounds inflicted on their complacent souls by his sharp criticisms, express in after-life their gratitude and sense of obligation to him for the service he had rendered them by his unsparing fidelity. They were ready to exclaim, "Faithful are the wounds of a friend."

There was in his manner in the class-room and elsewhere a certain air of dignity and high-breeding, which
sometimes seemed to students, with their unconventional
ways, to border on primness and formality, and perhaps
was occasionally in danger of falling into that extreme.
But it was not without its beneficial effects. There was
something in his bearing, in his neatness of dress, in his
elegance of language, that rebuked coarseness, vulgarity,
and untidiness in a manner not unsalutary to young men
living by themselves in dormitories and in commons hall,
when, secluded from general society, they so easily fell into
habits of carelessness concerning their dress, and became
neglectful of the ordinary courtesies of life. The fact
that he impressed them with his ideals of demeanor expressed itself in the current saying that no one who appeared in his recitation room with boots unblacked could
expect a high mark for his recitation. Of course there
was no truth in this. But the unconscious influence of
the teacher, who was always and everywhere so instinctively regardful of the proprieties and courtesies of refined
society, in making students mindful of them, is not to be
lightly valued.

In my time in college, Professor Gammell's instruction
in history was mainly confined to the constitutional history of England, though he gave a few lectures on the
history of the United States. His work was afterwards
broadened in its scope. But in all his historical teaching
he was intent on making his students observe and apprehend the development of constitutional liberty and of civilization. It was not dates and facts by themselves that
he sought to fix in their memory, but the progress of the
great principles whose triumphs have secured human progress. In his later years he became much interested in
some of the problems of international law. His special
historical reading had been ampler in the fields of English

and American history than in the history of continental
Europe, though he had studied with care the development
and the decline of feudalism in France and Germany.
The excellence of the articles on historical and political
subjects which he contributed to the "Providence Journal" and to the "New York Examiner," and of the papers
which he read before the Rhode Island Historical Society,
makes one regret that he did not devote the years following the resignation of his professional chair to writing
some historical work.

But after laying down the duties of his professorship
he did not lose his interest either in college questions or in
historical and political problems. He watched the careers
of his pupils with the deepest interest, and felt the greatest pride in their successes. He was ever ready to help
them by his counsels. He had constantly at heart the
welfare of Brown University. Of the many letters I
have received from him, I doubt if there is one in which
he does not speak of that college with earnest interest and
touch on some phase of current discussion of college
problems. His conversation always led speedily to the
same themes. He was conservative in his views of college
policy, as in all things. His last will and testament gave
touching proof of his devotion to the college and to American history.

He cherished a strong pride in the career of Rhode
Island. Himself a biographer of the founder of the
State and of one of its early governors, he was familiar,
as few men are, with her history. While not blind to her
mistakes, he loved to dwell upon the bright passages in
her record, and to discourse with hearty appreciation on
the strong men she has reared.

In instruction to classes, in writing for the press, and
in conversation, he was ever urging that educated men,
and especially rich men, should cultivate a deep interest

in public affairs and in public institutions. He never tired of emphasizing the importance of the nurture and growth of civic virtue. He illustrated his doctrine by his own active interest in the Rhode Island Hospital, the Providence Athenæum, the Rhode Island Historical Society, and other institutions, and in public affairs in general.

Mr. Gammell was fond of society. He was a fluent, vivacious, and agreeable talker. He was a welcome guest at any dinner-table. His conversation was often racy with sharp but not ill-natured criticism. He was not wanting in wit, and he keenly appreciated it in others. He had " the courage of his convictions," and defended his positions with spirit, but without loss of temper. He was a charming companion and a most faithful friend. His sympathies were quick and tender. He was a man of simple, earnest Christian faith, a believer of the broadest and most catholic type. He was the last survivor of that group of marked men who constituted the Faculty of Brown University when he joined it. None of them served that college with more faithful devotion than he. With all her wealth she has no richer treasure, no more precious endowment, than the memory of their lives and characters.

Yours very truly,   JAMES B. ANGELL.

The years 1843–1850 were years of literary labor outside the regular and engrossing academic work. Professor Gammell was asked to prepare two of the Memoirs in the " Library of American Biography," conducted by Jared Sparks, then McLean Professor of Ancient and Modern History at Harvard College. He entered at once and with zest into the undertaking, and his Memoir of Roger Williams appeared in 1845, in Vol. IV. of the " American Biography," Second Series. His monograph is more condensed than that of a previous biographer, Mr. Knowles. It is, however, no mere digest of Mr. Knowles's labors. Professor Gammell made his own investigations, and the result of his work is well stated in an appropriate notice of the book in the " North American Review: " [1] —

" Mr. Gammell, though he has consulted all the works of our colonial history relating to his theme, has not found occasion in any important point to vary from the opinions expressed by his predecessor. The memoir which he has prepared, as its position in a series of popular biographies required, is more brief and more closely confined to the life of the individual. The writer has shown more skill in the selection and arrangement of his materials, equal soundness of judgment in the views of individual character and of colonial policy, and very commendable impartiality in the narration of events, the history of which has been too often distorted and colored by prejudice or malevolence. The style is remarkably well suited to a work of this kind. It is chaste, easy, and animated, showing the taste and skill of an accomplished and accurate scholar."

The Life of Governor Samuel Ward was published in the following year, 1846, in Vol. IX., New Series, of the " American Biography." The latter volume cost him a somewhat extended research. He examined the " letters and private papers of Governor Ward, now in the possession of his descendants in the city of New York; also, the legis-

[1] Vol. lxiv. pp. 1–20.

lative records and the files of ancient documents in
the office of the Secretary of State of Rhode Isl-
and, as well as the published memorials relating to
that period of her colonial history." Nothing which
he ever published seems to have been prepared with
greater care. The narrative is flowing and graphic,
the salient points in Governor Ward's career are
brought into proper relief, the style is clear and
concise, and while a hearty admiration for his subject is manifest, his appreciative spirit does not sink
the historian in the eulogist. It is a critical estimate as well as a biography. The preparation of
the volume had one marked effect on Professor Gammell : it deepened his interest in Rhode Island history, and made him a more fervent admirer of Rhode
Island institutions. He records his opinion in the
Preface "that the services of the colony of Rhode
Island in the Revolution have never yet been duly
chronicled."

The writing of these two volumes qualified him
for another and weightier task in historical author-
ship. The Executive Committee of the American
Baptist Missionary Union requested him to write a
history of American Baptist missions. What the
work involved is best described in his own words :
"The subject relates to many different countries and
races of mankind, and comprises the personal adventures and philanthropic labors of a large number
of individuals, who, in the spirit of their Master and
in obedience to His great command, have toiled for
the extension of Christian truth among their fellow-

men. From a range of topics so wide and varied the author has aimed to select the incidents and scenes which may fairly represent the growth of each separate mission, and to form from them a series of narratives fitted to interest the general reader. In the execution of the design, the most difficult task has been to blend particular facts with general views, and from the scattered letters of many individuals to trace the gradual advancement of the enterprises in which they are engaged." To carry out his plan, it was necessary to examine carefully the journals of the missionaries, the published reports of missionary operations in the " Missionary Magazine," also records and papers in manuscript at the Baptist Missionary Rooms. He consulted the memoirs of missionaries and works on missions in different countries, as also works discussing the history and condition of countries in which the missions had been planted. He wove " into the narrative brief notices of such public events as have affected their progress and success." Aside from the general qualification for such a work which his historical studies and writings had given him, he had a special fitness springing from close studies of the great missionary field. It had been his habit to prepare for the Society of Missionary Inquiry in the college a monthly *résumé* of missionary intelligence. This was given on the evening of the first Sunday in the month, at the old chapel. Dr. Wayland was always present. The students of that day will recall the dimly lighted room, and the impressive prayers and addresses of Dr. Wayland, which followed Professor Gammell's presentation of missionary intelligence from all parts of the world. Nothing ever kindled Dr. Wayland's enthusiasm more than the story of missionary toil and sacrifices; and after Professor Gammell had read his selection of well-chosen facts gathered from the missionary periodicals, always skillfully grouped and lighted up by explanatory comments, Dr. Wayland closed the service by one of those off-hand moving addresses in which he was so powerful. The same service was subsequently repeated in the vestry of the First Baptist Meeting-House. From this wide survey of missionary operations, and still more from the deep sympathy with missionaries and their labors which this survey engendered, Professor Gammell had gained a special training for the office of a missionary historian.

His " History of American Baptist Missions " is a model of its kind. More than half the book is occupied in detailing the wonderful story of the Burman missions. From these the author passes to missions in Siam and China; then treats of the mission in Assam, briefly describes that to the Teloogoos, and, leaving the continent of Asia, details the history of the mission in West Africa. Not the least striking feature of the volume is its concluding portion, in which the history of Baptist missions in Europe is narrated. Each of those in Greece, in France, in Germany, and in Denmark is happily described. The book ends with an account of missions

among the Indians of North America. It is a volume
of only 348 octavo pages ; but so well proportioned
is the author's discussion of each mission according
to its importance, so well selected are the salient
points of missionary interest, dry and prolix details
are so skillfully avoided, striking incidents and significant crises are so carefully seized, the style is so
well suited to the subject, warmed at times into a
glow of Christian enthusiasm, that this History has
secured high rank in the literature of missions. The
" North American Review " heartily commended both
its style and execution :[1] " In point of style it is
chaste and elegant. It rejects all rhetorical embel-
lishments, and when the narrative is most exciting
its flow is still calm and dispassionate. . . . Professor Gammell deserves our high regard also for
the kindly spirit in which he has wrought out this
monument to the philanthropy of his denomination.
We look in vain for the language of bigotry, exclu-
siveness, or unkindness. The most generous notice
is uniformly taken of the missionaries of other sects,
and the ashes of buried controversy are in every
instance left undisturbed."

The reorganization of the University by President
Wayland, and the introduction of the " New System," as it was called, opened the way for a change
of professorship to Professor Gammell. His interest in historical studies had been steadily growing.
They were to assume a new importance and a much
larger field in the future course of study. For

[1] Vol. lxx. pp. 57-78.

fifteen years he had wrought laboriously and successfully in the rhetorical department. But there
was of necessity a drudgery in correcting essays and
supervising orations from which he naturally desired release. He had purchased the right to exemption from such toils. And when, in 1850,
history was constituted a distinct department, associated with that of political economy, he had abundantly shown his fitness for the new position. Accordingly, he was transferred from the chair of
rhetoric to that of history and political economy.

He was married a second time, September 22,
1851, to Miss Elizabeth Amory, daughter of Mr.
Robert H. Ives, of Providence, and with his bride
sailed for Europe, where they passed a year visiting
England, France, Italy, and Switzerland; returning
by England and Scotland in August of the year
following, in time for the opening of the college.
It was a year of rest greatly needed by him, and it
proved all that his best friends hoped. He was in
Paris during the stirring times of the autumn of 1851.
The *coup d'état* took place the day after he left
the capital, the news reaching him at the city of
Lyons. His interest in this foreign tour was not
concentrated on any specialties. It was various, keen
always, and fastening on every aspect of foreign
life, or manners, or institutions, or scenery.[1] His

---

[1] In 1879 Professor Gammell revisited Italy with his family. On
his return, he prepared and read before the Friday Evening Club the
paper *Italy Revisited*, printed in this volume. That paper reveals
in an interesting manner his habits as a traveler.

social gifts, as well as his wide intelligence and culture, gave him ready access to men of note, whose acquaintance he desired. Perhaps the most marked instance of this was his visit to Guizot, who had returned from his exile in England, and was then living in Paris. For him as a historical scholar Professor Gammell had great veneration. They discussed, in an interview they had, the problems of the day in their connection with mediæval history. He was wont to allude to this conversation with Guizot with profound interest, and his use of the " History of Civilization " as a text-book was one fruit of the discussion. He admired its method, sympathized with its views, and grounded his classes well in the generalizations expounded by Guizot.

He resumed his duties in the college immediately on his return, and for twelve years filled the chair of history and political economy. Professor Gammell made no claim to knowledge of speculative philosophy. He had no fondness and perhaps no aptitude for metaphysical studies. It would, however, be a great mistake, as well as an injustice, to conclude from this that he did not teach the laws as well as the facts of history. His method was certainly a philosophical one; not fully developed, perhaps, wanting in completeness, but still proceeding on lines of broad and well-considered generalization. The estimates of his work as a historical teacher furnished already by Professor Fisher and President Angell are well supplemented by the following from Professor J. H. Gilmore, of

Rochester University,[1] a graduate from Brown University of the class of 1858, who was his pupil when he was devoting his whole time to this department : —

UNIVERSITY OF ROCHESTER,
ROCHESTER, N. Y., *February* 25, 1890.

Pray excuse my seeming neglect in delaying to answer your letters. It is only seeming, as I have been absent from the city nearly all the time since the first one was received, and, when at home, have been so busy that it has been impossible to attend to any work that was not absolutely imperative.

Even now, I do not know that I can render you much service, but I will give you, at least, my impressions of Professor Gammell; and that with the greater interest, as I feel under especial obligations to him.

I do not think he was exceptionally popular with our class (perhaps it was not altogether his fault) ; but while my own relations with Professor Dunn and Professor Angell were more cordial than those that subsisted between Professor Gammell and myself, I liked him exceedingly, and thought, at the time, that I was getting more from him than from any other professor in college. As I look back upon my college course, I still feel under peculiar obligations to my professor of history. More time was then given to history at Brown than to any other study excepting Latin, Greek, and mathematics ; and it seems to me that the course of study in Professor Gammell's department was better organized than those in most of the other departments. Certainly, the instruction which I received from him has stood me very fairly in stead during all these years. But I think I especially appreciated (I know that I appreciated more than most of my class

---

[1] This University conferred on Professor Gammell, in 1859, the honorary degree of LL. D.

did) Professor Gammell's *obiter dicta*, his incidental remarks concerning men and things of our own day. He was animated by a sturdy contempt for humbugs and shams; and, as I recall his teachings, his influence seems to have been broadening and liberalizing beyond that of most of my professors. Only yesterday, after penning (or, rather, caligraphing) the sentence, " And, often, back of the mysterious editorial *we* there is masquerading some callow stripling, who lacks even the rudiments of a decent English education," I thought to myself, That's one of my old professor's sentences, — as, indeed, it might well have been, for the thraldom of the press was one of his favorite themes.

I do not think that Professor Gammell was particularly intimate with any of his students, — perhaps he did not care to be, perhaps they thought he did not care to be, — but I am certain that he was profoundly interested in their welfare. Once, when I had occasion to see him about another matter, he talked with me quite at length in regard to a very bright young man, a student for the Christian ministry, who was not getting that preparation for his life-work which he needed, because he was so eager for immediate work and immediate results. " He has no right to neglect his opportunities as he does," said Professor Gammell, " but it will not do for me to tell him so. He would only misunderstand me. Now, you are intimate with him, and religiously in sympathy with him, without neglecting your immediate duty. Could n't you influence him for good?" As I look back upon that conversation, it seems in every respect creditable to Dr. Gammell.

I wish, my dear Dr. Murray, that I could really give you something that would be of more value to you than these fragmentary reminiscences; but such as I have I place at your disposal.

Very truly yours,   J. H. GILMORE.

The following letter from Professor Fisher, of Yale University, gracefully expresses his feelings of indebtedness to his esteemed professor. Its occasion was the publication of Professor Fisher's "Outlines of Universal History."

NEW HAVEN, *January* 7, 1886.

MY DEAR PROFESSOR GAMMELL, — When you first led me to begin historical studies, you little knew that the ambitious and audacious spirit of your pupil would one day impel him to the bold task of writing a history of the world. Yet such is the fact; and for it I am afraid that you will have to be held in a large measure responsible. The least thing that I can do is to carry the fruit of the seed which you sowed back to your door. Accordiugly, I have directed the publishers to send to you a copy of my "Outlines of Universal History."

Very sincerely your friend and pupil,

GEORGE P. FISHER.

PROFESSOR GAMMELL.

In 1864 Professor Gammell resigned the chair of history and political economy, to which he had been called in 1850. It was with the deepest satisfaction to him that his pupil the Rev. J. Lewis Diman, of the class of 1851, was appointed by the Corporation his successor, as in 1850 his pupil the Rev. Robinson P. Dunn had succeeded him in the chair of rhetoric. Seldom has it been the fortune of a successful professor to leave his work in hands so well fitted to carry it on. Professor Gammell had now completed a long and honorable career of academic life. More than a generation of students had been graduated since he began his work as tutor in the University. His influence as a scholar and as a professor had steadily increased. He retired from the chair of history in the zenith of his powers. He was never more strongly interested in the high position he had secured than when he decided to lay aside his professional duties, and to find for the remainder of his life a sphere of usefulness outside the professor's chair. The following estimate of Professor Gammell's services to Brown University, from the pen of Professor John L. Lincoln, long associated with him in its Faculty, and who is so widely beloved and deeply honored, will be welcomed by every friend of his departed colleague. No tribute could be more gracefully rendered, and none could be of higher value.

PROVIDENCE, *March* 28, 1890.

You have requested me to give you, from my recollections, some views of the relations of our late friend, Professor Gammell, to our University as a member of the Faculty and a college officer. It is with pleasure that I comply with this request, as such a view takes me back in memory over the scenes and events of many years belonging alike to his and my own professional life; and yet it is a pleasure mingled with sadness, when I remember that he with whom I was then associated in college service, and to whom I was wont to look up as older in that service than myself, and who had also been my instructor, is now gone from among us; and that in his death I lost the last one of that company of good men and true who were my elders in the Faculty, when I entered it as a tutor in 1839, and as a professor in 1844.

Mr. Gammell came into the Faculty as tutor in September, 1832, the beginning of the second year after his graduation. That was the year in which my class entered college; and I remember well the kindly greeting he gave me on meeting me, on my first college day, as an applicant for admission to the Freshman class. He instructed our class the first term in all three of our studies; in our Sophomore year he was our instructor in rhetoric, being then Assistant Professor of Belles-Lettres, and in 1836, having been appointed Professor of Rhetoric, he had the sole charge of that department, and ours was the first class which he prepared for Commencement. The duties of that department, in class instruction and lectures, and in the conduct of the public literary exercises of the college, he discharged, as we all know, with efficiency and skill until 1851, in which year he assumed the professorship, then first established, of History and Political Economy; and the work of that important new department he organized and carried forward with zeal and vigor, and with marked educating influence, till the year 1864, when he resigned his professorship and retired from his place in the Faculty. In these offices and studies he had thus been occupied as a member of the Faculty from 1832 to 1864, — a period of thirty-two years. These were among the best years of his life, of his youth and manhood, — from the age of twenty-one to fifty-two. They were also years of important changes and great progress in the history of the University, in the increase of its resources, the widening of the range of its educational work, and the adoption of larger views of what constitutes a liberal education. These years cover a large part of Dr. Wayland's administration; indeed, if we include Professor Gammell's undergraduate life, he was a member of college during the whole of Dr. Wayland's administration, from 1827 to 1855. These years include also nine of the twelve years of Dr. Sears's administration. During this period, besides the professorship of History and Political Economy, there were also established the professorship of Chemistry, Physiology, and Geology, and that of Chemistry applied to the Arts. Then, too, in 1850, came, after long-continued reflection on the part of Dr. Wayland, and much agitated discussion in the Faculty, the introduction of what has been called the "New System;" which, while it embodied some measures that, being of a somewhat radical nature and of ambiguous benefit, were afterwards changed, yet has justified itself in the subsequent history of college education, as right and most important in its fundamental ideas, and progressive in its spirit and ends. During all this period of change and progress, Professor Gammell rendered valuable service as a college officer. In him Dr. Wayland, whom he always loved to speak of as his chief, found a faithful adviser and an untiring coadjutor. It was a marked characteristic of Professor Gammell that he never limited his thoughts and labors to his duties in the lecture-room as an instructor. Outside and beyond this sphere of professional work, he was wont to keep a vigilant outlook over every domain of college jurisdiction, wherever might be developed and cultivated elements and resources of the welfare and the prosperity of the institution. He was a truly academic man, and his academic life was identified with the life of Brown, his Alma Mater, and the sphere of his untiring filial devotion, in thought and effort. He kept himself in touch with all that went on in its history, rejoicing in everything that enhanced its fame and usefulness, and pained to the quick by anything which threatened to dim and diminish its good name and influence. In the earlier years of his professorship, he prepared the Annual Catalogues, either alone or in union with the President. So, too, he early interested himself, in connection with the late Hon. Theron Metcalf, in the preparation of the

Triennial Catalogue; and after Judge Metcalf had retired
from these labors, he was the sole editor of this Catalogue
till the year 1846. In this way he kept himself in communication with the graduates, and had probably a wider
and more accurate knowledge of their places of residence
and their occupations than any of his colleagues. Professor Gammell also rendered important and long-continued
services as a member of the Joint Library Committee of
the University. He came into the Faculty the year after
measures had been taken by Dr. Wayland for raising a
Library Fund, and two years after his accession this fund
had been raised, chiefly through the personal exertions of
Dr. Wayland and Dr. Caswell. The year 1835 was marked
by another signal event in the history of the library, the
erection and dedication of Manning Hall, and the appropriation of the first floor of that building, which was the gift
of the Hon. Nicholas Brown, to the uses of the library.
In 1839 the sum which had been raised for the fund had
increased at interest to $25,000, and the first dividend
from its income was paid in July of that year. Three
years after this new era in the history of the library, Professor Gammell was chosen from the Faculty a member of
the Library Committee; and then began a course of faithful service in promoting the interests of the library, which
continued till 1859, — a period of seventeen years. Later,
in 1871, after he had been elected to the Board of Fellows, he was chosen to represent the Corporation in the
Joint Library Committee, and remained in the committee till 1886, his whole period of service having been
thirty-three years. In 1843, the year after his first entrance into the committee, he prepared a circular, addressed to the graduates and friends of the college, inviting their coöperation in increasing the library, which was
printed and widely circulated, with immediate results of
important accessions of books and pamphlets. He also

wrote the annual report of the committee for that year, a document of substantial value, by its historical notices and its practical suggestions, in securing the after prosperity of the library. For seven years — from 1852 to 1859 — he was secretary of the Library Committee, and most of the annual reports during this period were the productions of his pen. As was his wont in all places of trust which he filled, he was uniformly regular and punctual in his attendance upon the meetings of the committee, and in union with his colleagues exercised a faithful supervision in the conduct of its affairs, in the selection and purchase of books, and in the planning and execution of measures for augmenting its usefulness. He held opinions on the province and functions of a college library, which, as the result of much reflection and experience, came to be an abiding possession of his mind; and though these opinions did not always coincide with those of his colleagues in their nature and workings, yet his maintenance of them illustrated the loyalty and fidelity which were marked qualities of his character. Besides these services, Professor Gammell promoted the interests of the college by his articles for the press, especially the " Providence Journal," by which he aimed to keep the college in touch with its alumni and friends and the public. If these articles, valuable for their information and their literary merits, could be gathered together, they would form a most useful and interesting contribution to the history of the University. In the inner work of the college, as done by the Faculty and its committees, Professor Gammell always bore a prominent part, striving ever, by counsel and action, to maintain wholesome discipline in the government and a high standard of scholarship and character in the students, and to preserve kindly and helpful relations between the instructors and their pupils. On all subjects which belonged to the jurisdiction of the Faculty he reached opinions of his own by reflection and experience, and these he maintained with firmness and constancy; and if these seemed sometimes to be pronounced in a somewhat positive and exclusive manner, yet they were recognized by his colleagues as emanating from the mind and will of a thoughtful educator and a loyal son of the college. When Professor Gammell resigned his professorship, he carried with him, as was expressed in the resolutions then passed, the warmest wishes of the Faculty for his continued welfare and usefulness, together with their hope, which was fully gratified, that his withdrawal would not lessen his interest in the institution with which he had been so long identified.

Upon Professor Gammell's resignation, with entire freedom from worldly cares, two courses of life were open to him. He could have devoted himself to some line of historical research, and have left behind him some elaborate historical work. For this he was fitted by bent of mind and by discipline. Not a few there may be who share in the regret that he had not done so, and thus have left his own best Memorial in some well-studied work on Rhode Island history, — always to him a fascinating theme. The other course was, to give himself to causes of benevolence, of learning, of public usefulness. He chose the latter. So had Dr. Wayland closed his long and noble career. So had Professor Chace decided to spend the honored close of his honored life. Professor Gammell found in the promotion of wise and noble beneficences, in the devotion to the University outside the professor's chair, the sphere which was congenial to him and in which he did a noble service.

The Rhode Island Historical Society was established in 1822. Only three institutions of the kind, organized in the United States, are older. It has always maintained a high rank in the prosecution of the noble purposes for which such institutions exist. Professor Gammell's interest in it dates from an early period in his career. He was chosen a member July 19, 1844. When the society opened its new cabinet on Waterman Street, November 21, 1844, he was chosen to give the dedicatory address. He surveyed the province of such societies in their general relation to the work of the historian, and then dwelt on their more specific relation to the history of the several States they immediately represent. He used the occasion to urge the claims of Rhode Island on her historical students. "The history of no State in the Union, we may safely say, presents claims upon the attention and study of her citizens so strong as does that of Rhode Island." [1]

He testified his interest in the work of the society by active participation in its efforts, contributing a remarkably interesting series of papers to its sessions. The list here given exhibits his varied interest in historical studies. A few of these papers are printed in this volume.

---

[1] When, some years since, it became necessary to open the grave of William Blackstone, Professor Gammell was present, carefully watched the removal of the few remains, and wrote with great feeling a notice of the occurrence. Such an event as the opening of an ancient historic grave drew out his liveliest interest. It was to him a pious care and a sincere joy that through the generosity of Blackstone's lineal descendants a suitable monument to Blackstone was reared on the spot.

ADDRESSES AND PAPERS READ BEFORE THE RHODE ISLAND HISTORICAL SOCIETY, BY THE LATE PROFESSOR WILLIAM GAMMELL, LL. D.

1. "Address at the Opening of the New Cabinet," November 21, 1844.

2. "The Loyalists of the American Revolution," March 5, 1857.

3. "Progress of Rhode Island History since the Formation of this Society," February 21, 1860.

4. "Contributions History has received from Certain Physical Sciences," October 16, 1877.

5. "Asylum and Extradition among Nations," March 9, 1880.

6. "The Monroe Doctrine, its Original History," January 26, 1881.

7. "Memorial Minute recorded in Honor of the Late Zachariah Allen, LL. D.," March 21, 1882.

8. "The Confederation Period of the Republic," October 31, 1882.

9. "The Huguenots and the Edict of Nantes," November 17, 1885.

10. "The Life and Services of the Late John R. Bartlett," November 2, 1886.

11. "Rhode Island refusing to adopt the Constitution," April 17, 1888.

12. "The Life of Rowland Gibson Hazard, LL. D.," July 30, 1888.

Also seven Annual Addresses: the first, January, 1883, the last January, 1889.

When, in 1882, the presidency of the society became vacant by the death of the Hon. Zachariah Allen, Professor Gammell was chosen to succeed him. An honor also highly appreciated by him was

his election, in 1873, as corresponding member of the
Massachusetts Historical Society. As President of
the Rhode Island Historical Society, he was called
on to give an Annual Address. On these addresses
he seems to have bestowed great care. They contained, according to well - established precedents,
some survey of the society's work during the previous year. But his addresses took a wider range.
He brought to the notice of the society important
lines of historical investigation, as yet not fully occupied. He pointed out matters of local history,
sustaining important relations to the history of the
country as well as possessing an intrinsic interest.
Thus in his first address, that of 1883, he calls
attention to the important place held by the history of the *towns* of Rhode Island, referring especially to the town of Newport, his early and his
later summer home. "I cannot forbear," he said,
"to express the earnest hope that some citizen of
Newport, with suitable qualifications, will soon be
induced to make use of the materials that may ere-
long be wasted or lost, and chronicle in a worthy
manner the instructive and fascinating history of
a town whose large agency in the early formation
of the State and in the subsequent development of
its institutions and interests has never been fully
appreciated nor understood." Specially he urged
that, among the chapters in such a work, "more
than one shall be devoted to those military fortresses which long ago were constructed at the
mouth of Narragansett Bay, alike on the islands

and on the mainland." He also called attention to
the need existing for a " new history of Providence."
The address for 1886 contains a spirited and eloquent plea for some adequate history of Rhode Isl-
and commerce in its earlier era. It is introduced
by a graphic picture of the barrier which Narragansett Bay interposed to any easy communication between the scattered settlements of the colony.

" Its shores, especially on the western side, were covered
with dense forests, in which, here and there, openings had
been made for Indian villages. It could be traversed only
in pleasant weather in any season, and in winter it was
effectually closed for at least two months by ice. When
we recall facts like these, it becomes evident that the conditions of intercourse among the towns of the colony, nay,
the conditions of their very existence, were somewhat
harshly prescribed and enforced by the stern mistress
whom they had not yet learned either to conciliate or to
control.

" But I must not be thought to disparage our noble
bay, which has done so much in the making of the State.
I am only saying that it was a somewhat formidable ex-
panse of water for our early settlers to traverse in nothing but row-boats and canoes. I know full well that it
was all the time training them to hardships, to self-re-
liance in dangers, to all the heroic qualities which were
needed to prepare them for a subsequent stage in their
social progress. The settlements, once united, became
prosperous and strong. The sea was still around them
on every side, but they had now learned to adapt themselves to its varying moods, and to make use of its forces
for purposes of their own. Industry had greatly increased

their resources. The little boats which necessity had taught them to build were soon supplanted by sloops, shallops, and snows, by brigantines and by ships; and these they built in great numbers, not only for themselves, but also for neighboring colonies. An active trade sprang up, not only with Boston, New London, New Haven, and Manhattan, but also with Barbadoes and the Spanish West India Islands. The struggle for existence was over, and the bay was no longer the dictator of their movements, but the willing servant of their interests. The forests on its shores were fast disappearing, its depths and shallows had been ascertained, and its harbors were inviting the commerce of Europe. I hope that before it is too late some worthy history of the era of Rhode Island commerce will be written. Should it be written aright, more than any other chapter in the annals of the State it will show how important was the agency of the bay, in all its length and breadth, in producing some of the noblest qualities in the character of the people. It enabled them to become a colony, in a large degree, of sailors and seafarers, of ship-builders and merchants. So great was the commerce of the colony before the troubles with England began that Newport was the rival of Boston as a port for foreign trade. This trade had also become large in Providence and at length in Bristol, while ships were built at Warren, at Wickford, and at East Greenwich, and the whole surface of our Rhode Island waters glistened with coasters from every part of New England. In the wars between England and France our sailors had been largely engaged in naval service and in privateering, and had become accustomed to those deeds of daring, which long lingered in the traditions of the colony. It was the spirit thus created and kept alive that in later days prompted the burning of the Gaspée, that produced Abraham Whipple for the continental navy and prepared the way for Commodore Perry and his Rhode Island companions at Lake Erie."

Professor Gammell's services, first as member and then as President of the Historical Society, are fittingly described in the appended paper from General Horatio Rogers, his successor in the office of President : —

"Professor Gammell's connection with this Society extended over a term of forty-five years, and at his death but two persons remained who had been members of it longer than he. In April, 1880, he was elected one of its Vice-Presidents, and twenty-seven months later he succeeded the Hon. Zachariah Allen as President, a position he continued to hold during the remainder of his life.

"For nearly threescore years and ten Professor Gammell lived in Rhode Island, and, though not a native of the State, few within its limits have surpassed him in familiarity with its history or in earnestness of zeal in its defense; and it is to be noted that during the sixty-eight years of the Society's existence he was the only one to attain to the presidency who was not a native-born Rhode Islander. Among his early services to the Society was delivering the address at the opening of its cabinet in 1844, and a few of the eloquent sentences uttered by him on that occasion will afford fitting illustration of his appreciation of the spirit of Rhode Island history.

"In referring to the exclusion of Rhode Island from the New England Confederacy, after inquiring into the motives that prompted such action, he said : ' Whichever of these may have been the motive, the act itself bespeaks a dark and malignant bigotry, which cannot be veiled, and for which it is vain to apologize, — a bigotry which, indeed, need not be dwelt upon, amid the general blaze of Puritan

virtues, but which we may well be proud to think has left
no trace of its existence in the history of the character of
Rhode Island. How different from all this is the spirit
which characterized *her* legislation, even at the same
gloomy periods of New England history! In turning to
consider it, we seem to have advanced a whole age in the
progress of civil and intellectual freedom.' Again, in
speaking of the literature of New England and the misrepresentations of the early annalists of Massachusetts
and Plymouth, he used these words: ' Many of these misrepresentations have been corrected by subsequent writers,
in the same States from which they emanated, and the
fame of Rhode Island has been brightened by their labors. But she still appeals to her own sons for a fuller
vindication; she claims it for the lessons she has taught
them, for the inheritance of freedom she has transmitted
to them. From these eminences in her social progress, to
which she has attained, she points us back to the scattered
graves of her original Planters, and demands of us that
we build monuments to their memory, — that we guard
their fame, and transmit their principles, undisguised and
unperverted, in the imperishable records of history.'

" Professor Gammell sturdily defended his adopted State
against attacks from without, but he was extremely pronounced as to any of her history that did not command
his own approbation. He was scathing in his denunciation of those that caused Rhode Island to delay her adoption of the Federal Constitution; and though it would
seem that the lapse of a century should, to the impartial
historian, have lightened some of the shadows of that
event by enabling him to look calmly through the partisanship of one of the most bitter periods in the annals of
Rhode Island, to the real moving causes beyond, yet Professor Gammell never beheld that light, and could award
no judgment to the country party of a hundred years ago

but a condemnation that admitted neither extenuation nor qualification.

"Two of his published works — the 'Life of Roger Williams' and the 'Biography of Governor Samuel Ward' — were essentially Rhode Island books, and the numerous papers he read before the Society, and many of his printed articles, especially in the 'Providence Journal,' were upon subjects germane to Rhode Island history. His polished periods were highly attractive, and his elegant English invested every subject he treated with a charm not easily resisted. The announcement that he was to read a paper never failed to draw a numerous audience, and none ever regretted going to hear him. The scope of his knowledge and his ready adaptation of it to practical use were amply illustrated by the remarks with which he invariably favored the Society after the reading of papers before it; and, as the subjects of those papers were exceedingly diverse, his intellectual stores must have been ample to permit such drafts at sight upon them.

"Formerly it was the practice of the librarian and cabinet keeper of the northern department to present a report at the annual meetings of the Society; but in 1880 President Allen deviated from former usage, and delivered an address in substitution of such report, a course he pursued the succeeding year. President Gammell in this respect followed the precedents of his immediate predecessor, and his annual addresses were always looked forward to with interest by the whole Society. Especially in the preparation of memorial minutes Professor Gammell had no superior, as the proceedings of the Society abundantly prove, and those upon his predecessors in office, the Hon. Samuel Greene Arnold and the Hon. Zachariah Allen, as well as upon the Hon. Elisha R. Potter and others, are models in this department of literature.

"Professor Gammell discharged all the duties of President of the Society with scrupulous fidelity. Regular and prompt in his attendance at the meetings, diligent in looking after the advisory and supervisory functions of the office, he spared no pains to advance the well-being of the Society under his charge, and he had the satisfaction of seeing his efforts thoroughly appreciated and bearing good fruit in the wide interest excited and in the general expansion of the usefulness of the institution. He presided at the meetings with great dignity. Naturally a lover of order and decorum, he conducted affairs with the gravest propriety, and he regarded with disfavor the introduction of business that had not first been submitted to him and received his approval.

" The Rev. Edwin M. Stone, a former librarian of the Society, informed us, in 1872, in surveying the half century of the Society's life, that the Rhode Island Historical Society ' was the first historical society to erect and own a suitable building for the reception and preservation of its collections.' Professor Gammell, as President, took great interest in having the Society adequately accommodated, and during the latter part of his life he was very active in procuring the means for enlarging the building, which had become too contracted for the growing needs of the institution. Through his own personal efforts a sum exceeding ten thousand dollars was added to the building fund, one thousand of which he contributed from his own purse. Though he did not live to see the addition commenced, yet the enlarged and completed structure will constitute a monument to his zeal and interest in the Society.

"The Rhode Island Historical Society has been fortunate in its past Presidents. Their fame has exalted the official position into one of honor, and their contributions to the history of Rhode Island have elevated the character of the State."

MINUTE

ADOPTED BY THE RHODE ISLAND HISTORICAL SOCIETY AT A SPECIAL
MEETING HELD APRIL 9, 1889.

The Society performs a painful duty in placing upon record the decease of its President, William Gammell, LL. D., which occurred on the 3d instant. He has been a member of the Society since July 19, 1844, and its President for the last seven years. Besides the official addresses with which he has closed each of these years, he has read thirteen papers at different meetings, probably a larger contribution than any single member has ever made.

For such work he was well qualified. Though not a native of Rhode Island, he had lived here from his boyhood, had thoroughly acquainted himself with the history of the State, and appreciated, while he criticised, its founders, its principles, and its institutions.

The study of history, the teaching of history, had occupied the ripest and most vigorous period of his academic life. He was more than a mere professor of history. He had the historic temper, the historic imagination, the constructive power, which enabled him to enter into and reproduce the events and the periods which interested him. He had facility in digesting materials, which in history are often rather indigestible, and working them into clear and continuous narrative. He rose readily from facts to principles, and generalized within the safe limits of induction without wandering into regions of speculation and vagary. His style was lucid, polished, elevated, correct without coldness and elegant without ostentation. The "Life of Roger Williams" and the "Life of Samuel Ward" in Mr. Sparks's "Library of American Biography," and the "History of American Baptist Missions" are the more considerable works of his pen. The minor writings which came from his busy hand would probably make other volumes of equal or larger amount.

The Society has occasion to remember not only his literary contributions and his historical work, but also the dignity and courtesy with which he presided over its meetings, the interest he has taken in whatever concerned its usefulness and its progress, but especially the successful attempt he made to secure a large subscription for the enlargement of its building, which was almost the last labor of his life.

Beyond all this, it takes pleasure and a certain pride in remembering the course of his long and honorable life; all he was as a citizen, a scholar, a teacher, a man, a Christian; his fidelity in all trusts, his devotion to the highest interests, the good name he has left behind.

At the annual Commencement in 1870, Professor Gammell was chosen a member of the Corporation of Brown University, and took his seat in the Board of Fellows. No man understood better than he the work and the wants of the institution. He had watched its growth from the time he entered as a student, in the first year of Dr. Wayland's presidency. He had labored successfully in two prominent departments of instruction. He had put his best strength into its development. It had become a part and a large part of his life. It was bound to him by ties of close association with his honored chief, Dr. Wayland; with his endeared friends, Professors Caswell and Chace, now among the departed, and Professor Lincoln, among the living. He had walked under the shadow of its elms for forty years.

He had seen all its buildings reared save the venerable University Hall and Hope College. He brought to the new post of duty the most active and sacred interest in the welfare of the college. Nothing but absence from the country ever prevented his attendance at the meetings of the Corporation. Indeed, his last earthly service was rendered at the meeting, March 20, 1889, when President Robinson laid down his office. On that occasion he made the following fitting address, an abstract of which is here given, as reported by Dr. Lincoln Wayland : —

"I can but recall at this time the honorable and successful manner in which President Robinson has discharged the duties of his office for the seventeen years of his incumbency. Any one who enters the college yard will notice the great changes and the marked improvements which have been made within that time. The grounds, which were plain and unadorned, have become a beauty and a delight. The number of new buildings and the important changes are without precedent in the history of the college. The John Carter Brown Library Building has been erected ; also the Slater Dormitory, a building suitable for the residence of students ; and Sayles Memorial Hall, the most beautiful and most costly building on the grounds. Also this ancient building, University Hall, has been renovated and made as good as any building connected with the college. The Metcalf estate, of very great value, and a lot on George Street, of great prospective importance, have been added to the college property.

"The funds of the University, which in 1872 were $552,430, were in 1888 $960,411, not including the gift of Mr. Duncan, $20,000, and a more recent gift of $20,000, and other gifts, which would make the total about $1,018,-000. The endowment has been very nearly doubled [not counting the Lyman bequest, from which $60,000 or $70,000 will be realized]. These gifts have come very largely from the community in which the college is located.

" For this prosperity we are greatly indebted to the judgment, the fidelity, the ability, and the diligence of President Robinson. During these seventeen years, he has never been absent from a college duty, from a recitation, or from a chapel exercise, except when called away by public duties. This fact indicates at once his vigor of constitution and his fidelity to his duties. How few professional men have a similar record !

" Of his instruction, I may speak with confidence, having had two sons under his teaching, and it having been my duty in various ways to know the internal condition of the college. The instruction has been of a very high order. He has done much to raise its standard; he has restored largely the spirit of the training of my old teacher, President Wayland, which had waned somewhat during the intervening period. I consider this a fair statement of the results of Dr. Robinson's labors. He is entitled to high praise for these services.

" He has now left the position at a more advanced age than any of his predecessors had attained while in office. I cannot say that this step is unwise ; it is surely better to lay down the office while one is in full intellectual vigor than to wait till a failure makes the step necessary. We do not to-day part with President Robinson ; and until we do so, we may defer such expressions as will be at that time appropriate."

How great was the value of the counsels which he

brought to the maintenance of the high standards
of the past, is better told by those who sat with him
in the Corporation. He always had the courage of
his opinions, never feared to be in a minority, and
as a venerable member of the Board said recently,
always " went for high things." When he died, it
was found that he had remembered the University
by a gift of ten thousand dollars, to be used in promoting the interests of historical study by devoting
its annual income to " the purchase of books relating to the history of the United States." But the
following estimate of his services, by the Rev. E. G.
Robinson, D. D., LL. D., ex-President, sets forth
the nature and extent of those services in impressive form : —

" Professor Gammell had resigned his professorship,
and was already a member of the Board of Fellows, when
I entered on my duties at Brown University, in the autumn of 1872. I had known him as professor of rhetoric,
during my undergraduate days, and had learned to hold
at a high estimate the value of his instruction. In after
years, our relations, though not intimate, were always cordial, and my editorial duties had given me frequent occasion to notice his skill as a writer, his wisdom as a critic,
and his sound judgment and high character as a man.
On my coming to the University, he was frank enough to
tell me that he had preferred for the place to which I
had been called his friend and long-time colleague, the
late Professor George Ide Chace, LL. D., a preference
which I fully appreciated as natural, as just and eminently
fitting ; but he assured me, that for all the good offices
and hearty support of which he was capable I might confidently rely on him. And most faithfully were his words

fulfilled. During the seventeen years through which we worked together, no member of the Corporation was more punctual in the performance of his duties, or more ready for any reasonable and useful service, however laborious it might be.

" Professor Gammell, from his long connection with the University, first as a student, then as a tutor, and afterwards as a professor in different departments, had come to know more of the last sixty years of its history, of its needs and its difficulties and its possibilities, than any other member of the Corporation. His care for the best interests of the University, founded on long experience and broad knowledge, was always preëminently intelligent, and it was also conspicuously unselfish. Differ as he might from others in his judgment of given measures, no one ever failed to recognize his disinterestedness. Thoroughly appreciating what the University had done for himself and others as students, and for the community in which it was placed, he was only intent on such measures as would strengthen and widen its efficiency for good. And so often was the wisdom of his judgment vindicated in the issue that his influence in the Corporation was never so great as in the last years of his life.

" During my connection with the University a variety of changes in its internal arrangements seemed to be imperatively necessary, — changes which the charter of the University required should first be sanctioned by the Fellows, and afterwards approved by the whole Corporation. To no one of the Fellows could I look as to Professor Gammell, with assurance that the necessity of the changes would be so fully understood, and when understood, be approved. One of the pleasantest of the recollections of my official connection with the University is that of the readiness, the interest, and the broad intelligence with which he entered into a discussion of whatever promised

an improvement in college work. And very few men, I
think, were ever better judges than he of what constitutes
good work in a college. The disciplinary effect of various
departments of study, alike in the development of intellect and in the cultivation of taste, had been carefully observed by him through a long series of years, so that his
theory of education rested not merely on *a priori* principles, but also on a basis of carefully collated facts.

"The tastes and acquisitions of Professor Gammell
were in the lines of English literature and history rather
than of science ; yet he never underestimated the value of
science as a factor in a liberal education, and came to regard instruction in the natural sciences as an essential
part of the training of a man who is to be fully fitted for
the duties of our time. His hearty coöperation in the
creation of new professorships of natural science in the
University was by no means the least of his many valuable services.

" To the questions whether advanced instruction should
be given in Brown University to graduates, and the degrees of Master of Arts and Doctor of Philosophy, after
given courses of study and rigid and satisfactory examinations, should be conferred, he gave careful attention,
taking the liveliest interest in discussing them. He held
that no institution of learning calling itself a university
could, without recreancy to its trusts, withhold such instruction and degrees from those who might ask and
prove themselves worthy to receive them. It was largely
through his influence and advocacy in the Board of Fellows that a beginning of such instruction was made, and
the degrees, to which candidates by examinations had
proved themselves entitled, were conferred.

"One of the last of the many services of Professor
Gammell was the preparation of an elaborate report on
the question whether the doors of Brown University

should be open to the admission of young women as candidates for degrees. The question had for two or three years been before the Corporation, and a numerical majority of its members were in favor of their admission. A strong and determined minority were opposed. Professor Gammell, as chairman of a committee to consider the subject, was requested to present a report on it. His report, prepared with great care, was submitted to the Corporation at its annual meeting, in September, 1888, and was so satisfactory to the advocates of both sides of the controversy that they unanimously asked for its publication; and it was voted that it should accompany the published report of the President at the end of the academic year then ensuing. On subsequent reflection he expressed to me an unwillingness to have the report published, and especially so without some revision and possible additions. I reminded him that before it would be necessary to print there would be the meeting of the Corporation in June, at which he could either decline their request or the desired changes could be considered. Alas! before June came he had passed from this world, and in compliance with his wishes his report was not published.

"Of the personal characteristics of Professor Gammell's service in the Corporation, the most marked, and that which gave it special value and influence, was his perfect frankness and transparency of motive. He seemed absolutely incapable of indirections. In his advocacy of a measure he never put forward plausible reasons while concealing the real ones. Politic men would have thought him deficient in tact. He evidently thought honesty not only the best policy, but the only principle of action by which an honorable and honest man, and specially a Christian man, should always and everywhere be actuated. In all my relations with Professor Gammell, I was never for one moment, in doubt, in any action of his as to what he really thought, or what he believed, or what were his motives. All were as clear as the sunlight. In his death Brown University lost one of the stanchest, most disinterested, most painstaking, and most intelligent of its guardians and friends."

In the founding of the Butler Hospital for the Insane Professor Gammell manifested the deepest interest. He was appointed one of its trustees, and it is touching to find in one of his letters to Professor Chace, written from Rome, Italy, in March, 1879, the following allusion to Butler Hospital, showing how strongly he felt his responsibilities: "I greatly fear that Mr. Hazard's absence and my own will occasion embarrassment to the Butler Hospital board. I wish now that I had resigned my place then, for I always fear that in such an institution the supervision may be allowed to become less and less careful. If the old standard is once lowered, it will not be easy to raise it again. It was fixed at the beginning by heroic devotion to the hospital, and I shall be grieved to have it changed."

On Professor Gammell's devotion to this institution and its kindred institution, the Rhode Island Hospital, Mr. William Goddard has written with so much discrimination and beauty that his words, with the resolutions adopted on the occasion of Professor Gammell's death, obviate all necessity for further enlargement on this theme: —

"On the 27th of January, 1875, Mr. Gammell was elected a trustee of the Butler Hospital for the Insane.

" His interest in this great charity had been fostered by an intimate acquaintance with its beneficent purposes, and by personal observation of its measureless blessings to those who were afflicted with the various forms of mental disease. His acute mind clearly discerned the importance to the safety of society of this place of seclusion and of restraint for those whose delusions were dangerous both to themselves and to their fellow-men. Before Mr. Gammell's election to this responsible office he had rendered important aid to the hospital by literary work, undertaken at the request of Mr. Ives, its first secretary. He was therefore, by familiarity with the work of the hospital, as well as by his mental endowments and by his sympathy with all forms of human suffering, exceptionally equipped for the high trust of its guardianship.

" I can bear testimony to the fidelity with which he discharged the varied and often trying duties of this office.

" He laid claim to no knowledge of mechanics, and he was always ready to refer to those trained in such matters all questions relating to the purely mechanical concerns of the hospital. In this respect he displayed a wisdom which gave the greater value to his opinions upon the subjects within the extensive range of his thought and study.

" The successful administration of a great hospital demands of its guardians something more than knowledge of construction and maintenance, of problems of ventilation and of sewage disposal, however vital these questions may be. It requires of them familiarity with statutes affecting the restraint of the personal liberty of patients, and with those universal laws that govern all human efforts for the cure of mental disease as well as the alleviation of the wretchedness which results from it. But more than all else is the constant appeal to the deepest sympathy with a form of misery to which ' all sorts and conditions of men ' are alike liable, from which neither youth nor age is exempt, and which in many of its aspects is far worse than any other disease with which the human being can be afflicted.

‘ Omni membrorum damno major dementia.’

" In exhaustless sympathy with sickness and sorrow, in that broad philanthropy, which counts no sacrifice too great for the good of the afflicted, and in the comprehensive conception of all the obligations of charity and the resources of science, Mr. Gammell was preëminent among the large-hearted and gifted men whose liberality and devotion have given to the Butler Hospital for the Insane its distinction among contemporary charities. He never neglected any duty devolving upon him, and often made his weekly visitations when almost disabled by illness. Of the annual reports, by which the work of the hospital is made known and its pressing wants are explained, no less than six proceeded from his graceful and earnest pen. Most of the occasional appeals of the trustees to the public and to the benefactors of the hospital during his long term of office emanated from him. His manners to the patients were singularly attractive and cheering, and he overlooked nothing that would diminish their sense of confinement or add to their slender store of happiness. His services will be long and gratefully remembered by his associates, and in the lucid intervals which sometimes come even to the clouded intellect of the insane his name is mentioned with respect.

" In the work which preceded the organization of the Rhode Island Hospital Mr. Gammell took a conspicuous part. His appeals in behalf of this noble charity awakened throughout the State that sentiment of personal obligation toward the sick and the helpless, which resulted in the foundation of a hospital that adds fresh honor to the name it bears. At its opening in 1868, he was chosen to deliver the address, which should commemorate the liberality of its founders and foreshadow its career of usefulness and philanthropy. The occasion was a memorable one, and the orator was worthy of it. The long toil was ended, and they whose hearts had yearned for the sight stood within a completed building, symmetrical in its proportions, equipped with the latest development of science, and to be dedicated to the solace of suffering and the cure of disease. He looked upon the faces of men and women whose Christian liberality had finished this great work, and he must have felt the invisible presence of those whose hearts had ceased to beat save in the renewed pulses of charity and human sympathy. The impulse that upon that day he gave to the Rhode Island Hospital has never spent its force.

" For more than twenty-five years Mr. Gammell was a Director in the Providence National Bank. His relation to this venerable institution was characteristic of the man. His studies had not fitted him to judge of credits, and only the experience of his later life had taught him the maxims and methods with which practiced merchants and bankers are necessarily familiar. But he brought to the discharge of his official duties that knowledge of broad and general principles which is one of the best fruits of academic training, and he regarded his office as a trust to whose every obligation he was always faithful. It is too much the fashion of the age for men to accept office, and to neglect its obvious or implied obligations. Directors and trustees are attentive to their duties more from motives of self-interest than from a sense of duty and a high conception of the meaning of a trust.

" Mr. Gammell yielded to no such heresy. He believed in the performance of every duty to the best of his ability, and the records of the Board of Directors show with what astonishing regularity he participated in its deliberations, and how fully he shared its labors and responsibilities. While never unmindful that the business of life demands hard work and unremitting energy, that the sluggard and the doctrinaire are certain to fail in the struggle for its prizes, he always impressed upon his companions that they were made for something else than to be 'hewers of wood and drawers of water,' and that educated men discharged but a small part of their duties to society by the mere getting of shekels of gold and silver. He knew that the triumphs of civilization are possible only in com-munities successful in the acquisition of wealth, but he also felt and inculcated the obligations imposed upon its possessors.

"Nothing could be more delightful than the relations of the scholar to this congregation of merchants and bankers, to most of whom he had taught the philosophy of life, the charm of letters, the full power of education, and the operation of those laws which are ordained for the moral government of the universe."

MINUTE

ADOPTED BY THE TRUSTEES OF BUTLER HOSPITAL.

By the death of Professor William Gammell, April 3, 1889, the Butler Hospital for the Insane lost a trusted counselor and an earnest friend.

For more than fourteen years he was a member of the Board of Trustees, and his quick sympathy, his clear, trained intellect, and his large experience were always freely devoted to the best interests of the institution.

Scrupulously faithful in the performance of every duty, his example was a stimulus to his fellow-trustees and to the officers of the hospital. His bright and cheerful words made him a welcome visitor to all the patients. Liberal without ostentation ; learned without pedantry ; an accurate thinker, yet tolerant of the mistakes of others; an earnest Christian without any of the bitterness of the sectarian; courteous and of polished manners, but uncompromising in his hostility to all shams, he won the respect and love of all who knew him, and his death is felt by each of his associates on this board as a personal loss.

The Providence Athenæum had been opened to the citizens of Providence as a public library in 1838, with an address by Dr. Wayland. In this institution Professor Gammell had the warmest interest, not only from his love of books, but from his conviction that such institutions are essential to the best interests of our municipal life. Long before he held any official connection with it, he had given his cordial support to its labors. But he rendered it a long and active official service. He was chosen one of its directors September 26, 1853, and held the office four years; was rechosen in 1864, serving it four years longer as director, and then made its Vice-President from 1868 to 1870. He was chosen President in 1870, and filled this office till 1882, — having thus, in varied capacities, devoted himself to its objects for twenty-two years. The minute from its records here given shows in what esteem his services were held by his associates: —

"The communication from Professor William Gammell, declining another election to the office of President, being called up for further action, the following minute in reference thereto was ordered to be incorporated in the record of proceedings.

"While the directors of the Providence Athenæum feel constrained to accept as final the conclusion of Professor

Gammell, it having been reached 'in accordance with a purpose formed some years ago,' yet they desire to make record of the fact that they accede to his wish with reluctance, and in disregard of their own judgment and feelings, both of which prompt them to continue him in a position which he has so long, so wisely, and so acceptably filled.

"Conspicuous as have been the predecessors of Professor Gammell for their devotion to the interests of the Athenæum, its directors wish to make an enduring record of their confident belief that no one of them ever did or could surpass him in the intelligent zeal, the untiring industry, and the deep interest with which he has discharged his duties as its President, and as chairman of its two most important committees.

"And in tendering him their grateful acknowledgment of his past services, they wish also to express to him their earnest hope that he may be spared for many years to come, to aid by his counsel and cheer by his presence those to whom the interests of this institution may be intrusted.

"And it is further ordered that a copy of this minute, signed by the President and the Secretary, be forwarded to Professor Gammell."

For fifteen years he held the presidency of the Rhode Island Bible Society. Christian scholar that he was, none knew better than he, from his historical studies, what a part our English Bible has played in English civilization, and what large and vital interests depend on its free circulation among the people. He followed with interest all the modern questions as to its interpretation. When the Revised Version appeared he studied it with some care, preparing a notice of it for the "Providence Journal."

He was too ripe an English scholar not to be profoundly appreciative of the King James Version as an English classic. But he was no blind worshipper of the past, kept his mind open to any improvements, and was ready to welcome the New Version if it gave a more perfect rendering of the Word of God. His devotion to the Bible rested, however, on the deepest foundations, not on scholarly tastes. He found a congenial field of labor in the duties of his presidency of the Bible Society. What he accomplished in this field of Christian work the following minutes from the records of the society will show.

PROVIDENCE, R. I., *February* 18, 1890.

He was elected President September 2, 1869, and served the society in this office until October 14, 1884, when he declined a reëlection. The following resolutions were presented and unanimously adopted at a special meeting held May 19, 1885.

Whereas, at the last annual meeting, Professor William Gammell, LL. D., on account of other pressing engagements declined a reëlection as presiding officer of this society, —

Resolved, That it has been with deep regret that the society has consented to his retirement from its presidency, which he has held for so many years, and which office he has filled with so much dignity, faithfulness, and efficiency. His energy and sound judgment have impressed themselves upon the action of the society in its explorations of the destitute portions of the State, and the wide circulation of the Holy Scriptures from year to year, through its agency, has been greatly promoted during his administration.

Resolved, That the thanks of the board are hereby tendered to the late President.

Voted, That the resolutions be placed on the records of the society, and that a copy be sent to ex-President Gammell.

He was also chosen a Vice-President of the American Bible Society in 1884. The managers of that society, at the time of his death, adopted a minute recording their high appreciation of his efficient efforts as President of the Rhode Island Bible Society in promoting the "Fourth General Supply of the United States." In discharging public trusts like these much of Professor Gammell's time was passed. They engrossed him. He gave to them not only his time, but his thought, and took no office to which he did not bring an earnest and willing service.

He had a high ideal of citizenship. Abhorring political partisanship, he had always a decided opinion on questions of the day. He stood in general aloof from party gatherings of any sort. He had little taste for popular assemblies, was wanting perhaps in popular sympathies. His historical studies as well as his inborn predilections gave him a strong contempt for the windy patriotism of the stump or the hustings. He failed, possibly, to realize what the modern mission of the scholar in politics involves. But one occasion stands out, when he with other citizens stepped forward to rouse as well as guide popular sentiment. When Charles Sumner was so brutally assaulted in the Senate Chamber of the United States, the citizens of Providence, without distinction of party, met in Howard Hall on the evening of June 7, 1856. His Honor Mayor Smith called the meeting to order. Alexander Duncan was chosen to preside. Dr. Caswell offered a series of resolutions, which were supported in vigorous addresses by Professor Gammell, the Hon. C. S. Bradley, the Rev. Dr. Hedge, and Dr. Wayland. It was a memorable occasion in the history of the city as well as the country. All the addresses on the topic which was absorbing the mind of the North were much above the level of ordinary popular addresses. That by Professor Gammell, while it disclosed the historical scholar in its allusions, revealed also the thoughtful but determined patriot. Free from all empty denunciation, it was weighty with righteous scorn and with just reasoning.

Mention has been made already of Professor Gammell's writings, but not of all his work in this line of literary effort. He was associate editor of the "Christian Review" for the years 1850–52. Not only did he contribute articles to its pages, but gave Dr. Cutting, its editor, the benefit of his counsels and help in maintaining it. A more important work, however, was the contribution of articles to the "Examiner," a weekly religious journal representing the Baptist denomination, and published in New York. During almost the entire period of the war for the Union, he wrote a weekly letter on the events occurring in the great struggle, and the principles involved in it. They attracted wide and special attention, and were complimented in the

warmest terms by the great war secretary, the Hon.
Edwin M. Stanton. At no period in the history of
the newspaper press has it been called to more arduous or more responsible service than during the fluctuating issues of that fearful strife. It was not
only the varying fortunes of the war, but it was the
very important questions which rose from time to
time, and on which the public needed enlighten-
ment; it was the need also of encouragement under
the frightful cost of the battles, not in money, but
in life, and of support against insidious foes in the
Northern household, which called for the strongest
and most constant service from the press.

Professor Gammell's articles were given a prominent place in the paper, and appeared under the
general title of " Thoughts on Current Events." A
glance at the titles of some of the more important
will show the range of discussion they took as well
as the aim they pursued. On July 11, 1862, one
appeared entitled " Proposals of Mediation, France
and England." It was succeeded in the issue of the
week following by one on " Sources of Solicitude."
After General McClellan's failure before Richmond,
Professor Gammell wrote, August 7, 1862, on " The
Present Hour and its Demands," followed in the next
issue by an article on " The Drafting Order." In
September, he had one entitled " Assailing the Government." He wrote in January of the next year
on the " Border States Becoming Free," and so to
the close of the gigantic struggle. After it was
over his pen was still occupied in discussing the

problems of the hour. Two significant articles appeared in the summer of 1865: one on " Wise Delays in Reconstruction," the other on " England and her Humiliation." The tone of these articles was conservative, but loyal to the core. He held throughout a courageous attitude. He never betrayed the slightest faltering in the darkest hour. He viewed the whole contest in the light of history. He brought his historical studies to bear on all his discussions. He had learned in that school to discriminate between eddies and the main current. He planted himself on general principles, and hence he was not easily shaken. Among all his good services to the community, this series of writings must always stand conspicuous. As one turns the files of the paper containing these timely, telling, well-considered articles, there is no wonder raised at Secretary Stanton's warm appreciation of them. They were worth squadrons in the field.

For many years, also, he furnished articles to the " Providence Journal," whose accomplished editor, the Hon. Henry B. Anthony, was his friend. In this he followed in the footsteps of Professor Goddard. His contributions took various shapes : sometimes reflections on current events, then discussions of matters pertaining to Rhode Island history, or the cause of education. Notable among them were his commemorative notices of prominent citizens. If these were somewhat stately in form, yet they were always in perfect taste, and delineated the life or the services with fidelity and felicity too. It is only

needful to recall such notices from his pen as those
on Dr. Isaac Ray, Mr. William T. Dorrance; on his
colleagues, President Wayland ("Examiner and
Chronicle"), Professors Caswell and Chace; on the
Hon. William S. Slater, Zachariah Allen, and Henry
B. Anthony. A kindred service was rendered the
college in the necrology of its graduates, which he
prepared for thirty years. It was read at the annual
Commencement, and was a model of its kind. He
followed closely the fortunes of the graduates, and
as they fell one by one at their different posts of
duty, the departure was chronicled in kindly words.
No matter how humble or obscure the position he
may have filled, if the graduate had done a good
work in life, a few well-chosen words recalled him
fitly to his brethren still in the march of life.

Thus far the sketch of Professor Gammell's life
has been mainly occupied with the outward manifes-
tations of that life in its professional and public relations. It has sought to disclose the scholar at his
work, and using his scholarly gifts in the service of
good causes. But did it stop here, some important
characteristics, some of the finer qualities of the
man, would be unnoticed. It is always, indeed, difficult to portray an inner life. It eludes analysis.
Even when "diaries" and "correspondence" furnish
clues to the more private and sacred experiences,
it is hard to transfer to any pages

> "The beaming eye, the cheering voice,
>   That lent to life a generous glow."

Professor Gammell impressed himself on life about

him largely by means of his superior social gifts. He had a ready flow of conversation, had at command a varied fund of knowledge derived from his converse with books, was full of a contagious cheerfulness, brought life into the discussions in which he took part, enjoyed deeply the wit of other men, and at times threw out flashes of his own in quick repartee or comment. The society of Providence for many years recognized in him one of its most accomplished leaders. If any man of distinction was to be honored socially, Professor Gammell was sure to be one of the invited guests. He was specially fond of coming in contact with those interested in literary pursuits, dispensed a charming hospitality to them in his own home. But in any general company he had the art of enlisting all in talk, and no one knew better than he how to avoid " shop " when general conversation was the proper demand. It is common to hear his manners spoken of as formal, courtly, with a touch of coldness or reserve about them. To the public this was his mien, but to the more private circles he was simply the genial companion or the kindly, gracious host. Perhaps his social gifts found one of their best expressions at the Friday Evening Club, whose story is told by Bishop Clark, in the following paper, with equal vividness and beauty.

PROFESSOR GAMMELL AND THE FRIDAY EVENING CLUB.

On the 16th of January, 1868, Professor Gammell, with a few other gentlemen, organized an association " for the discussion of literary, philosophical, æsthetic, historical, and scientific subjects," and it was arranged that they should meet in turn every alternate Friday night at each other's houses, when " each member in succession will be required to prepare and present a subject for discussion, either orally or in writing, — simple refreshments to be served at ten o'clock." The Club embraced representatives of the clerical, legal, and medical professions, — teachers of science, philosophy, history, and the languages, book-makers and book-collectors, a bank officer, and a manufacturer. It continued to meet, with its ranks unbroken by death or removal, until the year 1877, when Dr. Alexis Caswell, formerly President of Brown University, in a ripe old age and while his natural force was still unabated, suddenly passed away. In the course of a few years, the accomplished Professor J. L. Diman was taken from us, in the very prime of his days, and without the slightest premonition of his departure. On Friday, the 27th of February, 1881, the Club met at his house, and were entertained by him with his usual cordiality and cheerfulness, and on the following Thursday he had ceased to live on earth. Next followed Alexander Farnum, President of the Rhode Island Trust Company, and who had been the Secretary and Treasurer of the Club from the beginning: a man of wonderful gifts and varied learning, and who, amid the pressure of an active business life, always found time for careful study and reflection.

Then there dropped out of our ranks, in somewhat rapid succession, John R. Bartlett, who, in his earlier days, was at the head of the Mexican Boundary Commission, and afterward a well-known collector and writer of books, — holding for several years the office of Secretary of State in Rhode Island; Dr. Edward T. Caswell, an eminent physician, whose papers instructed us in matters of medical science which only an expert could be expected to expound; Professor George I. Chace, a profound thinker and a magnetic educator, who did his part in forming and stimulating the minds of many of our best and ablest men; the Hon. Charles S. Bradley, at one time professor in the Law School at Cambridge, a distinguished and successful jurist, and at the same time an enthusiast in art; Professor William Gammell, of whom we shall have somewhat more to say; and, last of all, the Rev. Dr. Samuel L. Caldwell, formerly pastor of the First Baptist Church in Providence, professor in the Theological Seminary in Newton, Mass., and afterward President of Vassar College, and who had just begun to collect the materials for a Life of Professor Gammell when he was suddenly called to the discharge of higher duties in a higher sphere.

It is not appropriate here to write at any length of the delightful and instructive meetings that were held on those winter nights in years gone by, when some of the ripest scholars and ablest thinkers in our community were willing to expend their best strength in the preparation of articles for the edification of the little circle of listeners who were wont to gather around our Club table. All shades of political and theological opinion were represented, and it was understood that every man was at liberty to express himself without reserve; but no unkind or discourteous words were ever spoken, and no discord disturbed the harmony of our meetings. The social element was as prominent as the intellectual, and the feeling seemed gradually to grow up amongst us that we formed a kind of family by ourselves, — a sacred brotherhood, bound together by peculiar and very intimate ties. It is sad to think that the lips of nearly all who so often electrified us with their brilliant talk are silent now. The memory of those pleasant evenings lingers in the air, like a strain of distant and melancholy music.

Professor Gammell was, from the beginning to the end, one of the most prominent, active, and loyal members of the Friday Evening Club. He was never absent from its meetings, unless by some great constraint, and he entered into our proceedings with an emphasis that seemed to excite and invigorate us all. The papers that he presented were carefully prepared and full of rich and instructive thought. The subjects of which he wrote are preserved in the records of the Club, and a somewhat full analysis of his earlier papers may be found there. The first of these was read on the 6th of November, 1868, on "The Nature and Results of Naturalization," and a brief outline of this paper will serve to illustrate the fullness and precision with which Professor Gammell was accustomed to treat any topic that he was called to handle. He begins with a careful definition of the term "naturalization;" stating the laws of the United States and of the chief states of Europe in relation to the subject; citing sundry cases which have arisen between our own and foreign governments in which were involved the rights of naturalized citizens under differing laws; showing that the most recent foreign legislation indicates a tendency towards a recognition of the doctrine of the right of complete expatriation, for which American statesmen have contended; and closing with a statement of some of the evils to which we are exposed by the present state of our naturalization laws and the methods of their enforcement, with suggestions as to the possible means of avoiding those evils.

The next paper was on "The Law and the Gospel of Divorce." Assuming marriage to be a divine institution as well as a civil contract, the professor proceeds to consider at some length the laws of divorce that existed in the great states of antiquity, with a sketch of the revolution that was wrought when the Latin Church pronounced marriage to be a sacrament, and therefore indissoluble. He then goes on to show how the teaching of the theologians of the Reformation has led to the recognition of marriage, in most Protestant countries, as a civil contract, which, under certain circumstances, may rightly be dissolved. The existing laws of divorce in various countries are detailed, followed by a careful examination of the argument from Scripture, the general conclusion being that divorce can be justified for only a single cause.

The third paper is on "The Future of Labor," showing how largely the future of civilization is involved in the future of labor; but we have not the space for giving a full analysis of this valuable contribution to a subject that is now to so great an extent agitating the community.

"Belligerency, Neutrality, and Peace" was the next topic presented by the professor; but as the outline of this treatise fills five or six closely written pages in the records of the Club, I must leave it without further notice.

The professor's fifth paper, on "The Agency of Cities in Modern Civilization," was particularly adapted to bring out the stores of historical knowledge which in a lifetime of study he had accumulated, and in a single hour valuable treasures were opened to us which it would have required weeks of patient toil to explore.

I must now confine myself to a simple recapitulation of the subjects presented to the Club by Professor Gammell, taking them in their order, as follows : —

"The Present Aspect of the Labor Question."
"International Arbitration as a Substitute for War."
"The Life and Travels of Marco Polo."
"The Epochs of Civilization in the United States."

" Asylum and Extradition among Nations."

" The Confederation Period of the Republic."

" History of the Adoption of the Constitution, by George Bancroft."

" Tendencies towards a General Use of Comparative Method in History."

" Italy Revisited."

" The Monroe Doctrine."

Not one of these topics was treated carelessly; in fact, Professor Gammell was incapable of anything like careless writing, and if he erred at all it was in the direction of an excess of refinement and polish. That he had been a teacher of rhetoric might be inferred from the stately flow of his periods and the delicate finish of his sentences; just as we might have known that he had been an instructor in history from the amount of historical illustration in almost everything that he wrote.

It was the custom of the Friday Evening Club, at the close of every paper, to call upon each member in his turn to pronounce judgment upon what had been presented, and on these occasions the professor was distinguished by the accuracy and copiousness of his criticisms, — it sometimes appearing as if he must have prepared himself for the symposium with more care than the essayist himself. His own opinions were very positive, and he was by nature and education a true conservative; and yet he was willing to listen to the opinions of others with respect, however seriously he might differ from them, and ready to accord to them the same right of private judgment that he claimed for himself. He was always pleasant and genial in his talk, and had a keen sense of humor, although he rarely indulged in it of his own motion. He did not deal in apothegms or in scintillating expressions; he was sensible, instructive, and entertaining, but made no special attempt to say brilliant and sparkling things. He was not at all given to pyrotechnical exhibitions. His humor was rather of the mild, Addisonian sort, and did not remind one at all of Carlyle or Sydney Smith. Still he was never dull, or prosy, or commonplace, and when he opened his mouth we were sure that we would learn something.

Professor Gammell was loyal to the Club from the beginning to the end, seeming to regard it as one of the chief enjoyments of his life; and when on the evening of the 21st of November, 1884, he found himself present at what proved to be its last meeting, with only four others present of the original members of the Club, the reluctance with which he relinquished his hold upon the old fraternity, and his unwillingness to do anything that might look like putting a deliberate end to its existence, is evident in the following extract from the minutes : —

" On motion of Professor Gammell the following vote was passed: ' Voted, that the meetings of the Friday Evening Club be suspended till such time as it may seem practicable to resume them, at the call of the Secretary *pro tem.*' "

That time will never come, and already two of the four original members who were present that evening have passed away.

It has interested me to find that the last entry made in the minutes of the Club is from Professor Gammell's pen, and reads as follows : —

" Since the last meeting of the Friday Evening Club, our greatly esteemed associate, Alexander Farnum, has been removed by death. He was the only officer the Club has ever elected, and in a fuller sense than is true of any other one of its members he was the representative and embodiment of its life and spirit." After a brief sketch of Mr. Farnum's career, he eulogizes him in language, which we transcribe, not only as a just tribute to the memory of a very gifted man, but also as a specimen of the professor's stately and flowing style: " Possessed of intellectual endowments of superior order, he had acquired that liberal and many-sided culture which comes from well-directed studies, from travel in many lands, and from practical acquaintance with the methods of business and the principles of finance. He had also collected for his own use a large and select library of the best books in the best editions, and among these he delighted to spend the leisure hours of every day. He had thus informed himself on a great variety of interesting subjects, and was familiar with most of the important questions of the time, whether political, literary, or philosophical. But over all his gifts and acquirements there shone a radiant and quick intelligence, a genial social spirit, and a responsive intellectual sympathy, which fitted him to enliven and adorn the social circles in which he appeared. He thus possessed in a remarkable degree those qualities of mind and character which always impart the most attractive charm to the meetings of an association like ours. Nowhere did he appear to better advantage than here. How nobly he performed his part, how well he filled his place among us, we shall never forget. How finished were his papers, how independent were his criticisms, how brilliant his conversation, how sprightly his wit, how much in every way he contributed to these ' Noctes Ambrosianæ' which we have passed together, will always be among the cherished memories of his associates in the Friday Evening Club."

After the last meeting of the Club in 1884, the professor cherished the feeling that it might still be revived under new auspices; but now that he has gone, the fraternity is extinct, and the little handful of us who remain can only look forward with the hope that we may be allowed to meet again in a nobler and purer sphere.

Only the few know what warmth of affection dwelt in his nature. He made, however, long and lasting friendships. If to some he seemed unsympathetic and distant, it was because he never cared to "wear his heart upon his sleeve." Two of these friendships are types of an intimacy so high and true that they well deserve a passing commemoration. His friendship with Professor Chace was formed in the years of college life, when together they were "nursed upon the selfsame hill." It was kept up through years of kindred association as members of the Faculty, in different chairs of the same university. It was preserved by devotion, each to the other's interests, as true as steel and more precious than gold. They shared the trials and triumphs of life — sorrows which darkened and joys which brightened its skies — more closely than brothers. It lasted to the end, — through fifty-seven years; and now, together in the land of light, we doubt not they have renewed its bonds.

Scarcely less notable was Professor Gammell's friendship with Mr. Robert H. Ives. It was of early growth. It deepened with every year. To him Mr. Ives gave his confidence freely. He was intrusted with confidences no one else shared. On all matters of literary taste or execution Mr. Ives sought his opinion, and deferred to it absolutely. Every day saw them together. Professor Gammell reverenced in Mr. Ives that noble elevation of character, that strong, massive comprehension of affairs, that modest, quiet demeanor, which so well became but never

concealed his strength. They had common responsibilities as members of the Corporation of Brown
University. In the work of founding the Rhode Isl-
and Hospital, of which Mr. Ives, bore so considerable a part, the sympathy between them was perfect. And it was one of many proofs of regard for
Professor Gammell given by Mr. Ives, that in his
will he bequeathed an annuity of ten thousand dollars and a life interest in the old family mansion to
his friend.

If the circle of Professor Gammell's more intimate friends was not large, it was choice. Among
his pupils he numbered some of these. They
shared his gracious and genial hospitality. How
warmly he followed their careers in life! How
ready and how full his gratification over their successes! How open to their desires for counsel!
Indeed, outside academic circles, his friendship was
a help and solace to some who knew him. "He
was the best friend I ever had," writes an accomplished Christian woman, whom he had known for
many years; indeed, from girlhood. In the time of
bereavement and consequent care, struggle, and
loneliness, he had proved the most sympathetic of
friends, cheering and sustaining her by almost daily
visits to her darkened home. The following tribute
to his memory by the Rev. J. G. Vose, D. D., while
it dwells on other points in Professor Gammell's
character and career, lays special emphasis on his
qualities as a friend.

"I learned to esteem Professor Gammell before I became acquainted with him. As I had not the honor of graduating at this University, I count myself very fortunate in having the early acquaintance, in my professional studies at home and abroad, — not the acquaintance only, but I may venture to say in some cases the intimate friendship, — of some of the choicest sons of Brown University: the lamented Diman and Dunn, and, among the living, such men as Professors Fisher, of New Haven, and Murray, of Princeton. From these men I first heard the name of Gammell, not as of an ordinary teacher, but spoken of with youthful familiarity; indeed, with an affectionate gratitude, as of one who had led them into the pleasant paths of literature, and inspired them with a desire for something pure and lofty, encouraging their youthful efforts. I learned to admire and respect our friend from them. His life had gone out into theirs, as is the case with all true teachers; not the precepts only, not the canons of literary taste, but a certain quality of mind and heart, a love of all high thoughts and generous emotions, that must be felt to be understood. Professor Gammell did the best of his work, perhaps, in the influence he exerted over others. He certainly spent many of the best years of his life in this service.

"I am not unmindful of his excellent writings; surely in this place we cannot forget his historical papers, his studies in special fields, or his wide acquaintance with the domain of history. But he gave a great deal of his life to the work of teaching. He spent some of his best years in those efforts which seem to many men petty and trivial, to correct the faults and prune the exuberance of youth, to impart to generous minds a sense of the sacredness of all truth and beauty, and the close relation there is between refined expression and a pure life. Few men have ever accomplished so much as he in that particular department of influence.

" It is common to look down on criticism ; no doubt it has been perverted. Men have themselves become limited and narrowed in attempting to employ it. Matthew Arnold tells us that Wordsworth had a low idea of criticism, and quotes this saying of his : ' That if the quantity of time consumed in critiques on the works of others were given to original composition, of whatever kind, it would be much better employed ; it would make a man find out sooner his own level, and do infinitely less mischief.' We can see reasons why Wordsworth should have thus spoken, in the shallow, unjust, and even spiteful criticism to which he was subjected. But the work of a critic who has a large heart and a quick perception of genuine excellence is far different from this, and may save to lifelong usefulness what would else be wasted. Such was the efficient work of our lamented friend for the young men of a generation ago in Brown University, who imbibed from him just views of expression, of a simple and manly style, enriched by all the wealth of heartfelt imagination and a sincere love of the beautiful. It was all the grander because it seemed humble, and must have cost an amount of patience and forbearance that can scarcely be realized. It was all the richer in its results because it touched life so near the fountain head ; and its influence has been seen in many a noble treatise, in oratory that has charmed the world, in a higher standard of journalism, in all the departments of literature and the utterances of moral and religious truth.

" And here we reach the secret of excellence in the character of our honored friend : that he gave so much of his life to others. Whatever knowledge and skill he possessed he held as a treasury, on which every man might draw who needed them. I can bear personal witness to his cordial readiness to give advice and encouragement in literary matters, such as few could bestow. His own stores were used to aid men, and not to hinder them. He cherished no contempts. He was full of all kind and friendly sentiments. His sympathies were not locked up in his own bosom. I shall not forget his coming to my house in a time of sickness, when I was suffering from the deepest parental anxiety, bringing with him that genuine fellow-feeling by which our burdens are made lighter and our faith in God strengthened. Nor will either you or I forget the great fortitude which he exhibited under the recent disappointment of his earthly hopes. Yet the prevailing characteristic of his life was a friendly cheerfulness. He put aside his own sorrows for the welfare of others. This was what made it always pleasant to meet him. The rare courtesy that characterized his outward demeanor was the product of a true gentleman's instinct, the desire to confer happiness wherever he went. If his manners seemed to some a little formal and precise, they were the courtly manners of the old school, and we felt beneath them the throb of a genuine hospitality at home and a hearty interest abroad. His air of leisure and of deference was in delightful contrast to the brusque and hurried greetings of modern times, such as we catch from the telephone, and which seem to come to us with the rush of modern inventions and of labor-saving machines and threaten to destroy the reverence of the young and the charm of social life.

"It was indeed a pleasure to meet him at any time. Like some of our good citizens on the hill, he often extended his walks far over on the west side of the city. His cordial greeting can never be forgotten. Rarely have I met him but he wished me to share his walk, and entered into genial discourse on matters of literature or morals, with frequent and kindly reference to the friends of early days. I seem to see him now at the corner of the street, near my house, where he lingered with me in the warm sunshine, but four or five weeks ago ; his voice, his smile, his figure, all are distinct before me. This is the every-day mystery of life, that those we value so highly vanish like a dream."

But if in the circles of friendship Professor Gammell's nature showed its capacity for large and generous affections, in the sacredness of home that nature displayed still more its affluent tenderness and beauty. The delight in children and grandchildren was a constant brightness in his life. He used to say that he thought it the highest privilege that he could live to see a third generation growing up around him. The birth of a grandchild always stirred in him new thoughts of tenderness. For his children his love took on often the shape of a solicitude which seemed to brood over every interest of their lives. He delighted in their society. His native cheerfulness of temperament kept itself fresh and hearty by his sympathy with them. When, in 1887, his son Arthur, a promising student of law in Harvard University, died, the bereavement, though accepted in all the meekness of Christian resignation, was an anguish to his spirit which only those near him ever knew. Outwardly calm, his suffering was like the quiet of those still, dark waters which sunlight does not pierce, and far below the surface of which we know are unsounded depths.

Any memorial of Professor Gammell which did not advert to the happiness of his home-life would be greatly wanting. It was what he emphasized as the token of a " gracious loving-kindness in his

Heavenly Father towards him." Those who ever shared the hospitality of that beautiful home by the sea, at Newport, will readily recall the cheerful, bright look as he sat at his table, or as he walked upon the lawn by the shore, looking out upon the sweep of waters. For thirty-eight years that home gave him "sympathy in his aims and labors." It gave him rest. It gave him in the growth of his children an ever present joy. The letters of those thirty-eight years show how perfect was the union of hearts. A sacred reserve forbids lengthened allusions to the inner life of that home; but how ample and rich were its blessings for him his own expressions tenderly record.

His religious character was decided and deep. He had an unquestioning faith in the great verities of the Christian revelation. It was not only unshaken by all the modern assaults on Christianity, but grew in strength and determination to the last. His religious life was inward, meditative, averse to all periodical excitements or enthusiasms, but pronounced in the observance of the Sabbath, in the worship of the sanctuary, and in the training of his household. On a regular and devout family worship he set the highest value, and visitors at his home will recall the fervency and aptness of his prayers at the household altar. That service he never allowed to be hurried nor lightly performed. " He was," said the Rev. Dr. Caldwell in the singularly just and beautiful tribute to his memory published in the " Providence Journal," just after his death,

" a man averse to pretense, sham, indirection, mere rhetoric, and yet he had no tolerance for anything like impropriety, vulgarity, low tone, in religious service. He cared most for what is true and spiritual, and yet he wanted the outward observance worthy of the humble, devout, adoring spirit. He learned the way of faith in his father's house, and he continued in it to the end of his days, unseduced, unshaken by any doubt. In the familiar intercourse of more than thirty years I never discovered any wavering in the confidence of his faith. His views were large enough and liberal enough, but his simple trust in Jesus Christ and belief in the gospel and kingdom of God were never disturbed." He was always glad to have conversation take a religious turn. It was natural for him to speak of religious themes, for they interested him deeply. On one occasion he remarked to a friend that he " was sorry there was so little doctrinal preaching. The laity needed instruction on such themes." Indeed, the sermons which interested and held him were sermons unfolding Christian truth to the understanding. He distrusted the hortatory appeals except in special cases, and when supported by a previous convincing exhibition of solid teaching. For everything that trenched on the dignity of the pulpit, for everything that bordered on the flippant or the coarse in pulpit teaching, he manifested a hearty disgust.

Both by hereditary ties and by firm conviction he was a Baptist. But no man was more catholic in his religious sympathies. He had the widest interest in the growth of Christ's kingdom, and could not tolerate any sectarianism which did not rejoice in all victories for that kingdom gained by any body of Christian disciples. He was a worshipper frequently in other sanctuaries than those of his own denomination, and his tolerance was as marked as was his quiet devotion to his own church.

Professor J. L. Lincoln, who has delineated so admirably Professor Gammell's career in the University, has also sketched his connection with the First Baptist Church of Providence : —

"You requested me to add to my recollections of Professor Gammell's relations to the college Faculty a mention of his relations to the First Baptist Church and Society of this city. Gladly do I accede to this request, as it is in the spirit and conduct with which he maintained these relations that the best qualities of his character found their crowning illustration and influence. I have spoken of his loyalty as a son of this college, the place of his education. This virtue of his character shone forth yet more conspicuously in a devotion to yet higher interests than those of education and good learning, — the interests of the Christian religion and of the kingdom of Christ. In his youth he confessed by baptism his faith in Christ and Christianity, and this faith grew with his growth and strengthened with his strength to mature manhood and age. He was a member of the First Baptist Church from 1837 to his death, a period of fifty-two years ; and for a still longer period — for sixty-two years, if we begin with 1827, when he entered college — he was a devout attendant upon its services. For six years he was a superintendent of the Sunday-school, and for a much

longer time he was teacher of one of the Bible classes.
He rendered most valuable service in promoting in the
church the interests of foreign missions, by his personal
efforts to increase its contributions to this cause, and also
by his addresses at its missionary meetings. A like active and useful part Professor Gammell bore in the promotion of the secular and financial interests of the church,
as a pew proprietor and member of the Charitable Baptist Society. On important committees he shared with
his colleagues responsible trusts of the Society, and gave
to it, in its deliberations and acts, the aid of his counsels,
and contributed generously on all occasions when its
finances needed aid. The records of the Society for more
than a generation are full of evidence of his efficient
labors in furthering all that pertained to its progress.
His death was felt to be a great loss to the Society as well
as to the church; and it was meet that, on the day of the
funeral, the services should be held in the meeting-house
where he had worshipped for more than half a century,
and that from that sacred place his remains should be
borne to their last rest."

The features of Professor Gammell's religious
life, so well delineated by the Rev. Dr. Thayer in
the tribute he has prepared, will be recognized by
all who knew him. His independence of spirit was
one of his more prominent characteristics. Whenever manifested, it was always maintained with just
deference to the opinions and feelings of others. It
added strength to his influence, and while it ac-
cented his individuality, as Dr. Thayer says, it never
isolated him from his fellow-Christians or from his
associates in the work of life.

NEWPORT, *March* 15, 1890.

I have been asked to join in a testimonial to Professor Gammell. My increasing intercourse with him of late years, has made me feel his loss too much not to comply with the request. One shrinks from a formal tribute to a friend. Yet it is a real tribute which I pay Professor Gammell in saying that through all the changes about him he preserved his identity. For all agree that a wonderful process of assimilation is going on, and everybody is becoming like everybody else. Perpetual contacts with all sorts of people are unconscious attritions that rub down personal peculiarities to an uninteresting sameness. Fashionable life renders its votaries indistinguishable by the enamel it puts on them. Politics bring men into disgusting resemblance, while our literature of all kinds is strangely alike, and forms its readers to its own average. What wonder, then, that men lose or greatly qualify their identities, that colleges are conforming to the pattern of the age, and that presidents and professors are becoming like the rest of mankind, — the presidents largely employed in collecting funds, and the professors no longer living and working in the college only, but playing the scholar in politics and acting in peripatetic universities? But Professor Gammell was wholly formed in Brown University when — defects and all — it was the old American college, and his life was concentrated there with singular devotion. That cast of character he never lost. Not obtrusively, but decidedly, it impressed you, and it was easy to conceive of him as in the class-room. His opinions were positive and given emphatically, but not offensively *ex cathedra*. He loved racy good English, taught it and used it, though I doubt not he exercised literary charity for his pupils and friends who have come to prefer poets and thinkers whose meaning is not plain to their readers, nor probably was to themselves.

Professor Gammell lived on the verge of fashion, yet had no heart for it, but cultivated the society of scholars and Christian gentlemen, who, among others, sometimes visit Newport. His own religious convictions were quiet, but assured, and he never failed in his testimony to the truth. Fully recognizing other Christian communions, he was faithful to his own, and his pen vindicated the claims of its worthies to the esteem of mankind. So he did not accept dilutions of doctrines, nor look with favor on Christianity held in solution, but believed and loved the simple, strong faith of his fathers. If some of his friends advanced towards a Protestant purgatory, or favored those who did, Professor Gammell, without interrupting his friendship, did not accompany them, since, trusting in the sufficiency of Christ's atonement and the abounding grace of God to his own soul, he was not wont to look for 'another probation.' He gloried in the work of missions, and found, as others do, chiefest hope for man in their progress. As years passed on, and from his quiet life he looked out on the great world, his thoughts grew more massive with ideas of God and Law and Providence, and his heart more responsive to Christ and his gospel. And then sorrow which 'comes to all' came to him. Very great was the disappointment in the loss of a most promising young life, exceeding dear to a father's heart, — very sad the loneliness. Old age feels more deeply than youth. But Professor Gammell bowed himself humbly, and those who saw him in private felt a chastened, mellowed tone that told of a blessed work within.

Very painful this breaking up of such a circle as existed in Brown. Yet very pleasant to recollect them as with varying gifts and genial feelings they pass before

the mind. Not the least worthy of affectionate memory
was the subject of this notice.

Yours, sincerely,   T. THAYER.

Professor Gammell's closing years were full of
vigor. In 1887 he showed some signs of failure.
He seemed far from well. His striking personal
presence, erect form, and bright eye were still observed, but there was less elasticity in his step and
less vivacity in his conversation. From all this, however, he rallied, and his health had been exceptionally good through the winter of 1888–9. He was
never more cheerful, and never entered with more
zest into life. He was seen, as of old, taking the
familiar walks, delighted most if some companion
would share them with him. But the end was unconsciously drawing nigh. On Tuesday evening,
March 26, he attended the monthly meeting of the
Historical Society, presiding as usual, and entering
with his accustomed spirit into all the exercises.
On the day following, a meeting of the Corporation
of the University was held to consider and act upon
the resignation of the office of President by Dr.
Robinson. He took an active part in the counsels
of the occasion, making one of his felicitous addresses. The long continued strain of the meeting,
without his usual meal in the middle of the day,
perhaps with some exposure to a biting wind in a
long walk taken after adjournment, seemed to ex-
haust him. On Thursday he was confined to the
house. During Friday and Saturday he resumed

his usual course of life. On Sunday, however, pneumonia set in. "I am taken sick," he said to his wife, "on the anniversary of our son's death." For a while the doctor encouraged hope of recovery. Some days later, in the morning, having been refreshed by an ice-bath, he was lifted from his bed to the couch, and asked for the "Providence Journal." He turned to the account of the Historical Society's recent meeting. It was the last act of the Christian scholar, but characteristic of his scholarly habits. He soon showed signs of growing weakness, and none more clearly, none so calmly, recognized the approaching end. With undimmed intelligence and perfect serenity of spirit, he expressed his trust in the Redeemer, as one who knew Him whom he had believed, and was persuaded that He was able to keep that committed to Him against that day. On the morning of the day before he died, he said to his devoted wife, "I am spared to you one day more;" and it was touching, during his last illness, to hear him "rejoice that he was taken first," and was not to be left as the survivor of his beloved wife. He made all the arrangements for his funeral, enjoining the utmost simplicity in all the services. Life drew gently, but swiftly, to its close. He died on April 3, 1889, in his seventy-eighth year.

His funeral took place on the following Saturday, April 6, from the First Baptist Church, where for sixty-two years he had been a worshipper. His pastor, the Rev. Edwin Brown, D. D., read selections from the Holy Scriptures. His friend of thirty years, who had also been his pastor, the Rev. Dr. Samuel L. Caldwell, since "passed into the world of light," made the prayer. And then he was buried in the beautiful cemetery of Swan Point, close by the grave of his son Arthur.

A few months later came the Commencement of the University. For more than half a century his presence had added to the life and interest of the academic gathering. With possibly two or three exceptions he had always been there to greet the old graduates. He loved the occasion consecrated to college memories and to the interests of good learning. All his love for the college then shone conspicuous. As the groups of returning alumni assembled, his name was mentioned, his labors were recalled, his long and faithful devotion to the honored Alma Mater was rehearsed, and the general grief that they "should see his face no more" found ready utterance. And when, in the course of the Commencement festivities, the alumni assembled in their annual session, the desire of all hearts was met in the adoption of a minute on his death. This biographical and memorial sketch, prepared by a grateful pupil, is best concluded by the graceful appreciative testimony of this minute to the exalted character and services of Professor Gammell : —

" It is with profound sorrow and a sense of great loss that the members of the Alumni Association, assembled at their annual meeting, record the death of Professor

Gammell, of the class of 1831. He will be sadly missed this week at the college anniversary occasions, public and social, which for so many years he has always attended, and to which his dignity of presence and gracious manners have always lent distinction. For more than sixty years, the period which covers his undergraduate and his subsequent professional life, and during which he has resided in Providence, and sustained intimate relations to the college, his name has been honorably associated with its prosperity and progress. We recall with gratitude the valuable services which he has rendered as a college instructor in rhetoric and English literature, and in history and political economy, bringing to these departments unusual qualifications by his literary tastes and attainments, and by his zealous pursuit of historical studies; promoting in the one, by his rhetorical instruction and lectures and by his discriminating criticism of rhetorical exercises, the literary culture of his pupils and the literary character and reputation of the college, and by his intelligent and faithful work in the other, inaugurating an era of historical instruction and study which has been most worthily perpetuated by his successors. Many are the classes, many the students, of our University who will ever cherish his name and the influence of his teaching among the choicest memories of their college life. We recall, too, the services which he rendered, after his retirement from the Faculty, by his counsel and action as a member for eighteen years of the Board of Fellows of the University. But, devoted though he was with a loyal affection to his Alma Mater, his labors were not confined to his offices of trust in her service. As a citizen he took a generous and active interest in good learning and liberal education everywhere, and in all worthy enterprises in philanthropy, morals, and religion which advanced the progress in this country and the world of a truly Christian civilization. And with all these remembrances of Professor Gammell's various and useful labors we gladly associate our recollections of those sterling qualities of his personal character and life which won for him the respect and affection of his numerous friends."

HISTORICAL PAPERS.

SAMUEL WARD, GOVERNOR OF RHODE ISLAND.[1]

I.

THE generation who peopled New England during the middle of the eighteenth century were witnesses of a series of events whose importance in shaping the subsequent character and the ultimate destiny of the colonies can scarcely be estimated too highly. It was the age in which was brought to a close the protracted struggle between England and France for ascendency upon this continent; in which were suffered the worst evils of the ill-devised legislation of the Parliament, and the earliest aggressions of the British ministry upon the rights of the colonies; and in which were seen the first acts of resistance that terminated at length in the war of American independence. To this generation belonged Governor Samuel Ward, the subject of the present sketch; and in the colony with which he was connected he was among the foremost of the patriotic actors in the stirring scenes of the age.

He was descended from an ancient and respectable family, of which the first representative in this country was his grandfather, Thomas Ward, who came to Newport, Rhode Island, soon after the restoration of Charles the Second. In England he had been attached to the republican party, and had been somewhat conversant with the affairs of the Commonwealth. He was highly respected in the colony, to which he rendered many valuable

[1] Reprinted from Sparks's *American Biography*.

services, both as a private citizen and as a member, at different times, of both branches of the colonial legislature. Thomas Ward died in 1689, leaving a second wife, whose maiden name was Amy Smith, and their only child, Richard Ward, who was born a few months before his father's death. Richard Ward, the father of the subject of this memoir, on attaining to manhood, was an active and exemplary citizen of Newport, engaged in commerce, and devoting much attention to the affairs of the colony, in whose service he was distinguished for his fidelity and probity of character. He was for several years Recorder, or Secretary of State, and afterwards Deputy-Governor, of Rhode Island, and was twice elected to the office of Governor, in 1741 and 1742; after which he declined a reëlection, and retired to private life.

Samuel Ward, the second son of Richard, was born at Newport, on the 27th of May, 1725. His mind was early subjected to the discipline of that best kind of education, which arises from the associations of a well-regulated family circle, of cultivated manners and liberal tastes. He was also sent to a grammar school in his native town, which in its day maintained a high celebrity as one of the best schools in the country. Here, aided, as is probable, by the instructions of his elder brother, Thomas, who graduated at Harvard College in 1733, he passed through a course of study which was probably more than usually extensive and thorough for one not destined for either of the learned professions.

For a considerable period prior to the American Revolution, the ancient town of Newport was among the most flourishing commercial towns on the Atlantic coast. Its capacious harbor made it the resort of much of the foreign shipping that visited the colonies. The enterprise of its inhabitants had embarked in nearly every branch of colonial trade, while the salubrity of its climate and the surpassing beauty of its ocean scenery were already attracting temporary visitors from less favored climes, and making it what it has since become, the most delightful watering place upon the continent. Amidst its external prosperity and its intimate relations with the mother country, the society of the town is said to have been distinguished for its polished manners and the intellectual spirit with which it was pervaded.

Here the philosopher Berkeley passed two years in maturing his generous plans for civilizing the Indians and educating young men of the colonies for the ministry of the gospel. This eminent man was much in the society of the town, and for a time assisted the rector of the Episcopal parish in the performance of his parochial duties. His active and generous spirit, enriched as it was by the most liberal culture and the noblest benevolence, must have exerted a controlling influence over every circle in which he moved. While residing at Newport, Berkeley is said to have composed his " Minute Philosopher," the most finished and the most enduring of all his writings, which has forever linked his name with the quiet shores of the beautiful island which was then his home. He also founded a literary and social club, made up of the gentlemen of the town, which, no doubt, was instrumental in elevating its character, and promoting a unity of feeling in relation to subjects of general concern. From this association, whose object was " the promotion of knowledge and virtue," at a subsequent period sprang the Redwood Library, which, had it been earlier started, would doubtless have received from Bishop Berkeley the valuable collection of books which, on leaving Rhode Island, in 1731, he distributed among the clergymen of the colony and presented to the colleges at Cambridge and at New Haven.

In the midst of a community whose social and literary

character was expanded by influences like these, Samuel Ward passed his boyhood and youth, enjoying, in addition, the best advantages for a common education which the colony in that age could afford. He is believed to have devoted himself to the acquisition of knowledge with earnest diligence, and to have derived from the advantages which he enjoyed what for the time was considered a remarkably good education. His father had long been extensively engaged in navigation, and was at the head of a trading house in Newport. He was also possessed of considerable estates in King's County, on the opposite shore of Narragansett Bay, which had also received a share of his personal attention. To the charge of the same interests Governor Richard Ward directed the attention of his second son; and, by the time he had reached his majority, he had become conversant with the business alike of a merchant and of a farmer. He married, in early life, Anne Ray, the daughter of a respectable farmer of Block Island, and soon after removed to Westerly, and settled on a farm, which he received from his father-in-law as the dower of his wife.[1]

Here, in a secluded portion of the colony of Rhode Island, Mr. Ward entered upon the duties of manhood, on a quiet plantation, which by his industry and judicious expenditures he soon formed into a valuable and beautiful estate. In accordance with the hereditary custom of his family, he also kept a store in the town of Westerly, and was often engaged in commerce both at Newport and at Stonington. In all these enterprises he was blessed with

---

[1] This lady was an elder sister of "Catherine Ray of Block Island," whose name frequently appears among the correspondents of Dr. Franklin, and to whom he addressed some of the sprightliest of his familiar letters. See Sparks's *Franklin*, vol. vii. pp. 85 *et seq.* The incidents referred to in the letter on the eighty-fifth page must have occurred while both Dr. Franklin and Miss Ray were on a visit at Mr. Ward's in Westerly.

a good degree of prosperity, and early became possessed of such pecuniary means as rendered him independent of personal labor, and enabled him to devote his time and energies to the interests of his native colony, whose service was soon to demand the most patriotic exertions of all her sons. Though living in retirement, he did not withhold his attention from the public events which took place around him ; and, as the subsequent course of this memoir will show, he was always sagacious in apprehending the questions at issue, and among the foremost in advocating, both in private circles and in the public offices with which he was intrusted, the interests of justice, and truth, and freedom.

For a considerable period after his settlement at Westerly, Mr. Ward appears to have devoted his principal attention to the improvement of his estate and the prosecution of the commerce in which he had embarked. He studied agriculture as a liberal art, and soon became distinguished among his neighbors for the success with which he applied its principles. He gave much attention to the improvement of the several breeds of domestic animals with which his farm was stocked, and was particularly celebrated for the specimens he raised of the Narragansett pony, a race of horses which has now become entirely extinct, but which in that day constituted a leading article of export from the colony, and was greatly admired for the ease and fleetness of its movements.

According to the traditions which are still preserved in Rhode Island, the farmers of the Narragansett country, for a long period before the Revolution, were generally men of a superior intelligence and a higher breeding than were often to be found in their brethren of the other agricultural districts of New England. Many emigrants of considerable fortune, who had come to this country in the early part of the eighteenth century, had been attracted to the beautiful and fertile farms which skirt the western shores of Narragansett Bay, and had planted there a large though scattered community, distinguished for intelligent enterprise, for accomplished manners, and for elegant hospitality. The mode of life then prevalent there combined much of the quiet and simplicity of the country with many of the characteristics of a commercial town. The distinctions of master and slave were still maintained; and negroes, most of whom were in servitude, and who then constituted nearly one tenth of the population of the colony, were to be seen in great numbers on every large estate. These features suggest to us a conception of agricultural life and of social relations such as would, perhaps, best be realized in our own day among the plantations of some of the upper counties of Virginia.

In retiring thus to the country, Mr. Ward by no means withdrew from the intellectual activity and cultivated society to which he had been accustomed at Newport. There were living around him some of the leading men of the colony, whose companionship, not only in his own chosen pursuit of agriculture, but in every other sphere of life, was fitted to improve, as well as gratify, an intelligent young man. These persons formed themselves into a club for social intercourse and intellectual improvement, and were accustomed to meet at each other's houses, to bring together at the festive board the results of their reading or experience, and to discuss the public events which were then beginning to assume an unwonted importance.

In this manner, interrupted only by occasional visits to Newport, and more rarely to Boston and New York, Mr. Ward passed the years of his early manhood. Living upon his own well-ordered estate, from which, with a grateful spirit, he received the bounties of Providence, surrounded by his family and in the midst of congenial neighbors and friends, he stands out in the foreground of a picture which any man might well aspire to realize. From this retirement, however, he was soon to be summoned forth to mingle in the agitating politics of the day; and, after engaging in the fiercest strifes of the politician, and reaping all his ephemeral honors, he was at length to act an heroic part in the opening drama of the Revolution.

His first appearance in the public service of the colony was in 1756, when he was elected to the General Assembly, as a deputy or representative from the town of Westerly; a post which he continued to occupy with but a slight interruption till May, 1759. In that early time the legislature of Rhode Island, though not inferior to other similar bodies either in the dignity of its forms or in the variety of the powers which it exercised, yet presented but a limited theatre for public debate. Its members were always few in number, and, being elected twice every year, they brought with them to its councils the fullest sense of the popular wishes respecting nearly every public measure. Hence their sessions were short, and their acts were usually passed with but little debate. In the proceedings of the Assembly Mr. Ward appears immediately to have taken an active part; and, though probably one of the youngest of its members, he early won for himself a wide and commanding influence. The frequent recurrence of his name upon the pages of its records indicates how intimately he was connected with the most important public measures which occupied its attention.

The irregular contest between England and France, which had been waged for more than two years in their respective colonies, had now broken out into an open war, which was declared on the part of England in May of the same year; and the several colonies were preparing to engage in it with their utmost zeal. A considerable number of French residents in Rhode Island, who had been seized by the colonial officers and thrown into the jails as prisoners of war, sent a petition to the legislature, praying for their liberation and the privilege of removing to some neutral port, and claiming an exemption, in the mean time, from the laws of war. Their situation excited no small interest among the people of the colony, and involved a principle which was likely to prove important in the subsequent progress of the contest. The whole subject, when presented to the legislature, was referred to a committee of which Mr. Ward was a member, who reported a bill authorizing the government to transport the Frenchmen in question to some neutral port, but refusing them any exemption from the ordinary fortunes of war, and requiring them still to be kept in jail; a measure which was doubtless thought to be necessary on account of the facilities they would possess, if set at liberty, of giving information to the king's enemies.

Mr. Ward was also a member of the committee for levying the annual tax, and proportioning it to the several towns of the colony, a work which was at that time considered among the most difficult and embarrassing of the duties of the legislature. So diverse were the interests and the resources of the several towns that scarcely a year passed away without occasioning a protest from some of them against the rates which had been assessed; the agricultural community now insisting that the commercial interests should bear a larger share of the public burden, and the southern towns now complaining that the growing capital of the north was regarded by the Assembly with too indulgent an eye.

Another of the services which he rendered to the colony in his capacity of legislator was in the investigations he made as a member of the committee on the violations of the laws of trade. The instructions which had been received from the king were urgent and peremptory, that the Assembly should "pass effectual laws for prohibiting all trade and commerce with the French, and for preventing the exportation of provisions of all kinds to any of their islands or colonies." The existing colonial statutes for enforcing the Navigation Acts of the British Parliament were but slightly regarded ; and an extensive contraband trade was carried on by merchants in all the colonies, in defiance of the authority of Parliament, and in most instances without the interference of their own legislatures. When the state of the trade was spread before them, the General Assembly, in accordance with the report of their committee, adopted such regulations as were necessary in order to comply with the instructions of the king, and in every way in their power prepared the colony to engage in the war as it became true and loyal subjects.

It was also during the year 1756 that the legislature of Rhode Island passed its first general act for the relief of insolvent debtors. It provided that persons who should give up their property for the benefit of their creditors, and make oath to the fidelity of the surrender, should be discharged from all claims preferred against them. The law was undoubtedly called forth by a few instances of failure, which, in the distresses of the times, had occurred among the merchants of the colony, one of the first and the most conspicuous of which was that of Mr. Joseph Whipple, a merchant of Newport, who at the time of his failure held the post of Deputy-Governor. The law which was then passed has served as the basis of all the subsequent legislation upon the subject of insolvency in Rhode Island, and does not differ very materially from that which is now in force in that state, and indeed in most of the other States of the Union.

The war with France was now becoming an engrossing subject of attention with all the northern colonies of

America. It had thus far been prolific of nothing but disaster and disgrace to the English arms. The colonists had engaged in it with their utmost zeal; but, such was the delay of the ministry, and such the incapacity of the generals who had been sent to conduct it, that every year had witnessed the gradual decline of the English power in America. The French, on the contrary, were every year gaining ground, and were gradually encircling the British possessions by the lengthening chain of their military posts, and, with the aid of their Indian allies, were spreading terror and dismay through the settlements.

Immediately on the formal declaration of war, in 1756, the Earl of Loudoun was sent to America with a large force, which, together with such as should be furnished by the colonies, he was directed to employ against the French. His arrival in America was greeted by the several colonies, and Mr. Ward was appointed one of a committee to prepare an address of welcome on the part of Rhode Island. One of his first acts, on assuming the command of the forces, was to levy four thousand troops from New England; and of these the proportion to be raised in Rhode Island was four hundred and fifty. The troops were raised, and were on their march for the rendezvous at Albany; but the season was too far advanced to admit of any effective operations, and they were dismissed at the beginning of November without having been employed in actual service, but were ordered to be in readiness when summoned again to the field in the ensuing spring.

It was early evident that the reverses which the English had experienced thus far in the war were not likely to be soon retrieved by the generalship of Lord Loudoun. He appointed a convention of the Governors and Commissioners of the several colonies to be held at Boston, in January, 1757; which seems to have terminated only in still greater distrust of the military capacity of the General-in-chief. The colonies, though commonly yielding a ready compliance with the requisitions which were made upon them, yet found serious cause of complaint in the unequal levies that were successively imposed; and the troops themselves were unwilling to be mingled with the British regulars, but demanded to be placed under the command of their own officers. Questions like these served only to embarrass the plans which the commander had set on foot, while, by the distrust and apprehension which they awakened, they added a deeper shade to the general gloom which hung over the colonies.

Rhode Island had a deep interest in the speedy termination of the war, as well as in all these questions relating to the terms of its continuance. She had already lost from ninety to one hundred vessels that had been captured by the enemy, a loss, which, according to a statement of her Secretary of State, made in 1758, was three times as great as that of New York, and four times as great as that of Massachusetts. She had added immensely to her public debt; and, in addition to fifteen hundred men, who were engaged as privateers in the war, she was obliged to maintain an armed vessel for the protection of her coast, and had also furnished to the campaign of 1757 not less than a thousand men for the service of the king. This was done at a period of gloom and dismay, when the whole number of her citizens between the ages of sixteen and sixty, then the legal limits of military service, scarcely exceeded eight thousand. It was an effort scarcely equalled by that of any other colony, for she had nearly a third of her whole effective force in actual service beyond the limits of her own territory.

In the winter of 1758, the Earl of Loudoun, finding himself still surrounded with difficulties and embarrassed by the jarring interests of the colonies, summoned another convention to meet at Hartford, in the month of February. At this meeting, Governor Greene, at that time the chief magistrate of the colony, and also Mr. Ward and Mr. John Andrews, were appointed to represent Rhode Island. The commissioners received full and explicit instructions from the legislature as to the course which they were expected to pursue. In these instructions they were directed, on arriving at Hartford: —

"1. To lay an exact state of the colony before his lordship with regard to its fortifications, cannon, warlike and military stores, the number of inhabitants, state of the treasury, and funds for supplying the same.

"2. To beg his lordship to lay the defenseless condition of the colony before his Majesty in the most favorable light.

"3. To request his lordship to make the colony such an allowance for the provisions and military stores furnished by this colony for the two last years as will correspond with his Majesty's gracious intentions signified unto us by his Secretary of State."

The commissioners were also directed to " request his lordship that the forces raised by this colony may be under the immediate command of their own officers, and no others, except the Commander-in-chief."

To these directions, which were probably open to all the commissioners who composed the convention, the General Assembly ordered the following to be added, which was to be regarded as a private instruction for the guidance of their representatives in adjusting the quota of troops, the most difficult and delicate part of their task: "And as to what aid or number of men you are empowered by virtue of your commission to furnish his lordship with, on the part of this colony, towards the ensuing campaign, you may agree to raise one fourteenth part of the number that shall be raised by the New England colonies; but, if that proportion cannot be obtained, you are then to agree to such other proportion as shall appear to you just and equitable."

These instructions aid us in comprehending the circumstances of the times, and illustrate the nature of the questions which were at issue, while they also serve to indicate the spirit of loyalty and of sacrifice for the general good which pervaded the people of Rhode Island.

Governor Greene was prevented by sickness from attending the convention, and the performance of the duty assigned to the remaining commissioners fell almost entirely upon Mr. Ward, who, on his return from Hartford, submitted to the legislature a full report of the doings of the convention. From this report, which is entered at length in the records of the Assembly, it appears that the Rhode Island commissioners proposed that the several colonies should furnish troops for the next campaign in exact proportion to their respective population; an arrangement by which Massachusetts would have raised 2,432 soldiers, Connecticut 1,582, and New Hampshire and Rhode Island each would have raised 425. This number on the part of Rhode Island was objected to by Lord Loudoun as smaller than that which had been agreed upon by the convention at Albany as the quota of the colony; and the commissioners were obliged to waive their proposal, and yield to the levy which his lordship demanded. They were, however, assured by the Commander-in-chief that no further difficulties should arise respecting the command of the troops, for he would take those from Rhode Island under his own especial command. The report of the commissioners was fully approved by the Assembly; the men, whose levy they had guarantied, were immediately ordered to be raised for the campaign of the following summer. This campaign, however, furnished far better illustrations of the valor and endurance of the colonial troops than of the skill and conduct of their commander.

II.

The period at which Mr. Ward entered upon public life in his native colony was one distinguished for the violence of the local jealousies and party animosities which so frequently appear in the history especially of small communities. The people of the southern counties of Rhode Island, from the first institution of the government, had been more or less at variance with those of the northern.

The town of Newport was at that time the only port of entry in the colony, and in point of commercial importance was one of the foremost towns along the entire Atlantic coast. It was the centre of the principal wealth, and the residence, probably, of most of the leading men, of the colony ; and, though the legislature was accustomed to hold its sessions in each of the several counties, yet Newport had long been the place where the offices of state were established, and was more than any other town the ·seat of the colonial government. Providence, standing at the head of the navigation of Narragansett Bay, was the older town, and was rising rapidly in wealth and importance, and already beginning to dispute the supremacy of the ancient capital. Amidst these relations subsisting between the two leading towns, a mutual jealousy had gradually sprung up, which had doubtless been fostered by the aspirants for office, and strengthened by the various local interests that had been incidentally involved in the issue, until it now divided the opinions and controlled the politics of the entire colony.

Among the incidental questions upon which this jealousy had fastened, the two most important were, the policy of the government in relation to supplies for the French War, to which allusion has already been made, and the famous question of paper money, which, in all the colonies of America, was a subject of endless perplexity and embarrassment, and in Rhode Island appears to have yielded its fullest harvest of social and political evils. The whole subject of the emission of paper money in the colonies, to the statesman and the political economist, would be one of the most curious and instructive connected with their history. For fifty years this deceptive currency spread its disastrous influence over the trade and the morals of the country, and was not wholly abandoned till the benefits of political independence had changed the relations of trade between America and all other parts of the world.

The earliest emission of bills of credit, to take the place of gold and silver in Rhode Island, was made in 1710. The colony had been at great expense in furnishing supplies for the war with France, in which the mother country had been involved ever since the accession of William and Mary to the throne. Finding the resources of the treasury inadequate to the exigency, the General Assembly, following the example already set by Massachusetts twenty years before, adopted the fatal though perhaps inevitable expedient of issuing bills of credit, and thus delaying the actual payment of the debts which had been incurred. The first emission did not exceed the sum of five thousand pounds; but this mode of postponing to the future the necessities of the present, having been once invented, was found to be too convenient to be readily abandoned. Other emissions followed in rapid succession, until, in 1749, after the lapse of nearly forty years, the bills which had been issued amounted to not less than three hundred and twelve thousand three hundred pounds, of which one hundred and thirty-five thousand pounds were still standing against the treasury, in one form or another; and these constituted the depreciated and almost valueless currency of the colony.

Every occasion of public expenditure furnished an excuse for the issue of a new *Bank ;* and though merchants were everywhere suffering from the policy, and frequently petitioned against it, and most intelligent persons were satisfied of its ruinous tendency, yet so captivating to the people is always the idea of plentiful money, and so clamorous were now the multitude of those who were largely in debt, that numbers of the Assembly constantly yielded to the popular will, and in some instances, it is said, actually legislated to meet their own private necessities. The currency which was thus created tended in no equivocal manner to impair the commercial contracts, and to prostrate the commercial honor, of the whole community, while it perpetually offered to the reckless and the profligate an opportunity, too tempting to be resisted, to counterfeit the bills of the colony; a crime of frequent occurrence, though punished in Rhode Island with cropping the ears and branding the forehead of the offender, together with the confiscation of his entire estate.[1]

Such is a brief outline of the subject upon which the two political parties in Rhode Island were accustomed most frequently to divide during the period of which we are now writing. The mercantile, and what was then regarded as the more aristocratic, portion of the community were usually opposed to the emissions of paper money, while those whose fortunes and avocations placed them in humbler life were arrayed in their favor. At the head of this latter party, which was also supported by some of the leading citizens of Providence, stood Stephen Hopkins, a gentleman whose name is conspicuous in the annals of the colony, and who, both as a determined opponent in the fiercest contests of local politics and an unwavering coadjutor in the far nobler struggle of the Revolution, was for

---

[1] For a full view of this curious subject, see a pamphlet by Elisha R. Potter, entitled *A Brief Account of Emissions of Paper Money made by the Colony of Rhode Island.*

many years intimately connected with the public life of
Samuel Ward. Supported principally by the northern
towns of the colony, Mr. Hopkins, in 1755, had succeeded
Governor William Greene as the head of the government, in opposition to the wishes and efforts of a powerful minority who were attached to the interests of the
south. The success of the Hopkins party raised to a high
pitch of excitement the animosity between the two districts of the colony, and, during the years in which Mr.
Ward was a member of the Assembly, this animosity was
frequently manifested in the action of that body.

In the political contest previous to the election of 1757,
when Governor Greene was still the candidate of the mercantile and southern party, in opposition to Governor
Hopkins, to whom strong objections had been raised, the
latter gentleman published an address to the freemen of
the colony, in which he insinuated that the legislature, in
its recent sessions, had pursued a policy hostile to the success of his administration. Mr. Ward was at that time a
member of the Assembly, and took occasion immediately
to come forward in its vindication. In defending it from
the charges of Governor Hopkins, he reviewed the Governor's administration, and stated at large the official acts
which had given offense to the people, dwelling particularly upon the conduct of the executive in relation to a
cargo of sugars which had been forfeited to the colony,
and also in relation to the liberation of some French prisoners of war, which had been made contrary to the acts
of the legislature.

For some cause or other, which, to one at all conversant
with party warfare in our own times, it is by no means easy
to assign, this vindication gave great offense to Governor
Hopkins, and, though at the time occupying the chair of
chief magistrate, he immediately commenced an action
for slander against Mr. Ward. The action was entered

in the Court of Common Pleas for the county of Providence, the county where the Governor had always resided, and which was warmly enlisted in the interest of the political party of which he was the acknowledged chief. In order to escape the prejudicial influence of party feeling, and to secure a fair trial, Mr. Ward petitioned the legislature to remove the cause to one of the other counties. On this petition being granted, Mr. Hopkins, who was now out of office, and was doubtless suffering from the mortification of recent defeat, immediately discontinued the suit, for the purpose of evading the legislative decree, and, on the rising of the Assembly, commenced another, still in the county of Providence. At length, however, after many delays and evasions on the part of Mr. Hopkins, which could have been suggested only by feelings of political rivalry or the exasperation of disappointment, it was agreed by the two parties that Mr. Ward should submit to an arrest within the territory of Massachusetts, and that the trial should be had before the court at Worcester, beyond the limits of the colony whose citizens were so generally embroiled in the question between their rival politicians.

The case appears to have excited no small interest, not only in Rhode Island, but also within the neighboring jurisdiction to which it was referred; and the distinguished name of James Otis is recorded as one of the counsel for the complainant. It would seem, however, that after the virulence of party feeling had somewhat abated by the lapse of time, Mr. Hopkins attached less importance to a judicial remedy, and, it may be, felt less confidence in the justice of his cause; for, when the trial came on at Worcester, in 1759, he did not appear at the court, and, after his counsel had made some slight attempt to have the case continued to another term, it went against him by default, and he was required to pay the costs of the prosecution.

Thus ended a case of political litigation, in which, as usually happens in such transactions, the gratification of party feeling was the end proposed, far more than the vindication of injured justice. Mr. Ward does not appear to have been guilty of anything like slander, or even of reprehensible severity, in his remarks upon the administration of Mr. Hopkins, which were strictly confined to his official acts. Indeed, were such a writing to be produced in our own day, and aimed at a public officer on the eve of an election, it would rather be considered as remarkable for its courtesy and forbearance, and the candidate would be pronounced little less than mad, who, for no greater cause, should follow the example of Mr. Hopkins, and bring an action for slander against its author. But the adjudication of the suit pending between the rival chiefs of the Rhode Island parties by no means allayed the political strife with which the colony had already begun to be divided. Both Ward and Hopkins were now candidates for the office of Governor, and they continued to stand in opposition to each other, at the head of powerful parties, for nearly ten years, in which each experienced alternate success and defeat.

In the year 1761, Mr. Ward, having failed to secure an election to the chief magistracy, was appointed by the General Assembly to the office of Chief Justice of the colony, which, according to the charter, was an office of annual appointment. He discharged its duties with fidelity during the year for which he was appointed; but his position at the head of a party whose success was identified with his promotion did not allow him to remain in the quiet sphere of judicial life. He was the following year again summoned to the strife for executive office, and at the election in May, 1762, he was found to be the successful candidate, and was installed in the office of Governor. The struggle of the two parties is said to have been violent in the extreme, and the towns of the colony were nearly equally divided; those of the south generally voting for Mr. Ward, and those of the north, with few exceptions, being strongly in favor of Mr. Hopkins.

It was the ancient custom of the freeholders of Rhode Island, as the voters were then termed, to meet at Newport, at the general election in May of every year, and deposit, in person, their votes for the Governor, Assistants, and other general officers. In later periods it had been allowed, to those who could not attend the general election, to send their votes by those who went, and thus to deposit them by proxy; still, as the population of the several towns increased, an immense multitude would thus assemble from all parts of the colony, presenting a mass of human passions, which might be easily inflamed by the party excitements of the day, and which the sternest resolves of the government were sometimes unable to hold in check. The scene which was here presented, in a sharply contested election, would have furnished many attractive features for the satiric pencil of Hogarth. There were gathered all who were hoping for office and all who were fearing to lose it; the leaders of either party exerting themselves, each to secure his own triumph, and the friends of each, confident of success and eager for the result, discussing their respective merits with the loudest vociferations, and sometimes enforcing their opinions with fists and canes; and at length, when the vote was declared, and the proclamation made in the public square, according to the ancient custom, before all the people, the triumph of the successful party would go beyond all bounds of decency and order, and the day would sometimes end in disgraceful riot and confusion.

To prevent the recurrence of scenes like these, and also to save the time and expense that were wasted by this perilous gathering of the people, an important alteration was made in the election law in 1760. An act was passed by the legislature, providing that for the future the voting should be done by the citizens in their respective towns, and that none but members of the Assembly should be entitled to vote at Newport on the day of election. The passage of this law was most seasonable, and its results, in every way, were beneficial; the protracted controversy between the friends of Ward and of Hopkins had already begun, and, if the people had been still in the habit of assembling at Newport during its more exciting periods, the peace of the colony might have been seriously endangered in the party strifes that would have ensued.

The year during which Mr. Ward now held the office of Governor seems not to have been marked by any important public events. It deserves, however, to be mentioned that during this period the project of founding an institution of learning in Rhode Island was first made a matter of serious interest and attention among the people. From the commencement of this important enterprise, Governor Ward took an active part in promoting its success. He belonged to that denomination of Christians by whom the idea was first proposed, and his own liberal tastes prompted him to give the full weight of his personal and official influence to the accomplishment of an undertaking fraught with so many blessings to the people of the colony.

He was present at the first meeting of gentlemen which was held to consider the expediency of the project. His name stands among the first of those who petitioned the legislature for the charter, and, when " Rhode Island College " was incorporated in 1764, he became one of the original trustees. This to him was no merely honorary post, but one that required of him a portion of his time and attention, which he freely gave to the interests of the infant institution. In 1767, he entered his son as a student in one of its earliest classes, and to the close of his life he continued its fast friend, as well as a member of its board of trustees.

Governor Ward's present term of office was a period of great suffering and anxiety among the tradesmen of the colony, in consequence of the extreme depreciation of the currency. The general scarcity of gold and silver and the uncertain value of the colonial bills depressed trade, and reduced especially the poorer classes of the people well-nigh to desperation. Murmurings and complaints arose from every quarter, and, notwithstanding the party then in power had always been known as the opponents of paper money, yet, in obedience to a natural propensity of the popular mind, strengthened perhaps, in this instance, by the intrigues of politicians, the evils of the time were very generally charged upon the administration; and, by means of the exertions which were made, the next election resulted in the defeat of Governor Ward, and the success of Governor Hopkins, who again took the oath of office in May, 1763.

At the close of his official year, Mr. Ward, who while he was Governor had resided at Newport, retired to his estate in Westerly, and, resuming the quiet occupations of the farmer and the trader, gave his time to the care of his family, to reading, and the society of his friends; a sphere of life in which he cultivated those elevated principles and amiable dispositions which not all the rude collisions of politics, nor the agitations of a troubled age, were ever able to pervert or to change.

The intervals which elapsed between the annual elections of general officers in Rhode Island seem to have passed quietly away, with but a rare collision of partisans, and only an occasional awakening of party feeling. But, as the political year drew to a close, and the season of general election came on, the whole colony became a scene of agitation and excitement. Every act that was performed, and every word that was uttered, by either of the candidates, became a matter of public interest, and, in the scarcity of newspapers, was repeated by political gossips in every place of public resort, and was borne to the fireside of every voter in the colony. Neighbor was arrayed against neighbor and family against family, in an irreconcilable feud, which, unless it should be checked, threatened to ruin the peace of the community, and to be transmitted from father to son.

Impressed with the disastrous consequences of their wide separation from each other, the leading men of both parties seem, at different times, to have entertained plans of reconciliation, and of thus healing the wounds which had been made in the peace of the colony. The first distinct proposal, however, for this purpose is believed to have come from Governor Ward, and is contained in the following letter, which he addressed to the General Assembly on the 28th of February, 1764, just as the arrangements for the annual election were about to be made : —

GENTLEMEN, — The many ill consequences necessarily attending the division of the colony into parties are too manifest to require any enumeration, and call for the serious attention of every man who hath the welfare of his country at heart.

Deeply affected with the melancholy prospect, and sincerely desirous to restore that peace and good order to the government, which have been too much obstructed, and without which we can never be extricated out of our present distressed situation, I beg leave to lay before you some proposals, which, in my humble opinion, might greatly tend to the accomplishment of these beneficial purposes.

1. As the Honorable Stephen Hopkins, Esq., and myself have been placed by our respective friends at the head of the two contending parties, I think it necessary, and accordingly propose, that both of us resign our pretensions to the chief seat

of government; for the passions and prejudices of the people have been so warmly engaged for a long time against one or the other of us that, should either Mr. Hopkins or myself be in the question, I imagine the spirit of party, instead of subsiding, would rage with as great violence as ever.   And so greatly anxious am I for putting an end to those bitter heats and animosities, which have thrown the government into such confusion, that I can sincerely declare that, for the sake of peace, I shall cheerfully resign all my pretensions to the office of Governor, or any other office.

2. As it is clear and evident, for many reasons, that Newport is the most proper place for the residence of the Governor, I would propose that the Governor, to be elected upon this plan, should reside there, and the Deputy-Governor in Providence.

3. That the Upper House be equally divided between the two parties.   This, I believe, would naturally tend to take away all pretense for a party.

When I made proposals of this nature to Mr. Hopkins about two years ago, the principal objection that he made to them was, that a number of his friends had been deprived of offices, and no provision was made for restoring them.   But as the case is since altered, and they are now restored, I hope every obstacle to the proposed plan is removed.

That this may be the case, and that we may all heartily unite for the public good, is the sincere wish of, Gentlemen,

Your most obedient humble servant,

SAMUEL WARD.

On the same day, but apparently without any knowledge of the foregoing letter, the following proposition was made to Mr. Ward on the part of Governor Hopkins, viz. :

The death of the Honorable John Gardner, Esq., having left the place of Deputy-Governor vacant, Governor Hopkins, and those in the administration with him, invite and solicit the Honorable Samuel Ward, Esq., to accept of that office ; hoping, as well as earnestly desiring, that such a measure carried into execution may put an end to the unhappy and destructive party disputes, which have too long been extremely injurious to the colony and its divided inhabitants.

STEPHEN HOPKINS, Governor.

Such were the proposals which were simultaneously made by each of the gentlemen who seemed to hold the peace of the colony in their hands. The terms in which they are both expressed, and the common spirit of apprehension which pervades them both, serve to indicate the fearful extent to which the party strife of the day had been carried. These proposals were respectively declined by each of the parties: Mr. Ward, it would appear from the correspondence, not thinking his acceptance of the post of Deputy-Governor likely to secure the peace of the community; and Mr. Hopkins regarding his surrender of the office of Governor as "having no tendency to put an end to parties, but as evidently calculated to perpetuate them." As we review the correspondence which passed between them, and recur to the ordinary principles of human nature, it is not too much to suspect that an unwillingness to be second to a rival chief may have strengthened the conclusion of the one, and a reluctance to surrender the fascinating gift of political power may have stimulated the patriotism of the other. The attempts of both parties, however, proved abortive, and the contest went on with as much virulence of feeling as ever.

In May, 1765, Mr. Ward was again elected Governor of the colony, and went from Westerly to reside at Newport, where, in consequence of a reëlection in the following year, he continued to reside till May, 1767. The two years during which he now held the chief magistracy were full of excitement, and were marked by events of high importance. A new spirit was rising in the minds of the colonists, and the petty distinctions of local party were for the time lost sight of in the deep indignation called forth by what were deemed the aggressions of the mother country on the rights of the colonies. In the preceding year the British ministry had already given intimations of their intention to tax America; and, soon after the election of Mr. Ward, the intelligence was received in Rhode Island that the Stamp Act had passed both Houses of Parliament, and had received the royal approbation.

At one of the sessions of the previous year, the Colonial Assembly had given utterance to the feelings of their constituents, in the petition which they had adopted and sent to the king; and, though a considerable number of the wealthier inhabitants of Newport and of some others of the southern towns were still unwilling to oppose an act of Parliament, yet, no sooner was it known that the Stamp Act had become a law than the minds of both the government and the people were made up to disregard its provisions. The act was not to go into operation till the following November, and the events of the interval only served to strengthen the determination to resist and to increase the irritability of the popular mind. Commissions were sent over, appointing the necessary officers to superintend the execution of the law, and the cruisers of the king, which seemed to multiply in all the ports of the colonies, became subjects of popular jealousy and hatred, on account of the closeness of their scrutiny and the arrogance of their demands upon the inhabitants.

During the summer of 1765, while the Maidstone, sloop of war, was lying in the harbor of Newport, the captain, whose name was Charles Antrobus, impressed some sailors belonging to the town, and detained them on board his vessel. On a complaint being made, Governor Ward immediately wrote a request for their release, which not being complied with, a band of people at one of the wharves seized a boat belonging to the Maidstone, and burnt it in a public square. This act of violence gave rise to a series of retaliations on the part of the commander of the sloop, which for a time suspended all intercourse, and came near producing open hostilities between the people of the Maidstone and the inhabitants of the town. The Governor, in his correspondence with Captain Antrobus, contended that "the impressing of Englishmen was an arbitrary action, contrary to law, inconsistent with liberty, and to be justified only by urgent necessity." "But, as the ship lay moored in an English colony, always ready to render any assistance necessary for his Majesty's service, there could be no possible reason sufficient to justify the severe and rigorous impress carried on in this port." He also firmly maintained the principle that the commander and crew of a ship lying within the jurisdiction of the colony were subject to its laws.

The men who had been impressed were afterwards given up, but not till they had been detained for several weeks, during which there were frequent collisions between the people belonging to the vessel and the inhabitants of the town. Incidents like this served only to array the feelings of the colonists still more decidedly against the officers of the crown, and doubtless prepared the way for the excesses which were soon afterwards committed against the vindicators of the Stamp Act and the officers who had been appointed to superintend its execution.

Mr. Augustus Johnson, a lawyer of respectable standing in Newport, had accepted the office of stamp master, in contempt alike of the arguments and the threatenings which were employed to dissuade him, and was preparing to perform its duties, when the day should arrive for the enforcement of the act. On the 27th of August, in open day, a few weeks after the affair of the Maidstone, a riotous collection of persons appeared in the streets of Newport, with a cart containing the effigies of Augustus Johnson, Martin Howard, and Dr. Thomas Moffat, the stamp master and two gentlemen who had written in de-

fense of the act, each with a halter upon its neck. The
images were drawn through the streets to a gallows which
had been erected near the town house, and were there
hung up till evening, to the gaze and derision of the multitude.   On the following day the mob again assembled,
and proceeded first to the house of Moffat, and afterwards
to that of Howard, both of which they stripped of their
furniture and nearly destroyed, the gentlemen themselves
having escaped to a ship of war lying in the harbor. The
house of Johnson was also assailed; but, by the persua-
sions of some of the principal men of the town, it was
spared, on his giving a reluctant promise that he would
not perform the duties of stamp master.[1]

Some efforts were made by the government of the colony to apprehend the persons who were engaged in these
outrages, and the matter was soon after brought to the
notice of the Assembly, by whom the Governor was requested to issue a proclamation commanding all officers to
arrest the rioters wherever they might be found. But a
similar scene had just before been enacted in Boston ; and,
in the excited state of the public mind, which then prevailed, though most well-disposed people disapproved, and
perhaps regretted the proceeding, yet none could be found
who were willing to come forward and bear testimony
against its authors.

The report of these outbreaks, which went home to
England, produced upon the administration an impression
most unfavorable to the reputation of the colony ; and, in
a letter which Governor Ward soon afterwards received
from the agent in London, it was stated that the Lords of

[1] See *Life of Augustus Johnson*, in Updike's *Memoirs of the Rhode
Island Bar*, p. 67.   Mr. Updike represents the riot as having occurred
in 1766, after the repeal of the Stamp Act ; but the recorded proceedings of the legislature, and a notice in the *Providence Gazette*,
fix it in 1765.

the Treasury had determined to withhold the money which was still due to the colony for the supplies she had furnished in the war, until full indemnification should be made to those who had suffered from the proceedings of the rioters. This information gave rise to a long correspondence between the government of the colony and the Secretary of State in England, in which the claim of Rhode Island to compensation was urged on independent grounds ; but the condition was still insisted on, and the money was withheld by the ministry.[1] Several attempts were subsequently made to get a bill through the Assembly to indemnify the stamp master and his associates, who had suffered at Newport, but in every instance without success ; and, as no restitution appears ever to have been made, it is presumed that the services of the colony remained unrequited, until the Revolution put an end to all urging of the claim.[2]

While these events were in progress, the Stamp Act was becoming a still more engrossing subject of popular attention ; and, as the time for its enforcement approached, the feelings of the community were raised to the highest pitch of excitement. The association of the Sons of Liberty, who pledged themselves to abstain from the use of

---

[1] Two letters relating to this subject, addressed by Governor Ward, one to Mr. Secretary Conway, and the other to the Earl of Shelburne, are contained in Almon's *Prior Documents*, pp. 102 and 118.

[2] A bill passed the House of Assistants, in 1768, making full indemnification for the losses of property sustained by these men ; but the claims which they presented were deemed exorbitant by the Lower House, and were also without satisfactory certificates ; they were accordingly dismissed. In 1772, the claims were again before the Assembly, and reëxamined by a committee appointed for the purpose. After undergoing considerable reduction by the committee, they were at length allowed by both Houses, and were ordered to be paid when the Lords of the Treasury should pay the debt due to the colony for its services in the war. This was never paid.

every article bearing the odious stamp, extended through-out the colony. Many of the towns held meetings, and instructed their deputies to urge the strongest measures in opposition to the act; and the Assembly, at its session in September, adopted the five celebrated resolutions which had been drawn up by Patrick Henry, four of which had just before been passed by the House of Burgesses of Virginia. The fourth resolution received an important modification by the omission of the words " his Majesty or his substitutes," and, as adopted by the Assembly, de-clared that their own body possessed "the only exclusive right to lay taxes and imposts upon the inhabitants of the colony." To these resolutions they also added another, breathing the spirit of a still bolder opposition to the aggressions of the ministry, in which they directed all the officers appointed by the authority of the colony " to pro-ceed in the execution of their respective offices in the same manner as usual, and that this Assembly will indemnify and save harmless all the said officers on account of their conduct, agreeable to this resolution." These resolutions, taken as a whole, are nearly equivalent to a declaration of independence, though no formal act of the kind had then been proposed. They appear to have been, at the time of their adoption, decidedly in advance of those of any other colony, in the tone of resolute independence which per-vades them, and were undoubtedly a true expression of the general feeling which reigned among the people.

At the same session the Assembly also appointed dele-gates to the Colonial Congress, which was soon to meet at New York, for the purpose of representing to his Majesty the views entertained by the people of America respecting the Stamp Act. The gentlemen selected for this delega-tion were Henry Ward, a younger brother of the Gover-nor, and Metcalf Bowles, both of them citizens of eminent standing, and holding high offices in the colony. The instructions which the Assembly voted to the delegates breathed the same determined spirit as the resolutions to which we have already referred, and evinced, in the most unequivocal manner, that they regarded the concerns committed to the Congress as "of the last consequence to themselves, to their constituents, and to posterity."

In the spring of the year 1767, the hostility subsisting between the political parties of the colony reappeared in all its violence. Mr. Hopkins was again the opposing candidate for the office of Governor, at the head of a ticket of general officers, who, with reference to the distracted condition of the community, were styled by their friends "Seekers of Peace." The contest which ensued was attended with unusual excitement in every part of the colony; the towns north of Bristol and Warwick all giving large majorities for Hopkins, while the southern towns gave their votes, with scarcely less unanimity, for Ward. The campaign resulted in the election of Mr. Hopkins by a larger majority than he had ever before received.

This election was the last in which these gentlemen appeared as candidates in opposition to each other. At the meeting of the Assembly in the following March, the season at which the arrangements for the annual election were usually made, Governor Hopkins, who had been elected as a "peacemaker," in behalf of himself and the friends who supported him, put forth substantially the same proposals for the pacification of the colony which Ward had made four years before, and which he had then rejected. These were, that both the rival candidates should relinquish all pretensions to the chief place in the government, and that the two parties should unite in forming an administration, in which one should nominate a Governor, and the other a Deputy-Governor, each from the ranks of its own opponents. The terms were readily accepted by Governor Ward and his friends ; and the two chiefs, who had so long been arrayed in opposition to each other, met first at Providence, and afterwards at Newport, and settled the preliminaries of what proved to be a lasting and happy coalition.

Thus ended what perhaps deserves to be regarded as the most remarkable contest of parties which has occurred in the history of Rhode Island. The inquirer at this distant day, who explores its half-forgotten records, finds but little to explain the length to which it was protracted, or the acrimony with which it was carried on. Though it was occasionally involved with questions of public policy, yet, in the main, it seems not to have depended on any important principle of government or any leading interest of society. It was a warfare between men and classes, and not between measures and interests. The gentlemen who for nearly ten years stood at the head of the respective parties were both persons of liberal minds, and, it would seem, were quite above the petty ambition which seeks office merely for the sake of its trifling rewards; and the strife in which they were so long and so warmly engaged can only be accounted for by referring it to the natural antagonism which, in certain states of society, always exists between persons of different classes and different occupations and habits of life. The portion of the community who supported Governor Ward regarded themselves as the most suitable guardians of the public weal, on account of their hereditary wealth, their intelligence, and their elevated position in society; while those who favored Governor Hopkins were perhaps at first thrown into the opposition by their jealousy of a class who claimed to be their superiors in social importance, and who had long been accustomed to wield the political power of the colony.

The continuance of the controversy had been productive of unnumbered evils, and, on account of the expense and

the excitement it occasioned, had doubtless become weari-
some to the leading members of both parties. Besides,
other questions had arisen, embracing wider interests than
those of a single colony, and new parties were already
forming on principles which involved the dearest rights of
Englishmen. Before these higher questions the petty
strifes of local politics necessarily lost their importance,
and the spirit which had hitherto animated them became
speedily merged in patriotic solicitude for the liberties of
the country.

III.

Previously to the period at which Governor Ward
closed his official connection with the government of the
colony, we have seen that he was more than once called,
in the discharge of his duty, to take a firm stand against
the encroachments which the ministry had already commenced upon the rights of the colonists. To the position
which he thus assumed, we have every reason to believe,
he was directed not less by his personal convictions than
by the dictates of official duty. From the beginning of
the contest with the mother country, he seems to have
given his whole influence to the colonial side of the questions at issue; and, as he was at the head of the party
then in power, he was doubtless largely instrumental in
promoting the unanimity of feeling which characterized
the opposition to the Stamp Act in the colony. After the
repeal of this act, however, and the passage of the revenue laws of 1767 and 1769, the issue which was presented
was thought to be different from that of former years,
and many of the wealthy merchants of Newport, and of
other towns of Rhode Island, who had acted with Governor Ward in all the contests of local politics, were now
willing to engage but feebly, if at all, in measures of resistance to the authority of Parliament.

To him, however, the questions which were presented were still the same, and his views of their importance to the colonies, or of the measures which it was necessary to adopt in opposing them, were not changed by the opinions of his former friends and supporters. He was now in private life; but he still watched with anxious interest the course of public events, and, through the medium of his correspondence, and of occasional intercourse with the leading patriots of New England, he contributed the influence of his own earnest views towards forming the public sentiment that ruled the events of the time.

After the renewal of the attempt to tax the colonies by the Townshend administration, the coast of New England was carefully watched by cruisers employed by the commissioners of customs, to repress the illegal traffic which was extensively carried on, and to aid the custom-house officers in enforcing the laws for collecting the revenue. For these vessels, the harbor of Newport was one of the principal rendezvous, and, being an important port of entry, it was constantly frequented by them. The harsh impressments, and the arrogant demands for supplies which were often made by their commanders, gave rise to frequent collisions between them and the inhabitants of the colony, and tended gradually to detach from the mother country the affections even of those who had hitherto taken no part in the resistance which had been made to the acts of Parliament. These insolent displays of authority, and the annoyances which were suffered in consequence in many parts of the colony, seem to have rendered the minds of the people peculiarly irritable, and, like the presence of troops among the inhabitants of Boston, to have kept alive a hostile feeling, which any slight occasion was sufficient to fan into a flame.

Such an occasion was presented in the summer of the year 1769. The armed sloop Liberty, commanded by

Captain Reid, brought into the harbor of Newport two vessels, one a sloop and the other a brig, which she had taken in Long Island Sound, on suspicion of their being engaged in the contraband traffic. The sloop appears to have been open to suspicion, but the brig had regularly cleared at the custom-house of the port from which she sailed. Both of them, however, were forcibly detained beneath the guns of the cruiser, and occupied by a guard whom Captain Reid had placed on board. The seizure was thought to be illegal by the people of the town, and their sympathies were warmly enlisted in behalf of the captured vessels. The commander of the brig, on finding himself thus stripped of his command, and even refused access to his personal wardrobe, was forced into an altercation and scuffle with the man who had been set over him, and afterwards, while passing to the shore in his boat, was fired upon by the crew of the Liberty. This was provocation enough to call forth all the indignant feeling which had long existed in the popular mind towards the cruisers of the king. The captain of the Liberty, being found on shore on the evening of the same day, was seized by the people, and compelled to send for his crew, in order that the person who had fired upon the captain of the brig might be identified. In the mean time, a party from the shore went off to the sloop, cut the cables which moored her, and, on her drifting to a neighboring point, dismantled her, and a few days afterwards burnt her to the water's edge.[1]

This destruction of the sloop Liberty, in the harbor of Newport, has been justly claimed as among the earliest, in point of time, of the acts of open resistance to British power, which terminated in the final separation of the colonies from England. It was followed, three years later, by the destruction of the schooner Gaspee, upon

[1] See Staples's *Gaspee Documents ;* and, for a fuller account of the affair, Bull's *Memoir of the Colony for* 1769.

the waters of the same bay, and within the jurisdiction of the same colony; and, though less important from the consequences it produced, yet, as an illustration of the spirit of the colony, it deserves a place in the history of the revolutionary struggle, on the same page which records that famous achievement. Immediately after the attack upon the Liberty, the Governor, with the advice of such of the Assistants as he could assemble, issued a proclamation, directing the officers of the king " to use their utmost endeavors to inquire after and discover " the persons engaged in the riot, and the commissioners of customs published a notice offering a reward of a hundred pounds for any information which should lead to their detection. But no judicial investigation was ever held, and neither the proclamation made by the Governor, nor the reward offered by the commissioners, in the state of feeling then prevalent in the colony, was sufficient to elicit any important evidence.

The destruction of the Gaspee, in addition to the numerous acts of resistance which had preceded it, created in the minds of the ministry the deepest dislike towards the colony, and a determination to humble its spirit by every means in their power. It is said they formed the purpose of quartering some regiments of soldiers in its two principal towns, and even advised the king to abrogate the charter, which had been granted by Charles the Second. For the purpose of investigating the circumstances attending the burning of the schooner, a court of commissioners was appointed under the authority of the great seal, with instructions to employ, if necessary, the troops of the king, in executing their commission, and to deliver the persons who should be found to have participated in the affair to the commander of one of the ships of war, to be transported to England for trial. The extraordinary powers and arbitrary proceedings of this high court of inquiry were subjects of widespread apprehension, and attracted the attention of the House of Burgesses of Virginia, who appointed a committee to inquire into their bearing upon the rights and liberties of the colonies. The investigations of this court, however, which were conducted with great assiduity for many weeks, were at length brought to a close, without leading to the detection of any of the offenders, notwithstanding the fact that they were well known to hundreds of the people of the colony.

The incidents which we have thus related illustrate the state of popular feeling in Rhode Island, in the early stages of the contest with Great Britain. That these acts of violence were illegal, and against the peace and good order of the colony, cannot be denied; and as such they seem to have been generally regarded at the time. But, when viewed in their connection with the revolutionary struggle, which was already commencing, they are not to be condemned as crimes against society. They were rather the natural consequences of the injurious laws of Parliament, and especially of the oppressive manner in which those laws were executed by the officers of the king, who were sent to the colony.

These officers were in the habit not only of searching every vessel that came within their reach, which sometimes occasioned a detention of several days, but they would often seize upon the market boats which plied upon the bay, for the trifling purpose of examining the freights which they contained, and would subject their crews, who were usually farmers from the country, to every species of indignity and oppression. They seldom took the trouble to exhibit their commissions to any of the magistrates of the colony, but seemed to hold themselves above the laws, and to sport with the interests and rights of the inhabitants. As they were perpetually hovering upon the coast, and seldom remained long in port, legal redress for the injuries they occasioned was impossible ; and it is not strange that they should have occasionally experienced the vengeance of an insulted people.

The sky was now growing dark with clouds that portended still more violent commotions. The impression which had been produced by the destruction of the Gaspee, and by the proceedings of the commissioners who were appointed to inquire into the affair, instead of humbling the spirit of the colony, as was intended, served only to prepare the minds of the people for still further acts of resistance. Reverence for the authority of Parliament was rapidly passing away, and the necessity of boldly withstanding the enforcement of the revenue acts was every day becoming more apparent. Agreements of non-importation and non-consumption had been formed among the inhabitants of Newport and Providence, as early as 1769 ; and though they seem not in all cases to have been very faithfully adhered to, yet they served to organize the opposition that was now very generally felt towards the proceedings of Parliament.

The tax on tea was still continued ; and the unusual facilities for its importation into the colonies, which had been granted to the East India Company, created among the people, especially of the commercial towns, an apprehension that they might at length be obliged to submit to the tyranny that threatened them. In this apprehension Rhode Island largely shared, for she presented the most accessible port upon the coast, and numbered among her eminent merchants a few, at least, who might have consented to act as factors of the Company, for the sale of the tea.

During the whole period through which we have thus traced the early progress of the revolutionary contest in Rhode Island, Governor Ward had lived in comparative retirement upon his estate at Westerly. He was here surrounded by his numerous family and by an extensive circle of friends. He had not been exempt from the melancholy changes incident to every human lot, but had buried several of his kindred and his dearest friends; and, though he had lost none of his children, he had been stricken with a still heavier calamity in the loss of his wife, the amiable and worthy companion of many years, who died in December, 1770. In addition to the care of his family and the management of his estate, his attention had been in part occupied by a vexatious suit at law with a troublesome neighbor, in which he had been compelled to engage, in vindication of his title to a tract of land lying in the Narragansett country. The suit was at length decided in his favor, after being protracted through several years, during which his opponent attempted to enlist against him the partisan feeling which still survived the controversy in which he had formerly been engaged.

But he was also a close observer of the course of public events; and, though dwelling apart from the excited feeling which now pervaded the larger towns, he was not the less informed of the progress of liberal sentiments, nor the less able to estimate with calm judgment the magnitude of the issues to which they were leading. It was his habit frequently to attend the sessions of the General Assembly, and, though he held no official connection with the government, his position in the colony enabled him to exert a wide influence upon the popular mind, and rendered his advice and sanction exceedingly important in the decision of every question of great public interest.

Thus far in the contest, the opposition which had manifested itself to the measures of the ministry in the several colonies had resulted from accidental causes, rather than from any concerted plan which had been agreed upon for the purpose. The state of the question, however, had now become such that some arrangement for circulating important intelligence and for promoting unity of action was absolutely essential. For this purpose, the House of Burgesses of Virginia, on the 12th of March, 1773, appointed a standing committee of correspondence and inquiry, whose duty it should be to obtain the earliest intelligence of all measures of the British government relating to America, and to maintain a correspondence with such committees as should be appointed for a similar purpose by the other colonies, to whom the adoption of the measure was earnestly recommended. The recommendation of Virginia was immediately adopted by the Assembly of Rhode Island at its session in the following May, and seven of the leading citizens of the colony were appointed a committee of correspondence, one of whom was Mr. Henry Ward, a younger brother of the Governor, at that time holding the office of Secretary of State.

From this period the colony of Rhode Island was among the foremost in activity and zeal, both in devising and executing measures for the promotion of the common cause. Soon after these arrangements had been adopted for securing a greater unity of sentiment and of action among the colonies, the shipment of several cargoes of tea was made by the East India Company to some of the American ports, and serious apprehensions were entertained by many of the friends of liberty in Rhode Island that boxes of the obnoxious article might be clandestinely entered at Newport. In order to provide against such an occurrence, and to secure a more perfect organization throughout the colony, Governor Ward, in December, 1773, a few days after the destruction of the tea at Boston, addressed a letter, signed by himself and several others of the inhabitants of Westerly, to some of the leading gentlemen of Newport, urging the establishment of a committee of correspondence in each of the towns of the colony, and suggesting that Newport, as the seat of the government and the emporium of trade, should take the lead in carrying forth the measure.

This letter, which breathes the spirit of a cautious and wise man, who clearly saw the storm that was gathering over the colonies, was submitted to the people of Newport at a town meeting; and the suggestions it contained were soon afterwards adopted and carried into effect. He also addressed similar letters to leading men in other towns of the colony; and early in February, 1774, having himself accepted the post of chairman of the committee of correspondence of the town of Westerly, he introduced a series of resolutions, at a meeting of the town, which, taken as a whole, form a complete embodiment of the principles maintained by the colonies, and of the grounds upon which they rest. For the purpose, as is probable, of instructing the citizens of the town respecting the cause in which they were embarked, the resolutions recited very fully the grievances which were complained of, and earnestly, yet calmly, urged resistance as the only remedy which was left, and as a high civic duty, which they owed not less to themselves than to the whole British empire and to posterity.

The English ministry had already become thoroughly incensed at the spirit which the colonies, especially Massachusetts Bay, had constantly evinced towards all their measures for raising a revenue in America; and, on receiving intelligence of the destruction of the tea at Boston, they immediately determined to avenge the insult which had been offered to their authority. Accordingly, within a month after the intelligence was received at London, they carried through Parliament, by a large majority, the three celebrated bills, known as the Boston Port Bill, the Bill for the better regulating of the Government of Massachusetts Bay, and the Bill for removing persons accused of certain offenses to another Colony, or to England, for trial. These famous bills were regarded as special acts of ministerial vengeance, and the alarm which they everywhere occasioned formed one of the most powerful of the agencies which hastened forward the crisis of the Revolution. Instead of the olive branch which many had hoped to see, the colonists now saw that only a naked sword was held out to them.

The sufferings of the people of Boston became a subject of universal sympathy, and a general Congress of delegates from all the colonies soon began to be talked of. The first distinct proposal of such a Congress, however, by any public body, it is believed, was made by the town of Providence, at a meeting held on the 17th of May, 1774. At this meeting, the deputies of the town were instructed " to use their influence at the approaching session of the General Assembly of this colony, for promoting a Congress, as soon as may be, of the representatives of the General Assemblies of the several colonies and provinces of North America, for promoting the firmest union, and adopting such measures as to them shall appear the most effectual to answer that important purpose, and to agree upon proper methods of executing the same." [1] The citizens of Providence, at the same meeting, also directed the committee of correspondence to assure the people of Boston of the sympathy they felt for the distressed condition of that town, and that they regarded their cause as the common cause of the whole country.

The session of the General Assembly was held at Newport on the second Monday in June; and though none of the other colonies had at this time taken any formal action respecting the proposed Congress, yet the spirit of its members was already prepared to respond to the in-

---

[1] Staples's *Annals of Providence,* p. 235. This date is four days earlier than the action of any other public body on the subject.

structions of the deputies from Providence. The subject was taken up at the beginning of the session, and, after mature consideration, the Assembly, on the 15th of June, adopted a series of resolutions setting forth the condition of the colonies, and declaring that a convention of representatives from them all ought to be holden as soon as practicable. By the same resolutions, Stephen Hopkins and Samuel Ward were appointed to represent the colony, and were specially directed "to endeavor to procure a regular annual convention of representatives from all the colonies." In this vote, which was adopted with great unanimity, all party feuds were buried forever; and the political leaders who, in former years, had so often been arrayed against each other were henceforth to be united as friends and fellow-patriots in the council that planned the Revolution. In this council their appointment bore the earliest date among those of all its members; and, until separated by death, it is believed, they shared each other's confidence and sympathy in all the arduous duties in which they were engaged.[1]

The views with which Mr. Ward accepted the important trust that was now committed to him were of the gravest and most serious character. He was no frantic patriot, who supposed that vaporing resolutions and exciting speeches were all that was needed for the crisis which he saw was approaching. A large acquaintance with human nature made him distrust the hope, which many entertained, that the determinations of the ministry would be changed by any remonstrances or threatenings

---

[1] The delegates from Massachusetts were appointed on the 17th of June, which has generally, though erroneously, been considered as the date of the earliest appointment. So far as is now known, it was at a Rhode Island town meeting that the first public proposal of a Congress was made, and at a session of the Rhode Island Assembly that the first delegates to that Congress were appointed.

of the colonies; and the religious sentiments which he had early imbibed, and which were now woven into all his reflections, imparted a deeply moral aspect to all the questions which were likely to be presented to the body to which he had been appointed. But he had already decided on which side the right certainly lay, and he did not waver from the decision to which he had come. In a letter to his brother, written in the following year, but referring to this period, he says of himself: —

"When I first entered this contest with Great Britain, I extended my views through the various scenes which my judgment, or imagination (say which you please), pointed out to me. I saw clearly that the last act of this cruel tragedy would close in fields of blood. I have traced the progress of this unnatural war through burning towns, devastation of the country, and every subsequent evil. I have realized, with regard to myself, the bullet, the bayonet, and the halter; and, compared with the immense object I have in view, they are all less than nothing. No man living, perhaps, is more fond of his children than I am, and I am not so old as to be tired of life; and yet, as far as I can now judge, the tenderest connections and the most important private concerns are very minute objects. Heaven save my country, I was going to say, is my first, my last, and almost my only prayer."

The delegates of the several colonies were at length all chosen, and the place was fixed upon at which the Congress should assemble. Mr. Ward left his home about the middle of August, attended by a faithful family servant, and arrived at the place of meeting on the 30th of the same month. The journey was made on horseback, and, on the day after his arrival, he acknowledged with pious gratitude, in a letter addressed to his children, the kind Providence which had watched over him amidst the perils of the way. On the morning of the 5th of September, 1774, the "Old Congress," as it is now familiarly known in our history, commenced its sessions, in Carpenter's Hall, in Philadelphia. The place but ill corresponded with the real magnitude of the occasion. No tapestry bedecked its walls, no images of sages and heroes of other days looked down upon the scene. Yet, to one who could read the future, it would have presented a simple grandeur, such as we may now look for in vain within the majestic halls of the Capitol and amidst the imposing forms of the Constitution.

The forty-four individuals who met on that day for the first time, were men of different characters and different opinions, for they had come from the extremes of the continent; but they came together unfettered by partisan or sectional feeling. The simple Quakers of Pennsylvania, the high-spirited Cavaliers of Virginia and Carolina, and the resolute Puritans of Massachusetts and Connecticut, all were represented in that body of grave and earnest-minded men; yet, amidst all differences of temperament, of creed, and of opinion, the pervading sentiment was catholic and patriotic. They had been roused from the repose of their homes by common grievances, and they only sought a common redress.

Their resolution of secrecy, the first which they adopted after their organization, was so sacredly kept that a veil has rested upon their proceedings to this day, which even the publication of their " Secret Journal " has aided us but little in removing. But tradition has reported the eloquence of their debates, and the recorded results which they achieved fully show that their daily sessions were seasons of unremitted deliberation upon the questions before them. Among the different classes of measures which were proposed to the Congress, Mr. Ward, if we may judge from the occasional allusions in his correspondence, was always an advocate of the moderate counsels which so eminently characterize its published documents. Cooler and more quiet in his temperament than some others of the New England delegates, while he regarded a separation from the mother country as sooner or later inevitable, he was still in favor of first trying every pacific measure, and of thus placing the cause in the best possible light, both before the colonies and the world.

The Congress closed its session on the 26th of October, after appointing another session to be held on the 10th day of the following May, unless the public grievances should be removed before that time. The results of its six weeks' deliberation were then probably but imperfectly comprehended, even by those of its members who looked farthest into the vista of the future. The consultations which were held and the friendships which were formed, blending with the common interests and common dangers of the whole country, became enduring bonds of union to the colonies, which no subsequent differences of opinion, nor all the gloomy disasters of the Revolution, were able to break asunder.

The delegates from Rhode Island returned immediately to their homes; and at a meeting of the General Assembly, called specially for the purpose, they made a full report of the proceedings of the Congress. Its several acts were unanimously approved, and the delegates, having received the thanks of the Assembly, were immediately appointed to attend the next Congress, and charged with suitable instructions as to the objects to be accomplished.

Before the meeting of the second Congress, the fields of Lexington had been reddened with blood, spilt in the earliest engagement of the Revolution. Tidings of the battle were received in Rhode Island on the evening of the 19th of April, and companies from the northern towns of the colony made immediate preparation to march to the assistance of the people of Massachusetts. On the 22d of the same month, a special session of the Assembly was held at Providence, and acts were passed for putting the colony in a posture of defense, and for raising fifteen hundred men, to act with similar quotas from Massachusetts and Connecticut, as an army of observation. At the same session, Nathanael Greene was advanced from the station of a private in the Kentish Guards, the company of his native town, to the rank of Brigadier-General, and was placed at the head of the troops from Rhode Island.

To these spirited proceedings of the Assembly, the Governor, Mr. Joseph Wanton, and the Deputy-Governor, and several of the Assistants, entered a formal protest, on the ground that they were unnecessary, and might still further disturb the relations of the colonies with the mother country. But, in an emergency like this, the protest of men who had been intrusted with the government of the colony was not to be endured by the people. So high was the excitement among the members of the Assembly that the Deputy-Governor and the recreant Assistants were obliged to resign their places; and the Governor, though he had just before been elected for another term, was suspended from the exercise of all official authority. A few months afterwards, the office was taken from Mr. Wanton by an act of the Assembly, and bestowed upon Mr. Nicolas Cooke, an eminent merchant of Providence, who held it with dignity and firmness for three successive years, during the most trying period of the Revolution.

In this disordered state of the colonial government, the delegates from Rhode Island again departed to join the Congress at Philadelphia. Their credentials bore only the signature of Henry Ward, Secretary of State, whom the legislature, on account of the defection of the Governor and his Deputy, had authorized to sign the public papers of the colony. Mr. Ward appeared and took his seat on the 15th of May, five days after the session began. The papers relating to the battle of Lexington had already been presented by Mr. Hancock, on the first day of the session; and, in promoting the measures which were now proposed for the defense of the colonies and for raising and equipping troops, he engaged with the utmost zeal. His son, Samuel Ward, Junior, who had been recently graduated at Rhode Island College, had just received a captain's commission in the service of his native colony; and this circumstance, in connection with the views which he had long taken of the nature of the contest and the necessity of preparing for the worst, may have strengthened his interest in the military establishment of the country. In carrying forward all these measures, Mr. Ward earnestly coöperated with John Adams, the far-sighted leader of the New England delegations, who at this very time was writing those delightful Letters, which now throw so much light upon the deliberations which were held at Philadelphia.

On the 26th of May, when the House resolved itself into a committee of the whole, "on the consideration of the state of America," Mr. Ward was called to the chair by Mr. Hancock, who had then just been elected President; and from this time onward he seems to have been selected to preside in the committee of the whole, whenever the Congress gave this form to its deliberations. In this situation he was, of course, precluded from engaging in the debates of the committee; but, on the questions which were discussed in the House itself, he was accustomed to deliver his sentiments with manly clearness and earnest eloquence. Every day's deliberations only served to unite the minds of all the delegates in the opinion, which a few had entertained from the beginning, that a reconciliation was not to be expected, and that vigorous measures must immediately be adopted for defense and resistance. This sentiment is everywhere expressed in the letters of Mr. Ward, written, at this period, to his friends in Rhode Island, and to his kinsman General Greene, and his son Captain Ward, at the camp before Boston. With these and some other officers in active service he maintained a frequent correspondence, that he might the better ascertain the views of the troops, and judge of the public measures needed for their discipline and efficiency.

General Greene, on the 4th of June, writes to him his opinion that " all the forces in America should be under one commander, raised and appointed by the same authority, subjected to the same regulations, and ready to be detached wherever occasion may require ; " [1] and on the 15th of the same month, we find in the Journal of Congress the following entry : —

" Agreeable to order, the Congress resolved itself into a committee of the whole, and, after some time, the President resumed the chair, and Mr. Ward reported that the committee had come to further resolutions, which he was ordered to report. It was then resolved, That a General be appointed to command all the Continental forces raised, or to be raised, for the defense of American liberty.

" The Congress then proceeded to the choice of a General by ballot, and George Washington, Esq., was unanimously elected."

Though the full importance of the step which was now taken could not then have been realized, yet there were those who saw clearly that they had staked the destiny of the colonies upon the election which they had made. Mr. Ward had formed the acquaintance of Washington in the

---

[1] The same letter contains the following, at that time, remarkable passage : " Permit me, then, to recommend, from the sincerity of my heart, ready at all times to bleed in my country's cause, a declaration of independence ; and a call upon the world, and the great God who governs it, to witness the necessity, propriety, and rectitude thereof."

session of the preceding year, and appears immediately to have conceived for him that sentiment of mingled reverence and esteem which his character never failed to inspire in every ingenuous mind. The vote which was adopted a few days after the election, and which pledged the delegates to maintain and assist the Commander-in-chief with their lives and fortunes, was on his part a pledge of the deepest and sincerest devotion. A month or two later, in a letter written to the General in the hurry of public business, he says : " I most cheerfully entered upon a solemn engagement, upon your appointment, to support you with my life and my fortune; and I shall most religiously, and with the highest pleasure, endeavor to discharge that duty."

In August, 1775, the Congress took a recess for a month, and Mr. Ward passed the interval with his family in Rhode Island. During this period he also attended the meeting of the General Assembly, and, in connection with his colleague, Mr. Hopkins, made a report to that body of the condition of the colonies, and the measures which had been adopted for their common safety. He found the people of Rhode Island, though still animated with the same devotion to liberty, yet more than usually distressed at the depredations of the ships of war which now covered the Narragansett Bay, and frequently sent their tenders marauding along its shores. A large proportion of the towns of the colony border upon navigable waters, and the property of their citizens was thus continually exposed to the incursions of an enemy who had full possession of the harbor of Newport, and withal was not without the confidence of some of the leading citizens of the town.

The great body of the people, however, had long since espoused the American cause, though, as their fidelity had been put to severer tests than that of most other towns, it had not wholly escaped suspicion. The commerce, which had hitherto supported the town, within a single year had been reduced to less than a third of its former extent, and the sources of its long-continued prosperity were rapidly drying up. Mr. Ward, whose sympathies were warmly enlisted in the sufferings of his native town, foreseeing the doom that must descend upon it when hostilities should assume a still sterner aspect, earnestly advised its inhabitants, who were true to the country, to remove their families and effects to other parts of the colony. The people of Providence also offered to make provision for the reception and support of some hundreds of the poor families of Newport. The proposal, however, seems not at the time to have been generally accepted; and the long possession of the British and the melancholy desolations of war annihilated the prosperity of the town, and at the close of the Revolution left nothing of her former glory save the changeless beauties of nature which surround her.

For the purpose of protecting the trade of the colony, the General Assembly, in June, 1775, chartered and equipped two vessels of considerable force, and placed them under the command of Abraham Whipple, to whom was given the title of Commodore. He also received private instructions to clear the bay of the tenders of the British frigate Rose, that lay at its mouth; and in his first cruise, after a slight engagement, the first concerted naval engagement of the Revolution, he captured one of the tenders, and brought her to Providence. In August this armament was increased by the addition of two row galleys, carrying thirty men each; and, on the 26th of that month, the General Assembly adopted a resolution instructing the delegates of the colony " to use their whole influence, at the ensuing Congress, for building, at the Continental expense, a fleet of sufficient force for the protection of these colonies, and for employing it in such manner and places, as will most effectually annoy our enemies, and contribute to the common defense of these colonies." [1]

This resolution was the earliest proposal for a Continental navy. It was the natural result of the maritime experience of the colony, and of the several encounters of her citizens with the cruisers of the king. The annoyances which they had thus experienced enabled them to appreciate the advantages which might be derived from a naval armament, and their familiarity with the sea led them earnestly to engage in its establishment.

These instructions were presented to the Congress on the 3d day of October, and were ordered to lie upon the table. Several vessels of different force were soon afterwards either built or chartered for the service of the colonies, and Esek Hopkins, at that time a Brigadier-General in the army of Rhode Island, was appointed to the command of the infant navy. He repaired to Philadelphia immediately on receiving his appointment, in November, 1775, and in the following February sailed with the entire fleet on an expedition against one of the Bermuda Islands. The expedition seems to have been undertaken without any precise orders from the Congress, and, though in some respects eminently successful, it failed to receive their entire sanction.

In consequence of the urgency of other business, the instructions to the delegates of Rhode Island were not taken up for the action of the House till the 16th of November, though several of the intervening days had been assigned for their consideration. On this day Mr. Ward wrote to his brother in Rhode Island: " Our instruction for an American fleet has been long upon the table. When it was first presented, it was looked upon as per-

[1] Staples's *Annals of Providence*, p. 265 ; also *Schedules of the General Assembly of Rhode Island.*

fectly chimerical; but gentlemen now consider it in a very diffcrent light. It is this day to be taken into consideration, and I have great hopes of carrying it. Dr. Franklin and Colonel Lee, the two Adamses, and many others will support it. If it succeeds, I shall remember your ideas of our building two of the ships." The matter, however, seems not to have been brought to a final determination till the 11th of December; for in the Journal we find the following entry for that day: —

" Agreeable to the order of the day, the Congress took into consideration the instructions given to the delegates of Rhode Island, and after debate thereon, Resolved, That a committee be appointed to devise ways and means for furnishing these colonies with a naval armament, and report with all convenient speed."

This committee brought in their report on the 13th of December, and recommended that thirteen ships, five of thirty-two guns, five of twenty-eight guns, and three of twenty-four guns, be built and made ready for sea as soon as practicable. The report of the committee, after being fully debated, was adopted by the Congress, and the ships were ordered to be built at the expense of the united colonies. On the day following the final adoption of this measure, Mr. Ward again wrote to his brother: " I have the pleasure to acquaint you that, upon considering our instructions for a navy, the Congress has agreed to build thirteen ships of war. A committee is to be this day appointed, with full powers to carry the resolve into execution. Powder and duck are ordered to be imported. All other articles, it is supposed, may be got in the colonies. Two of these vessels are to be built in our colony, one in New Hampshire, etc. The particulars I would not have mentioned. The ships are to be built with all possible dispatch."

We have thus seen that the first establishment of a

Continental fleet is to be traced back to the instructions of the Rhode Island Assembly, and to the exertions which were made in obedience to them by the delegates of the colony. The measure was on every account an important one, and the merit of originating and supporting it, at that opening period of the struggle for independence, ought not to be lightly estimated. It is alone sufficient to entitle the colony to an honorable distinction in the history of the Revolution, and may be regarded as the early pledge of the brilliant deeds which have since been achieved by her sons upon the decks of the American navy.

IV.

In the Journals of the Continental Congress for the session of 1775, and the early part of the following year, few names, after those of the immediate leaders of the Revolution, are more frequently mentioned than that of Samuel Ward. Though not unused to debate, it is probable that his most important services were performed in a less conspicuous sphere of action. Indeed, the real work of such bodies is usually accomplished away from the scenes of brilliant oratory, in the confinement of the committee room or the seclusion of the private chamber, where business is prepared and plans of public policy are elaborated and matured. Of this class of labors Mr. Ward sustained a large share. He entered into the duties of his station with a patriotic zeal, that shrank from no sacrifice of personal ease, however great it might be. He was exceedingly regular in his attendance upon the House, and uniformly accepted, without hesitation, every work which was assigned to him to perform.

After the reassembling of the Congress in September, in addition to the service he almost daily rendered in the chair of the committee of the whole, he was appointed a member of the secret committee, to contract for arms and munitions of war, and of this committee he was subsequently chosen chairman. He was also a member of the standing committee on claims and accounts ; a post which required his attention to an infinite number of details, and which compelled him to become conversant with all the operations of the army, and with the services performed by each of the respective colonies.

In addition to these two appointments, each of them of the most arduous and confining nature, he served upon a large number of special committees, some of which were charged with the most delicate and responsible duties. His colleague, Mr. Hopkins, was at this time disabled from writing, on account of physical infirmity ; and the official correspondence of the delegation with the government and the citizens of the colony was thus thrown wholly upon Mr. Ward. To the close confinement thus imposed upon him by the duties of his station he makes frequent allusions in the familiar letters addressed to his family. In one of these, written in the month of October, he says : " I am almost worn out with attention to business. I am upon a standing committee of claims, which meets every morning before Congress, and upon the secret committee, which meets almost every afternoon ; and these, with a close attendance upon Congress and writing many letters, make my duty very hard, and I cannot get time to ride or take other exercise. But I hope the business will not be so pressing very long."

Our own times are so remote from the period of the American Revolution that we often are able to gain only an imperfect idea of the questions which perplexed the patriots of that day, or of the personal feelings with which they regarded the scenes that were passing before them. There were among them men of every hue of character and every degree of decision ; men who were prompted by impetuous temperaments, by selfish hopes, and by a high sense of duty; men who were timid champions of the cause and were always hoping for a reconciliation, and those who staked their all upon the issue, who early saw that reconciliation was impossible, and were only waiting for the separation which they believed to be inevitable. In which of these classes of the patriots, who composed the Congress of the Confederation, Governor Ward deserves to be ranked has already been indicated; it may, however, be more fully seen by the following extracts from familiar letters written to his brother in Rhode Island, during the autumn of 1775. On the 30th of September he writes: —

" No news from England since my last. The gentlemen of Georgia deserve the character I gave you of them; they are some of the highest sons of liberty I have seen, and are very sensible and clever. Mr. Wythe and Mr. Lee, of Virginia, have been under inoculation since my last, so that I can say no more of these than I did then. Saving that unhappy jealousy of New England, which some weak minds are possessed with, great unanimity prevails in Congress; our measures are spirited, and I believe we are now ready to go every length to secure our liberties. John Adams's letter [1] has silenced those who opposed every decisive measure; but the moderate friends, or, as I consider them, the enemies of our cause, have caused copies of it to be sent throughout the province, in hopes, by raising the cry of independence, to throw the friends of liberty out of the new Assembly, the choice of which commences next Monday; but I believe they will fail, and that the House will be

---

[1] Two of the private letters of John Adams had been intercepted and published. The originals were sent to England, and are now in the State Paper Office in London. Mr. Sparks has published extracts from the originals, in *Washington's Writings*, vol. ii. p. 499. The one referred to in the text was addressed to James Warren, then President of the Provincial Congress of Massachusetts. See, also, *John Adams's Letters to his Wife*, vol. i. p. 268.

more decided than ever. One comfort we have, that divine wisdom and goodness often bring good out of ill. That the issue of this same contest will be the establishment of our liberties I as firmly believe as I do my existence ; for I never can think that God brought us into this wilderness to perish, or, what is worse, to become slaves, but to make us a great and free people."

On the 2d of November he writes again in a strain equally characteristic : —

"The evening before last, two ships arrived from England. The advices which they bring (amongst which is a proclamation for suppressing rebellion and sedition) are of immense service to us. Our councils have been hitherto too fluctuating: one day, measures for carrying on the war were adopted ; the next, nothing must be done that would widen the unhappy breach between Great Britain and the colonies. As these different ideas have prevailed, our conduct has been directed accordingly. Had we, at the opening of the Congress in May, immediately taken proper measures for carrying on the war with vigor, we might have been in possession of all Canada, undoubtedly, and probably of Boston. Thank God, the happy day which I have long wished for is at length arrived : the southern colonies no longer entertain jealousies of the northern ; they no longer look back to Great Britain ; they are convinced that they have been pursuing a phantom, and that their only safety is a vigorous, determined defense. One of the gentlemen, who has been most sanguine for pacific measures, and very jealous of the New England colonies, addressing me in the style of 'Brother Rebel,' told me he was now ready to join us heartily. 'We have got,' says he, 'a sufficient answer to our petition; I want nothing more, but am ready to declare ourselves independent, send ambassadors,' etc., and much more which prudence forbids me to commit to paper. Our resolutions will henceforth be spirited, clear, and decisive. May the Supreme Governor of the universe direct and prosper them !

"The pleasure which this unanimity gives me is inexpressible. I consider it a sure presage of victory. My anxiety is now at an end. I am no longer worried with contradictory resolutions, but feel a calm, cheerful satisfaction in having one great and just object in view, and the means of obtaining it certainly, by divine blessing, in our own hands."

Congress was at this time exceedingly perplexed and embarrassed on account of the condition of the army, the headquarters of which were at Watertown, in Massachusetts. The troops had been enlisted, and brought into the service, under the authority of the colonies to which they respectively belonged ; and the conditions of their enlistment, and the periods for which they were engaged to serve, were exceedingly various. Even after the appointment of the Commander-in-chief and the other general officers, and the commencement of the Continental system, the men were still unwilling to serve far from home, or under any other than their own officers. The letters which General Washington addressed to the Congress, at this period, contain frequent allusions to the difficulties he constantly encountered in the arrangement of the army. In addition to the information thus communicated, Governor Ward held a correspondence with General Greene, from whom he obtained the most accurate views respecting its actual condition and the difficulties inherent in its organization. His own letters are full of expressions of the solicitude he felt upon this subject, and they often refer to efforts which he made to induce Congress to take some decisive measures for averting the evils which threatened the service of the country.[1]

The councils of that body, however, were far from being unanimous respecting the extent to which the Continental system should be carried. Not a few of its members were exceedingly jealous of anything like an abridgment

---

[1] See Johnson's *Sketches of the Life and Character of General Greene,* vol. i. p. 35 *et seq.*

of the authority of the colonial governments, while others were for merging the whole of that authority, so far as the common cause was concerned, in the new central power which the exigencies of the times had called into being. These differences of opinion, and the feelings of jealousy and suspicion which were connected with them, enhanced the difficulty which attended the remodeling of the army, and filled the minds of those who were acquainted with its condition with the gravest apprehensions. Governor Ward was heartily in favor of the Continental system, and earnestly advocated the offering of a bounty by Congress in order to facilitate the enlistments; but he still thought that the attachment of the troops to their respective colonies was a matter too important to be broken up, or even disregarded, in framing the conditions of enlistment. He accordingly was exceedingly desirous that Congress, in building up its authority and in regulating the military service of the country, should avoid everything which might have a tendency to weaken the attachment which the soldiers felt for the colonies to which they belonged.

His views upon this subject may be best learned from passages contained in the letters which he addressed to his friends during the autumn of 1775, especially to his brother, the Secretary of State in Rhode Island. To this gentleman he writes, on the 21st of November : —

" By letters from camp, I find there is infinite difficulty in reënlisting the army. The idea of making it wholly Continental has induced so many alterations, disgusting to both officers and men, that very little success has attended our recruiting orders. I have often told the Congress that, under the idea of new-modeling, I was afraid we should destroy our army. Southern gentlemen wish to remove that attachment which the officers and men have to their respective colonies, and make them look up to the continent at large for their support or promotion. I never thought that attachment injurious to the common cause, but the strongest inducement to people to risk everything in defense of the whole, upon the preservation of which must depend the safety of each colony. I wish, therefore, not to eradicate, but to regulate it in such a manner as may most conduce to the protection of the whole.

"I am not a little alarmed at the present situation of the army. I wish your utmost influence may be used to put things upon a proper footing, and must beg leave through you to recommend the matter to the immediate attention of the Governor. There is no time to be lost."

The letters written at this period to Governor Ward by General Greene, from the camp near Boston, breathe a similar spirit, and contain many facts which were undoubtedly the basis of the views above given. The correspondence which Washington held not only with the Congress, but with the Governors and public men of several of the colonies, indicates how deep was his anxiety on account of the condition of the army, and how gloomy a period the autumn of 1775 must have been to all the far-sighted patriots of the Revolution. It is from such sources as these that we derive the means of estimating aright the nature of the attachment which the people, especially in New England, felt for the respective colonies to which they belonged, and the difficulty with which this attachment was identified with their interest in the common cause of resistance to the ministry. Though great confidence was generally reposed in the wisdom of Congress, and high expectations were entertained concerning the results of its deliberations, yet the idea of a Continental sovereignty, independent of the authority of the colonies, was of slow growth in the popular mind, and the indistinctness with which it was conceived was a fertile source of embarrassment and confusion in the early stages of the Revolution.

But events were steadily, though slowly, advancing towards the consummation which a few had anticipated from the beginning. The successive arrivals from England only confirmed the opinion that the ministry were determined to persevere in enforcing the measures which they had adopted, and were preparing additional forces to decide the contest by the sword, in the approaching spring. In the mean time, some of the more active and fearless spirits in the colonies had conceived the idea of separation; and it was already beginning to spread among the people, though there might still be found those who fondly clung to the hope of reconciliation. The wife of John Adams, writing from the heart of Massachusetts, was urging separation upon the mind of her husband with all the ardor of woman's eloquence. General Greene, in his letters to Governor Ward, many months before, had begun to recommend a declaration of independence, and had often declared that the people were beginning to wish for it. The Congress, however, was still inactive and uncertain in its opinions. The subject had not yet been discussed, nor had the word " Independence " been uttered in any of its debates. Its members, as they are described in the letters of John Adams, sat brooding " in deep anxiety and thoughtful melancholy," with only rare and remote allusions to the mighty question, and waiting for the occurrence of some critical event to decide their course of action.

Governor Ward, if we may judge from the tone of his letters, was more patient of this delay than were some others of the delegates from New England. He felt confident that independence would be the ultimate destiny of the colonies; and, when the troubles on account of the Stamp Act first appeared, he had often predicted this result in the friendly intercourse of private life. His most earnest desire was to see the different portions of the country united in the maintenance of their liberties, and to have the army thoroughly organized. With this preparation, he was willing patiently to wait the slow progress of events, and to leave the issue of all with the justice of Heaven.

The colony of Rhode Island was now suffering the worst evils consequent upon its exposed situation. The ships of the enemy, under the command of Captain Wallace, were lying along all its shore, and parties of marauders were constantly making depredations upon the property and threatening the lives of the inhabitants. Bristol had been attacked, and, after being laid under heavy contribution, was nearly destroyed. The islands of Conanicut and Prudence had been ravaged with more than usual brutality; and the town of Newport, in which the British commander still had influential friends and supporters, was compelled to furnish periodical supplies to the fleet, which had exclusive control of the harbor and the adjacent bay. The commerce of the colony was entirely prostrate; some of the wealthiest inhabitants, refusing to engage in the Revolution, had moved away, while the poor people, who remained, were reduced to the extremity of suffering by the severity of the winter, the scarcity of provisions, and the heavy restrictions which were placed upon them. So large a portion of the men who were fit for service were enlisted in the Continental army, or were otherwise employed away from home, that those who remained were wholly insufficient for the protection of the long line of sea-coast which bounded a large part of the colony.

In this general distress of the people, the Commander-in-chief, at the request of the Governor of Rhode Island, sent General Lee with a small detachment to Newport, to observe the condition of the town, and recommend such measures for its relief as he might deem practicable. The

General Assembly passed an act making it a crime for any
person to convey intelligence to the British ministry or
their agents, to supply their armies or fleets with arms or
military stores, or to serve as a pilot to an English vessel of
war ; and providing that whoever should be found guilty
of the offense should be punished with death and the confiscation of estate.[1] Several persons, who had rendered
themselves obnoxious to this penalty, and who refused to
make any promises for the future, were taken into cus-
tody, and their estates declared to be confiscated. The
Assembly also adopted an address to Congress, in which
they set forth, in the most urgent terms, the condition of
the colony, the exertions which they had made, and were
still making, for its defense, and their inability longer to
sustain these exertions, or to keep the colony from falling
into the hands of the enemy, unless they should receive
timely aid from Congress. A copy of this address was
forwarded to Mr. Ward at Philadelphia, and another was
sent to General Washington, with a request that he would
second the views which it contained by such recommendation as his knowledge of the colony would enable him to
give.[2]

[1] The town of Newport was excepted in this act, and, under certain restrictions, its people, in accordance with their own request,
were allowed to furnish supplies to the ships of Captain Wallace,
which lay in their harbor. This was suffered as a measure of safety
to the town, though its expediency was called in question in other
parts of the colony, and by General Washington in his letter to Governor Cooke. Sparks's *Washington,* vol. iii. p. 227.

[2] This address, which bears the date of January 15, 1776, together with the letter from General Washington to the President
of Congress concerning it, is contained in the *American Archives,*
vol. v. p. 1148. It is a document of no small importance, as illustrating the exertions and the sufferings of the people of Rhode Island
at this early stage of the Revolution. From the account there presented, it appears that the colony, besides minutemen and militia
not yet called into service, had, at this time, not less than 3,743 sol-

The Commander-in-chief, when he communicated the paper to Congress, fully indorsed the statement it contained respecting the condition of the colony and the sufferings of its inhabitants, and expressed his conviction that it was highly necessary that measures should be adopted to relieve their distress and to furnish the aid they required. The delegates of Rhode Island did not immediately bring the address to the public attention of Congress, but preferred, according to the instructions which they received from the Governor of the colony, to consult some of the leading members upon the subject in private. A few weeks afterwards, Mr. Ward writes to Governor Cooke that "this had been done; and from their generous concern for the colony, and a universal approbation of our vigorous exertions for the common defense, I have not the least doubt but the two battalions raised by the government will be taken into Continental pay."

The countenance which was received from General Washington and the assurances of aid from Congress, together with the spirited acts of the Assembly, gave new energy to the people of the colony, and served to dissipate the gloom which had settled around their prospects. In Newport, the influential men, who still adhered to the ministry, and who maintained frequent intercourse with the British officers attached to the ships in the harbor, were thoroughly humbled by the visit of General Lee to the town, and by the bold stand which he took against them.

diers and sailors, exclusive of officers, in actual service, of whom 1,700 were in the Continental army, and at least 200 more were on board armed vessels, beyond the limits of the colony. The whole population, in the year 1774, amounted to only 59,678 souls, and of these 5,243 were Indians and Negroes. The number of families was 9,437.

The peace of the town, however, was still almost entirely at the mercy of the British commander, whose numerous acts of insult and brutal violence in different parts of the colony called down upon his name and character the direst execrations of the people. In his moods of malice, which, it was said, were made more vindictive by frequent intoxication, he would often ravage the shores of Narragansett Bay, pillage the neighboring farms and hamlets, and sometimes take the lives of the inhabitants, in a manner that would be expected only of the outlaw chief of some horde of pirates. The distresses of his native colony, and especially of those portions of it with which, from infancy, he had been most familiar, enlisted the deepest sympathies of Governor Ward, and the numerous passages in his letters relating to the subject show how earnest were the efforts he made for their relief, both in Congress and in his communications to the colonial government.

In September, 1775, a detachment of eleven hundred men had been sent, under the command of Colonel Benedict Arnold, on an expedition to Canada, for the purpose of weakening the British forces stationed there, and of conciliating the good will of the Canadians towards the cause of the colonies. When volunteers for this distant and perilous expedition were called for by General Washington, two hundred and fifty of the troops belonging to Rhode Island had presented themselves for the service. Among them was Samuel Ward, Junior, who, as we have already mentioned, had in the preceding spring received a captain's commission in the Continental army.

Upon the formation of the character of this young man, now in the twentieth year of his age, Governor Ward had bestowed the care which might naturally be expected of a fond and high-minded father. Having sent him to receive his classical education at the College of Rhode Isl-

and, he had seen him bear its highest honors at the period
of his graduation, and, at the opening of the Revolution,
he had given him up, the hope and the pride of his family, to the service of his country. He had early instilled
into his mind his own spirit of self-sacrificing patriotism,
and had constantly enjoined upon him the practice of virtue and the fear of God.

After Captain Ward had joined the camp near Boston,
and while the period of his enlistment was still undecided,
his father wrote to him a letter which contains a full expression of his views concerning the duty which a citizen
owes his country in times of calamity or distress.

" With regard [says he] to your engaging in the public service during the war, my sentiments are these: that so long as
my country has any occasion for my service, and calls upon me
properly, she has an undoubted right to it ; and I shall ever esteem it the highest happiness to be able, in times of general distress, to do her any material good. Upon these principles, you
will give me the highest satisfaction by devoting your life, while
Heaven graciously continues it, to the public service. The poet
justly said, ' *Dulce et decorum est pro patria mori.*' I can as
justly add, *pro patria vivere.*"

With these sentiments, rendered more forcible by parental example, to guide his conduct in the army, Captain Ward early attracted the notice of the Commander-
in-chief, and, though at an immature age, he was permitted to join the troops from his native colony, who had
been under the command of Colonel Christopher Greene,
in the expedition to Quebec. Full of hope, and eager
for the service in which they were to be engaged, the
volunteers, under the command of Arnold, left the camp
on the 15th of September, and arrived at the mouth of
the Kennebec River on the 20th of the same month.
Here they commenced their march through an untraveled
wilderness, amidst the severities of an inclement season,

without provisions, and but poorly clad; and, after enduring hardships such as were scarcely paralleled in all
the struggle of the Revolution, they reached the bank of
the St. Lawrence, opposite Quebec, on the 15th of November. A few days from this date he writes to his sisters at Westerly : —

"We were thirty days in a wilderness that none but savages
ever attempted to pass. We marched one hundred miles upon
short three days' provisions, waded over three rapid rivers,
marched through snow and ice *barefoot*, passed over the St.
Lawrence where it was guarded by the enemy's frigates, and
are now about twenty-four miles from the city, to recruit our
worn-out natures. General Montgomery intends to join us immediately, so that we have a winter's campaign before us; but
I trust we shall have the glory of taking Quebec."

This expectation, which was also confidently entertained
both in Congress and at the camp of the Commander-in-
chief, was doomed to a melancholy disappointment. A
few days after the arrival of Arnold, General Montgomery joined him on the plains before Quebec, with three
hundred men from Montreal, and took command of the
expedition. Though the force was still too small for the
reduction of the city, yet the General, relying on the disposition of the Canadians to favor the cause of the Americans, commenced the attack on the morning of the 31st
of December. The event proved but too clearly that this
reliance was wholly misplaced. The heroic commander
fell early in the battle, and his men were repulsed. The
detachment led by Colonel Arnold was engaged at another
point of the city. It had already forced one of the
barriers, which had been thrown up for its defense, and
was approaching a second, when Arnold was borne
wounded from the ground. The troops, however, led on
by Colonel Greene, were still maintaining the assault,
when they were attacked in the rear, and their retreat

cut off by a party of the enemy, and nearly four hundred of them were made prisoners. Among these were Captain Ward and a large portion of the company under his command.

On the 17th of January, 1776, the news reached Congress, by despatches from General Schuyler, of the disastrous fate of the expedition to Quebec and of the fall of Montgomery. The intelligence was received with no common emotion. A brave officer, high in rank, had been snatched from the service of the country; and the hopes which had been indulged, that the people of Canada would join the colonies in their resistance to the ministry, were blighted at the very moment when they were the strongest and most ardent. But in the mind of no one in Congress, who on that day listened to the melancholy recital contained in the letters of General Schuyler, was a deeper anxiety excited than in that of Governor Ward. As a warm-hearted patriot he mourned the loss of the gallant General, and, with a father's pride and a father's solicitude, he learned the heroic conduct and the unhappy fate of his son, the youthful captain, and his soldiers from Rhode Island. He was immediately appointed one of the committee to whom the communications of General Schuyler were referred; and on the 21st of January, so soon as the duties of the committee had been discharged, he addressed a letter to his son in Canada, which will illustrate his character both as a patriot and a father: —

My dear Son, — I most devoutly thank God that you are alive, in good health, and have behaved well. You have now a new scene of action, to behave well as a prisoner. You have been taught from your infancy the love of God, of all mankind, and especially of your country; in a due discharge of these various duties of life consist true honor, religion, and virtue. I hope no situation or trial, however severe, will tempt you to violate those sound, immutable laws of God and nature. You will now have time for reflection; improve it well, and examine your own heart. Eradicate, as much as human frailty admits, the seeds of vice and folly. Correct your temper. Expand the benevolent feelings of your soul, and impress and establish the noble principles of private and public virtue so deeply in it that your whole life may be directed by them. Next to these great and essential duties, improve your mind by the best authors you can borrow. Learn the French language, and be continually acquiring, as far as your situation admits, every useful accomplishment. Shun every species of debauchery and vice, as certain and inevitable ruin here and hereafter. There is one vice which, though often to be met with in polite company, I cannot but consider as unworthy of a gentleman as well as a Christian. I mean swearing. Avoid it at all times.

All ranks of people here have the highest sense of the great bravery and merit of Colonel Arnold, and all his officers and men. Though prisoners, they have acquired immortal honor. Proper attention will be paid to them. In the mean time, behave, my dear son, with great circumspection, prudence, and firmness. Enter into no engagements inconsistent with your duty to your country, and such as you may make keep inviolate with the strictest honor. Besides endeavoring to make yourself as easy and comfortable as possible in your present situation, you will pay the greatest attention, as far as your little power may admit, to the comfort and welfare of all your fellow-prisoners, and of those lately under your immediate command especially.[1]

During the winter of 1776, the attention of Congress was earnestly directed to preparation for the campaign, which it was expected the ensuing spring would open upon the country. The fall of Montgomery and the failure of the expedition to Quebec undoubtedly had a tendency to give a still more serious air to their deliberations. He was the first officer of the Continental army,

---

[1] The letter from which this is an extract was published in the *American Annual Register*, vol. vii. p. 407.

high in rank, who had fallen in the service; and the fathers of the country mourned for him, as for one who had died an heroic martyr to the common cause. The committee who were appointed to consider the subject made a series of successive reports, which resulted in sending a deputation from Congress to visit Canada, and in reinforcing the army which was stationed there.

The military operations of the Continental army were also greatly extended; new posts were established, and arrangements set on foot for undertaking the defense of the entire continent, as the common territory of all the colonies was then termed. The attitude of Congress, however, had not changed. It was still that of deep anxiety and painful suspense, in which its members were waiting for some decisive event to determine the course they should adopt. Independence was only mentioned in the privacy of familiar intercourse, or in the correspondence of confidential friends. In the hall of Congress the word had not yet been uttered. But among those grave and thoughtful men suspense was not a natural state of mind, and it could not long continue. Beneath the solemn exterior which they presented a discerning eye might detect many a current of deep and earnest feeling, whose sure and silent flow was bearing the whole body insensibly onward to some mighty crisis.

These were the settled views which now regulated the conduct and shaped the opinions of Governor Ward; and the familiar letters, which have guided us in framing this memoir, alone can show how deeply he was interested in the plans which Congress was now adopting, and in the approach of the events which he felt confident were hastening on by the appointment of a destiny which no earthly power could withstand. He also, at this time, as was natural from the troubled condition of his native colony, experienced great anxiety on account of his domestic affairs. Eleven children had survived the death of their mother, which took place in 1770. Of these, one had died during his attendance at the session of the first Congress. The three elder sons were now, in imitation of their father's example, in the service of the country, two of them holding places in the army and one in the navy. The two elder daughters were recently married, and the remaining children, still of a tender age, were dwelling, without the protection of a parent, in the mansion at Westerly, in one of the most exposed situations along the coast of the colony. To that once cheerful and happy home of his family his thoughts would often revert, and his warm, parental affection would urge him to abandon the public service, that he might watch over the tender years of his children, and save from wasting and decay the beautiful estate which his industry had acquired.

But such were not the views of duty which became a patriot statesman of the Revolution. To him the present was of little importance; the future was all in all. Never, perhaps, in the history of mankind, has there been a period distinguished by so striking instances of the sacrifice of every private interest to the general good. The individual was but a unit in the mighty mass, whose freedom and happiness were of immeasurable importance. It was in accordance with this higher sentiment of duty to his country that Governor Ward at this time decided against the dictates of parental affection, and resolved to remain in the Congress, and there abide the issues of the contest. In the month of February, of this long and anxious winter, he thus writes to the sister to whom he had especially committed the charge of his family: —

" When I consider the alarms, the horrors, and mischiefs of war, I cannot help thinking what those wretches deserve who have involved this innocent country in all its miseries. At the same time, I adore the divine wisdom and goodness which

often overrules and directs those calamities to the producing of
the greatest good. This I humbly hope will be our case. We
may yet establish the peace and happiness of our native country upon the broad and never-failing basis of liberty and virtue.

"When I reflect upon this subject, and anticipate the glorious
period, the dangers of disease, the inconveniences experienced in
my private affairs, the almost unparalleled sufferings of Samuel,[1]
and all that my dear children and friends do or can suffer appear to me trifling. I am sure your own love of liberty and
your fortitude of mind will not only support you, but will enable you to encourage and support all around you in the hour
of danger. My dear little boys and girls, I know, need me
much; but my duty forbids my return. I can only recommend
them to God, to you and my other sisters, and to their older sisters. Do all you possibly can to encourage them in the paths of
virtue, industry, frugality, and neatness, and in improving their
minds as far as their situation admits."

Such were the labors, the anxieties, and the hopes
which occupied the mind of Governor Ward, when death,
coming at an unexpected hour, suddenly put an end to
them all. In the pressure of the many concerns which
had engaged his attention while in Congress, he had neglected to adopt the usual preventive against the smallpox, at that time one of the most dreaded of the diseases
with which humanity could be afflicted. It frequently
appeared with great malignity, especially in the large
towns of the country; and Governor Ward had received
repeated admonitions, while at Philadelphia, to resort to
inoculation, the only preventive measure at that time
known; but though, as would appear from his letters, he
dreaded the contagion with peculiar apprehension, he
would never allow himself to be inoculated.[2]

[1] His son, Captain Ward, now a prisoner at Quebec.
[2] He is said to have had an invincible repugnance to this mode of
taking the disease. Indeed, a strong prejudice had always existed
in the colonies against inoculation, since its first introduction in 1721.

In the Journal of Congress for the 13th of March is found the latest mention of his participation in the business of the House. On that day he presided in the committee of the whole, through a protracted discussion of several memorials and other papers relating to the trade of the colonies, and, on reporting to the House the progress of the debate, obtained leave to sit again. He also accepted an appointment as a member of a special committee, which was instructed to devise ways and means for defraying the anticipated expenses of the campaign that was soon to open. These duties, however, were not for him to perform.

On the two following days he was still in his place in Congress, with his characteristic punctuality and devotion to business. From this time his seat was vacant. The disease, which had already begun to be felt in his system, now appeared in its worst malignity, and on the 26th of March, 1776, put an end to his useful and honorable life, in the fifty-first year of his age. In the published " Letters " of John Adams, the event is thus noticed a few days after it happened : —

" We have this week lost a very valuable friend of the colonies in Governor Ward, of Rhode Island, by the smallpox in the natural way. He never would hearken to his friends, who have been constantly advising him to be inoculated ever since the first Congress began. But he would not be persuaded. Numbers who have been inoculated have gone through this distemper without any danger, or even confinement. But nothing would do; he must take it in the natural way, and die. He was an amiable and a sensible man, a steadfast friend to his country, upon very pure principles. His funeral was attended

Vaccination was first adopted in England, by Dr. Jenner, in 1798, and was introduced into America, about the year 1800, through the agency of Dr. Benjamin Waterhouse, a native of Newport, and at that time a lecturer at Harvard College, and also at Brown University.

with the same solemnities as Mr. Randolph's. Mr. Stillman, being the Anabaptist minister here, of which persuasion was the Governor, was desired by Congress to preach a sermon, which he did with great applause." [1]

He was interred in the burial-place of the First Baptist Church, amid the solemnities of religious worship, in the presence of the members of Congress, of the General Assembly of Pennsylvania, and a large concourse of the citizens of Philadelphia, among whom his amiable manners and exalted character had won for him many admiring friends. A monument was ordered to be erected to his memory at the place of his interment by a vote of Congress, and afterwards by an act of the General Assembly of Rhode Island.

The course of this memoir has furnished but few opportunities to refer to the religious opinions or the religious character of Governor Ward. He was, however, a sincere and humble Christian. He was connected, as were his ancestors before him, with a church of the Sabbatarian persuasion ; a name given to what was then a large and highly respectable denomination of Christians in Rhode Island, who practiced the rite of baptism by immersion, and adhered with singular tenacity to the ancient Jewish Sabbath as the appointed day of public worship.[2] He was at all times a careful observer of the simple forms of the church with which he was connected, and was withal a truly devout and conscientious as well as a high-minded and honorable man.

His patriotism, which was deeply tinged with his religious feelings, was of the most constant and self-sacrificing nature. To be useful to the cause of American liberty,

---

[1] *John Adams's Letters to his Wife*, vol. i. p. 92.

[2] Among his papers is a confession of his faith in the fundamental doctrines of Christianity, which was submitted to the church on his admission as a member.

then struggling with mighty foes, to see his country successful in the great contest she had undertaken, and to win for himself the approbation of Heaven, "as a faithful servant and soldier of Jesus Christ," — these, we may well judge, were the controlling aspirations of his mind, when death summoned him to the scenes of immortality, and to a nearer communion with the spiritual realities which he had so long contemplated from afar.

His death took place on the eve of great events, which no man had more clearly foreseen, and which few men had done more to hasten forward. His sun went down ere the star of his country had risen, and while gloom and night yet hung round the whole horizon. Had his life been prolonged but for a little season, he would have beheld his native colony taking the lead of all the others in asserting the doctrines which he cherished, and becoming the first to throw off the allegiance that bound her to the British throne.[1] He would also have affixed his signature to the Declaration of American Independence, and thus linked with his name an enduring title to the gratitude of posterity, and won perhaps a prouder place in the annals of his country.

But this high guaranty of fame he was not permitted to attain ; and we close this narrative of his life and services with the following estimate of his character, from the pen of one who knew him well, and who, while in Congress, relied with unwavering confidence on his fidelity, his wisdom, and his patriotism. The late John Adams, near the close of his venerable old age, in a letter dated January 29, 1821, and addressed to one[2] of the descendants of Governor Ward, thus speaks of his character : —

---

[1] The act of allegiance was repealed by the General Assembly in May, 1776.

[2] Richard R. Ward, Esq., of New York.

"He was a gentleman in his manners, benevolent and amiable in his disposition, and as decided, ardent, and uniform in his patriotism as any member of that Congress. When he was seized with the smallpox, he said that if his vote and voice were necessary to support the cause of his country, he should live ; if not, he should die. He died, and the cause of his country was supported, but it lost one of its most sincere and punctual advocates."

The life of Governor Ward was abruptly closed at a gloomy period in the history of his country. But his generous patriotism and his manly spirit did not die. He had instilled them with parental care into the mind of the son who bore his name, and to whose early service in the army of the Revolution we have already alluded. The father descended to the tomb in the meridian of his days, but the leading features of his character were inherited by the son, who in his own career worthily exemplified the precepts and counsels which had guided his youth.

Samuel Ward, Junior, was born at Westerly, on the 17th of November, 1756. He was graduated at Brown University, with distinguished honors, in the class of 1771. At the early age of eighteen, he received a Captain's commission from the government of his native colony, and in May, 1775, marched with his company to join the army of observation, which Rhode Island was at that time raising for her own and the common defense. In the autumn of the same year he volunteered, with a large body of the troops of Rhode Island, to accompany Colonel Arnold on the expedition to Quebec, — an expedition attended with sufferings and privations such as were scarcely surpassed, if indeed they were equalled, during the war. They were bravely encountered and heroically endured ; but the expedition terminated in disaster and defeat. With a large number of his gallant associates, Captain Ward was overpowered by superior force, taken prisoner, and carried to

Quebec, where he was still detained at the period of his father's death.

In the course of the year 1776, he was exchanged, and, on his return to Rhode Island, married the daughter of William Greene, of Warwick, who was afterwards Governor of that State. Soon after his exchange, Captain Ward was commissioned as Major in the regiment of Colonel Christopher Greene, who had been his brave associate in the toils and disasters of the expedition to Quebec. Under this gallant commander he bore a distinguished part in the celebrated battle at Red Bank, in which Fort Mercer was successfully defended from the assault of the Hessians under Count Donop. Of this action, at the order of his Colonel, he drew up the official account, which was forwarded to the Commander-in-chief, and which is now contained in the published correspondence of General Washington.[1] He was also in the camp of Washington during the dreadful winter in which the army was quartered at Valley Forge.

In 1778, the regiment of Colonel Greene was detached for special service in the colony to which it belonged, and was placed under the command of General Sullivan, whose headquarters were then at Providence. The General was preparing an expedition, which he had been ordered to undertake against the island of Rhode Island, for the purpose of dislodging the British forces, and driving them from the shores of Narragansett Bay. In this expedition Mr. Ward, though holding only a Major's commission, was intrusted with the command of a regiment. The enterprise proved unsuccessful, and the army of General Sullivan was obliged to retreat from the island ; but the youthful officer, though charged with a responsibility above his commission, behaved with prudence and gallantry, and contributed his share to the order and success

[1] Sparks's *Washington*, vol. v. p. 112.

with which the retreat, so mortifying to the commander and so calamitous to the colony, was conducted.

In April of the following year, he received the commission of Lieutenant-Colonel in the first regiment of the division from Rhode Island; and in this command he passed two years in Washington's army, while stationed in New Jersey and upon the Hudson River. In many of the important operations of this period he bore the part becoming to his rank; he endured patiently the toils and privations which the service of his country imposed upon the army, and won for himself a share of the glory which belongs to all those who, amidst disappointment, disaster, and the keenest suffering, were still faithful to the cause of the Revolution.

Near the close of the war, Colonel Ward retired from the army, and engaged in mercantile pursuits in the city of New York. While thus employed, he made several voyages to Europe and the East Indies, and was among the first to display the flag of his country in the China Seas. He also resided in Paris during some of the early stages of the French Revolution, and was present at the scene when Louis the Sixteenth was beheaded. On his return to the United States, he retired from the mercantile house with which he had been long connected, and settled with his family on an estate near East Greenwich, in Rhode Island. Here, amid the quiet pursuits of agriculture, he revived the studies of his early years, and to the end of his life maintained a scholar's familiarity with Cæsar, Ovid, and Horace, the classic writers who had been the favorites of his academic days. On the death of his wife, in the year 1817, he removed to Jamaica, in the vicinity of New York. Here and in the metropolis itself, where some of his children were now settled in business, he lived for many years in the enjoyment of congenial society, and blessed with the filial love of a numerous family, and with the confidence and respect of a wide circle of friends.

Colonel Ward, though well qualified for public life by his talents and education, as well as by his varied experience of human affairs and his familiar acquaintance with most of the leading men of the country, yet was too strongly attached to the quiet scenes of his own home, and was withal too little ambitious of political distinction, ever to engage with relish in the exciting labors of the politician. He was twice, however, chosen to represent his fellow-citizens in what were then deemed important public bodies. One of them was the Commercial Convention which assembled at Annapolis, in 1786; the other was the Convention which met at Hartford, in 1812.

With these solitary exceptions, his days were passed in the humble occupations of a private gentleman. Yet he was not indifferent to the fortunes of his country. He had been taught to love her from his infancy, and had spent the first years of his early manhood in the achievement of her independence. But now that this had been secured, he yielded to the love of quiet inherent in his nature, and felt at liberty to keep himself aloof from her public concerns. He died at New York, in 1832, at the age of seventy-five years.

The recollection of the person and the character of Colonel Ward is still vivid in the minds of many who knew him as he appeared in society in the later years of his life. One of these, who can well judge of the qualities he specifies, has pronounced him to have been "a ripe classical scholar, a gentleman of most winning urbanity of manners, and a man of sterling intellect and unblemished honor." [1]

[1] Notices of the early graduates of Brown University by William G. Goddard.

THE MONROE DOCTRINE.[1]

IN the year 1823, James Monroe was in the third year of his second presidency of the United States; John Quincy Adams was Secretary of State; Richard Rush was Minister of the United States at the Court of St. James, where George Canning was Minister of Foreign Affairs, virtual head of the English cabinet. The presidency of Mr. Monroe, from the beginning, had been singularly free from partisan bitterness and political agitations of every kind. The old Federal party had gone to its final rest. The passions engendered during the War of 1812 had become extinct, and his second election had been well-nigh unanimous. The acquisition of Florida had gratified the national appetite for territory, the Missouri Compromise had for the time pacified the sectionalism of the South, and the rapid extension of settlements beyond the Mississippi proclaimed the beneficence of the government and the prosperity of the people.

In Europe, however, a very different spectacle was presented. The wars of the French Revolution had come to an end, but their end had brought neither public peace nor private contentment. The armies of allied Europe, which had been engaged in the overthrow of Napoleon, were still kept on foot, and were now employed in the reconstruction of the continent on the principles of legitimacy, and in destroying every vestige of the freedom which revolution had anywhere secured. The Great

[1] Read before the Rhode Island Historical Society, February 8, 1881.

Powers were resolved not to abandon their efforts at subjugation till absolute monarchy should be again established in every country in which free institutions had
gained any foothold. To Austria had been assigned the
work of popular subjugation in Italy and Switzerland ;
and the restored monarchy of France, with the support
of Russia and Prussia, had sent an army into Spain to
destroy the liberal constitution which the Cortes had
forced upon their faithless Bourbon king, Ferdinand VII.
England had been associated with these powers in the
wars against Napoleon, and had for a time continued in
their bad company. When Mr. Burke, thirty years before, wrote his " Reflections on the French Revolution,"
he penned a passage of brilliant apology for the repres-
sive measures which the madness of the Revolution then
seemed to require, closing it with the sententious apho-
rism, " Kings will be tyrants from policy when subjects
are rebels from principle." But the time for such apology
or for any apology had long passed in England. She
looked with alarm and disgust upon the reactionary movements in which the allies were engaged, and found herself
compelled by every requirement of her free constitution,
as well as by all the best impulses of her Saxon blood,
to declare against them.

It was in these circumstances that in August, 1823,
Mr. Canning took occasion to confer with the American
Minister, Mr. Rush, as to the alarming designs of the
allies, and also to make known to him the fact, which had
come privately to his knowledge, that these designs now
distinctly embraced the restoration to the Spanish crown
of the American colonies which had been wrested from
it by revolution. Mr. Canning's design was to unite
this country with Great Britain in a determined protest
against any forcible interference with the Spanish-American colonies, then struggling for their independence, and

he concentrated his views in the highly suggestive, perhaps artful question, " Are the great political and commercial interests which hang upon the destinies of the New World to be canvassed and adjusted in Europe without the coöperation or even the knowledge of the United States ? "

The conversation, or conversations, for there were several, which were entirely confidential, were carefully reported to the State Department. Mr. Adams, the astute and practiced secretary, immediately comprehended the situation, and lost no time in deciding as to what he should advise the President to do. The United States had already acknowledged the independence of the Spanish-American republics, and had formally urged Great* Britain to do the same. But she had delayed, and now, instead of acknowledging them herself, Mr. Canning had proposed that the two governments should join in a solemn protest against the contemplated proceeding of the Holy Alliance. With this proposal Mr. Adams had no thought of complying. He saw at a glance that, by joining with England, this country would perform but a secondary part in a matter of transcendent importance to her interests and even to her destiny. Accordingly, in laying the whole matter before the President, he urged upon his attention the fact that here was a great opportunity to define and declare the position of the United States as to the movements in question, and at the same time to afford special encouragement to the new republics whose independence we had very recently acknowledged. This, Mr. Adams suggested, could most properly be done in the annual message to Congress.

Mr. Monroe, it is understood, did not readily adopt the views of his secretary. He had intended to advert in his message to the dangerous proceedings and more dangerous doctrines of the Holy Alliance, but he shrank from adopting the bold declarations of Mr. Adams. He apprehended that their utterance might bring embarrassment to his administration, in whose quiet, easy-going character he greatly delighted. He at length, however, waived his objections, and wrought the sentiments with which Mr. Adams had inspired him into the message which he sent to Congress at its assembling on December 3, 1823. These sentiments are embodied in separate paragraphs in different parts of the message. It should also here be mentioned that a dispute was then in progress between the United States and Russia respecting the claims of the latter to what was at that time vaguely known as the Oregon Territory, and that in this dispute Great Britain was incidentally involved on account of the still unsettled boundary between her possessions and those of the United States in the same Territory. After giving an account of the question then at issue between us and Russia, the message contains the following sentence, which, though without any bearing on the Holy Alliance or the Spanish-American republics, has always been considered a part of the so-called "Monroe Doctrine:" "The occasion has been judged proper for asserting, as a principle in which the rights and interests of the United States are involved, that the American continents, by the free and independent condition which they have assumed and maintain, are henceforth not to be considered as subjects for future colonization by any European power."

It was, however, in a subsequent part of the message that he set forth, in several paragraphs, the views which he had been persuaded to present concerning the threatened interference of the allied powers of Europe in the political affairs of the western continent. The paragraphs are too long to be recited in full; they are indeed only repeated expressions of one and the same general idea, and of this idea the essential declarations are as follows:

" The political system of the allied powers is essentially different [in this respect] from that of America. This difference
proceeds from that which exists in their respective governments. . . . We owe it, therefore, to candor and to the amicable
relations existing between the United States and those powers
to declare that we should consider any attempt on their part to
extend their system to any portion of this hemisphere *as dangerous to our peace and safety.* With the existing colonies or dependencies of any European power we have not interfered, and
shall not interfere ; but with the governments who have declared
their independence and maintained it, and whose independence
we have, on great consideration and on just principles, acknowledged, we could not view any interposition for the purpose of
oppressing them, or controlling, in any other manner, their destiny,
by any European power, in any other light than as the manifestation of an unfriendly disposition towards the United States."

" In the war between those new governments and Spain, we
declared our neutrality at the time of their recognition ; and to
this we have adhered and shall continue to adhere, provided no
change shall occur which, in the judgment of the competent authorities of this government, shall make a corresponding change
on the part of the United States indispensable to their security."

In a subsequent paragraph the message sets forth the
marked difference between the policy prevailing among
the powers of Europe as to interfering in the political affairs of foreign States and the policy early adopted by
the United States in regard to all those powers. It then
points out that in regard to these American continents
"circumstances are eminently and conspicuously different." It goes on to declare again that "it is impossible
that the allied powers should extend their political system to any portion of either continent without endangering our peace and happiness."

These are the several declarations which together constitute what has received the name of the " Monroe Doctrine." The significance of the doctrine, as intended by

President Monroe, is to be determined by reference to the circumstances in which it had its origin and the avowed objects which it was designed to accomplish. These fully show: 1. That this second part of it was prompted solely by the threatened interference of the powers of Europe in the political affairs of the American States, for the purpose of controlling their destiny. 2. That its single design was to prevent this and all similar interference. 3. That the doctrine, as put forth by Mr. Monroe, was declared and promulgated solely in the interest of the United States, and because the interposition in question would inflict injury upon this country. 4. It did not promise or imply military aid to the Spanish-American States in their existing struggle with Spain. On the contrary, it expressly declared that neutrality would be strictly maintained between the belligerents, unless there should arise a necessity for departing from it. 5. Nor was it a declaration against the existence of monarchical institutions in the western hemisphere; for such institutions were already existing in Brazil, in Cuba, in Canada, and they had scarcely ceased to exist in Mexico, whose first independent government was an empire. It had to do, not with existing governments or colonies already here, but solely with European interposition for the purpose of oppressing them or in any way controlling their destiny.

The other, or first-mentioned, part of the doctrine — that which relates to colonization by any European power — had a different origin, and it would probably have had a place in Mr. Monroe's message, even if the allied powers had never thought of intervention in America. It had been repeatedly asserted before in the diplomatic correspondence of the government. But it is manifestly only another declaration of the same underlying fact, and this fact is that every part of America — both North and South — had now become the property of some established government, and that, consequently, no portion of it could now be claimed or colonized by any country of Europe in virtue of any right of discovery or of bargain with its aboriginal proprietors. The two declarations go naturally together. They unite to form one doctrine of public law, because they are both parts of one and the same political idea, viz., the recognized jurisdiction of some established government over every part of the two continents of America. These continents, therefore, are henceforth no more open to European colonization than is the continent of Europe open to American colonization.

It should here be especially observed that this doctrine was at the outset, and still remains, simply a passage in an annual message of President Monroe. It declared that European intervention in the political affairs of North or South America, or the colonization of any part of its territory by any European power, would be regarded " as the manifestation of an unfriendly disposition towards the United States." It did not, however, declare what the United States would do in case of such intervention or colonization by the allied powers ; still less did it promise to the other American States any protection or military assistance of any kind. What would be the consequence was left for them to imagine, and this was to give it the greatest possible effect. It was to the former a matter of indefinite apprehensions, while to the latter it was an occasion of indefinite expectations. It was designed solely for moral effect, to deter the great powers of Europe from their contemplated interference by assuring them that we should regard it as " endangering our peace and happiness." It is also to be said that this doctrine has never been sanctioned by any enactment of Congress, nor has it, in any other way, been established as a uniform principle of public policy for the United States. President Monroe reaffirmed it in his annual message of December,

1824; Mr. Adams, his successor, reiterated it in 1825; and it has since been repeated again and again by other Presidents.   The first attempt to secure for it the sanction of Congress was made in 1824, by Mr. Clay, at that time Speaker of the House of Representatives.   He introduced in the House a resolution for that purpose, and advocated it with all his brilliant oratory, but the effort was without success.   On several subsequent occasions, similar attempts have been made, but they have uniformly resulted in failure.   It has, however, always been a power in American diplomacy.

But notwithstanding these limitations and drawbacks which may be connected with it, this declaration of President Monroe, it must still be said, produced a profound impression on the public mind of this country, and a scarcely less profound impression on the public mind of the leading nations of Europe.   It was one of those fortunate and significant utterances which mean more than they at first seem to mean.   It expressed a national sentiment just at the moment when it was forming in the minds of the people.   It published to the world what was in the national heart, though no one had ever uttered it before.   It embodied at once our American sympathy with popular freedom, our hatred of absolute governments, the dictates of our national pride, and the aspirations of our national ambition.   In this country it was hailed as a sort of Declaration of Independence for the whole western hemisphere.   Nor was this popular appreciation of it essentially different from that which was entertained even in advance by Mr. Jefferson.   Weeks before the message was prepared, Mr. Monroe, while considering the proposal of Mr. Canning, that the two governments should unite in a solemn protest to the allied powers against their intervention in Spanish America, had asked the advice of Mr. Jefferson, who answered in these earnest words : —

"The question is the most momentous which has ever been offered to my contemplation since that of independence. That made us a nation ; this sets our compass, and points the course which we are to steer through the ocean of time opening on us; and never could we embark on it under circumstances more auspicious. Our first and fundamental maxim should be, never to entangle ourselves in the broils of Europe. Our second, never to suffer Europe to meddle with cisatlantic affairs. America, North and South, has a set of interests distinct from those of Europe, and peculiarly her own. She should, therefore, have a system of her own, separate and apart from that of Europe. While the last is laboring to become the domicile of despotism, our endeavor should surely be to make our hemisphere that of freedom."

Nor was the effect of this declaration abroad less marked than at home. Mr. Rush records that "it was upon all tongues; the press was full of it; the Spanish-American deputies were overjoyed. Spanish - American securities rose in the stock market, and the safety of the new States from all European coercion was considered as no longer doubtful." It was hailed with the utmost satisfaction by the liberal statesmen of England. Lord Brougham, Sir James MacIntosh, and Lord John Russell expressed their gratification in the House of Commons. Nor did Mr. Canning, though a Tory, withhold his full approval of the declaration against interference, though it was not precisely what he desired, while the declaration against colonization was very different from what he desired. It was everywhere regarded as a bold assertion of American spirit and character, and the United States and the American continent all at once assumed a conspicuous position in the thoughts and interests of Europe. The allied powers still offered their assistance to Spain in the war with her rebel colonies, but England immediately declared that the first act of intervention would be a sufficient ground for recognizing their independence.

Such was the origin of the Monroe Doctrine, and such the interest with which its first promulgation in 1823-24 was received on either side of the Atlantic. So far as the intention and design of its author were concerned, it had to do only with the conjunction of events which called it forth. It has, however, long survived these events, and has been connected with several interesting public questions of our national history.

The first of these is the question of the Panama Congress. Early in the administration of John Quincy Adams, Mexico, Central America, and Colombia invited this government to send envoys to a Congress of American States, which was to meet in the following spring at the city of Panama. The general object of the meeting was to consider what means should be employed by the several States to defend themselves against the attempts of any European power either to interfere in their civil affairs or to colonize their territory. These States sought to consult as to their common interests, and their motive in inviting our government to meet with them undoubtedly was, that they might thus have the benefit of our longer experience and superior wisdom as a nation. The idea of the Congress was a natural result of the declaration of Mr. Monroe, and some such conference seemed to be required in order to give that declaration practical effect. The President immediately accepted the invitation, and in his first message in December, 1825, he communicated the fact to Congress, and soon afterwards sent to the Senate the names of John Serjeant of Pennsylvania, and Richard C. Anderson, of Kentucky, to be confirmed as envoys. The question also came up in the House of Representatives as to the appropriation that would be required. It was thus, in one form or the other, before both houses at the same time, and no question of the day gave rise to so protracted debate or excited so widespread public interest.

The President and his advisers attached extraordinary importance to the proposed Congress. They saw in it an unprecedented opportunity, and they expected from it great results, that would contribute to the advancement of the South American States in civil and religious freedom, in good government, and in all commercial and social development. Mr. Gallatin was at the outset invited to be one of the envoys, and, in urging his acceptance of the invitation, Mr. Clay, the Secretary of State, wrote to him as follows : " I think the mission the most important ever sent from this country, those only excepted which related to its independence and to the termination of the late war." The instructions, also, which were prepared for our envoys were liberal and comprehensive as well as careful and well guarded. They were designed to afford the utmost encouragement to the new States which it was in our power to give. The measure could have done no harm ; it promised to do great good. The two houses of Congress, however, were at this time largely composed of the factions which had just been defeated by the election of Mr. Adams to the presidency, and they, with one accord, seized upon this novel recommendation as an opportunity for bringing annoyance and odium to the administration. It immediately became the object of bitter and virulent attack. The proposed Congress was denounced as a " Council of Amphictyons," — as likely to form a sort of Holy Alliance in America in feeble imitation of that in Europe. It would entangle us in the dubious fortunes of the South American republics and compel us to become their protector. It would involve us in war with Spain, and perhaps with all Europe. The Monroe Doctrine itself was condemned as unsound and dangerous ; and the House of Representatives went so far as to adopt a resolution declaring that the United States ought not to become a party with the South American States or any one

of them to any joint declaration even for preventing European interference or colonization in the continent of America. This resolution was, of course, the same thing as to
annul, so far as the House of Representatives was concerned, the whole practical import of the doctrine, and
render it utterly nugatory.

Mr. Adams sent repeated messages to Congress in order
to remove these erroneous impressions. He declared that
there was no intention of binding the United States to
any compact; that the Monroe Doctrine never contemplated any guarantee for the South American republics or
any concerted action with them, save that each State, in
its own way and by its own means, should resist the attempt of any European power to interfere with its independence or to colonize its territory. It was all in vain.
The opposition cared only to annoy and embarrass the
administration. But what, in those days of Southern
domination in this country, did most to concentrate hostility against the project was the demand of John Randolph in the Senate to be informed whether the Congress
would not recognize the Black Republic of Hayti, or rev-
olutionize Cuba and Porto Rico, and free their slaves!
After this, the measure could not pass save with restrictions and conditions that would strip the envoys of the
United States of everything like prestige or authority,
and make them merely silent and useless spectators of
what the others might do. The nominations, however,
were at length reluctantly confirmed, and the appropria-
tions were voted, but not till the season had become so
late that Mr. Serjeant refused to encounter the unhealthy
climate, and Mr. Anderson, the other envoy, was Minister
of the United States in Colombia. The latter commenced
the journey from Bogota, but died on the way to Panama,
from the fever of the country. Others of the envoys
and their secretaries narrowly escaped a similar fate.

The Congress met only to adjourn till autumn to a place in Mexico; but by that time the President, or Dictator, of that republic had become hostile to it, and it did not assemble again. Its total failure was undoubtedly owing to the want of interest in its objects manifested by the United States, and the only importance which now belongs to it in American history arises from its connection with the positive refusal of one house of Congress and the manifest unwillingness of the other to give anything like practical effect to the Monroe Doctrine; and that, too, within less than three years after its first promulgation.

The next conspicuous assertion of the Monroe Doctrine was made by President Polk, whose administration began in 1845, while the Oregon question with Great Britain was still pending. The rallying cry of the party which elected him had been "54° 40' or fight," and in his first message to Congress he recurred in vigorous words to the declarations of his predecessor of twenty years before, and asserted that these declarations would be maintained, and that "no future European colony or dominion shall, with our consent, be planted or established on any part of the North American continent." When, however, the negotiations were begun, it was seen that the parallel of 54° 40' could not be maintained, and the government was obliged to accept that of 49° for the boundary. Mr. Polk, in spite of his brave words, did thus consent to the opening of a territory of more than five degrees of latitude, with a longitude extending across nearly half the continent, to both "colonies and dominion" from Europe.

Three years later (in 1848), during the Mexican War, he sent to Congress a message stating that Yucatan, nominally one of the States of Mexico, had appealed to the United States for protection against the violence of its own Indian population. A similar appeal was, at the same time, made to Spain and to England. The Presi-

dent took the ground that the appeal should be regarded
by our government, because either England or Spain
would otherwise interfere, and this would be in disregard
of our traditional policy, as declared in the Monroe Doctrine. The suggestion was bitterly assailed in the Senate
by Mr. Calhoun, who had been a member of the Monroe
cabinet. He denied that the doctrine was capable of any
such application, and it again failed to receive the sanction of the legislature, and was also abandoned by the
Executive, — and that even when urged by considerations
of humanity.

In 1850 was concluded the convention between Great
Britain and the United States which bears the name of
the "Clayton-Bulwer Treaty." The special object of this
treaty was to fix the relations of those two powers to the
republics of Central America, and its stipulations very
largely involve the considerations which are embodied in
the declarations of President Monroe. But they expressly
disclaim, on the part of the United States, any interest,
rights, or advantages in connection with those Central-
American States other than such as may pertain to Great
Britain or any other European nation. The executive
branch of the government here took the lead in abandoning the ground which before it had so constantly assumed
and so generally maintained. The treaty, however, has
never been acceptable to the country, nor has it been much
regarded on either side. So early as 1852, it was wantonly
violated on the part of Great Britain by her claim of a
protectorate over "the kingdom" of the Mosquito Indians
in Nicaragua, and her subsequent occupation of the "Bay
Islands" on the coast of Honduras. These proceedings
led to the introduction in the Senate, by Mr. Cass, of a
series of joint resolutions, which were designed to enact as
a law of Congress the declarations of Mr. Monroe. The
resolutions were debated through several weeks by most

of the leading statesmen then in the Senate; but they
again failed of adoption. The Monroe Doctrine, however,
still continued to be urged by the Executive in the diplomacy of the government; and England, at the demand
of Nicaragua and Honduras, in 1860, abandoned her
claims both to the protectorate and the islands. By this
proceeding, the last remaining trace of European intervention in the affairs of this continent was brought to an
end.

But this exemption was not to continue long. Four
years had scarcely elapsed when an enterprise, by far the
most daring and dangerous which had ever been undertaken against the independence of American States, was
carried into full execution in Mexico by the Emperor of
the French. It was the gloomiest moment in the war of
secession, when the French expedition, with Maximilian
at its head, landed at Vera Cruz, and with slight opposition made its way to the capital, where the destined Emperor was proclaimed, with the seeming approval of the
clergy, the notables, and the most respectable of the population. It was the most brilliant pronunciamento that
Mexico had ever witnessed. The republic shrank to a
single province or two, where it continued to maintain a
precarious authority and to carry on a guerrilla war in its
own defense. The government of the United States had
sent its reiterated and earnest protests to the Emperor
of France against this reckless menace to all American
States, but he had treated them with undisguised contempt, for he was persuaded that the Union was hope-
lessly destroyed, and that the Southern Confederacy would
soon be his ally. Meanwhile. the American Minister in
Mexico had remained with Juarez, the President of the
republic, and had given to him the entire moral support
of our government. No notice whatever was taken of
Maximilian or his empire, which had come from Europe.

The enterprise thus went on for more than a year, and seemed to be a complete success. Louis Napoleon boasted of it as the greatest achievement of his reign, and was already dreaming of a still more comprehensive union of what he called the Latin races in America, under the protection of France. But the new empire was already on the verge of annihilation. In the summer of 1865 the Union had subjugated secession and suppressed rebellion. The Monroe Doctrine, as again uttered by Mr. Secretary Seward, now sounded in the ears of Louis Napoleon like the voice of a triumphant and united nation, with a victorious army of a million of men fresh from the battlefields of the war. He immediately heeded its demands, which were that his troops should be withdrawn from Mexico, and that the question between the empire and the republic should be left for the people themselves to decide, without foreign coercion or dictation. Never did American diplomacy win a nobler or more righteous triumph. Never did the peaceful pressure of a great national idea secure a more momentous result. We may indeed pity the tragic fate of Maximilian and Carlotta, the innocent dupes of Napoleonic ambition, but we must still rejoice in the complete vindication of a great idea, which is essential to the political independence of every nation on the continent of America.

And now has arisen the question of the Isthmian Canal, to which the Monroe Doctrine is again sought to be applied. The limits of this doctrine, it is true, have never been very carefully fixed, but until now they have not been imagined to be broad enough to embrace a question so remote as this. President Monroe announced that no part of the American continent was any longer open to colonization, or to any kind of political intervention by a European power, and that any such intervention would be regarded as " the manifestation of an unfriendly disposition towards the United States." This declaration, put forth fifty-seven years ago, is now made to include the construction of a canal, designed to be, like the ocean itself, a grand highway for the commerce of all the world. This is certainly neither colonization nor intervention, but it has been assailed with as much hostility as if it combined all the evils and dangers of both. Our government is urged to declare and to maintain not only that no canal across the isthmus shall be constructed by any European government, but also that none shall be constructed by any corporation chartered by a European government; in a word, that it must be built, if built at all, only by a corporation chartered in the United States, and that, when built, the canal must be under the single guarantee and control of the government of the United States. All this, it is claimed, is a part of the Monroe Doctrine; and the reason given is that the construction of this great work by an European corporation will involve the planting of settlements whose inhabitants will be subjects of an European government, and that thus a colony will be established at our very doors. This, it is said, is only another mode of bringing about the very result which Mr. Monroe designed to prevent.

It cannot be denied that there are grave questions connected with this Isthmian Canal which have a very important bearing on American interests, and demand the most careful consideration of our government. But among these questions there can hardly be one of smaller consequence than whether it is or is not at variance with the Monroe Doctrine. This doctrine has, no doubt, done good service in its day. It made an imposing show before the designs of the Holy Alliance. It proved to be decidedly effectual with Louis Napoleon and Maximilian in Mexico. But it is clearly not equal to solving the momentous problem of how a ship canal from ocean to ocean, designed to be open to all nations and neutral in all wars, is to be constructed and controlled in harmony with the sovereignty and the interests of the United States. This new application of the doctrine is, however, so much in accordance with certain currents of public opinion in this country that it requires a moment's consideration.

I. In the first place, it is to be remarked that the claim that the United States alone shall build and control this and every transit across the isthmus is obviously equivalent to a claim of sovereignty over the State through which it may pass. Colombia, as an independent nation, has already given the right to build to a French company, with which she has also entered into very heavy pecuniary engagements. This she had an undoubted right to do. How are we to annul those engagements except by a forcible intervention of our own, or, in other words, by a war with both Colombia and France? And what can be the issue of such a war but to retard the progress of every interest of civilization, and to bring dishonor and reproach upon our national character? Our Monroe Doctrine, which we have been so fond of parading before the world, was originally designed to protect the independence of every State on the American continent; but this new application of it, which is now attempted, threatens the destruction of every State when our interests shall seem to require its destruction. If these Central American States are to be thus subjected to foreign intervention, they may well ask us the significant question whether we saved them from the Holy Alliance only that we might swallow them up ourselves.

II. Again, it is also to be kept in mind that this new assumption that we alone must build and control the canal is wholly at variance with our entire policy and agreements concerning it. The project of thus connecting the two great oceans did not originate with us. It is as old as the discovery of the continent. Columbus believed that a connecting strait already existed, and he made his latest voyage for the special purpose of finding it. After the discovery of the Pacific, the kings of Spain constantly instructed their officers in America to see if a water communication could not be opened with it from the Atlantic. Subsequently expeditions were sent to the isthmus by England, by Holland, and by France, some of them before the United States were in existence, and all of them before we had begun to manifest any interest in the undertaking. So soon, however, as our republic had extended its territory to the Gulf of Mexico, by the acquisition of Louisiana and Florida, the project began to be regarded with peculiar interest by the American people. This interest has deepened with the lapse of years. It has acquired new force from every new development of our resources, from the annexation of Texas, from the rapid growth of the Pacific States, and, most of all, from the grander national life which has burst forth in every direction since the overthrow of slavery and the triumphant close of the civil war.

We began to treat on this subject with the Central American States so soon as they became independent. But our treaties never had any other aim than to secure absolute and perpetual neutrality of any canal that should be built, and our own right to use it on the most favorable terms. In one or two instances, we have agreed to guarantee its neutrality and security, and to induce other nations to unite with us in the guarantee. But we have never before sought to own or control it, much less to acquire sovereign jurisdiction over it. On the contrary, in the Clayton-Bulwer Treaty with Great Britain, in 1850, the two countries bound themselves by a solemn engagement that neither shall ever obtain or exercise any control over the canal, or erect forts commanding it, or exercise dominion over the country in which it is built, or seek to obtain any advantage for the citizens of either over those of the other. And what is here to be specially observed, the two countries agree to "give their encouragement and support to such persons or company as may first offer to commence the same," and also " to guarantee its neutrality, so that the said canal may be forever open and free, and the capital invested therein be secure."

Under the implied invitation of the stipulations of this treaty, numerous routes have been surveyed and reported upon by eminent engineers of several different countries. Our own engineers have given preference to the route across Nicaragua, while those of France and England have declared in favor of that across Panama at Darien. It is along this latter route that the Count de Lesseps, the eminent constructor of the Suez Canal, has obtained the requisite concessions from the government of Colombia, has organized his company of French capitalists, and actually begun the work of construction. Meanwhile, all that we have done about it, during the two years in which this preparation has been going on, is to denounce the whole scheme as at variance with the Monroe Doctrine, as a movement which "cannot be regarded in any other light than as the manifestation of an unfriendly disposition towards the United States ; " for this is the meaning of President Hayes's message on the subject, and also of the resolutions now before both houses of Congress. Certainly, no one can expect that a great enterprise in the interest of commerce and civilization, undertaken by private capitalists, is to be arrested and defeated by fulminations such as these.

There is, however, one way, and so far as I see it is the only way, which it would become a great and magnanimous people to adopt, in order to arrest the building of the canal at Darien by a corporation chartered in France ; and that is, immediately to build another and better one ourselves by the Nicaragua route, — a route nearer our coast by two hundred and fifty miles, and making the voyage from New York to San Francisco or to China shorter by twice that distance. This it is now proposed to do, if the sanction of Congress can be obtained. A company has been formed, a very liberal concession has been secured, and the work of construction is ready to be commenced, with General Grant to direct it. Under such leadership, and with so many advantages and inducements as attend the enterprise, it will be a strange result indeed if we cannot do this work far more successfully than the Count de Lesseps with his French company. If we cannot and do not, then let us cheerfully concede that he is fully entitled to all the success he may achieve.

Of the Monroe Doctrine it only remains to be said that, in its proper and historical meaning, it has done its work and had its day. The country has passed beyond the exigency which called it forth, and any new exigencies which may come hereafter will probably demand new doctrines for themselves. Indeed, this is even now true of the question of the canal. It is beyond the reach of the Monroe Doctrine. But its name has already been appropriated by a certain sentiment long existing among the American people, — a sentiment which makes them believe that the whole of North America, if not the whole of the western hemisphere, belongs, by reversionary right, to this republic, and that we are bound to repel every agency from abroad that may hinder or delay our final and early occupancy and possession. Under the influence of this sentiment we have become wholly indifferent to the fortunes of the other American States, and now regard these States very much as temporary occupants of territories which "manifest destiny" has assigned to the republican empire that is to embrace the cisatlantic world.

This, there is reason to apprehend, is fast coming to be the only meaning which will hereafter be attached to the Monroe Doctrine.

THE PERIOD OF THE CONFEDERATION.[1]

THE origin of the United States as a nation was in part a growth and in part a creation. As a growth it had been silently and unconsciously preparing through the whole colonial period; more rapidly and surely after the troubles with England began in 1765, — still more rapidly after the meeting of the first Continental Congress in 1774. The subsequent collisions of arms between colonists and troops in Massachusetts, and the later Congresses of 1775 and 1776, completed the preparation. These Congresses had formed the colonies into United Colonies, and this name they had already assumed. They had also exercised large powers of a national, or, as it was then styled, a continental character. They had voted to raise an army and a navy, had appointed a commander-in-chief, assessed a revenue, established a post-office, and advised the colonies to adopt separate measures to secure the rights of the people, and, last of all, they had incurred a public debt. All these measures of high public authority, and many others of similar import, were adopted only as measures of defense of the rights belonging to the colonies as a part of the British Empire. They held themselves to be justified by the British Constitution, and they acted in imitation of the great examples of the illustrious champions of British freedom in all ages, of the barons who obtained the Magna Charta from King John at Runnymede, and of John Hampden, who resisted the ship money

[1] Read before the Rhode Island Historical Society, October 31, 1882.

of Charles I. They, however, had done more than they imagined. They believed themselves to be only resisting the unjustifiable taxation of Parliament. They were, in reality, even then an embryo nation, and on the very verge of a separate national existence. It needed but the Declaration of Independence to make this existence an unalterable fact.

The Congress of 1776, like those of the two preceding years, was in reality a representative popular assembly, to the fullest extent that was consistent with the habits of the age and the condition of the country. In those colonies in which royal governors were in power, its members were chosen by the popular branch of the legislature as the obvious representatives of the people. In here and there a colony where the entire government was opposed to the popular movement, they were chosen either by a colonial Congress, or by the action of committees of public safety, or by such local assemblies of the people as were possible in the circumstances. In Rhode Island and Connecticut, which had charter governments, they were, at the beginning, chosen by both houses of the Assembly, and were commissioned by the Governor. All the members of this Congress came together, — in some instances with specific instructions, in all instances with the fullest information as to what their constituents desired them to do. So soon, also, as the Declaration was made it was accepted and ratified alike by legislative action and by popular demonstrations in every part of the country. It unquestionably breathed the spirit and embodied the wishes and determinations of the great majority of the people of the colonies.

It was therefore the Declaration of Independence, thus adopted, proclaimed, and ratified, that called into being the new political society, — the United States of America. It created a new sovereign body politic, which from that time has claimed and maintained an equal place among the nations of the world. Up to this time, the colonies, though taking vigorous measures of redress, had not ceased to regard themselves as dependencies of England and subject to her dominion. By the Declaration, however, their people formed themselves into a separate sovereignty, and each colony, having now become a State, came to sustain to this sovereignty relations in some respects similar to those hitherto sustained to Great Britain. It was by the direction and authority of Congress that each State now formed for itself a new constitution or modified its existing charter, to suit its new relations. These relations, it is true, were left wholly undefined, except that they were of necessity, for certain purposes, relations of subordination to the United States, while for certain other purposes they were left quite independent. It was never, then, claimed that the Declaration created thirteen independent sovereign States. Independence and sovereignty, in their full sense, were accorded to the United States alone. The nation, from the beginning, was expected to conduct the War of Independence; to protect, if necessary, every State from Indian depredations; to maintain foreign relations; and, in the words of the Declaration, "to do all other acts and things which independent States may of right do." It was, from its very nature and in the name of those who created it, to act for those high national ends and interests in which all the people and all the States had a common concern. No single State ever dreamed of winning its own separate independence, or of sending its own ambassadors to the courts of foreign nations, or, indeed, of performing any other act of independent sovereignty.

In the loose mode of thinking on social questions and among the inadequate views of jural rights and obligations which then prevailed, it is not probable that the

relations of the States to the Union were fully comprehended or that they really engaged much attention. Indeed, the leading embarrassment of the time arose from
the fact that all political ideas and interests were exceedingly narrow and local. Intercourse had always been restricted. The colonies, fringing the Atlantic coast for
nearly a thousand miles, were of necessity but slightly
known to each other, and their social bonds were of very
slender character. Besides this, it must also be admitted
that the words of the Declaration bearing on these relations were much less precise and explicit than they ought
to have been, and that, to say the very least, they did not
fail to suggest the idea that, after all, it was the States
which had declared themselves independent, and that the
States were now sovereign. Nor, indeed, was this suggestion different, in a certain sense, from the actual fact.
They were, by their very organization, in many respects,
independent of each other as well as of Great Britain.
They were also sovereign, for certain purposes, and these
purposes were liable to be multiplied according as the interests or the conceits of States might demand. Ideas
of independence and sovereignty, once entertained, are
highly stimulating to the popular mind, especially in infant
nations. It is not very surprising, therefore, that the
States almost immediately, in their legislative acts and
in some of their constitutions, began to style themselves
sovereign and independent, and to accustom the people
both to the phraseology and to the idea which it expressed.

But, notwithstanding all pretensions and all declarations to the contrary, the nation, for all executive purposes, at least, was always held to be greater than any
State or all the States by themselves. And it has ever
since remained the practical principle of our American
institutions that the Union alone is the depositary of su-

preme and sovereign power, that the Union alone is the nation, and that to the Union every citizen and every State are bound by obligations of paramount allegiance. There have been questions of nullification, questions of secession, and questions of dissolution, but it has never been seriously maintained that, so long as the Union exists, it alone may of right exercise the higher attributes of sovereignty for all its component parts. And this is equally true whatever may be the government which, for the time, may be administering its affairs; for it is not the mode of its government that makes it a sovereign, but the jural obligations which its people have assumed, the solemn agreements which bind them together and constitute them a nation.

The United States existed in fact as a nation for nearly five years without any written instrument of government. It was, however, as sovereign then as it has been since. The only government which directed national affairs was the Congress which had been called into existence for obtaining redress of the public grievances, and which, in obedience to the voice of the nation, had made the Declaration of Independence. It was from the beginning a purely revolutionary assembly, possessed of no formally delegated authority, but it was expected to do everything that might be necessary for securing the independence which had been declared by its authority. No American Congress of later times has ever assumed functions more important or exercised powers more absolute. On one occasion, in the first year of the war, it proceeded to invest the commander-in-chief of the army with unlimited military authority, such as the Roman Senate sometimes gave to the Dictators; and, notwithstanding its revolutionary origin, it continued to be the only general government of the country from 1776 to 1781. It was not till this latter date that the "Articles of Confederation" were adopted and set in operation. The duration of this second government extended to the adoption of the present Constitution and the inauguration of President Washington in 1789. It is this period of eight years, lying between the government of the revolutionary Congress and the government established by the present Constitution, that is in this essay designated " The Confederation Period." It is not a period in which the student of our political history finds much to gratify national pride or to awaken patriotic sentiment. It illustrates, however, the character of our American institutions, and points out the origin of the evil tendencies and the conflicting forces that have done so much to shape our career as a nation.

I have said that the Articles of Confederation went into effect in 1781. They were, indeed, framed and placed before the country long before they were adopted as the fundamental law. On June 10, 1776, the very day on which the committee was appointed to draft the Declaration of Independence, a separate committee was also named " to prepare and digest the form of a confederation to be entered into between these colonies." This latter committee reported a form of confederation on the 12th of July, thirty-one days after its appointment. This was frequently the subject of debate till the 20th of August, when its form was somewhat changed. The whole subject was then laid aside for nearly eight months, till the 8th of April, 1777. The Articles were then again taken up for debate ; many amendments were proposed, and at least one that shows the bad ideas of the times was agreed to, and was embodied in Article 2: " Each State retains its sovereignty, freedom, and independence, and any power, jurisdiction, and right which is not by this Confederation expressly delegated to the United States in Congress assembled." With this unfortunate provision superadded to them, the Articles of Confederation were adopted by Congress and sent to the States for ratification on November 15, 1777, nearly seventeen months after they were first reported. They were to go into effect when ratified by the legislature of every State.

They were styled "Articles of Confederation and Perpetual Union between the States," and they created what was only a league of state governments, in which the people of the country had no direct participation or agency of any kind. The characteristics of this first written Constitution of the United States are so well known that I need refer only to here and there an illustration. 1. The new Articles were not much more than a mere embodiment in writing of the general mode of proceeding which had been observed in the revolutionary Congress already existing. Beyond this crudely extemporized method of carrying on public affairs it would appear that the committee were unable to stretch their comprehension. 2. According to this unfortunate model, they vested all the powers of the government, executive, judicial, and legislative, in a single assembly, which was still to be called a Congress, composed of not more than seven, nor less than two members from each State, chosen as the legislature might direct, and making a body which, when fully attended by the States, might have ninety-one members for its maximum and twenty-six members for its minimum. In this body each State was to have a single vote, which was wholly lost if only one delegate was present; and all measures of importance must receive the votes of at least nine States, and other measures the votes of at least seven States. 3. Members of the Congress were not eligible more than three years in any six, and no member could be chosen President of Congress for more than one year in succession. 4. The members were to be paid and controlled by the state governments. This composition of the Congress of the Confederation was singularly fatal to anything like unity or efficiency in a body designed for managing national affairs. But this was really the least important of the inherent defects of the whole system. It was full of contradictions. The proposed Articles gave to a Congress in which was embodied the entire national authority the sole power to declare war, to make peace, to regulate weights and measures, to form treaties, to borrow money, and incur all the necessary expenses of conducting national affairs, but they withheld the power to collect any revenue whatever. The States alone had the right to levy duties and to collect taxes as well as to fix the rate of both, nor was there a single source of revenue in the country that was under the control of Congress. The Articles provided for a general treasury, but it was to be supplied solely by means of assessments made on the several States. Congress, though it had the power to declare war, could not enlist a single soldier. It could appoint foreign ambassadors, but it could not support them while abroad. It could contract debts, but it could not pay them. It was required to assume all national responsibility and to discharge all national obligations alike in peace and in war, but it must depend for the means of doing this on the uncertain and reluctant votes of the state legislatures. In doing this it could enact, but it· could not execute. It could make treaties, but it could not secure their fulfilment. It could vote levies of money on the States, but it could not collect a dollar of these levies even for the most pressing necessity, unless they were allowed by the legislatures.

Such, in its general outlines, was the government of the Confederation. It seems to have been all that the collected statesmanship of Congress could then contrive for the new republic. It is one of the foremost marvels of American history, not to say one of the chief humiliations which it records, that a government so crude and ill-devised was proposed by Congress, ratified by the States, and suffered to bring its calamitous consequences on the country. One asks in vain where were the illustrious leaders of the age when such a wretched caricature of all national authority was proposed for the American people? A few of them, we know, saw and deplored the inherent feebleness of the system, but amidst the narrow views and local jealousies which then prevailed, they were powerless in making it better. Most of them, however, it must be confessed, wholly failed to discern its total inadequacy for the necessities of the country.

The " Articles of Confederation and Perpetual Union " were adopted in Congress on November 17, 1777, and were immediately sent to the States with a circular letter urging their ratification by the legislature of each before the 10th of March, 1778. But when that day came, very few of the state legislatures had acted upon them, and the matter was not called up in Congress till the 10th of the following July. In the course of that month the ratifications of ten States were officially reported by their delegations. The remaining three were New Jersey, Delaware, and Maryland. Amendments, meanwhile, had been proposed by at least nine of the States, but not one of them was adopted by Congress.

But what especially delayed the ratification of New Jersey, Delaware, and Maryland was the question as to the ownership of the western lands claimed under the charters of Massachusetts, Connecticut, New York, Virginia, North and South Carolina, and Georgia. These lands had been the property of Great Britain, and were styled " Crown Lands." It was contended by the non-claiming States that whatever lands had belonged to the crown should now belong to the United States; that the right to possess them had been secured by the common sacrifices and blood of all the States, and that it would be both unjust and injurious to allow them to become the property of a few separate States, to the exclusion of the others. Virginia and New York made the largest claims, but at least three other States deemed their own to be too valuable to be readily abandoned. Rhode Island had no claims of any kind, and scarcely any territory, but greatly to her credit she was among the earliest to ratify the Confederation, an act which was prompted by purely patriotic considerations, and by the generous belief that the question of the lands would be finally settled on an honorable basis. The country was already taunted with its want of organized national authority, and Congress expressed its apprehensions as to the effect of this on its foreign relations, especially on its relations with France. In these circumstances New Jersey decided to waive her objections, and to accede to the Confederation, in November, 1778; she was followed by Delaware in February, 1779; both these States adopting substantially the form of ratification which had been used in Rhode Island, and trusting to the justice of their sister States. Maryland now stood alone in her refusal. Congress again appealed to her patriotic sentiments. She replied that nothing would separate her from the cause of American independence, but that the allowance of the claims of Virginia would be fatal to her own interests, and also fatal to the interests of the Union.

This repeated refusal of Maryland gave the greatest uneasiness to the other States, especially as the substantial justice of her position could not be denied. In this condition of affairs, New York decided, by an act of legislature in February, 1780, to fix the boundary of the State and to surrender the lands beyond it to the United States. Congress now appealed to the other States claiming such lands to follow this example, and at the same time again entreated Maryland to accede to the Confederation. That patriotic State, confident that the example of New York must soon be followed by Virginia, and desirous to show her attachment to the common cause of national independence, proceeded to ratify the new government on January 30, 1781. But as Maryland, for some time, had but a single delegate present in Congress, her ratification was not formally presented and carried into effect till the first day of the following March. The Confederacy was now completed by the accession of the thirteenth State to the Articles of Confederation, at the end of three years and nearly four months after they were sent to the States for ratification, and of four years and nearly nine months after they were first reported in Congress by the committee that prepared them in July, 1776.

It was on the following day, March 2, 1781, that Congress was first organized under the new fundamental law. One of the members of that body, a citizen of Rhode Island, then in Philadelphia, wrote to the Governor on the 5th of March as follows: "The Confederation was completed last Thursday at twelve o'clock, and at the same time was announced by the discharge of a number of cannon, both on the land and on the Delaware. The President of Congress gave a general invitation to the members of Congress, the President of the State, his council, and the House of Assembly and the civil and military officers of Congress, to wait upon him at his own house at two o'clock, where they partook of a cold collation. In the afternoon Captain Jones fired a *feu de joie* on board the Ariel. In the evening a number of fireworks were played off, and the whole concluded in the greatest harmony to the great satisfaction of every true friend of his country and mortification of the infamous Tories, who have long plumed themselves with the vain hope that our Union would soon crumble to pieces. Our State was not represented." I do not know that the event was cele-

brated anywnere else in the country even with this " cold
collation " enthusiasm which it seems to have roused in
Philadelphia. It really touched no chord of patriotic
sentiment in the hearts of the people. Nor was there any
reason why it should. The new government most unfor-
tunately was a mere league of the state legislatures, about
which the people had not been consulted and in the making of which they had taken no part. This first " ship of
State " had been five years in building and many of its
timbers were already rotten, while some of the most essential were wholly wanting, and only here and there one was
really sound and in its right place. It was to be commanded not by a captain chosen by the American people,
but by a council of its thirteen owners. Who could be
expected to rejoice over the launching of a craft which
may be well described as

> " that fatal and perfidious bark
> Built in th' eclipse and rigg'd with curses dark " ?

With auspices such as these the Articles of Confederation, the first written Constitution of the United States,
were adopted and set in operation. The event, however,
produced no important change in the proceedings of the
government save that these proceedings were now subject to an inflexible law. They had been made to conform very nearly to the existing mode of conducting public affairs. The presence of at least two delegates from a
State was now required in order to cast its vote. With
less than two its vote was wholly lost, a provision which
soon after, for months in succession, left Congress without a working majority. The ineligibility of members
for more than three years in any six, and of the presiding officer for more than one year in succession, not only
tended to make that body inefficient by the exclusion of
its experienced members, but to take from it all attrac-

tions as a theatre of statesmanship, and to render it anything but a school in which men were to learn the lessons of public service. The result was that the service of the States became vastly more an object of ambition than that of the United States. In this manner the Congress of the Confederation soon presented a marked decline especially from the early Congresses of the Revolution. They had sprung suddenly into being at the bidding of the continental will. They placed themselves at the head of a mighty movement for independence, and they were expected to do and to ordain whatever that movement, in its successive exigencies, should demand. The Congresses of 1775 and 1776 had exercised vast powers, and to these powers there was no limit that could be assigned. Not so with the Congress of the Confederation. Its powers were limited by a written fundamental law, so worded and so contrived as to leave only the semblance of authority to the national government. It no longer represented the spirit and energy which had asserted the essential rights of man, which had declared the independence of the colonies, which had summoned the continent to arms and defied the power of the British empire. It no longer spoke and acted with the authority of the nation. Its members ceased to act for the American people, but now, as mere envoys of the States, they were compelled simply to execute the will of their respective legislatures. It bore the name of a government, but it possessed scarcely an attribute of government. For a time it favorably impressed the courts of Europe, till its inherent feebleness came to be understood, and this was its only advantage over the revolutionary government which it supplanted.

But far more than this is true of the Articles of Confederation. They were at variance with the true spirit and the real attitude of the American people in the work of national organization. They were an illogical and illegitimate conclusion from the doctrines of the Declaration of Independence. They made the United States appear no longer a sovereign nation, with vast resources in its control and vast possibilities within its reach, but a loosely formed compact of state governments, of which the design would seem to be to render the central government as weak as possible, and the state government as strong as possible. How different is all this from the ringing utterances of the men who were present in the Congress which called the nation into being! Of Patrick Henry, who exclaimed in the Congress of 1774, "The distinctions between Virginians, Pennsylvanians, New Yorkers, and New Englanders are no more. I am not a Virginian: I am an American." Of Wilson, of Pennsylvania, who said : "As to those matters which are referred to Congress we are not so many States ; we are one large State. We lay aside our individuality when we come here." Or of John Adams, who said in the Congress of 1776, "We shall no longer retain our separate individuality, but become a single individual as to all questions submitted to the Confederacy." Sentiments like these had utterly vanished from the public councils when the Confederation went into operation. Whatever its framers may have intended, and Wilson was one of them, its practical effect was exactly the opposite of anticipations such as I have cited.

A falling off so signal and deplorable in the whole construction of this first national Constitution from the original spirit and the obvious necessities of the country is not readily explained. Von Holst, a recent writer on our constitutional history, ascribes it very largely to the fact that the Confederation was framed by Congress and ratified by the legislatures of the States, instead of being framed by a National Convention and ratified by a convention in each of the States. There can be no doubt that this was a political blunder of the gravest character, and that neither Congress nor the state legislatures had any authority to frame or ratify a Constitution for the United States. The entire proceeding, in its form, was wholly at variance with the American idea of popular sovereignty. But this alone did not make the Confederation the thing it was, nor is there any reason to believe that it would have been essentially different had it been framed and ratified in any other mode which was at that time practicable. It undoubtedly reflected the prevailing views of the kind of government which the country needed. The trouble was of deeper origin. The views themselves, alike of statesmen and of people, were lamentably narrow and one-sided, and wholly inadequate either to the emergency of the time or the well-being of the country. With such views controlling the minds of the people, the Confederation could not have been essentially different from what it was, however it had been framed or however it had been ratified. Indeed the country, as distinct from the States, was in reality a matter of very little concern. The minds of the people had not learned to take it in. A sovereign nation had been called into existence, but its own people did not comprehend their relations to it, or have any but the crudest conception of its true character and office. It was taken for granted that all would be well with the United States if all was well with the separate States, and to secure this latter result each State devoted its energies to taking care of itself, to reconstructing its own government, and to looking simply after its own local interests. Thirteen populations so distinct as those of the early States could not be wrought into a nation in so brief a space of time. Until the struggle for independence began they had never acted together or had interests in common. The mother country had till then been their only bond of union, and now

that this was swept away, they had in its place the United
States, which thus far was little more than an abstract
idea, a vague sentiment, not yet embodied in any national insignia or officers of state, or other representatives
of sovereign power. In this manner the States almost
unconsciously looked upon the Union, not as the supreme
and essential head of the political framework, but as a
mere contrivance of their own which had been devised
for securing for themselves a place among the nations of
the earth.

Besides this pitiful narrowness of political thinking,
there sprang up very early in the States an intense jealousy of all power not belonging to themselves. They
were haunted by the idea that they were likely, in some
way, to lose their liberties even before they had fully
secured them. They thought that liberty was the only
end to be provided for in civil society. The *vultus in-
stantis tyranni* glared continually on their morbid imaginations as a constant menace of their independence, — as
the only danger in their pathway. Even the feeble and
half-fed army that was fighting their battles was regarded
with ceaseless apprehensions. Both the States and their
public men gave only a reluctant and imperfect confidence
to the illustrious commander-in-chief who, more than any
mortal man before or since, was bearing on his own shoul-
ders the fortunes of his country. But this unreasonable and
idle jealousy found its most conspicuous object in the central authority that represented the nation. The States very
early began to regard this new power that seemed to be
above them all with feelings of distrust and aversion, such
as when colonies they had constantly cherished towards
Great Britain. They chained it by their Articles of Confederation ; they disregarded it ; they evaded it ; they even
defied it when it restricted their authority or thwarted
their purposes.

Considerations and facts such as these, I think, show that the nation, at that time, was absolutely incapable either of framing or of approving a mode of administering national affairs essentially different from that of the Confederation. They also show that, even then, there were planted in the minds of the American people those conceits of state sovereignty which, after seventy years of struggle, were at length destroyed only on the bloody fields of the civil war.

In a condition of public opinion like this, the government of the Confederation was set in operation on March 2, 1781. It is little to say that it was a failure from the beginning. It was much more than a failure. It had been before the people for four years before its adoption, its principles were familiar, and its demoralizing power had already been felt in every part of the country. It proved to be probably the most lamentable instrument of government ever devised among a free people for degrading the national character, for debasing the national conscience, for blighting generous sentiments and heroic purposes, and for destroying the essential unity and integrity of civil society. It was not corrupt; it was not despotic. It was only feeble, timid, and incapable ; and this because it was powerless for the very purposes it was designed to accomplish.

I. In October, 1781, the united arms of France and America won the victory at Yorktown, and virtually decided the question of independence. Had Congress now possessed the requisite energy and power, peace would have soon followed. It made its requisitions for money and men on the States, but as usual they were not furnished. The legislatures criticised the assessments, and called in question the purposes for which they were made. In some States they even suggested that France ought to bear the expenses of the coming campaign. In this disgraceful emergency, as in nearly every other that arose during the war, Congress was compelled to ask Washington to use his influence with the state authorities in securing the quotas that were needed.

II. The officers and soldiers of the army had continued without pay almost from the beginning of the war, because the States did not respond to the requisitions of Congress. Several plans of adjustment had been proposed, but without successful result. In consequence of the feeling of injustice now prevailing, certain regiments, first of Pennsylvania and afterwards of New Jersey, rushed like a tumultuous mob to Philadelphia to demand satisfaction of Congress. The story of the Newburgh Addresses affords a still graver illustration of the desperation to which even officers of rank and of high character were wrought by the seeming indifference and contempt as well as the gross injustice with which they were treated by the government of the country. Had it not been for the unequalled judgment and the peerless influence of Washington, the government of the Confederation might then have come to an ignoble and perhaps a violent end.

III. Meanwhile Congress continued to decline both in efficiency and in public estimation, and in its own self-respect. Few of the ablest men of the country were now among its members, and it constantly illustrated its want of capacity to maintain its position as the representative of the national sovereignty. The war was now ended, and Washington, after depositing with the Treasury an exact statement of his expenses as commander-in-chief, and refusing all compensation for his eight years' services, requested that a day should be named for him to submit in person the resignation of his commission. The occasion was one of transcendent interest and unequalled moral grandeur. But it was not till the 22d of December (1783), six weeks after the session began, that twenty members, and these from only seven States, were present to do honor to the illustrious chief of the Revolution and the country's foremost benefactor. The treaty of peace with England had been signed on the 3d of September, and now waited ratification by Congress; but even this great consummation was delayed till January 14, 1784, because the delegations of nine States, the requisite number, could not be brought together to act upon it.

IV. Equally humiliating was the civil administration of the government both at home and abroad. The public debt was not only without any provision for its payment, but its interest was largely in arrears. Even the restoration of peace did nothing to revive the sentiment of national honor. The state legislatures disregarded the provisions of treaties and broke the solemn pledges of the nation. The treaty of peace could not go into full effect because of state laws in conflict with its provisions, which the legislatures refused to repeal. Applications for foreign loans and offers of treaties with foreign nations were alike greeted with the derisive inquiry whether the States had authorized them, or only the nation by itself.

V. This demoralization, so conspicuous in public affairs, did not fail to show itself in the condition of society. Following the example of Congress and the state legislatures, citizens refused to pay their honest debts. Courts were flooded with suits of recovery, and jails were crowded with debtors and criminals. The most signal instance of this widespread demoralization was seen in the disturbances in Massachusetts known as Shays's Rebellion, which was only a local outbreak of the general disregard of legal and social obligations. That was happily suppressed by the Massachusetts government; but it was because of the alarm awakened that, under the pretext of quelling some disturbances among the Indians, Congress voted to raise from New England several regiments for the emergency, and attention was again turned to Washington, now in his retirement at Mount Vernon, as the only champion of peace and order whom the country could rely on. It was in reply to a letter thus addressed to him by Arthur Lee, and asking the aid of his influence, that he wrote the famous passage, prompted no doubt by the bitter recollection of many a similar request in other years: "You talk, my good sir, of employing *influence* to appease the present tumults in Massachusetts. I know not where that influence is to be found, or, if attainable, that it would be a proper remedy for the disease. *Influence is not government.* Let us have a government by which our lives, liberties, and properties will be secured, or let us know the worst at once."

But even in this prostration of all public interests and this degradation of public honor, high-minded and far-seeing men were not wanting, though in the hampered councils of the country they found no sphere for statesmanship or for great achievements. The period, however, affords one illustrious exception — one solitary act in which the Congress of the Confederation broke loose from the trammels of the state legislatures and accomplished a work whose beneficent results cannot be estimated too highly. They will last as long as the republic itself. This was the Ordinance for the government of the territory northwest of the Ohio, — a territory which was acquired by the United States through the patriotic surrender by several States of the lands embraced in their charters and now occupied by the States of Ohio, Indiana, Illinois, Michigan, Wisconsin, and a part of Minnesota. Anticipating the creation of imperial States like these, it dictated to them in advance a perpetual contract of national unity. It prohibited slavery, it guaranteed to their inhabitants civil and religious freedom, and secured to them the essential elements of a high civilization and a magnificent social destiny. The framer of this renowned Ordinance of 1787, as has well been said, is entitled to a place among the most illustrious lawgivers of the world.

The Confederation was now hastening to its end. It had thoroughly done the only work of which it was capable, and that work was to demonstrate its own exceeding worthlessness. The Convention for framing a new Constitution was already in session. In that Convention was sitting a young man of scarcely thirty years, who, ingenious for constructive statesmanship, was equalled by no one of his contemporaries. At the age of twenty years he had been appointed an aid of Washington, and at the headquarters of the great commander, where the anxieties and sufferings of the whole country were all brought together, he had learned the solemn lessons of the time, and had since sought to impress them upon his countrymen. Since the close of the war, his one endeavor had been to secure nationality for the nation. He was, I believe, the youngest member of the Convention, but he was also the foremost master of the difficult problems it had to solve. Older statesmen, more closely in sympathy with the popular mind, modified many of his opinions and shaped the new Constitution to the necessities of the time; but the mighty and heroic work of preparing the way for that instrument, of explaining it to the country, and of securing its adoption, is to be very largely ascribed to Alexander Hamilton. In the continually darkening sky of the Confederation period, his luminous genius shone as the morning star of the brighter era that was soon to dawn on the distracted and declining republic.

I have thus traced here and there an outline of the period which was controlled by the Confederation. In its political aspects, it is the dreariest period of American history. It fully justifies the words of Mr. Hamilton:

" A nation without a national government is an awful spectacle." And, indeed, if we may rely upon the testimony of contemporaries, its social and moral aspects were far from radiant with either personal or civic virtues. Washington writes of it thus : "From the high ground we stood upon, from the plain path which invited our footsteps, to be so fallen, so lost, is really mortifying ; but virtue, I fear, has in a great degree taken its departure from our land, and the want of a disposition to do justice is the source of the national embarrassments." Unless the army of the Revolution presented an exception, this could not have been the heroic age of the nation. The astonishing fact is that, with such a government, national independence was ever achieved, and that, when achieved, it was not immediately lost. The period, however, is full of instruction. It was not wanting in specimens of illustrious character, and it produced at least one that will shine forever in the annals of mankind. But its chief lessons are those of warning for later times. It was the period in which were developed the ideas and tendencies which have done most to disturb the peace, to degrade the character, and to peril the life of the republic. The chiefest satisfaction connected with it is that it was inevitable at our national beginning, that it prepared the way for all that has followed, and most of all that, without having the humiliations of the Confederation, we could not have had the triumphs of the Constitution.

THE HUGUENOTS AND THE EDICT OF NANTES.[1]

Gentlemen of the Historical Society:

The twenty-second day of October just past was the two hundredth anniversary of the revocation of the Edict of Nantes. It has been commemorated by descendants of the Huguenots in many different parts of the country. Several of you have united in a request that I begin our winter course of Historical Papers with one relating to "The Huguenots and the Edict of Nantes," and it is in accordance with this request that I present to you the following : —

The Protestant Reformation in France had a comparatively brief career, and finally came to a disastrous overthrow. While it lasted, however, it was associated with resolute and unfaltering faith, with heroic courage, and with sufferings scarcely paralleled in any other country or at any other period of history. Its beginning was nearly coeval with its beginning in Germany, though well-nigh independent of it, and it maintained substantially the same character in both countries. It was in both an uprising of the human mind against the principle of absolute authority in matters of religion. In both it asserted the supremacy of the Holy Scriptures over the traditions, the usages, and the authority of the Church. In neither country was it really the work of any single leader. It began in the minds of thoughtful people before any lead-

[1] Read before the Rhode Island Historical Society, November 3, 1885.

ers appeared, and it was the expression of a prevailing sentiment, of which leaders were only the asserters and exponents. Indeed, they became leaders only as they publicly declared the ideas and beliefs, the cravings and aspirations, which already existed in multitudes of minds. The Reformation demanded that the Scriptures be given to the human race for whom they were designed, instead of being confined to the priests alone. The invention of printing had just made the Bible an accessible book to all who could read, and multitudes everywhere were searching for its hitherto unknown teachings and promises. In palaces and in hovels they read its sacred pages or heard them read, that they might learn the truths which it contained, but which had never before been within their reach.

In France, more generally than in Germany, the doctrines of the Reformation were for a time regarded with great favor by the more intelligent classes of the population. The relations of the Gallican Church and the Papacy had been disturbed, and the popular fear of the Vatican had been diminished in consequence. This was especially true in the southeasterly portions of the country which were nearest to Switzerland, in whose freer air these doctrines were received with singular readiness. Their votaries were called "gospellers," because they encouraged by precept and by example the reading of the New Testament, and the doctrines which they held and which they everywhere taught to the people were styled "the religion," as if they were a new gift to mankind. Many of its early ministers were men of learning, who had been trained at the Sorbonne in Paris, the most illustrious school of mediæval theology. It also early numbered among its votaries men and women of rank, officers of distinction in the service of the country, and even princes of the royal blood. But its most efficient propagators for a considerable period were undoubtedly to be found among the travelling traders of the age, many of whom had now added the New Testament to the wares in which they trafficked alike at castle and at cottage, all over southern France. They were the humble beginners of rural commerce and rural handicraft, whom history seldom mentions, but who rendered invaluable services in the centuries to which they belonged. Those who have looked over the writings or the life of Palissy the Potter will recall the service he thus rendered, as he travelled over the country, in promoting that beautiful process of enameling clay, which he had so laboriously invented. Wherever he went in the practice of his art, with which he at length decorated some of the grandest castles and palaces of the age, he bore with him copies of the New Testament, which he sold or gave to all who would receive them. He was a simple "gospeller," without church and without creed, — a man of extraordinary genius and of heroic Christian faith, whom threatenings did not disturb and persecutions did not destroy. So quietly for a time did " the religion " thus make progress in the minds of the people that in many places its services were frequented almost as largely as those of the ancient faith. Rural churches were opened for conducting them on Sundays, and they were often attended by many who had already celebrated the mass and listened to the teachings of the priests.

The city of Meaux for a time became the centre of this singular tolerance. Here lived James Lefèvre and William Farel, men of education and learning, who had been among the earliest preachers of the new faith. They had prepared for their congregations a new translation of the Evangelists, and when it was finished they submitted it to the kind-hearted bishop of the city, who not only approved what they had done, but gave them assistance in publishing it. He also found many of his priests to be non-resident and without vicars, and he invited Farel, Lefèvre,

and others to preach in their vacant pulpits, and himself
assisted in circulating their Four Gospels among the poor
of his diocese. The effects of this new agency of divine
truth were soon visible in the improved morals and better
lives of the people of the city and its environs. But a
still more remarkable promoter of the new faith appeared
in the person of Queen Margaret of Valois, the sister of
Francis I., King of France. She, while residing in Paris
at the court of her brother, introduced certain Reformed
preachers into the pulpits of that city, acting, possibly, on
the principle that both sides were entitled to a hearing.
It thus seemed for a time as though the new faith might
have at least a fair field in which to assert and maintain
its doctrines. It was also at this time that its professors
began to be called Huguenots. They had not, thus far,
attacked the institutions of the Church. Nor had they denounced the priesthood and the Pope, as had been done so
fiercely by the reformers in other countries. They had
simply searched the Scriptures and proclaimed the great
ideas which they had thus discovered. They were, therefore, scarcely regarded as reformers, nor did they desire
to be so called. The origin of the name of Huguenots,
which they now began to bear, has received not less than
fifteen different explanations. It was probably given to
them in derision, and taken from that of some obscure or
despised representative of their cause. They, however,
seem to have preferred it to every other, and to have
clung to it till all others were abandoned. The name soon
became synonymous with heretics, and they were placed
beyond the protection of law and proscribed as enemies
of the Church in every country in Catholic Christendom.
That they had been encouraged by the Bishop of Meaux,
and, still more, that they had been favored by the sister of
the king, soon stirred the wrath of the ecclesiastics and
called forth the remonstrance of the Pope. The fickle and

timid monarch, dreading the papal displeasure, made amends for all that had been done, by a proclamation of atrocious cruelty, which proved to be but the beginning of that long series of cruel enormities which finally obliterated nearly every vestige of Protestantism from France. In January, 1535, at the most magnificent fête which in that age Paris had ever beheld, Francis I. solemnly proclaimed his determination to punish all heresy with death, and not to spare even his own children if they should be guilty of it. This declaration of the king was received with the utmost delight by the fanatical multitude to whom it was addressed. It was regarded as a permission — perhaps as an invitation — to begin the work of slaughtering heretics at that very time and on the spot where it was uttered. The ceremonies of the fête closed with the burning of six Huguenots, suspended from six beams made to revolve in succession over a flaming furnace, into which they were dropped at each revolution till they were burned to death. Thus was planted in the French nature that appetite for Huguenot blood, which for more than a hundred and fifty years fed itself on massacres and butcheries, on murders and slaughters, the enormities of which no history has fully described and no imagination has fully conceived.

Thus far the Huguenots, though they had become very numerous, were without any recognized leader. In this same year (1535), John Calvin published at Basle, in Switzerland, his "Institutes of the Christian Religion," a book which not only united the French Protestants in a common faith, but also wrought their persecuted congregations into an ecclesiastical body of self-governing believers who acknowledged him as their patriarch and chief. A self-denying scholar who, as a student at the Sorbonne, had been sent away from Paris because of his heresies, he had studied the profoundest problems of reli-

gion with an ability and a zeal which no man has ever
surpassed. With a mind of the acutest and most comprehensive order, he embodied in his Institutes the doctrines
which not only gave character and organization to the
Protestants of France, but have ever since exercised a
controlling influence on the religious thought of at least
half of Protestant Christendom. Seldom in human history has the power of a single mind been so deeply and
so widely felt, not only in his own but in subsequent ages.

Thus organized as a religious body, they took another
step, and in 1569 made themselves also a separate political body, — a Christian State, — framed in accordance
with the theories of Calvin, though not with his special
approval of the proceeding. Thus, in an age of violence
and of brutal war, they became a religious republic, and
sought to be recognized among the great estates of the
realm which were subject only to the king. The effect of
this was that they came to be regarded by aspiring nobles
and ambitious princes as a power that might be concil-
iated and used for their own advancement. They soon
began to be courted and flattered, their cause was pro-
fessedly and often sincerely espoused, in order to induce
them to become tributary to political schemes wholly foreign to every interest of religion. Placed as they now
were, with an ecclesiastical and civil organization of their
own, in the midst of the factions and combinations of a
tumultuous age, it is perhaps not surprising that they were
drawn into the civil and political struggles which were
going on around them. They received assurances of assistance from one and another of the great leaders in these
struggles, some of whom had earnestly accepted their own
religious faith. They saw no escape from destruction
save by some sort of alliance with those who were contending with their common enemy and destroyer. Their
numbers had become so great and their importance so

considerable that they were able to dictate terms of union which gave promise of security to their religion, — the great end which they always kept in view. It was thus that they allowed themselves to make alliances with those who sought to become the controllers and masters of the State : at one time with the Family of Bourbon, at another with the party of the Politiques, at another with the Princes of Condé, and last of all with the chiefs of the House of Navarre, who were soon to become the rulers of France. But whatever their motives may have been, whatever the promises of advantage that were made to them, these alliances were always a mistake, and always disastrous to the interests of religion. As religious reformers, their sole work was to cherish and proclaim the teachings of Jesus Christ, to set them forth in their writings, to illustrate them in their lives, and to teach them everywhere to their fellow-men. It is thus, and thus only, that Christianity in all ages has won its splendid triumphs in all the earth. It is only degraded and dishonored when its disciples league themselves with princes or accept the services of armies to accomplish religious ends. It was this forgetting of the essential and unchangeable fact that the kingdom of Christ is not a kingdom of this world, which more than any other cause — more indeed than all other causes — very early involved them in disasters, and finally prepared the way for their greatest sufferings and for the humiliating failure of all their heroic endeavors to establish the Protestant Reformation in France.

The immediate consequence of this mingling of the religious struggles of the Huguenots with the politics and cabals of the age was the outbreak of the Wars of Religion, as they are styled, of which the narratives fill so many repulsive chapters of French history. They were really civil wars among rival factions, in which the Huguenots

became enlisted. They lasted for forty years, and the trage-
dies which are connected with them are amongst the most
revolting in which human beings have ever been the actors.
The belligerent Huguenots gained occasional advantages,
and for a brief season they expected to triumph. But in
the end they utterly failed. They were corrupted by bad
associations. They lost the religious character which they
originally possessed. They caught the worldly spirit of
the ambitious adventurers with whom they were allied.
They contended no longer for their faith, but for power to
rule. They even followed the example of their enemies
and avenged their sufferings by needless atrocities. In
at least one most lamentable instance, one hundred and
twenty defenseless Catholics, of whom seventy-two were
prisoners of war, were massacred in cold blood by one of
their military bands at the city of Nismes. It is true that
the outrage was a solitary exception to the general conduct of their campaigns, and was condemned by their ministers and their military leaders. It may be, even, that it
was perpetrated by ferocious soldiers acting without orders; but it was done in their name, and it was sure to be
avenged a hundred fold by their malignant enemies. It
undoubtedly became a precedent and a provocation for the
far more fearful massacres of 1562 at Vassy, at Paris, at
Senlis, at Meaux, at Chalons, at Epernay, at Tours, and
at so many other towns inhabited by Huguenots. It was
even cited in justification of that most atrocious of all
slaughters recorded in modern history, the massacre of
St. Bartholomew's Day, on the 24th of August, 1572, —
a slaughter perpetrated at the command of the royal
authorities of France, the beginning of which in Paris
was witnessed by the weak-minded King Charles IX., and
his intriguing mother, Catherine de Médicis, a woman who
deserves the detestable distinction of having suggested or
sanctioned all the Huguenot murders of that sanguinary

period of violence and persecution. This queen-mother was so much delighted with her bloody work of three days in Paris that she immediately dispatched letters to Philip II. of Spain, to the Duke of Alva, and to Pope Gregory XIII. at Rome. Philip, on receiving the tidings of what had been done, is said to have laughed aloud for the first and only time in a life made morose and gloomy by a fanaticism which knew no joy but in the persecution and destruction of heretics. At Rome the occasion was one of extraordinary jubilation. A Pontifical salute was fired at the Castle of San Angelo. Gregory XIII. and the College of Cardinals went in procession from one church to another " to render thanksgivings (such is the ancient record) to God, the infinitely great and good, for the mercy which He had vouchsafed to the See of Rome and to the whole Christian world." A painting of the massacre was ordered for the Vatican gallery, and a medal of gold was struck, with the head of the Pope on one side, and on the other the Destroying Angel exterminating the Huguenots, with the inscription *Hugonotorum Strages.* In Paris the whole body of the clergy celebrated the massacre with public processions, and established an annual jubilee to commemorate it. They also had a medal prepared in honor of the event, bearing the legend " Piety has Awakened Justice." The feeble-minded king, by whose authority these dreadful deeds of blood had been perpetrated, soon afterwards lay upon his death-bed, — his intellect well-nigh extinct, and his wild fancy peopling every scene with the victims of the massacre, as he wasted away under the power of a slow poison, believed at the time to have been administered by his mother.

I have thus given a hasty outline of the bitter experiences of the Huguenots under the last five kings of the House of Valois, through a period of fifty years. The reign of each, happily for his subjects, had been brief, for,

as has been truly said, "bloody and deceitful men shall
not live out half their days." The name of Huguenot
had become more odious than ever, and the policy of the
government had now left them without protection to the
fanatical hatred of their proud and vengeful enemies. In
this condition of affairs, after the brief and uneventful
reign of Henry III., the throne descended to his successor,
Henry IV., son of Anthony of Navarre. His mother was
Jane D'Albret, a Protestant alike by birth and by choice,
and a champion of the Protestant faith. Henry had been
excommunicated for heresy by Pope Sixtus V., and his
right to the throne had been annulled. On this account
he was compelled to contend in arms for its possession,
and at length to make his submission to the Papal Church.
In consequence of these hindrances, he was not crowned
till 1594, nearly six years after the death of his predecessor. His character has received an estimate higher than
it intrinsically deserves, because it is compared with those
of his predecessors and those of his immediate successors.
His great merit is that in a critical period he dared to act
as the head of the nation, and to take measures to secure
its unity and peace.

France had become so distracted and wretched that it
was constantly exposed alike to internal decay and to foreign subjugation and dismemberment. It is the merit
and the glory of Henry IV. — a merit and glory, however, tarnished by many a vice and many a folly — that
he made one heroic endeavor to put an end to the merciless persecutions which now for fifty years the Protestants
had been compelled to endure from their Catholic fellow-
subjects. So soon as his seat on the throne had been
fully secured, he called before him, on separate occasions,
the representatives of both, and after a patient consulta-
tion with each, he caused to be prepared and promulgated
the Edict of Nantes, — an edict which has usually been

styled the Charter of French Protestantism, and which certainly is a noble and generous attempt to secure a cessation of the bloody religious strife that had blighted the happiness and well-nigh destroyed the prosperity of France. The Edict bears the date of April, 1598. It contains the substance of several other edicts relating to the Huguenots which had been issued in former reigns, and is expanded through ninety-two articles. It is supplemented by three additional documents, of which two are entitled secret articles, and the remaining one is styled *Brevet;* the secret articles qualifying and in some instances enlarging the provisions of the Edict itself. They together, in the only form in which I have seen them, fill some forty closely printed crown octavo pages, and are certainly very dull reading. Their prevailing tone is very kindly, and shows the utmost desire on the part of the king to eradicate and destroy the religious animosities which had so long disturbed the peace and order of his kingdom. In this respect it is undoubtedly intended to be equivalent to an act of indemnity and oblivion, and for this purpose it provides several items of pecuniary compensation to be paid from the royal treasury. It is only when we examine it as a charter of liberties for the future that its inadequacies present themselves, though even thus considered it may be all that ought to be expected from an age and a country in which constitutional liberty was wholly unknown. It was undoubtedly intended that the people of France should have the right to choose between the two religions, but this right is hampered by so many restrictions and reservations that it could never be freely exercised.

The Edict recognizes two distinct classes into which the subjects of the king are divided : first, those who profess " the Catholic, Apostolic, and Roman religion ; " and, second, those who profess " the Pretended Reformed re-

ligion." The former of these religions it declares to be
the established religion of the country, and wherever it
has been overthrown or abandoned it is to be reëstablished
in full possession of all its former rights. The latter, or
the Pretended Reformed religion, on the other hand, is
placed on an entirely different foundation. Those who
profess and cherish it are admitted to certain privileges
rather than rights, and these privileges are conceded to
them, not from any principle of justice, but wholly from
considerations of expediency, and because of the trouble
they have occasioned and may occasion again. Through
all its concessions it presents the votaries of the "Pretended Reformed religion," not only as an inferior part
of the population, but as persons having no claims whatever to the privileges which it confers. It was thus incidentally fitted to inspire, in full measure among the more
favored class, that haughty contempt, that disdainful intolerance, which a national church, supported by law and
protected by government, always cherishes for those whom
it scornfully styles dissenters and schismatics and heretics. It allowed them simply to exist, but only by suffer-
ance. Though the Protestant Reformation in France,
even after sixty years of almost ceaseless persecution, now
numbered as its adherents scarcely less than a million of
Frenchmen, among whom were princes of the royal blood,
noblemen of illustrious lineage, officers of distinction in
the army and navy of the king, and a most respectable,
industrious, and thrifty portion of the population, yet the
tone of the Edict is one of condescension and of reluctant
interposition in behalf of an inferior class, who had been
deluded with troublesome doctrines and were practicing
strange rites of religion, rather to be indulged and borne
with than to be approved or respected.

If we pass from its general tone to its special provisions, we find that it permits every person to select the

Reformed religion without hindrance or restriction of any kind, but he can make no public exercise of it save in certain districts and places which are specially named. These places and districts are those in which it already exists. From all other places its public exercises are expressly excluded, and among these are comprised the city of Paris and the country around it to the extent of five leagues, in which their worship could not be held. The professors of the Pretended Reformed religion are made eligible to all public offices and employments, and also to all schools and colleges, and all hospitals and charitable institutions. They may reside in any part of the kingdom, but they may hold their worship or any public exercises of their religion apart, or keep for sale books relating to it, only in the specified places. It is obvious from restrictions such as these, especially in an age when intercourse was difficult and exceedingly limited, that the reformers could look forward to no organized growth and to no prolonged future for their religious faith. They could cherish it in their own hearts provided they kept it to themselves. They could not commune with each other in any religious exercise, still less could they explain their doctrines to others anywhere but in the districts and towns specified in the Edict; and wherever they might be, they were required to "observe the festivals in use in the Church, Catholic, Roman, and Apostolic, and on such days not to sell or to expose for sale in shops, or to engage openly in any work." Numerous sections of the Edict relate to the manner in which justice shall be administered in all civil suits and processes which affected them, and in this connection special officers were appointed to act in their behalf in several of the high courts of the realm. As I have already mentioned, the Huguenots had organized themselves into a sort of Christian State, — a political body without reference to territory, — which had, in some respects, been recognized by the government. This recognition was ratified in the Edict, and several fortresses in the districts assigned to them were placed under their control to give military importance and strength to their State.

No sooner was the Edict of Nantes promulgated than it was denounced in almost equal measure by both Catholics and Huguenots. The former regarded it as a boon too great to be given to heretics; the latter as a concession too small for them to receive. The former declared it to be a proof of the insincerity of Henry's conformity to the Church; the latter styled it the treacherous work of a renegade Protestant, who had abandoned the faith of his ancestors that he might receive the crown and sit upon the throne. Henry himself clearly thought it to be all that could be done with any advantage to either. His great aspiration was not so much to benefit either religious party as to bring peace and order to his distracted kingdom. It was in reality a great and beneficent act of royal authority, — an act whose true significance reached far beyond the subject to which it related, and which proclaimed that a new mode of government had begun in France. It was an assertion of prerogative on the part of the monarch which gave notice to feudal lords and local authorities of every degree that their importance was henceforth to be merged in the sovereign importance of the king himself. Henry was the first of the Bourbon race of kings, a race that created a new era in France only to show how incompetent they were to guide its spirit or to meet its necessities. The absolute monarchy which Henry founded made France a nation, but it also, in the hands of his successors, brought on the Revolution which, for the time, destroyed both nation and monarchy.

But the Edict was yet to be sanctioned by the Parliament of Paris, and by the other local Parliaments which in those times performed the functions of legislative assemblies, with something like the conceited independence and provincial narrowness which were so frequently displayed by our own state legislatures in the days of the old Confederation and the Continental Congress. It was in these bodies that the Edict of Nantes assumed its true political and historical significance. With them it was not merely a recognition of the Huguenot churches and their religion, but it was an act vastly more vital in its bearings. It entered into the very springs and sources of public authority, into the political life of the nation. It was an act such as that which our English ancestors in the days of Cromwell, fifty years later, used to style a Root and Branch measure. A new age had come, and but few were aware of its advent, and fewer still knew what kind of an age it was to be. Henry comprehended the exigency of public affairs and determined to meet it. He commanded the Parliaments to sanction the Edict, and they obeyed. In spite of his Huguenot training he was far from being a saint. He was licentious in his life, and to a large extent a votary of expediency in his morals. But he was kindly in his spirit, and more just than his predecessors in his acts. He found the country ruined by rival factions and religious wars. Civil society was falling to pieces amidst the universal prevalence of jealousies and hatreds, of intrigues and cabals. Life was without security and had but little value. The single explanation of this social disorganization and decay was to be found in the fact that there existed no government strong enough to become a guarantee of order and security ; no single force paramount over all other forces, that could limit their action and control the manner of their operation. The Edict of Henry IV. was thus the first great exercise of royal authority in France. Had he lived to carry it into full operation and complete development, its revocation might have become impossible.

Henry IV., like his predecessor, fell by the hand of an assassin in one of the streets of Paris, in 1610, after a prosperous reign of sixteen years. The Huguenots now discovered how great a friend he had been to their cause. The provisions of the Edict soon began to receive new constructions. New annoyances were contrived for their humiliation and new restrictions were placed on their worship. Under the bad influences which still controlled them, they at length rose in armed insurrections, and in 1629, after they had been subdued with needless cruelty by the soldiers of Louis XIII., they were pardoned and restored to their religious rights, but deprived of their political organization and their military fortresses, and made simple subjects of the king. This was what Henry IV. himself had foreseen would be necessary, and it proved to be the greatest boon they had ever received from the government. They were now deserted by the great nobles and military leaders who had acted with them. They gave up the engrossing business of governing themselves, and devoted their energies to agricultural industry, to commerce, and to the useful arts with a success which had never before been witnessed in France. Even in their worst days they had not ceased to read the Bible, to listen to sermons and prayers, and to sing their hymns of devotion and thanksgiving. They had thus kept alive the essential rudiments of religious life, which neither war nor worldliness had wholly destroyed. Their industry and prosperity soon became characteristic features of the regions which they inhabited. Indifferent to the holidays of the Church, their labor was remitted only on Sundays and on some occasional festival of thanksgiving or some chosen day for fasting and prayer. Their industrial year was thus nearly one third longer than that of their Catholic neighbors. In addition to this they conducted their work with a self-directing intelligence which never fails to insure the highest industrial success. Hence it came to be remarked that wherever the harvests were most abundant, wherever the vineyards yielded the most delicious grapes and the finest wines, wherever the silk and the woolen manufacturers were the most prosperous, wherever in the ports, either of the Mediterranean or the British Channel, the largest ships bore away the richest cargoes and brought back the most ample returns, there the Huguenots were to be found in the greatest numbers. So much better is quiet industry than war or than politics as an occupation of life. So much more beautiful and attractive, so much more effective over all human hearts, is the example of Christian faith when ruling in the daily lives of its disciples than it ever can be when courting the alliance of rank and power, or soliciting the favor of princes and monarchs. These were the best years of the Huguenots, — years in which they engaged in no wars and no cabals, in which they asked for nothing from the government but to be let alone. Louis XIII., in dissolving their political organization, became incidentally their greatest benefactor.

Louis XIV. came to the throne in 1642, at the age of five years, and his reign lasted till his death, in 1715, a period of seventy-three years. When he was at the age of fourteen, he declared himself qualified to reign, and on the death of Cardinal Mazarin, in 1661, he became his own prime minister, and assumed the entire management of the government. He was a man of extraordinary administrative abilities and of singular power of controlling other men. That centralization of power which Henry IV. had begun he carried to the fullest completion. He made the government of France not only an absolute monarchy, but an Oriental despotism, in which the word of the king was the law. His leading idea was that the country and its people of every degree, with all that they possessed, were his property, to be used at his discretion. *I am the State* was the maxim that controlled his reign. He made war on the grandest scale. He lavished the wealth of his subjects on the adornment of his capital, on palaces, churches, fortresses, on libraries and museums. He gathered around him scholars and men of genius, great statesmen and great soldiers, and made his reign the most brilliant in the history of France. It was fortunate that for a considerable period he gave little attention to the religion of his subjects. His spiritual advisers, writes the historian Sismondi, limited their counsels to two essential precepts: 1. Abstain from incontinence; 2. Exterminate heretics; and it has been said of him that " if he fell short in the first of these duties, he certainly wrought works of supererogation in the second." The extraordinary zeal and the still more extraordinary cruelty of Louis XIV. in the destruction of Huguenots had their origin in part, at least, in his imperial passion for unity of every kind in his kingdom. With him nonconformity in religion was rebellion, and he treated it as such. Whatever spirit of fanaticism he had was breathed into him, in a large degree, by Madame de Maintenon, a woman of disreputable celebrity, strangely enough of Protestant descent and training, who was first the teacher of his children, and afterwards his wife. She controlled what was called his conscience. She claimed and perhaps deserved the distinction of converting the king, by which she meant that she made him the foremost of religious persecutors in modern times. He did not massacre the Huguenots, as his predecessors had done. He adopted a different mode of proceeding. He began with a proposal, in full accordance with his magnificent ideas, to purchase the conversion of the entire body of the Huguenots at an average price of five livres a head, and for this purpose he set apart one third of the entire revenue of all the vacant benefices of the kingdom, as a special fund, which was styled the Bank of Conversion, and was administered by agents, called Converters. Multitudes of the baser sort took the money, but when the lists were published it was observed that they were not Huguenots, but persons — not scarce in any country or in any age — always ready to be bought or sold, and that very many of them had been paid for several conversions.

Enraged at his failure, he soon devised new methods of securing Catholic unity among his subjects. He ordered that all sorts of people should conform in outward observances to the Established Church. To promote this end, he suppressed the synods of the Huguenots ; he forbade them to be employed in the charge of estates and in all kindred positions. He forbade Catholics and Protestants to intermarry, and the children of such marriages he declared illegitimate. None but Catholics could be employed in any domestic service. Catholics becoming Protestants were visited with the severest penalties, while Protestants becoming Catholics received special privileges, one of which was the extension of their debts for five years. All public positions of every kind, the practice of all professions, and admission to all schools were denied to Protestants. Children of seven years might be brought to Catholic baptism without the consent or knowledge of their parents, and, once in the Church, they could not leave it. Multitudes of parents, in agony and despair, sent their children to England, to Holland, and to Denmark to be cared for. Huguenot families, also, in great numbers, began to seek homes in foreign countries. This, however, was immediately forbidden under the penalty of being sent to the galleys, but their ministers were encouraged to depart, and not suffered to return. These are but specimens of the harassing despotism which was brought to bear upon them, in total disregard of the Edict of Nantes.

In 1681 the quartering of soldiers on Huguenot families was first resorted to for "missionary purposes," as it was styled. This practice had not been unknown in France in times of war or national necessity. Now, in the province of Poitou, they were compelled to receive these dreadful guests, and feed and lodge them, often to the number of a hundred in each house, if their estates were large. But beyond the insufferable annoyances and outrages it involved, this first attempt at military conversion was not regarded as a success. Three years later, however, in 1684, it was renewed on a far broader and more terrific scale in nearly all the Huguenot provinces. For this purpose dragoons were selected as the most available, and likely to be the most effectual, instruments in the work. The enterprise thus received the name of *dragonnade*, a new word then added to the French language. Chosen squadrons of these terrible troopers lighted like filthy birds of prey on the homes of the Huguenots alike in cities and provinces, wherever they were found. They carried with them the whole machinery of agony and despair, — insult, outrage, degradation, the destruction of estates, the wanton violation of every sanctity, the inhuman practice of every atrocity, save murder alone. It was probably the most appalling form of wholesale persecution ever visited upon a civilized people. Human nature broke down beneath the infliction. Despair, insanity, and suicide marked its progress. City after city, province after province, professed their submission to the Church on the approach of the dreadful *dragonnade*. Nismes was converted, as was said, in twenty-four hours. Swift couriers bore daily reports of the universal surrender, till the king and his courtiers were made to believe that there were no longer any heretics in France. He had often professed his unwillingness to annul the Edict which had been proclaimed by his grandfather, though he had repeatedly violated every one of its provisions. But now, said he, it is no longer needed, for the Huguenots have all become Catholics. Deceived by false reports, flattered by courtiers and priests, elated by what he deemed the greatest of triumphs, he signed, on the 22d of October, 1685, the Revocation of the Edict of Nantes, which had been proclaimed by Henry IV. eighty-seven years before. This act removed every semblance of protection that remained, and let loose upon them the wildest fury of their enemies. The revocation was applauded in the splendid eloquence of Massillon and Bossuet, the most illustrious preachers of the age, but it gave a shock to the French people. It was the first break in the spell which had enthralled the nation. It occasioned the loss of at least three hundred thousand of the bravest, the most industrious, and the most intelligent of the population of the country, — a loss which well-nigh destroyed several of the great industries in which it most excelled. Their emigration was prohibited, and the coast was constantly watched; but amidst dangers, privations, and sufferings which no pen has fully described, they fled to England, to Germany, to Holland, and to the colonies in America, bearing with them not only immense wealth, but industrial skill, commercial enterprise, and high character, which enriched and adorned the countries that received them.

But I cannot linger on the scenes connected with this stupendous expatriation and exile. As they are portrayed in history they are the perpetual shame of our common humanity, the foulest reproach that has ever rested upon Christian civilization. We are not, however, to imagine that the spirit which produced them is confined to a single church or to a single type of Christianity. Religious intolerance belongs to human nature, and manifests itself in a vast variety of ways. Its most common device has been to seize upon the fatal assumption that the State is

bound to prescribe or support the religion of its people.
When Louis XIV. exterminated the Huguenots and put
an end to the Protestant Reformation in France, this assumption was well-nigh universal among Christian nations.
It is scarcely too much to say that religious persecution
or religious restriction, in one form or another, was at
least possible, if it was not practiced, in nearly every State
in Christendom. It had been made impossible in Rhode
Island alone by the very terms of the social organization.
Here, and here alone, the body politic had no power to
prescribe, or control, or in any way to affect the religion
of its members. It was an idea far in advance of the age,
and was everywhere derided and disparaged. But how
splendid are the triumphs it has won, — how manifold are
the blessings it has brought both to religion and to the
State! It has made persecutors like Catherine de Médicis
and Louis XIV. no longer possible in civilized nations.
It has brought together warring churches in the bonds of
a common faith, and animated them with new zeal in pro-
claiming the gospel to all mankind. It has emancipated
Christianity from a debasing bondage and restored it to
its original freedom. It has compelled the State to become the equal protector of every creed however despised,
of every worship however humble. Thus it is that the
seed planted here by our exiled founders two hundred and
fifty years ago has become a mighty tree, " and the leaves
of the tree are for the healing of the nations."

THE EPOCHS OF AMERICAN CIVILIZATION.[1]

THE first hundred years of American history are about to close. They have witnessed a national growth and a development of civilization different in many respects from any other hitherto known among mankind. Both the nation and the civilization which it embosoms have encountered perils and have been engaged in struggles which have tested their temper and their endurance, and now, at the end of a hundred years, these perils and struggles may be deemed not unworthy of such brief review as the hour may admit.

The elements of American society, and of the civilization which it has created, were wholly of transatlantic origin. Unlike those which were brought from Europe to other portions of the continent, they have remained uncontaminated by any admixture borrowed from the aboriginal races. They were also mainly English, including in that designation both Scotch and Irish. It is true there were settlements made here from other countries. The Dutch were the original occupants of New York; the Swedes mingled largely in the settlements of New Jersey and Delaware, the Germans in that of Pennsylvania, and the French Huguenots in that of South Carolina. But these soon became absorbed by the English, and as all the colonies became possessions of England, so they all took on an English character, spoke the English language, and came to be controlled by English ideas. This was most slowly accomplished in New York and Penn-

[1] Read before the Friday Evening Club, December 31, 1875.

sylvania, in the former of which States, more especially, another race had long a foothold, and many of their families exerted an important influence not only upon social manners and modes of thought, but also upon political events.

It is not true, however, that all the elements of the English social system were ever represented in the colonies. 1. There were here no branch of the royal family and no families of the feudal nobility of England. The nearest approach to the former was the brief possession of New York by the Duke of York, afterwards James II., and the only real feudalism we ever had was to be found among the Dutch Patroons of the same State. 2. There never existed here any uniform ecclesiastical establishment. Religion was provided for by law in all the colonies except Rhode Island, but it was in several different forms of ecclesiastical organization. At the period of the Revolution, when our survey begins, there was everywhere a substantial religious freedom. 3. While social distinctions were still marked in a manner somewhat rigid, yet the political ideas which ruled in all the colonies were essentially democratic, and the theory of the social organization rested upon the equality of its members. 4. In addition to this we must not omit to mention that negro slavery still existed in every colony, but flourished most especially in those south of Delaware Bay. To the north of this point, on the coast, it had proved unprofitable, and had also become the subject of moral reprobation among considerable classes of the population, especially in Massachusetts and Pennsylvania.

The civil and social elements which had been introduced by the settlers had also undergone some important modifications during the colonial period by the operation of the new forces which were brought to bear upon them. They had been planted in the wilderness, in a climate different from that of England, and amidst scenes and influences of nature which necessitated a ceaseless struggle for existence, in which only what was hardy and enduring could by any possibility survive. There were thus created both a sentiment and a condition of social equality. Few of the colonists belonged to the higher classes of English life, few were men of wealth, and these were scattered among colonies which were wholly distinct from each other, which indeed had scarcely anything in common save their English origin and their dependence on the mother country. All public interests were thus exclusively provincial. Their settlements skirted the Atlantic coast from New Hampshire to Georgia, and extended but little way into the interior. They were connected by no political and few social ties; their inhabitants, even in New England, were strangers to each other, and the policy of England was to prevent as far as possible any intercourse in the way of trade.

A civilization thus transplanted and isolated from its parent stock by an intervening ocean must of necessity deteriorate. At the period of the Revolution the colonists were thought, in England, to have degenerated in their wilderness life. They had at least grown to be different from Englishmen, and this fact, far more than any real oppressions which they were obliged to endure, was the cause of their political separation. The British civilization which they had brought with them had undergone a change, and this change now made distasteful the laws and restrictions and the entire rule which England continued to exercise over them. The traditional principles of British constitutional law had come to be differently understood and applied by the two divisions of the English race. Here, amidst the looser freedom of colonial life, these principles seemed to forbid restrictions, to demand self-government, and even to justify resistance to taxation, unless levied by colonial consent. There, the principal thought was of the power of Parliament, the expense incurred in defending the colonies in the war with France, and the best way in which they could be made to reimburse the treasury. The views of the colonists were rather vigorously put forth in petitions and documents of various kinds, often rudely written, but breathing strongly the ancient spirit of English freedom. The views of the government were embodied in acts of Parliament and in innumerable state papers of the ministers, while the average tone of British opinion was pretty faithfully reflected in literary productions like Dr. Johnson's "Taxation no Tyranny." The materials which had thus been collected in these scattered English settlements of the Atlantic coast, modified as they had been by the trials and struggles of colonial life, were now to be wrought together in a new political organization, and, under the new forces brought to act upon them, were to be formed into a new civilization, whose diffusion over the continent is the most remarkable social phenomenon of the last hundred years.

The epochs or periods in the progress of our civilization may be most naturally made to conform to certain periods in our political history to which they correspond, though these periods are not very precisely fixed, and at many points they run into each other. My general purpose is to set forth the agencies which throughout the century have shaped this civilization and made it what it is, rather than to point out any precise stages of its progressive development. These periods may be stated as follows: 1. The period of the War of the Revolution and the organization of the constitutional government, extending from 1776 to 1789. 2. The period in which American nationality became fully asserted and established, which also includes the purchase of Louisiana. This period ends with the peace of 1815. 3. The rapid development of the internal resources of the country, the growth of the leading American industries, and the rise and prolonged discussion of great constitutional questions to 1850. 4. The formation of sectional parties on the question of slavery, the war of secession, and its consequences to the present time.

There is certainly one aspect in which the War of the Revolution is a most unattractive subject for history to describe ; and this is found in the want of unity in the colonies, the petty jealousies which separated them, and the unmitigated selfishness which so generally controlled the action of their legislatures. Independence was declared long before any political organization was formed for maintaining it. A Congress, as it was called, had assembled in 1774 to consider what ought to be done, but its members had no power to bind those whom they represented. They were not indeed representatives. A second Congress met in 1775, but it had no power to do anything, and all its resolutions were mere recommendations. It, however, in some sense raised an army, appointed a general-in-chief, and, on receiving permission from the colonies, it made the Declaration of Independence, a Declaration which was ratified and repeated over the whole country. But as yet there was neither government nor nation, save in a very limited and inadequate sense. Never in history has a great war been carried on to a successful issue under an authority so ill contrived and so little suited to the purposes which it had undertaken to accomplish. But the colonies persistently refused to make this authority any stronger or to invest it with any greater efficiency. To create a nation in any true and proper sense was not at the outset an aspiration of the colonial legislatures. All they aimed at was independence. They aspired rather to be thirteen States,

like the cantons of Switzerland, and they would then have
shrunk from giving up their several sovereignties in order
to become one nation. Fortunately, the American Revolution accomplished far more than its original aims. If
it had not done so, it would have been an event of little
importance to the progress of civilization. Along with
the independence which it finally secured, it also gave the
colonies an impulse towards that national unity without
which independence would have been of but secondary
moment. It raised them above the narrow political ideas
which had ruled the minds of the people. It lifted them
out of their isolated provincial existence, and imparted to
them the rudiments of a national life. In this way, and
in this alone, the dreary War of the Revolution was civilizing in its agencies and its results.

But after independence was once secured, national sentiments seemed for a time to decline. The prevailing idea
was that the work to which the colonies had been called
was already done, instead of being just begun. The spectacle is a melancholy one to contemplate. The concep-
tions of what was requisite in order to be a nation and to
have a permanent place among the nations of the world
were all of the most meagre character, save as they existed
in a few broad and far-seeing minds. The country was
still, as it had been from the beginning, without a government. Articles of Confederation had been proposed by
Congress as early as 1776, but they had not been adopted
till 1781, near the close of the war, and even the feeble
restrictions which they imposed upon local sovereignty
were scarcely heeded. Congress had established a post-
office and a national flag, and beyond these there was little, if anything, to remind the people of the States that
the United States existed. Each State still collected the
revenues, levied all the taxes, and exercised every attribute
of sovereignty except treating with foreign powers, and

each State paid its share of the public expenditures with
such promptness or such tardiness as best suited its own
convenience or inclinations. The Congress of the Confederation was at best merely a legislative body, and that only
in a very loose and uncertain way ; for its subjects were
not citizens, but impracticable and unmanageable sovereign
States. There existed neither executive nor judicial authority. It could not pay its debts, it could not suppress
insurrection, it could not fulfill its treaty stipulations. The
greatest and most useful work it ever did was to demonstrate its own incompetency, and the necessity of creating
a government that should be able to rule the country, to
take possession of its resources, and to compel submission from the local democracies into which its population
was distributed. That such a government was so speedily created, and that, too, without tumult or distraction,
was the proudest triumph of the age, — more creditable to
American character than all the endurances and all the
achievements of the war. The latter secured independence, but the former secured nationality, without which
independence would have been of little importance, and
any brilliant career in civilization impossible. Fortunately, the framing of the new government fell into the
hands of no professional constitution - makers, such as
were so common in Europe after the French Revolution.
It was the work of practical rather than philosophical
statesmen, and it carefully provided for the great and obvious necessities of the country without attempting to re-
construct the social organization. It was such as grew
naturally out of the existing condition of the country. It
was republican, because all the social antecedents of the
country required that it should be so. It was federal, not
from any choice, but because the population from the beginning had been grouped in Colonies and States, and it
could not now be changed. It protected slavery in the

States that chose to tolerate it, because without such protection no constitution could be adopted and no government could exist. It had also the great peculiarity of containing no provision for the support of religion. In this respect it was the first experiment that had ever been made. Though all admitted that no other plan could be adopted, yet the experiment was deemed to be full of dangers, and was regarded with the gravest solicitude by many of the best and most patriotic men of the time. As a whole, however, it was a work of singular wisdom. It forms a brilliant and triumphant close of the first period of American civilization; the harbinger, also, and in some sense the guarantee, of all that has thus far followed in the social and political progress of the country. That it was so readily adopted and set in operation by nearly all the States, in the face of prejudices and difficulties that seemed insuperable, is a result to be gloried in; that it was accepted by majorities so small in some of the States, and was for a time rejected by our own, only suggests how nearly they all came to missing the only career that could lead them to greatness and power. The work, then, of this first period was to create a nation capable of guaranteeing the individual and social progress in which civilization consists.

The second epoch opens with the inauguration of President Washington in 1789. Already a more national tone inspires the public councils, broader ideas prevail among the people, and the statesmen of the country are animated by loftier hopes. The great name of the President, however, was still the only basis of confidence with other nations. The conspicuous task of the new government was to satisfy the nations of Europe that the colonies had achieved a truly national independence, and were determined to maintain it. This was the essential work of the

period now under consideration. England had retained
the military posts within our frontiers ostensibly because
the Confederation had not been able to fulfill its part of
the treaty of peace, but really, as her ministers declared,
because she expected soon to recover her lost possessions,
and to this end was her policy directed. The contempt
for the Americans, rooted so deeply in the English mind
when the Revolution began, had not been eradicated by
the events of the war. It prompted every sort of inso-
lence which British officials dared to show. They interfered with our rights of fishery; they insulted our flag
on the seas; they kept alive with all sorts of encouragement the revengeful passions of the Indian tribes that
prowled around our settlements, and still hoped, with British help, to regain the hunting-grounds which they had
once possessed. It was no wonder that the masses of the
people were filled with intense hatred of England, and,
though the suggestion was ludicrous, it was scarcely
strange that they were soon ready and even clamorous for
another war with the mother country. Barely was the
new government in full operation when the world was
startled by the most exciting event of the eighteenth century, — the overthrow of the French monarchy and the
proclamation of the French republic. Most exciting was
this event in the United States. France had followed
our example in overthrowing kingly power! A sister
republic had proclaimed death to tyrants and was claiming American sympathy within fifteen years from the
Declaration of American Independence! The appeal was
irresistible. The new republic rushed into the arms of
the American people with gushing declarations of liberty and fraternity. She solicited our closest friendship.
She reminded us of the aid given us by France, and without delay she began to use us as confederates in her wild
propagandism of revolution. The affectionate embraces

of France soon became more dangerous to national independence and dignity, and no less offensive to national
pride, than the open insults of England. Both these nations, though in different ways, treated the American people with an effrontery which not only outraged the national
sovereignty, but showed that they held us not as their
equals, but as their inferiors. Never was the firmness of
Washington so severely tried. He was determined that
this country should remain neutral in the wars of the
French Revolution, and most heroically did he carry his
determination into effect, though in doing so he periled,
and for a time lost, his unequaled popularity among his
countrymen. War either with England or France seemed
inevitable; but he postponed it with either, though it came
a few years later with both. Nations decline in self-
respect and true glory, and civilization takes on an inferior character, when they submit to be underlings to others.
To save the republic from this humiliation was the chief
work of the period we are now considering.

So soon as the country recovered from the impoverish-
ment of the war of separation, American commerce opened
trade with the great marts of the world. On entering the
Mediterranean, it immediately encountered the tribute
which the States of Barbary had long levied, with the
connivance of England and France, on the ships of all
nations. Our vessels refused to submit to the lawless ex-
action, and their crews in great numbers were carried into
Mohammedan slavery. The war with Tripoli which ensued, and the gallant exploits of Preble and Decatur, of
Truxton and Morris, may be said to have created the
American navy, and to have demonstrated how formidable
a power we might become upon the seas. This country
thus became not only the first to refuse the tribute exacted
by the Algerines, but also the first to proclaim the freedom
of the seas.

Of similar origin was the war with England in 1812. It grew out of a series of studied insults to the American flag and outrages on American citizens. Though it left unsettled the particular questions for which it was avowedly waged, yet it demonstrated the national strength and exalted the national character. With this war became extinct the great political party which had formed the Constitution and set its machinery in motion, which had sustained the administrations of Washington and Adams, which had withstood the fascinations of a French alliance, which had kept the peace with England in the face of mighty provocations to war, and which, though out of power for ten years, had steadily opposed the War of 1812. The Federal party, though probably the purest in American politics, had yet aimed at what was impossible, and what was undesirable even if it were possible. The spirit and manners of the American people were from the beginning essentially democratic, and it was inevitable that the popular will would sooner or later make itself directly felt in the action of the government. The extinction of this party altered the fortunes of the country, and in some sense the character of the government. From that time all parties have been essentially democratic, and the people have been the controlling force in national affairs, and have held in their own hands the destiny of the republic. Hence have arisen universal suffrage, a rapid and vast development of popular talent, energy, and ambition, and the continual rise of men of eminence and renown from the humblest ranks of social life. All this was attended by an immense increase of national sentiment, which, had it not been for counteracting agencies, would have created a vigorous national unity that no state-rights theories could ever have harmed.

But, considered in its ulterior consequences, no event belonging to this epoch was so important as the purchase of Louisiana from France in 1803. Prior to this, Spain, and afterwards France, had held control not only of the mouth of the Mississippi, but also of its entire western bank, — a fact that was sure to be productive of unnumbered woes. This transaction, in its bearing on our American destiny, is to be associated with the previous cession to the United States in 1784, by New York, Pennsylvania, and other States, of the great territory northwest of the Ohio. By the Ordinance of 1787 — one of the few illustrious enactments in the dreary legislation of the Continental Congress after the Revolution — this splendid tract was organized into a territory, out of which five future States were to be created, from all of which slavery was to be forever excluded. It was in connection with this that the Louisiana purchase assumed its vast significance. It stretched from the Gulf of Mexico northward to British America, and from the Mississippi westward, in indefinite lines, to the Pacific Ocean. The purchase was admitted to be beyond the constitutional authority of the government, and was strongly opposed by the Federal party. Even Washington recorded his opposition to it. But it was deemed to be justified by its great importance, even when that importance was only partially developed and dimly perceived in the distant future.

These two imperial possessions have ever since been the unconscious guardians of the republic and the architects of its destiny. In the first place, the mighty river that rolls between them, and washes one or both of them from its sources to its mouth, makes them one country, which no hand of man can separate or divide. In the second place, they furnished the most important theatres in which the stupendous struggle between freedom and slavery for the mastery of the government was to be mainly decided. As should be the occupants of these central regions, so would be the fate of the republic. The early exclusion of slavery from the former pledged its people to the cause of freedom by their own organic law, while all but two of the great States that have been formed in the other sent their hardy sons to battle for the Union. It was in Kansas, too, that the two forces first met in open conflict for the possession of the embryo State, and the issue of that preliminary conflict foreshadowed the grander issue of the Civil War. Though the extent of this magnificent purchase was imperfectly known either by the government that sold it or the government that bought it, its importance to this country was but narrowly estimated by Napoleon, then First Consul, who said to the commissioners that signed the treaty, " This accession of territory establishes the power of the United States, and I have now given to England a rival that will sooner or later humble her pride."

The third epoch of our civilization I make to extend from the close of the war with England to 1850, when slavery had become the controlling question in American politics. The position of the republic was fully assured among the nations, and was the subject of unlimited satisfaction to all its inhabitants. The cessation of party strife which followed soon after the war was especially favorable alike to new enterprises of maritime commerce, to the development of new industries, and the exploration and settlement of the new regions which had been added to the public domain. With these, too, were mingled widespread popular sympathies in the revolutionary movements then going on in Spanish America. It was a period of immense activity and enterprise, in which the whole country appeared to be filled with a full consciousness of its greatness and strength. All this, it must be admitted, was attended with drawbacks and dangers, which were specially felt in American civilization. The prosperity of the country and its geographical dimensions seemed all at once to enlarge the importance of every one of its citizens, and to give to them an inordinate faith in its manifest destiny. We became a nation of braggarts, with manners that made us particularly disagreeable to foreigners. We also were seized with an appetite for new territory, which, for a generation and more, was well-nigh insatiable, and which continually prompted us to measures, both of peace and of war, that were of the most dubious rectitude. During the period now in question Florida was purchased of Spain, in 1820 ; the republic of Texas, at its own solicitation, was annexed as a State in 1845; and California, Utah, and New Mexico were added to the republic at the close of the Mexican War in 1848. To explore and settle, to organize and govern, the vast regions beyond the Mississippi has, ever since their acquisition, been the ceaseless and still unfinished work of the American people. It has offered the fullest scope to their migratory propensities, and it has been greatly stimulated and abundantly rewarded by the unimagined resources which have been brought to light.

It was not to be expected that the civilization of the thirteen colonies, which a century ago contained only 3,500,000 white people, could thus be expanded over the continent without being diluted and enfeebled on its way. The civilized man of necessity parts with some elements of civilization when he moves to the frontier, and there fights the battle of life with the mighty forces of nature and with barbarians. But more than this is true. The vast western emigrations which have been going on through the entire century, and especially through the last fifty years, have retarded our civilization even in its original seats. For its higher developments it requires compact communities, where public interests, intellectual culture, and social refinement are concentrated. Nor were the settlements in the new States made by our own people alone. The emigration from the various countries of Europe, from the close of the Revolution to the present time, is estimated at six millions of people, comparatively few of whom have been above the standard of our own civilization, while the immense majority have been below it. It is not surprising that our progress in higher civilization has fallen far behind our progress in material prosperity. It was inevitable. The real occasion for surprise is that our civilization has borne as well as it has the tremendous drains which have been made upon it, and especially that it has received into its bosom, and assimilated to itself with so little deterioration, the diversified elements that were poured into it from beyond the Atlantic. What has been done required not intellectual culture and æsthetic tastes, but rather a vigorous manhood and the ability to subjugate nature, or what perhaps is the same thing, the common sense that learns her laws and makes them subservient to its own purposes. It should be added that this work was immensely facilitated by the great watercourses which were long the only highways of westward emigration. Afterwards came the roads and canals, which were built either by the national government or the States. When to these were added the steamboat, a purely American invention, the tide rolled westward with a tremendous volume. The later appliances of the railroad are only completing the exploration and settling of our public domain.

It was during this period, also, that there arose those great questions of public policy and of constitutional interpretation, which, while they profoundly agitated, also educated the minds of the people and made them familiar with the principles of our government. It was the age of parliamentary eloquence and of famous national orators, whom multitudes flocked to the Capitol to hear, and whose

printed speeches were read not only in the cities of the
Atlantic States, but in log-cabins on the remotest frontier.
These questions at first related to the power of the general government to impose tariffs and make internal improvements. Then came the more vital question, born of
our very organization, whether we were a nation or only a
league of sovereign States. Behind all these there gradually forced itself on public attention the still graver and
more exciting question of slavery, which from an early
period in the present century had darkened the horizon of
the republic. These questions were debated with an eloquence never equaled in American annals. So long as
they related to state-rights and federal authority alone,
they were not sectional questions. The people of both
South and North were on both sides of them. Slavery,
however, was always making use of them to strengthen
its own position. So anomalous was its character in the
midst of our democratic freedom, so wanting was it in
any moral basis to rest upon, that it instinctively sought
to protect itself by every species of alliance and by all
possible safeguards of its interest. Until 1830 its morality was still an open question in the South. It soon,
however, became so profitable and so vital to Southern
prosperity that differences of opinion were no longer tolerated, and all voices of dissent were effectually silenced
both in Church and State. The Southern people, with
few large cities, with an industry almost wholly agricultural, and with only two or three staple productions, cared
little for national roads and canals, and were especially
averse to tariffs. The result was that they soon organized themselves into a vast society for the protection of
slavery. On other questions they might be divided, but
on this they stood together in solid phalanx, without wavering and without hesitation. They had long insisted
that the number of Slave States and of Free States should

be kept equal, and that for any new free State a new slave State should be admitted into the Union. As the northwestern territory had been consecrated to freedom, they demanded, as an offset, that the whole Louisiana purchase should be open to slavery, though they at length accepted the Missouri Compromise in 1821, which limited slavery to the parallel of 36° 30' of north latitude. As we now recur to the debates of those eventful years, the statesmen of the Free States often appear to have performed no other part than that of mere temporizers and trimmers, so uniformly did they modify their principles to suit their circumstances. They held forth in their speeches the bravest views of the supremacy and power of the Union, but they invariably shrank from carrying them into effect. They sometimes spoke of trying the strength of the government to enforce the laws of Congress against a rebellious State, but when the crisis came they always avoided it by a compromise. General Jackson, it is true, was ready to strangle nullification in South Carolina, but that necessity also was avoided by a compromise. Indeed, on this class of questions compromise was then the only statesmanship that was possible. Nor is this to be set down to a want either of wisdom or of courage. The interests of slavery in the South were closely connected with the interests of industry in the North, and they were supported by a powerful political party. Besides, the early aims of the abolitionists were avowedly at variance with the Constitution. In these circumstances I cannot think that the statesmen of that day are now to be condemned for urging forbearance and concession to their utmost limit of endurance, rather than put in jeopardy the transcendent blessings of the Union. Thus, though in the midst of unequaled prosperity and with the greatest apparent strength both at home and abroad, the government was continually shrinking from the threatened collision with a State. This was remarked by De Tocqueville as early as 1831. One half the States were now holding their allegiance to slavery as paramount to every other. For its preservation new territory was continually demanded. It had been contended that slavery was to follow the law of the soil. The French had held a few slaves in the territory out of which Louisiana and Arkansas had been created, and slavery was of course to be admitted in these States. This rule would have excluded it from New Mexico and Utah, for there slavery had been abolished by Mexican law. The ground, however, was now changed, and the right was claimed to carry it into every territory by the force of the Constitution itself. California was made free by its own choice. But its admission as a State was violently resisted, and was secured at length in 1850 only by another compromise, of which Mr. Clay was the author. It provided: 1. That California be admitted as a free State. 2. That New Mexico and Utah be organized as Territories, without restriction as to slavery. 3. A pecuniary compensation to Texas for the surrender of her claims to certain territory. 4. The enactment of a new fugitive slave law. 5. The suppression of the slave-trade in the District of Columbia. This was the Compromise of 1850, the last ever consummated between freedom and slavery under the government of the United States.

Thus we reach the latest epoch of American civilization, — an epoch which was only to bear the fruits of all that had gone before, to reap the bitter harvest of suffering and war, of which the seeds had been planted in our original social organization. It embraces twenty-six years, of which eleven were years of growing sectional alienation and strife, five of open war, and the remaining ten of reconstruction and recovery. For the first

time since slavery had begun to assert its claims as a political power, the Compromise of 1850 had left the advantage with the Free States, but with the fugitive slave law
as a tremendous offset. The compromise produced anything but contentment on either side. In the South the
alarm was well-nigh universal lest it would speedily lose
its control in the republic. It put forth its utmost efforts
to people Kansas with slave-holders, in order to make it
a slave State, but it utterly failed, and experienced the
most ignominious of defeats. Virginia and Kentucky, the
great slave-breeding States, " the Congo," as Lord Macau-
lay called them, " of the other States," could not produce
slaves enough to meet the wants of their cotton growing
sisters. In this emergency a frantic movement was made
to reopen the African slave-trade, and some cargoes of
slaves were unquestionably landed on the coast. So complete, however, was the debasement of the Southern mind
that even this atrocity received only a qualified rebuke,
and that on the grounds of expediency and good policy.
Not only all public interests, but all sanctions of morality
and all teachings of religion, were forced to be subservient
to the maintenance and perpetuity of slavery.

In the Free States the hostility to the institution was
constantly increasing among all classes of the people.
By far the most numerous class, however, comprised
those who were willing to accord to it its constitutional
guarantees in the States where it already existed, but were
determined by all legal means to resist its extension into
the ·Territories of the United States; a second but much
smaller class were comparatively indifferent to the whole
question, and were quite willing to let the South have its
own way; while a third class, most especially feared and
hated in the South, comprised the open abolitionists, who
aimed to overthrow and extirpate slavery from the country, though into doing it they should hurl the Constitution

and the Union into common ruin. The general conscience of the people in the Free States was fast declaring itself at variance with the slavery provisions of the Constitution. Multitudes of the people felt called upon by the highest sentiments of duty to act against an institution to which the laws gave their protection. A condition of affairs like this in the two great sections of the country insensibly wrought a demoralization that was well-nigh universal, and threatened serious disasters to all high civilization. In one part of the country all moral sentiments were held in absolute subordination to the despotism of slavery. In the other they assumed a position and prompted an action at variance with the Constitution and laws of the Republic. In the former there was a growing brutality which burst forth on the slightest provocation, in spite of the utmost effort that could be made to repress it. In the latter there was open resistance to law as often as it was invoked for the rendition of a fugitive slave; and this too not among the lawless and criminal classes, but on the part of citizens of character and standing, often distinguished for their piety and worth, who appealed for their justification to a law higher than any human enactments. Fortunately, the continuance of all this was short. The outbreak of the Civil War put an end to it all. And when that war was ended not a vestige remained of the malignant power which had threatened such disasters to American civilization; which had enthralled the bodies of four millions of black men and the souls of thirty millions of white men. The triumph was complete. The cost indeed was tremendous, but not greater than it was worth; for it was a triumph not over secession and slavery alone, but over barbarism and wrong which were debasing the conscience and degrading the character of the American people. After what was then accomplished, whatever our future may be, it certainly cannot be like the past.

I. It must be admitted, I think, that our civilization
during the century has been distinguished rather for its
wide and rapid diffusion than for the elevation which it
has attained. Its special work has been to subdue the
forest and people the prairie, and this work is scarcely
compatible with high refinement either of thought or of
life. It has reclaimed multitudes from barbarism rather
than raised a select few to the highest excellence of which
they were capable. It has produced a high average of
popular intelligence and character rather than eminent
examples of genius or learning or intellectual culture. De
Tocqueville remarked of the United States that " in no
other country in the world does one find either so few
men of great learning or so few men of great ignorance ; "
and the remark is even now almost as true as it was fifty
years ago. Until recently there was nothing in our education to encourage tastes for special studies or acquirements, nor were such tastes appreciated in the country.
Our educated men knew a little of many subjects, but
they mastered none. We also became early possessed of
an inordinate national conceit which was unfriendly to
anything like thorough or careful culture. Mr. Adams
has lately reminded us that a committee of the House of
Representatives prepared an address to President Washington, in which they styled him the Chief Magistrate of
the freest and most enlightened nation of the world, and
this too at a time when all our science and all our literature were to be found in the writings of Dr. Franklin
and of Phillis Wheatley, the colored poetess. We dwelt
too exclusively on ourselves, and too readily thought our
popular freedom not only a cure for all the ills of society, but a guarantee for every excellence. We wor-
shiped utility in intellectual culture as in everything
else. Our intellectual activity was long expended almost
wholly on practical inventions, in which we certainly

achieved eminent success. All this, however, if it has not ceased to be true, is far less true than it was thirty years ago.

II. Much has been said in disparagement of our civilization, on account of its democratic spirit. We have been so often told, that we almost believe it to be true, that this is necessarily unfriendly to cultivated manners, to superior intellectual culture, or to success in literature, science, or art. But every word of this disparagement, as time is showing, has been premature. There have been faults and disagreeable peculiarities enough in American character and life. But none of these are essential or permanent. Our visitors and critics from abroad used to delight themselves in showing them up, and in ascribing them to the democratic spirit of our society, greatly to the disturbance of our sensibilities as a people. The early volumes of our older magazines abound in elaborate and often angry rejoinders to these irritating criticisms. Our critics assumed that our civilization must always be inferior. But no one now believes that there exists here any actual hindrance to the indefinite progress both of man and society, in all that constitutes the highest civilization. We have dispensed both with princes and aristocracy, and the century has shown that large-minded and patriotic citizens have done all, and more than all, that princes and nobles in other countries have ever done for the intellectual training of the people, and for collecting the means of the highest culture. It is the peculiarity of our civilization that, far more than any other, it makes every man the master of his own social destiny, and places the destiny of society in the hands of its members rather than of its rulers. As they are so will civilization be.

III. A paper recently read to the Club indicated how complete is the revolution which has taken place during this century in the relations of religion to the State. It has ceased everywhere throughout the country to be a matter of which legislation takes any direct cognizance. It is the one thing before every other which legislation studiously avoids. The State, by the very terms of its fundamental law, no longer cares whether its people are Christians, Mohammedans, or Pagans, or unbelievers in all religion. This is, perhaps, the natural result of our views of religious freedom, which have been pushed to some wild extremes in this country. It still remains true, however, that the essential life of all high and lasting civilization is in the religion of the people. To keep it alive, and to make it efficient in the formation of character and the guidance of conduct, is a work that cannot be dispensed with. Indeed, taking into consideration the whole nature of man, it is not too much to assert that the true end of civilization is to make society a theatre as favorable as possible for the moral probation of its members and their preparation for the life to come. It is a serious question whether an American theory of the State is entirely adequate to conducting civilization to any such end as this.

IV. The triumphant issue of the civil war has secured new advantages for American civilization. It was a triumph of what was best over what was worst in our political organization. It not only subjugated secession, but it put an end to those theories of state sovereignty which have always stood in the way of national unity and national advancement. And what is far more important in its bearings on every national interest, it overthrew and utterly annihilated slavery, the transcendent bane and disgrace of our social system. The republic, thus victorious in the mighty contest, towers in grandeur and renown, and steps forward to a place among the foremost powers of the world. In this altered position there is an inspiration such as has never been felt before, as there always is in a nation's history after heroic sacrifices and great achievements. The life of nations, as of men, is a perpetual struggle, and the future of both is always uncertain. It is, however, safe to say that our civilization is as likely to last as any other. It has no liability to disaster or decay which every other does not share with it. A thoughtful English writer has lately pointed out what he styles "Rocks Ahead," political, economic, religious, in the pathway of all existing civilizations. But if such "Rocks" exist, they are not more numerous in our pathway than in that of every other people, and we are at least as able as others to avoid them. We must not ask for exemption from the trials and dangers that belong to all human institutions. It is enough that our future is at least as fair and as inviting as that of other nations. With this we will be content,

> . . . "Nor bate a jot
> Of heart or hope : but still bear up and steer
> Right onward."

THE FORMATION AND ADOPTION OF THE CONSTITUTION OF THE UNITED STATES AS EXPLAINED IN MR. BANCROFT'S VOL-UMES.[1]

THE volumes of Mr. Bancroft which describe the formation and adoption of the Constitution of the United States were published when their author had more than half completed the eighty-second year of his life. A work so thorough in its research, so elaborate and accurate in its preparation, and so clear and condensed in its style, is certainly to be regarded as a rare exemplification of industry unabated and of intellectual powers unimpaired in the lapse of years. While, however, in these respects it bears no trace of intellectual decay, I cannot but hesitate to say that it was altogether wise for him to attempt so great and difficult a task at so advanced a period of life. But the fact that it had been his cherished aspiration for fifty years to close his History only with the inauguration of Washington disarms criticism and almost rebukes regret. The work is undoubtedly creditable to the genius of the venerable historian. The only drawback is that it is not in every respect all that the subject demands. Over and above thoroughness of research, judicious selection of materials, and accuracy of narration, to treat a critical epoch such as this with the best effect requires that the faculties of historic generalization and of historic imagination be in undiminished vigor and fullest activity. It is in those features of the work

[1] Read before the Friday Evening Club, November 23, 1883.

in which these faculties would be displayed, and possibly in those alone, that the careful reader discerns the difference between the volumes which were written in Mr. Bancroft's youth and those which have been written in his advanced age.

In his copious and interesting preface he writes, "That which I attempt to do is to trace the formation of the Federal Constitution from its origin to its establishment by the inauguration of its first President. The subject has perfect unity, and falls of itself into five epochs, or acts. I have spared no pains to compress the narrative within the narrowest limits consistent with clearness. In weighing authorities, I have striven to follow with strict severity the laws of historical criticism; ever careful to discriminate between those materials which are sources and those which are but helps or aids." But even with this purpose so distinctly announced, his two volumes are not exclusively the history of the formation of the Constitution, but rather the history of the United States during the period in which the Constitution was prepared for and formed, beginning precisely where his last preceding volume had ended. The volumes thus embrace passages and events which have no direct connection with the subject whose "perfect unity" he has so well set forth in his preface. They also become a continuation of the History of the United States, in which the change of the government from the Confederation to the Constitution is the most conspicuous event. This disregard of the essential unity of his plan may have been almost unintentional, and in many cases it would have been wholly unobjectionable. But here, it seems to me, it both disappoints and troubles the reader, and also embarrasses the author. The amazing changes in the minds of the American people, that led to the formation of the Constitution and rendered its adoption possible in the States, constitute the real subject of the volumes. It is a subject of very great importance, and is worthy to be treated by itself. Indeed, unless it be so treated it cannot be presented in its full proportions and effects, and made to teach its proper lessons for subsequent generations. Associated as it is, in these volumes, with the general course of events, and made merely a part of the general history of the period, it loses its distinctive unity and is divested of much of its impressiveness and interest. The deliverance of the republic from the Confederation and its settlement under the Constitution, next to the triumph of the Union arms in the civil war, I regard as the most honorable and most significant event in American history, and I regret that our illustrious historian has not made it stand forth by itself in all the historic and political importance which belongs to it.

Another serious disadvantage attends the modified unity which Mr. Bancroft has allowed to shape his volumes. He fails to supply to the reader any adequate classification of the agencies and events by which the grand consummation was accomplished. He in reality deals with all that belongs to the period, both those events and agencies which relate and those which do not relate to his special subject. The result is that the reader is obliged, to a large extent, to do the work of selection and classification for himself, instead of having it done for him by the historian. The subject, as is suggested in the preface to the volumes, is one of perfect unity, and is capable of a dramatic development of great interest and effect, such as I have no doubt the historian designed to give to it, but which his method made impossible. The result is that the most momentous and vital moral and social change recorded in the history of the country still remains to be adequately treated. Let it not be thought, however, that the narrative is not clear and well wrought, or that any material facts are omitted, still less that it is not discriminating and fair, and after all, perhaps, the best history of the formation of the Constitution which has thus far been written. What most of all is wanting is a more perfect unity of design, a more adequate grouping of the social forces which were at work among the American people, and possibly still more the exercise of that historic imagination which alone can transfer to the pictured page the majestic march of public events. That these are wanting in a historian of more than fourscore years is only what is to be expected. The extraordinary fact is that other faculties are in full vigor, and that the work as a whole is pervaded with an accuracy and thoroughness not surpassed in any previous volumes which have come from the pen of the venerable writer.

The government of the Confederation was not, save in a very vague sense, the creation of the American people, nor did it have the people for its subjects. It was in direct antagonism with the ideas of popular sovereignty which now prevail, for it was framed by the Revolutionary Congress, and adopted, not by the people, but by the state governments, and the state governments were its only constituents and its real masters. Indeed, popular sovereignty, though much blazoned in the Declaration of Independence and other political manifestoes, was then but imperfectly understood. In those days the people of the States chose their legislatures very much as some of the great corporations of our own days choose their directors. They vested them with full authority, and then left them to conduct the affairs of the State as they thought best. It was assumed that the legislatures were wiser than the people, and that whatever they might do the people would of course ratify and approve. All the powers of the Confederation government were vested in a single body known as a Congress. It had no separate executive head, it had no judiciary. This Congress assumed to govern the United States of America, — the new civil society which the Declaration of Independence had called into existence. It had assigned to itself all the legislative, executive, and judicial authority which pertained to this society. It conducted its correspondence with foreign governments by the agency of a Secretary of Foreign Affairs, its military administration by a Secretary of War, and its financial business by an officer whom it styled "Financier." Each State had a single vote. In all important matters the delegations of at least nine States must be present; in matters of mere form or routine those of seven States were sufficient. But no State could cast a vote at all unless two members, a majority of its delegation, were present. The members of Congress were paid by their respective States, and the States cared very little whether they were present or not, and often preferred to avoid the expense of supporting their delegations in Congress. The result of such an organization of the only governing body of the Confederation was that for a large part of the time it was without the number of delegations required for a quorum. It often made appeals to the absent States to send forward their delinquent delegations, but seldom with much effect. The little real business which Congress had the power to transact was thus continually delayed, and sometimes wholly frustrated. So long as the War of Independence engrossed the interest and attention of the country, Congress retained at least an appearance of importance and a shadow of authority. When this was ended, it sank into impotency and contempt. The leading men of the country ceased to be members, in part because of the rule of rotation prescribed in the Articles, but more largely because the public service of the States had become more attractive and more honorable than that of the United States.

The functions of this ill-devised and almost powerless government had to do, first, with the state governments, for it had no direct relations with the people; second, with the creditors of the country, both at home and abroad; and, third, with the governments of foreign nations, including the Indian tribes. It is not easy to determine in which one of these three departments of its agency it soon proved to be the most inefficient, or in which its ultimate failure was the most signal and disastrous.

I. As to the States. The Confederation as a government was from the beginning regarded by the States as a sort of disagreeable necessity, made indispensable only by the exigencies of the war. So soon as the war came to an end they looked upon it with constantly increasing jealousy and aversion. They thought of it, even in its weakness, as a perpetual menace to those conceits of state sovereignty with which their imaginations were filled. There was really nothing that Congress could do without the consent of the States. It levied quotas of troops, it made requisitions of money, it negotiated treaties, it contracted debts; but not one of these acts could go into full effect without the consent of the States. They were always ready to restrict it. In many of them it was regarded as a special favor if the requisitions of Congress were taken into consideration at all by the local legislature. During the five years immediately preceding 1787, of the requisitions made by Congress for national purposes, New Hampshire, North Carolina, South Carolina, and Georgia had paid nothing whatever; Connecticut and Delaware had each paid one third the amount; Massachusetts, Rhode Island, and Maryland had paid one half, Virginia three fifths, Pennsylvania nearly all, and New York more than all; while New Jersey had not only not paid, but had distinctly refused to pay, giving as the reason that New York had stripped her of her revenues by levying duties on all the commerce of the bay that washed the shores of both States.

II. With such inattention on the part of the States to requisitions for money, it is easy to see how impossible it was for Congress to deal with its creditors, both at home and abroad. Fisher Ames wrote that "it had bare revenue enough to buy stationery for its clerks and to pay the salary of its doorkeeper." Certificates of the indebtedness of the United States sunk to one tenth of their nominal value. This depreciation gave rise to unlimited distress in all mercantile classes. Merchants of unquestioned credit were compelled to pay discounts of thirty to fifty per cent. on their notes. The army had been disbanded in 1783. Its unpaid officers went to their homes in poverty, and multitudes of the unpaid soldiers, disabled in the service, obtained their daily bread only by beggary. The currency of the States was in inextricable confusion, while the Continental paper money was to silver as forty to one. Financial ruin brooded over all enterprises of business, and among the ignorant classes of the population was appearing that recklessness of social and moral obligation which always presages social decay. The insurrection in Massachusetts in 1786 was the natural result of the real sufferings and the dangerous theories that were prevalent all over the country.

III. This condition of affairs soon became partially known in foreign countries, and created the utmost distrust of all American obligations. The representatives of the government were treated with indignity at European courts, and were distinctly asked whether they represented the States as well as the United States. The Duke of Dorset, the British Minister of Foreign Affairs, wrote to the commissioners of the United States, who had come to London in 1785 to negotiate a treaty, that "the apparent determination of the respective States to control their own separate interests renders it indispensable that my court should be informed how far they are authorized to enter into engagements which any one of the States might not render totally useless and inefficient." English statesmen regarded it as a mistake that a treaty of peace had been made with the United States. They thought it would have been better merely to have acknowledged independence, and to have made commercial arrangements with such of the States as desired them. Both England and France believed that the American Union was a failure, and that the republic was fast tending to disintegration and ruin. So dilatory and irresponsible as to all public interests were the members of Congress that Marbois, the French minister, on arriving at Philadelphia, found there neither Congress nor any representative of the government to receive him. He wrote back to his court, " There exists no general government in America, neither Congress nor President, no head of any one administrative department," which at the time was literally true, though it was nearly a month after the session ought to have begun.

It should not be inferred, however, that the Confederation Congress was unmindful of the evils which had befallen the country, or of the inherent defects of the system which had been devised for its government. It had made repeated and most earnest endeavors to obtain larger powers from the state legislatures that always held it in control. So early as 1783 it had earnestly solicited from its sovereign masters the power to levy a duty of five per cent. on the imports of each State. With much difficulty and after long delay, consent was obtained from the legislatures of all the States with the single exception of Rhode Island. Her refusal annulled the whole measure. Mr. Hamilton was requested to prepare a remonstrance, but his arguments were of no avail with the legislature. New

York and Virginia subsequently revoked their consent, and though Congress in later years more than once repeated its solicitation, it was always without effect. Other amendments were proposed for increasing the powers of the central government, but they constantly failed of success; and it is a singular fact, especially in the light of our subsequent history, that the Articles of Confederation remained unaltered to the end of their existence. Every change required the consent of the legislatures of all the States. The most insignificant of the States could thus thwart the wishes of all the others. It was undoubtedly fortunate for the country that all these attempts to increase the powers of Congress ended as they did. Had they succeeded they would only have prolonged its useless life. The republic could be saved only by abandoning the Confederation, and with it all the false and pernicious ideas on which it rested.

From the midst of this general decay of all national sentiments and aspirations, from this prevailing predominance of local ideas and influences, this debasing jealousy between States and sections, how were the American people to be led up to the creation of a government which should rescue them from the frightful evils and perils of the time, and guide them onward towards the happy destiny that still loomed before them through the shadows of the future? The deliverance of the country from the humiliations of the Confederation and its establishment under the guidance of the Constitution were a work which transcends in importance all other achievements of American statesmanship. This work involved a social and moral transformation whose magnitude can scarcely be overestimated, and even to the broadest and wisest statesmen of the age, who contemplated it in advance, it seemed to be beyond any reasonable expectation. For, it is to be remembered, it was one thing clearly to point out the ex-

isting evils, and another and far more difficult to devise
a new government which the ill-instructed and wrongly
guided people of the States could be persuaded to adopt.
The political conceits of the time were monstrous and appalling. It was fondly believed that this was the only
country on which civil liberty had ever dawned, that
everywhere else the governments were tyrannies and the
people were slaves, and that the only danger to be watched
for and guarded against was the loss of liberty, and, worst
of all, that for a free people very little government was
required. The prevailing idea of the people was that by
their example they were to become the emancipators of all
the world. They vastly overestimated themselves. They
read almost incessantly the Declaration of Independence.
They breathed in its inflations. They became intoxicated
with its spirit. They looked with ignorant contempt on
other nations. There was really no more impracticable
or unamiable specimen of civilized humanity to be found
on earth than the free and independent American of the
first five and twenty years after the close of the war of
separation. By what agencies were such a people at length
induced to surrender the loose freedom of the Confederation, and place themselves under the obligations and
restraints of the Constitution? It is to this question
that Mr. Bancroft devotes several of the best chapters
of his work.

First of all, he reminds the reader that there still lingered in the country certain uniting influences, which
kept the States from final separation far more than their
written articles of agreement. Among these the most
important were : 1. A prevailing attachment to the Union.
In spite of the common conceits of state sovereignty, the
idea of the nation did not cease to stimulate and delight
the minds of the people. 2. The Articles of Confederation had specially provided for inter-citizenship among

the States, which had done much to promote intercourse and to diminish the importance of state lines. 3. More powerful than either of these was the interest which was felt by the States in the vast territory which had been surrendered to the United States, and had become the common property of the American people. The feeling had become general that every citizen had a right to the benefits of this magnificent national domain, which would be forfeited by a separation of the States. 4. The hostile commercial policy of England also greatly tended to strengthen the sentiment of nationality. The undisguised purpose of her ministry had been to divide the Confederation. They did not believe that it could last long, and they sought to hasten its overthrow, expecting it to be dissolved into separate republics, like those of Greece and Italy. The treatment the Confederation received from England helped to prevent this result and to hold it together.

But agencies such as these were effective merely for delaying or hindering separation. They were of themselves wholly insufficient for working the radical change that was needed in the opinions and modes of thought of the people. Coincident with these, however, were more positive influences, exerted by the foremost minds of the country, which had long been slowly working out the preparation that was required. Foremost among these was the personal authority of Washington. The Confederation had scarcely been submitted to the States, certainly it had not been adopted by them all, before he pointed out its inherent and fatal weaknesses. No man in the country had suffered as Washington had suffered from the incompetency and inefficiency of Congress. He never lost an opportunity of setting forth the necessity of a stronger government for the republic. In his Farewell Address to the army he had urged every officer and every soldier to use their influence in securing a change. He had done the same in his Address to the Governors of the Several States, at the close of the war. In subsequent years he appears to have written scarcely a letter to any public man in which he did not advert to the engrossing subject. Indeed, it is not easy to conceive how any single man could have done more to present to his countrymen the perils that threatened the republic from the weakness of the Confederation.

Next to Washington, Alexander Hamilton was undoubtedly the most efficient advocate and promoter of the change. He shared all the views of his great leader, and he thought even more profoundly on the manner in which the defects of the government were to be remedied. Mr. Bancroft makes less mention of his services in this respect than might naturally have been expected, — possibly for the reason that Hamilton, after the war, was but little in public life. He left Congress because he could do nothing in that body. He was, however, a member of the Convention, but on the withdrawal of his two associates the vote of New York was lost on the questions which subsequently arose. But his clear views of the strength which the government ought to possess, as they were put forth on many public occasions, and embodied with persuasive force in several series of articles in the journals of the time, attracted the attention of the whole country more than any other publications on the subject. And when the Constitution was framed and submitted to the conventions of the States, he wrote in its defense and explanation nearly all of those masterly papers now known as the " Federalist," and in every other way gave his constant efforts to securing its adoption.

Mr. Madison was more conspicuous in the Convention than Mr. Hamilton, and undoubtedly did more to shape the details of the Constitution, and he receives much stronger applause from Mr. Bancroft. He certainly deserves to be ranked among the foremost leaders of the movement towards a better government. Jefferson and John Adams were absent from the country, but many others might be named who contributed their full share to the work of bringing about the deliverance of the country from the dominion of its own follies and conceits. But even after a change was seen to be indispensable there was little agreement as to what the change ought to be, and neither Congress nor any one of the States was ready to take the first step. In this condition of affairs it fortunately happened that commissioners from Maryland and Virginia met at Mount Vernon to adjust the long-standing difficulties between these two States relating to the navigation of Chesapeake Bay and its tributary rivers. It was one of a large class of controversies between States with which the country was afflicted. The agreement of the commissioners was adopted by Maryland in December, 1785, and in communicating its action to Virginia the legislature proposed that all the States should be invited " to meet and regulate the commerce of the country." Virginia readily acceded to the proposal, and arranged a meeting to be held at Annapolis in September, 1786. This meeting was attended only by Virginia, Maryland, Delaware, New Jersey, Pennsylvania, and New York, though delegates were appointed by Massachusetts, Rhode Island, and New Hampshire, but failed to attend. The manifesto of this Convention, prepared by Hamilton, proposed still another step: that the States there represented should urge all the other States to meet with them in Philadelphia on the second Monday of the following May, to consider and to report to Congress what further provisions were needed to render the Articles of Confederation adequate to the exigencies of the Union. Madison immediately secured the unanimous approval of the Virginia legislature, and the Governor transmitted its action to Congress. But that body was unwilling to act on the recommendation of a State. After considerable delay, however, when delegates had been chosen by several States, it adopted an independent resolution, calling a convention to meet at the same place and on the same day, but without reference to what had been done either at Annapolis or in Virginia. Thus the object was accomplished, and Congress seemed to originate the measure which Virginia had forced upon its attention.

According to the dilatory habits of the time, the Convention did not have a quorum till more than two weeks after the appointed day. Its members, like those of Congress, were chosen by the state legislatures, for no distinct idea of popular sovereignty had yet been developed in American affairs. They were, however, wisely chosen, for among them were the ablest and most experienced statesmen of the country. Washington was President, and Franklin, at the age of eighty-four, was the senior member. Many of them had made special studies of the great masters of jurisprudence, in order to be qualified for the work before them. There was among them the utmost diversity of opinion as to what the Convention ought to do; whether merely to amend the Confederation in a greater or less degree, or to frame an entirely new government with powers hitherto unrecognized in the republic. The task which necessity demanded, and which it really performed, was one of surpassing difficulty. It was to frame a new constitution for a federal republic, — the most complex form of civil society. To found a monarchy would have been comparatively easy, had there been any material for such a government and a public opinion that would make it possible. The work to be done, in its essential peculiarities, was then without a parallel in history. All the existing governments of the world were growths, — not one was an original creation, — and they could afford no incidental suggestions in what was here to be done. If we add to this the clashing opinions of the country, the existence of negro slavery as a local institution, the crude ideas of government, the false theories of liberty, the jealousies and strifes that prevailed among the States, with all the bad precedents and bad influences of the Confederation, the probabilities of success appear exceedingly small.

The Convention sat with closed doors, and secrecy was enjoined on its members. At its opening session the Virginia delegation presented to the body through Governor Randolph a plan for a new constitution, which had been prepared by Madison as a basis for discussion. In its essential features it was mildly national rather than federal. Other plans were subsequently submitted, but the Virginia plan, more than any other, though with a multitude of modifications, was the groundwork of the Constitution. The first great question which it raised was whether the States should be on an equality in all respects, as they were in the Confederation. This question, with all that it involved, was debated with the utmost acrimony, and the votes that were taken repeatedly showed the same number of States on either side, with others divided and not voting. At the end of thirty-four days the Convention had made no progress, and members despairingly wrote to their friends that nothing could be done. At this juncture, Franklin made his famous speech, in which he said, "The wit of man is exhausted. I firmly believe that, unless the Lord build the house, they labor in vain that try to build it," and proposed that the daily sessions be opened with prayers. The whole matter was then referred to a committee, and through their agency the great compromises of the Constitution were prepared and adopted, and positive nationality became its pervading character. Had this not been secured, the Convention would have ended in ignominious failure.

But after all these great adjustments had been made, there still remained the stupendous work of devising the machinery by which these essential agreements should be carried into effect. It is here quite as much as in the agreements themselves that the real statesmanship of the Convention is displayed. The compromises of the Constitution were dictated by the necessities of the country. The Convention was compelled to accept them. Not so with the innumerable contrivances and adjustments which are designed to combine the different branches of the government into a harmonious whole, to give efficiency to every part, and to concentrate the united strength of the whole for the enactment and maintenance of law, and for the defense alike of the Union and of every State. Arrangements like these in other countries have slowly grown up in the lapse of ages. Here they had to be created in advance, and in doing this the far-seeing statesmen of the Convention achieved, perhaps, the most wonderful part of their work.

The sessions of the Convention had begun on the 14th of May; they terminated on the 17th of September. For several of the closing weeks, the Constitution, which had been substantially agreed upon, was in the hands of committees, who perfected its provisions and gave the final touches to its forms of expression. Its closing article provided that its ratification by the Convention, chosen by the people of nine States, should be "sufficient for the establishment of the Constitution between the States so ratifying." On the 17th of September it was finally adopted by the delegations of the eleven States that were represented in the Convention, though three conspicuous members refused to give it their signatures. Many did not believe that it would be accepted by eleven States;

some perhaps did not desire it to be. The general feeling, however, was that they had done better than they anticipated, and the best that was possible. Mr. Bancroft says: "The members were awestruck at the result of their councils; the Constitution was a nobler work than any one of them had believed it possible to devise. They all on that day dined together and took a cordial leave of each other. Washington at an early hour of the evening retired ' to meditate on the momentous work which had been executed.' "

The instrument was now in the hands of the people, who were to choose the state conventions. It was immediately assailed with a violence and fury which it is now difficult to explain. It certainly sprang from no well-grounded objections to the Constitution itself. The new government was denounced in advance as a rich man's government, an aristocracy, a gilded bait, a triple-headed monster, a stepping-stone to monarchy, and by a multitude of similar names suggestive of the low tone of the popular mind and the narrow range of the popular intelligence. Delaware was the first to accept the Constitution, which she did unanimously on December 6. Pennsylvania adopted it on December 12. These were followed by New Jersey, Georgia, Connecticut, Massachusetts, Maryland, South Carolina, and New Hampshire, on June 21, 1788. Nine States had now adopted the Constitution, the number required for its establishment. But there continued to be great anxiety among its friends. It was easy to see that without Virginia, and especially without New York, the Union would still be dangerously incomplete. Four days later, on June 25, Virginia gave her ratification, and New York on July 26, by a majority of two votes. North Carolina did not adopt it till November, 1789, eight months after the inauguration of the government, and Rhode Island not till May, 1790, when the government had been in full operation more than a year, and then by a majority of two votes. The great character of Washington at the head of the nation had already done much to subdue the opposition of these dilatory States, and to draw the whole people towards a government of which he was the head. Mr. Bancroft does not state it too strongly when he writes that " but for him the country could not have achieved its independence; but for him it could not have formed the Union; and now but for him it could not have set the federal government in successful motion." [1]

Nowhere was hostility to the Constitution so bitter as in Rhode Island and New York. These were the only States in which the passions of the people broke out in riotous proceedings. Rhode Island, especially, clung to the Confederation with a tenacity unequaled in any other State. The people of her rural districts seemed to delight in its impotence and inefficiency, for it left them undisturbed in the delusions of their paper money, with which they sought to pay their debts. Her legislature, under the control of its rural majority, had refused to send delegates to the Convention, giving as a reason that it had no power to do so, inasmuch as the delegates to Congress, since March, 1777, had been chosen by the people of the State, which was true. It refused on seven different occasions to call a convention of the State to act on adopting the Constitution, but submitted it to the people in their town meetings, a mode of procedure wholly at variance with the requirements of the instrument itself. Five of these seven occasions were after it had been adopted by nine States, and was therefore sure to go into effect, and two were after it had really gone into effect, and the federal government had been organized according to its provisions. The State also continued

[1] Vol. ii. p. 360.

to vote for delegates to the Confederation Congress, just as if that body had not been superseded. Like the English Jacobites, she still clung to the old dynasty after it had been destroyed. The reason which she gave for this display of irrational and offensive oddity was that the State, though she stood alone, was bound by the Articles of Confederation till they were legally set aside. The real reason was that the men then in power were too ignorant and narrow to understand the obvious interests of the State, and so wedded to their paper money that they could not be induced to do anything which would threaten its overthrow. The State was treated with the utmost indulgence by the new government. On the petition of the merchants of Providence, Newport, and Bristol, Congress fixed a day so late as the 15th of January, 1790, as the time when her vessels must be treated as foreign in the ports of the United States. The time was afterwards extended to the 15th of April; but they were not molested even then, for the legislature, after its seven refusals, had now called a convention to act upon the Constitution. A little longer delay, however, would have subjected her citizens to very great embarrassments and sufferings. A continued persistence in her experiment of separate existence as an independent State would have led, of necessity, to her dismemberment, and destruction.

Her conduct at this time of infatuation brought an injury to her character from which the State did not soon recover. She was visited with contempt and every kind of obloquy. Her name became a by-word in nearly every part of the country, and it was not till another generation had arisen that she began to recover from the consequences of the bad influences which then controlled her action as a State.

The conduct of New York was scarcely less discreditable and vastly more harmful than that of Rhode Island.

She had persistently disregarded the maritime rights of
her nearest neighbors, New Jersey and Connecticut, and
had long been the centre of an unyielding and reckless
opposition to every measure that was designed to give to
the government the control either of revenues or of commerce. She sent only three delegates to the Convention.
Two of these were determined anti-Federalists, and they
withdrew so soon as that body decided to frame a Constitution, and not to amend the Articles of Confederation.
The remaining delegate, most fortunately for the State
and for the country, was Alexander Hamilton. He could
not give the vote of his State, but he did give the whole
weight of his commanding influence and his great abilities to the success of the Constitution, and to him its
final adoption by New York is mainly to be ascribed. Its
foremost opponent was Governor George Clinton, who
presided in the state convention and controlled a large
majority of its members. But neither he nor his followers dared wholly to reject it. This would not only
have destroyed the union of the States, but it would have
compelled New York to maintain an army and a navy in
order to preserve the commercial supremacy which she
had already attained. New York, no more than Rhode
Island, could prosper out of the Union. The aim of the
opposition, therefore, was to embarrass the question as
much as possible. They proposed a multitude of amendments, and sought to make their incorporation into the
Constitution a condition of its adoption by the State, and
at the same time they voted to invite all the States to
meet in a second convention for framing another Constitution. The Federalists were alarmed at the situation.
Hamilton was their acknowledged leader. For months he
had given his days and nights to the success of the Constitution. He had organized a system of rapid communication among its friends in every State. He published the

successive numbers of the "Federalist." He wrote many letters. Swift riders brought him intelligence from New England, which, by others equally swift, he dispatched to Madison, in Virginia or in Congress. To him Hamilton now submitted the question whether any concession ought to be made as to a conditional adoption. Madison immediately replied that a conditional adoption is not an adoption. The crisis was one of great difficulty and danger. Hamilton, however, and his associates succeeded in getting the call for another national convention and the vote for adoption, with the words " on condition that " changed to " in full confidence that," both united in a single resolution. - This finally passed the Convention by a majority of two votes, the same majority as in Rhode Island, and even then it was something less than an unqualified adoption. But the qualifying clause was happily made nugatory by the amendments immediately recommended by Congress and adopted by the States, in the mode prescribed by the Constitution itself. Thus, as it were, against the determination of her own people and their representatives, did the great State of New York ratify the Constitution of the United States; and it is to be observed that neither here nor in Rhode Island, the two States in which the vote was the smallest, nor in any other State, did there appear the slightest dissatisfaction with what had been done. The defeated party was as submissive to the new government as the triumphant party. The members of the one immediately became as loyal as those of the other ; and both were equally ready to accept the offices and to discharge the responsibilities which the Constitution had called into existence.

I have thus suggested the outlines of the momentous moral and social as well as political transformation which was wrought in the minds of the American people at the period of the formation and adoption of the Constitution.

The magnitude and the results of this change amazed even those who had labored most earnestly to bring it about. It transcended their utmost expectations. It was as if the nation had been born into a new political life. A new blood seemed to flow in its veins and new joys glowed in its heart. In the place of dangerous political theories, of narrow ideas, of local prejudices and inflated political conceits, there immediately sprang up national sentiments, comprehensive interests, patriotic aspirations. The people of the States began to abandon their notions of state sovereignty, their groundless alarms lest a new tyranny should be imposed upon them, and, in obedience to the voice of the public reason, they accepted a frame of government whose essential features were directly repugnant to all that they had been struggling to secure. There is no other proceeding recorded in Mr. Bancroft's twelve volumes of American history which does so much credit to American character. The resistance to British taxation, the Declaration of Independence, the war of separation, all were less remarkable than the result of this great struggle between the good and the evil tendencies then embosomed in the republic. In other struggles they had won victories over their enemies; in this they conquered themselves. Before they had contended for independence and for greater liberty; now they gave up a portion of their independence and placed wholesome restraints on their liberty — a vastly higher achievement, as self-denial is always higher than self-indulgence.

Professor Seelye, in his lectures on "The Expansion of England," refers to the separation of the American colonies as, perhaps, the event foremost in importance in the history of the English race, for it called into being another Britain greater than the island "that rules the waves." But of how little importance might this separation have proved to be, had the Constitution not been formed, or, when formed, had it not been accepted, and the loose and disjointed union of the Confederation been left to shape the then dubious destiny of the American States! Both Spain and Portugal had colonies in America, and like those of England, they too separated from the mother country. But no greater Spain or greater Portugal had sprung, or is likely ever to spring, from them. It is the Constitution of the United States — the guarantee of liberty regulated by law, combining in harmonious relations the local governments of many separate States with the central government of the single united nation — self-governing provinces wrought together in a self-governing union, — it is this solution of the most difficult of problems that has given paramount and ever-increasing importance to the separate nationality of the English colonies in America, and has secured for the widespread English race a leadership among mankind such as otherwise it could not have attained. Great Britain now looks proudly abroad over another Britain vastly greater than herself, but still an expansion of herself and of the civilization which she represents, spreading over nearly one quarter of the planet. Of the greater part of this expanded Britain she is still the mistress and ruler. If she is able to keep together and govern this stupendous empire, she must do it very largely, as her own statesmen admit, by employing the methods and following the example furnished by the Constitution made by her American children nearly a hundred years ago, of which Mr. Gladstone has given his estimate in the following familiar sentence, inscribed by Mr. Bancroft on the first page of each of his volumes: " As the British Constitution is the most subtle organism which has proceeded from progressive history, so the American Constitution is the most wonderful work ever struck off at a given time by the brain and purpose of man."

ASYLUM AND EXTRADITION AMONG NATIONS.[1]

As I rise to read the paper of the evening before this Historical Society, I cannot forbear, first of all, to give some brief utterance to the sense of loss which we all experience in the death of our distinguished associate, Professor Diman. To me it is like a personal bereavement. Elsewhere, and on other occasions, his character will be delineated as a scholar, a professor in the university, a Christian minister, and an eminent citizen. Here we think of him in his connection with this Society, and the pursuits in which we are engaged. We all recall his readiness to instruct us by his papers, and to contribute his services in the work of collecting and preserving the materials for our state history. We remember, too, the volumes pertaining to Rhode Island which he has so carefully edited, the public discourses in which he has celebrated our local anniversaries and the characters of our distinguished citizens, and above all, how important was his influence in promoting historical studies, in his capacity as professor of history in the university. The professorship of history was not established till about the time of his graduation, but in such incidental work as was then done, I well remember the taste and aptitude for this class of studies which he evinced. Twelve years later, when the professorship became vacant, I was invited by those charged with making the appointment to name

[1] Read before the Historical Society of Rhode Island, March 9, 1880.

some son of the college who might be selected to fill it, and without hesitation I named Mr. Diman, then settled as a minister in Brookline, Mass. It was a well-considered suggestion, and I look back upon it with proud and perfect satisfaction.

He entered upon his work in the university in the autumn of 1864, and for more than sixteen years he has prosecuted it with ever-growing and brilliant success. His instructions embraced the long period which has elapsed since the fall of the Roman Empire, and were designed to explain the origin and formation of the states of modern Europe, and to trace the progress of modern civilization. Upon this subject, in all its departments, he had gathered large stores of information from the literature of many languages. But it is not learning alone that constitutes the true qualification for a professor of history. Professor Diman was penetrated with that comprehensive, liberal, and Christian philosophy which looks beyond the facts into the laws that govern them, which searches for the hidden meaning of the changes alike in states and in the opinions of mankind, and which in the long sequence of ages recognizes the process by which the Divine Ruler of the world unfolds the destiny of man and society.

He worked easily and cheerfully, with a candid and unbiased spirit which imparted itself to those whom he taught. Nor was his influence or his work confined to the university. They spread themselves over the community. He taught classes of ladies, beginning in many cases when they had just ceased to be school-girls, and going on after they had become women and heads of families. For several years, also, he had given courses of lectures on the constitutional history of the United States to the State Normal School, which were received with very great satisfaction and interest, and drew large assemblies at their delivery.

The Usage of Asylum, or, as it is styled in recent times, the Right of Asylum, is of very ancient origin, and is very widely spread among mankind. It would seem to be as old as civil society itself, and it has prevailed so extensively in early periods of history as to have acquired a special and mysterious significance. It was long associated with religion, but religion seems not to have been the source from which it sprang. It is to be regarded rather as the expression of a sentiment of dissatisfaction, which springs spontaneously in the minds of men, with the institutions and operations of all human justice, — a sentiment which revolts from the taint of selfishness and tyranny, of private hostility and revenge, that so generally affected the making and the execution of all human laws. This sentiment, especially in early ages, when individual rights were insecure, created a certain sympathy with the offender, and made men not only unwilling to assist in his arrest and punishment, but willing to afford him, if not assistance, at least some forlorn opportunity to escape the penalties he had brought upon himself; to open for him some place of refuge in which he might be secure from the seizure of those who pursued him in the name of the public authority. This sentiment finds less to justify it in civilized ages, but it has not become wholly extinct even in the most civilized countries. Religion very easily took this usage of asylum under its own sanction and care, and for many ages it was associated exclusively with religious institutions. Religion thus proclaimed that no criminal should be taken from its temples or altars, or any of its sacred places, and that all who had found a refuge in these places should be beyond the reach of the civil power, at least till their cause could be examined and decided upon by its own ministers, acting under the sanction of the divinity.

The oldest historical trace of this usage of asylum is

found among the Hebrews. By the provisions of their laws six cities were especially set apart as cities of refuge, to either of which the slayers of men might flee, and remain beyond the reach of that terrible agent of Jewish justice, the avenger of blood. The temple, also, and the altar of burnt-offerings appear to have afforded the same protection. This Hebrew law was doubtless only a formal recognition of the custom of a still earlier time, — an authoritative declaration of a sentiment which the Jews had long shared with other portions of mankind. Its design, its effect everywhere, was to rescue human life from the violence to which it was exposed in ages when personal passion and revenge so often assumed the name of justice, and usurped the authority of law.

Among the early Greeks the same usage prevailed. The groves and temples, and all places sacred to the divinities, were made asylums for criminals, and indeed for persons of every description who were fleeing from those who sought to injure them. No punishment could be inflicted, and no violence of any kind could be used, within these sacred inclosures, nor could any one be taken from them by force to be punished elsewhere. In later ages different temples were especially designated as asylums for different classes of fugitives, as that of Diana at Ephesus for fugitive debtors, and that of Theseus at Athens for fugitive slaves, and the shrines of Mercury everywhere for thieves. Here the religious idea had become conspicuous, and the sacredness of the place seemed to be the controlling consideration. The fugitive was protected, in appearance at least, not because of any sympathy which he deserved, but rather because the divinity would be offended if he were molested. It is probable, however, that humane feeling may still have prompted the usage, and that religion only gave it its sanction, and invested it with its own sacred authority, and thus made it more effective in its benevolent agency.

With equal distinctness is the same usage traceable among the early Romans. If there is any truth in the legends recorded by Livy, Romulus had scarcely completed the walls of his city, when he made it an asylum for the criminals and outcasts of all Italy, and invited them to come and share its rising fortunes. There was no period of Roman history, from the days of the earliest kings to those of the latest emperors, when the various sacred places of all the Roman cities were not constantly resorted to as asylums; not by fugitives from justice alone, but also by those who sought to escape from every form of outrage or oppression. The usage was the common law of the state long before it was enacted by the senate or decreed by the emperors. Indeed, it was so thoroughly wrought into the social system, that it at last proved to be difficult for either senate or emperor to modify or control it. The right of asylum became greatly extended as the sacred spots grew more numerous, and as nearly all the divinities of the world one after another set up their shrines in and around the imperial city. After the empire was established, the statues of the Cæsars were made to rank with those of the gods, and criminals who were able to touch them, or reach the inclosures in which they stood, claimed the same privilege as if they had fled to a temple, or to the wayside shrine of a divinity.

But wholly independent of any influence of either the laws of Moses or the mythology of Greece or Rome, the same usage of asylum also appeared among the Franks, the Visigoths, and the Germans, on their settlement in Western Europe. It became especially conspicuous in Lyons and Vienne, and in some German cities it lingered, as it has also in Edinburgh, almost to our own times.

A prescriptive institution like this would be sure to be constantly abused by those who resorted to it to escape the penalties of the law. The temples of the gods and the sacred places of religion were often crowded with the guilty and the depraved, who sought to place themselves beyond the reach of the public prosecutor. The right of asylum, thus perverted from its original uses, was often disregarded by the civil authorities, and well-known criminals were taken from its protection even at the risk of every penalty which the divinities could inflict. This is more than once mentioned in the Greek annals. In Rome the abuses became still more flagrant, but so powerful were the priests, and so superstitious the masses of the people, that for many generations no government dared to attempt their reformation. Tiberius is said to have been the first who succeeded in arresting these abuses, and imposing effectual restrictions on the usage of religious asylum. He was able to accomplish this mainly by securing a wiser and juster administration of the laws, and by preventing, to a great extent, the wrongs and outrages which this usage was designed to remedy. He limited it to the temples and altars of certain divinities, and designated certain crimes for which the offender could not take refuge in them. He narrowed the inclosures within which it could take effect, and he reduced the number of asylums in all the cities. The abuses, however, returned, and so long as the line of pagan emperors lasted, the temples of the gods continued to offer impunity to every sort of crime, and thereby to swell the dangerous multitude of the lawless and the dissolute.

When Christianity established itself in the empire and became the religion of the state, the asylum of the ancient temples was immediately transferred to the churches. Christianity had, from the beginning, been the religion of the poor and the oppressed. It was always opposed to violence and tumult and strife. It had no sympathy with the guilty. It did not care to shield even the fugitive unless he was innocent. For a long time the change was most salutary. But the empire was already falling to decay, and ere long the barbarian took possession of its ruins. In the universal wreck of society the Christian Church was the only organized and vigorous social force that survived, the only one that possessed either the courage or the ability to interpose in behalf of justice and right and humanity. The duties that were thus forced upon the Church contributed to make her ministers the leaders and lawgivers of the new kingdoms that sprang up in Western Europe. In every one of them the right of asylum, or of sanctuary as it had now come to be called, was fully recognized, and the churches and sacred buildings in many of them soon began to be the resort of criminals and fugitives of every description. The ends of justice were frequently perverted just as they had been in the days of the heathen temples. Great ecclesiastics clung to the usage just as the pagan priests had done before them, and it was as much abused and as firmly rooted as it had ever been. Governments complained of it, but they dared not destroy it; the best men of the Church were ashamed of it and denounced it, but they could not shut their eyes to the manifold benefits that were mingled with its vast abuses. The masses of the people demanded its continuance as a prescriptive right, which in those ages of depotism and violence they could not afford to surrender. It had its root, too, in the universal sentiment that the civil authority was still too vengeful and arbitrary, and in all respects too barbarous, to be allowed an unobstructed sway over the interests and lives of those whom it assumed to govern.

From causes like these this ecclesiastical sanctuary, though restricted by the later popes and often for a time disregarded by the more powerful of the temporal sovereigns, continued to be a recognized custom in every state

in Europe till the close of the Middle Age. As governments became more fully established, and more humane
and just in their administration, the necessity for such a
custom was diminished. In Italy, where the Church was
powerful and the State was weak, it prevailed to the
greatest extent, and survived in a modified form down to
the occupation of that country by Napoleon in the early
part of the present century. Indeed, the environs of the
papal palaces and the houses of the cardinals at Rome
still served as sanctuaries for fugitive debtors even so
lately, as 1871 when Victor Emmanuel, King of Italy,
made that city his capital. In Germany it was always
more limited than in any other country, and it wholly dis-
appeared there with the coming of the Reformation. In
England it was in full force till the reign of Edward III.
(1487), when it was first restricted by a papal bull. In
the reign of Elizabeth the privilege was denied to all who
were charged with treason and several other crimes, but
was continued to debtors. In that reign it appears to
have been a subject of unusual popular interest. Shake-
speare has not less than twelve references to it, and in
" Richard III." he makes the cardinal express the importance which was attached to it by the Church.

> "God in heaven forbid
> We should infringe the holy privilege
> Of blessed sanctuary ! not for all this land
> Would I be guilty of so deep a sin."

It survived the Reformation for the benefit of debtors, and
was not finally taken from the churches in England until
1697, in the reign of William III. The latest remnant
of it in Scotland is still attached to the palace of Holy-
rood, an ancient abbey, which retains the right of afford-
ing temporary sanctuary to certain classes of innocent
debtors.

Wholly independent of the sanctuary which the Church so long maintained and so reluctantly surrendered was the asylum which was afforded by the feudal towns during the latter portion of the Middle Age. These little hamlets which sprang up on the domains of the great proprietors, almost from their origin, made it a point to protect the fugitive serfs who sought refuge at their gates. Once within the limits of a town, the right of the feudal proprietor over them was sure to be contested by force. At length it was wholly abandoned. This usage of asylum came to be allowed by common consent, and was at length enforced by decrees of the sovereigns, who ordained that any serf residing in a town "a year and a day" should be free and entitled to be ranked among the burghers. The operation of this form of asylum was always beneficent. It afforded a way of escape from feudal servitude. It aided largely in increasing the population and strength of the towns, and did its part in creating the early institutions of civil liberty in Europe. It had not any necessary connection with religion, though it may have often invoked the sanction of the Church. It had its origin in a love of freedom and a hatred of feudalism, in a sentiment of humanity, and in the common interest which the burghers had in the growth of their free communities.

But this usage of asylum presents itself in its most imposing form in the relations of nations with one another. When the temples of paganism, the churches of Christianity, and the cities of the feudal age had all ceased to afford shelter to the fugitive in his own country, he has in later times found it in a foreign land. The states of Europe long sustained only loose relations with each other. Their boundaries were vaguely defined They were often at war. They were rivals in trade. They were jealous of each other's strength. The legal *status* of their subjects when away from their country was uncertain and precarious. But in spite of all this the first instinct, even of the feeblest sovereignty, always was to resist any inroad of a foreign jurisdiction, any exercise of a foreign authority within its territory. Under this impulse no government would consent to surrender a fugitive of any description who had crossed the border and sought its hospitality. This determination too would be strengthened by considerations of humanity, by a sensitiveness to its independence, and often, perhaps, by a desire to add to its population. Nations, too, then as now, differed in freedom and in the justice of their laws. Refuge would be sought and emigrations would be made from the less free to the more free. It thus became a dictate of humanity as well as of self-interest that every country should proclaim itself an inviolable asylum for those who placed themselves under its protection. The fugitive and the exile, the victims of despotic power, of popular hatred, of religious persecution, as well as of legalized justice, were all safe if they could touch the soil of a foreign country.

This international asylum had its origin, no doubt, in mixed motives, as do all human institutions, but its necessity in the age in which it began was never seriously questioned, and it has long been accepted as an essential principle of public law. It began to be asserted in an age of intense international hatreds and of fierce religious wars, — in an age when popular freedom was beginning its long struggle with prescriptive despotism, and multitudes of the noblest spirits in Western Europe hastened to take advantage of it. Its beneficent agencies have given it an importance and a sanctity which never rested on the sanctuary either of pagan temple or Christian church. The French Huguenots, to the number of 500,000, hunted down in their own country, sought the shelter of this asylum in foreign lands.   The persecuted Puritans of England, in like manner, fled for refuge to Switzerland and Holland.   In later ages, the proscribed scholar and the crushed artisans have made themselves exiles on foreign shores in order to secure an intellectual or industrial liberty which was denied to them at home.   The right of asylum has proved itself equally benignant to princes and their subjects.   How many a monarch, when driven from his throne, has had recourse to a foreign asylum for his own life and those of his family and followers!   The last three sovereigns who sat upon the throne of France saved themselves from the revolutionary fury of their own subjects only by seeking the inviolable sanctuary of British protection ; and there have been periods in our own history when no inconsiderable portion of our foreign-born population were exiles, and could not have safely returned to the country of their birth.

I have thus illustrated at length the progress and the agencies of the ancient usage or right of asylum in the several forms in which it has prevailed.   It is evident, I think, that in each one of its forms it has been a most beneficent custom, notwithstanding the perversions and abuses to which it has been so frequently liable.   In its origin it was prompted by humane instincts in the minds of men, which barbarism did not wholly obliterate, and which civilization has not wholly outgrown.   Within the last hundred years there has arisen among the leading nations of the world another practice, of an entirely opposite character, which is now urging its claims to universal recognition.   The practice I refer to is that of surrendering to the government of their country certain classes of the criminals who have taken refuge in other countries.   It is obvious that this usage is, in its operation, directly at variance with the usage of asylum, and indeed that, so far as it goes, it is a positive infraction of the principle on which asylum rests. It is claimed, however, that, in the present relations of civilized nations with each other, both justice and good policy require this infraction to be made, and the right of asylum, in certain cases, to be sacrificed to a higher end which cannot otherwise be attained. Portions of the world the most widely separated from each other have been brought near together by the modern facilities of intercourse. The same line of railroad now often runs through many different countries. Steam navigation has bridged the broadest rivers, and has closely connected the opposite shores even of the Atlantic. The perpetrator of a crime may now reach a distant land almost before his guilt is discovered, if he has friends to assist him and money to pay his way. Besides this, criminals are no longer, as they once were, obscure and powerless members of the community. They often hold prominent positions of public or private trust ; they have the control of wealth, and not unfrequently they are even able to dictate the terms on which their crimes may be compounded, and their offense is permitted to go unpunished. In these altered circumstances of mankind, it is urged that, unless justice is to be set aside by the increased facilities for escaping it, the right of asylum ought, in certain cases at least, to be waived, and the fugitive criminal who has taken advantage of it ought to be surrendered for trial and punishment in the country whose laws he has violated. This surrender has come to be denominated extradition.

It should be observed that, in the absence of a special agreement for the purpose, a surrender of this kind has not hitherto been deemed to be a matter of obligation ; nor is it an act which one nation, in the absence of agreement, has any right to demand of another. The practice has thus far been regarded as purely a matter of international comity, and as made obligatory only by the express stipulations of treaties. Such treaties are now not uncommon among nations. They always specify the crimes for which the extradition of the criminal may be demanded, the nature of the evidence that is to be insisted on, and sometimes other particulars relating to the manner in which the transaction shall be accomplished. All these specifications are designed to secure such judicial carefulness and formality as ought to attend so grave a proceeding.

But while, as a general rule, fugitive criminals are not surrendered, save in accordance with treaty agreements to this effect, such a surrender has not unfrequently been made as an act of comity in the interests of justice, in cases where no such agreement existed. It is certainly an act which every nation has a right to do if it chooses. Two notable instances of this kind have occurred in our own recent history. In 1864, in the height of the civil war, the government of Spain represented to that of the United States that a Spaniard named Arguelles had committed a crime repugnant alike to justice and humanity, and had escaped to New York; and that, as no treaty of extradition existed between the two countries, his surrender would be accepted as an act of special comity by her Catholic Majesty, the Queen of Spain. Arguelles was an officer of the Spanish army, and also deputy governor of a district in the island of Cuba. In this latter office, he was especially intrusted with rescuing a cargo of over one thousand African slaves, which had been brought into a Cuban port contrary to the laws of Spain. He seized the negroes and held them, ostensibly for restoration to Africa, and, for his success in doing this, received a large reward from his government. But while they were in his charge, he conspired with others and made sale of one hundred and forty-one of them to planters in Cuba, representing to the government that they had died, and fled to New York with the proceeds of his treacherous and nefarious traffic. The President of the United States immediately caused the man to be arrested and delivered to an agent of the Spanish government, by whom he was taken back to Cuba for trial. The surrender called forth sharp criticism ; first, because it was made in the absence of any treaty agreement ; and, second, because it was not attended with any judicial inquiry into the evidence of the man's guilt. A resolution of censure was introduced in the House of Representatives. This resolution called forth from Secretary Seward a communication which, in thoroughness of discussion, is scarcely surpassed by any state paper which the secretary ever produced. It secured the defeat of the resolution by a very large majority. It is unquestionably one of the fullest presentations of the whole subject of extradition that can be found in the annals of American diplomacy. It vindicated completely the right of the President to make the surrender, and at the same time demonstrated his obligation to make it, not only on the ground of justice, but also on account of many similar acts of comity which our government had asked and received from Spain, in days when our West India commerce was threatened by pirates who were constantly taking refuge in her colonial ports. We were also in the midst of a civil war which had been brought upon us by slavery, and it was not for the government to hesitate in delivering up to justice a fugitive slave-trader. The vindication thus made has been accepted as complete, so far as the surrender in the absence of a treaty was concerned, but I think it has been generally held that even in so clear a case, there should have been a formal and public examination, before a court, of the evidence on which the man's guilt was made to rest.

The second instance to which I have referred was the surrender of Tweed, the famous financial politician of the city of New York. What diplomatic correspondence took place in relation to this proceeding I have not been able to ascertain. The fact appears to be that, after many tribulations at home and long wanderings abroad, he landed in Spain. Almost as soon as he stepped on shore he was arrested by the police, on the evidence of his resemblance to certain photographs in their possession, and, with as little formality as had attended the case of Arguelles, was placed on board a national vessel of the United States, brought to New York, and delivered, not to the government of the United States, nor to that of the State of New York, but to the municipal authorities of the city. The Spanish police who arrested him, it is said, thought their prisoner was the abductor of Charley Ross, and they regarded him with great abhorrence. The two cases resemble each other in the absence of all judicial inquiry as to the evidence of guilt, or even as to that of personal identity, and the prompt surrender of Tweed has been commonly understood to have been an act of reciprocity for the surrender of Arguelles.

Concerning treaties of extradition as they now exist, several considerations are worthy to be mentioned.

I. Such treaties, by common consent, do not embrace political offenders. Whether the exception is inserted in the treaty or not, no nation ever fails to make it in practice. Such offenders always remain safe in the asylum to which they have fled. It is, however, generally conceded that, while enjoying this security, they are not to be permitted to do anything to harm the country or the government of the country from which they have escaped. They are not to make their new-found home the theatre of conspiracies against the life of the government, or the base of hostile operations of any kind. In 1858, the Emperor Louis Napoleon came near being assassinated in

the streets of Paris by an infernal machine prepared by
Orsini, an Italian, who was one of a large company of
republican refugees residing in London. The French
government complained to that of Great Britain that it
was harboring assassins within its asylum. The charge
was indignantly repelled, but there was no doubt that the
conspiracy to murder the emperor had been formed by
the refugees in England, and that they were continually
plotting against other governments in Europe. The ministry, recognizing their obligation to prevent such crimes,
introduced in the House of Commons a bill entitled the
" Conspiracy to Murder Bill." The principle of the bill
was undoubtedly right, but the opposition raised the cry
of French dictation. The result was the House of Commons refused to pass it, and Lord Palmerston, one of the
strongest and most popular of ministers, was compelled to
resign. The bill, however, three years later, became a
law without opposition.

Indeed, it is due to the English government that this
exemption of political refugees, during their good behav-
ior, from all liability to extradition has come to be a
recognized doctrine of international law. Nowhere has
the great principle of asylum been so persistently maintained as in England, and that, too, amidst difficulties and
embarrassments of the gravest character. During the
long era of revolutions in Europe, at the close of the past
and the beginning of the present century, England became the common asylum of the persecuted and the oppressed of every nation and of every party. Thousands
of such exiles flocked to her hospitable shores. The
countries from which they fled still feared and hated
them, for they were in many instances eminent as statesmen, as ecclesiastics, as scholars, or as soldiers; and
England was constantly urged to deliver them or drive
them away from her protection. But she never yielded

to the importunities addressed to her. She watched over her unbidden guests with constant vigilance; she gave them all the rights of her free asylum; she even fed them from her bounty; but she did not suffer them to violate her laws or abuse her hospitality. Her courts were always open to foreigners, and almost at the same time presented the extraordinary spectacle of the Emperor of Russia and the First Consul of France prosecuting for libel English journals edited by refugees, and each of them winning a verdict from an English jury.

II. Extradition treaties impose no obligation for surrender except for the crimes specially named in them. Demands for persons accused of any other crimes are not recognized. Those crimes only are mentioned which are of such heinous nature as to be generally condemned by the moral sentiments of civilized nations, and also such as with both parties to the treaty receive substantially the same punishment. It is generally held that an accused person ought not to be given up to a punishment severer than that which he would receive in the country in which he has found refuge.

III. Great Britain and the United States are the only important nations which consent to the surrender of their own citizens or subjects. Most other states refuse to make treaties for the surrender of their own subjects for trial and punishment by a foreign state. The limitations in this particular are by no means uniform.

IV. Every act of extradition must be founded on proofs, formally presented, of some particular crime among those named in the treaty. When the surrendered person has been tried for that crime, if acquitted, he cannot be tried for any crime previously committed, at least without the consent of the country delivering him. The reason for this is that he was surrendered for a particular purpose, and for no other. Indeed, it is maintained by some high authorities that he has the right, in such a case, *i. e.*, arrest for another crime, if he so elect, to be restored to the asylum from which he was taken, and this, too, at the expense of the party that claimed him. On this point of trial for another crime arose the recent discussion between Great Britain and the United States respecting the case of Winslow, the Boston forger. Our demand for this man's extradition was refused, save upon the condition that the government would promise that he should be tried for no other crime than forgery, the crime named in the demand. This condition was declined by Secretary Fish, because it was not warranted by the terms of the treaty, and a somewhat sharp though miscellaneous correspondence ensued. Meanwhile, the treaty was for a time suspended by our government, but was renewed by consent of both, on the assurance of Mr. Fish that we had no thought of trying Winslow for any other crime. By this time he had been released, I believe by a writ of habeas corpus, and his extradition proved a failure. The discussion, however, brought out the fact that neither government had before been careful on this point, but that Great Britain had determined to be hereafter. There can be no doubt that the ground taken by her government in that case, though not recognized by the treaty, is generally sanctioned by the usage of nations and by the best authorities in international law. That it be mentioned in treaties is by no means essential.

V. It has been already remarked that agreements among states for the extradition of criminals are of modern origin. A century ago, Great Britain had no treaty of the kind with any foreign country. Indeed, the word did not exist in the English language. The first provision for this purpose in a treaty of the United States is found in the British treaty of 1794, known as Jay's Treaty. The agreement was limited to twelve years, and expired in

1806, and the only crimes named in it were forgery and murder. It led, I believe, to only one surrender on the part of the United States, and that was made in 1799. The circumstances in which that surrender was made, and the consequences to which it gave rise, rendered it exceedingly odious to the American people, and were made use of in effecting the overthrow of the administration of John Adams. After this inauspicious beginning, there was little disposition to introduce extradition engagements into our treaties with foreign nations. It was far enough from the policy of the general government to send out of the country any one who had come to it for refuge. Some attempts were made to secure the rendition of fugitive slaves escaping to the West India Islands. The period was one of great political agitation in Europe, and it was the aspiration of the United States to become the chosen asylum of the oppressed and the discontented of all nations. Fugitives flocked to our shores in vast numbers, some of whom became eminent citizens of the country. But among them were doubtless very many who might well have appropriated to themselves the lines of the bard of Botany Bay : —

> " True patriots all ; for be it understood
> We left our country for our country's good."

They were seldom molested. The national authorities discouraged all applications for surrender in the absence of treaties, and here and there a state took up the work of occasional extradition on its own account, according to the crude notions of state sovereignty which then prevailed.

It was not till 1842 — after nearly fifty years — that a second treaty containing an extradition agreement was made by the United States. This was the Ashburton Treaty with Great Britain, which is still in force. The crimes for which extradition may be demanded by either country, under this treaty, are seven in number, viz., murder, assault with intent to murder, piracy, arson, robbery, forgery, the utterance of forged paper. It is also expressly stipulated that a person charged with either of these crimes shall be delivered only upon such evidence of criminality as would justify his arrest and commitment for trial in the country which is called upon to make the surrender. Since the adoption of this treaty the usage of extradition has entered very largely into our foreign relations, and not less than thirty treaties for that purpose have been made. The list embraces states as insignificant as the Hawaiian Islands, the Dominican Republic, and the Orange Free States, and even some of the free cities and petty principalities which have since been absorbed in the German Empire. The crimes named in them do not vary very materially from those named above, though in the later treaties it is to be observed that embezzlement by public officers or by salaried persons has been added, and also that the specifications respecting crimes have become more minute. It is pretty certain that our extradition treaties are much more numerous than those of any other country, — a fact which would seem to indicate that most other countries expect to find their fugitive criminals in the United States. Our recent experience with Great Britain in the Winslow case has developed the fact that our agreements in relation to extradition are especially liable to adverse constructions, and it has also given rise to the apprehension that they have often been carelessly made and loosely interpreted in practice.

The great question relating to extradition is whether, after all, there is any sufficient reason to justify its prevalence among nations. Is it really in the interest of humanity and of civilization? It claims to be the growth of the highest and broadest sense of justice. It is in the name of universal justice that it demands that the rights of asylum be set aside. It is for the ends of justice that it claims to stretch forth its arm across national boundaries, over dividing rivers and mountains, beyond the ocean itself, to seize the fugitive criminal, it may be in the remotest part of the world, and bring him back to be punished by the country whose laws he has violated. The essential idea of asylum, on the contrary, has been clemency and mercy. It holds the escape of the criminal beyond the jurisdiction of his crime as equivalent to civil death, by which the proper demands of justice are satisfied. It recognizes in perpetual exile a substitute for the penalty which the laws of the country would inflict. If the country which shelters him chooses to take the risks which belong to a character and a life like his, his own country ought not to be permitted to visit him with its vengeance for the crimes of the past.

The question thus raised has recently been discussed with much earnestness in a series of articles in the " Albany Law Journal," by the Hon. William Beach Lawrence, than whom this country has no more learned or eminent writer on public law. The articles were called forth by the correspondence between the government of Great Britain and that of the United States concerning the Winslow case. Mr. Lawrence appears to entertain the opinion that the importance of extradition has been vastly overrated, and that its operation is attended with drawbacks and evils which counterbalance, or more than counterbalance, all the benefits it ever produces. He urges : —

I. That, after all, but very few criminals are, in this manner, ever brought to punishment. Our present treaty with Great Britain has been in force thirty-five years, and thus far the number of applications made under it by the United States to Great Britain is eighty-eight, of which only thirty-four resulted in surrender; and the number of applications made by Great Britain to the United States is forty-eight, of which only nine resulted in surrender. In addition to these, Mr. Lawrence states, there have been nineteen surrenders from the United States to the British Provinces, while the United States has recovered in return thirty-one criminals who were demanded for justice.

II. That the inviolability of asylum is of greater importance than any results of extradition are likely to be. To have this asylum imperiled by treaties and practices at variance with it involves injury to society and to civilization itself.

III. He maintains that the idea of asylum is that those whom it receives are to be treated as citizens and subjects, amenable to the same laws, entitled to the same rights and privileges, and protected by the same muniments as the other inhabitants of the country. How, he asks, can a government containing so many guarantees of freedom as does that of Great Britain or the United States ever legally surrender a fugitive, whether native or foreigner, to be dealt with by a despotism, or indeed by any government whose fundamental ideas of human right are essentially different from Magna Charta and the Bill of Rights?

IV. He contends that exile is of itself a sufficient punishment for any crime. The ancient Romans regarded it as the greatest of all punishments, and there are few criminals having experienced it who have regarded it as anything less.

On the other hand, it is to be said : —

I. So far as criminals, by any means, escape the punishment of their crimes, the authority of law and the prevalence of justice are diminished in any country; and if the criminals who· thus escape are conspicuous and likely to become notorious as examples, law and justice lose their power everywhere.

II. It is manifestly for the interest of every country that the crimes perpetrated in it should be punished as they deserve, and it is, therefore, for the interest of all countries that they should assist each other in securing this end.

III. The time has passed, if there ever was such a time, when any interest of humanity required a nation to afford asylum to fugitive criminals of other nations. Such an idea is a perversion of the right of asylum. A criminal has no claim to protection anywhere, and the sooner he is brought to punishment the better.

IV. It may also be urged that, in the progress of civilization, nations are adopting common views of justice and of the true methods of securing it. The objection that extradition may sometimes deliver an accused person to unjust modes of trial, or to inordinate punishments, is losing its force. Nations, too, are becoming more closely linked together by the bonds of common interests and a common civilization, and it is claimed that the reciprocal surrender of fugitives who are guilty of great crimes will tend to strengthen these bonds. It is in accordance with views like these that our own country has been so ready to take the lead in making treaties for this purpose, alike with powers that are strong and with those that are weak. And it was only a step in advance of such views that a Senator of the United States, some years since, proposed in the Senate a plan by general law, without the agency of any treaty, for the extradition of all fugitives from justice, upon proper application being made and adequate proofs submitted; and also for refusing asylum to all criminals, and removing them from the country. The proposition, however, has never been acted upon in the Senate.

In the present condition of civilized nations and their relations with each other, there is clearly no reason why the ancient usage of asylum should any longer be employed for the special protection of fugitives from justice who are guilty of heinous crimes. There is not now anywhere in the civilized world any such inhumanity in the administration of justice as will justify this protection. The continuance of it, and the sensibility with which any infraction of it is so generally regarded, save in accordance with the express stipulations of a treaty, would seem to have outlived the age to which they properly belonged, and in which they were useful to the interests of humanity.

Besides this, states are moral beings, and are bound to coöperate with each other in the promotion of general justice and right in the world. This they certainly are not doing if they afford asylum to criminals, and make it as difficult as possible for each other to obtain them and bring them to punishment. So soon as a state is satisfied by judicial examination that the fugitive under its protection is probably guilty of the crime with which he is charged, is there any sufficient reason why he should not be surrendered? Extradition would thus become a matter of positive obligation, which could not be refused among friendly states. Treaties do not create obligations; they only recognize them, and contain agreements to fulfill them. Such obligations are recognized in all confederations of states, and, as civilization advances, nations become bound to each other by something like confederate bonds.

This view I find to be fully sustained by President Woolsey, who, more than most living writers on the subject, makes international law rest on ethical principles. He thinks that asylum should be less and less afforded to criminals, and that extradition, when properly demanded, is to be conceded as a matter of right. We may thus conclude that the time is not distant when the fugitive criminal guilty of a great offense will be surrendered to the nation whose laws he has violated by that to whose asylum he has fled, with something like the readiness and the facility with which the same surrender is accomplished among the States of the American Union. Clearly, the man who has committed a great crime ought not to be secure in any country to which he may flee. Even if no requisition is made for his surrender, it would be but just and right, if his guilt be great, that he be required to depart and become, like the first murderer, a fugitive and a vagabond in the earth. Had a monster like Arguelles been protected from punishment by the asylum of the United States, the world's sense of justice would have been outraged, and gigantic atrocities of every kind would have received new encouragement. On the other hand, the summary extradition of a political peculator like Tweed, and the disgrace and ruin which came upon him in the city which he so shamelessly governed and plundered, proclaim to the official thieves of every city and every country that the world has no retreat in which they can hide themselves from the retributions which their crimes deserve.

ITALY REVISITED.[1]

MY first visit to Italy was made in the winter of 1851–52, when I was there nearly four months. My second visit was made in the winter of 1878–79, — twenty-seven years later, — and it extended over nearly an equal time. It is my purpose here to sketch some of the most conspicuous changes which had taken place within this interval, alike in the condition of the country and in the experience of the traveler. Before doing this I ought perhaps to say that in my earlier visit I was accompanied by my wife alone, while in my late visit I had the company of my wife and of five of my children. The party of which I had the charge numbered in all nine persons, — a fact which of itself made a very marked difference in the journey.

The local characteristics of Italy of necessity undergo but little change in the lifetime of a single generation. Centuries, indeed, have come and gone and have witnessed scarcely any important alteration. The face of nature there remains singularly the same. The aspect of most of the great towns and the condition and modes of life of the people were stereotyped in the Middle Age, and, with here and there an exception, they remain substantially as they then were from one generation to another. The spell of a strange and mighty past rests on its population as it does nowhere else in Europe. It turns their thoughts backward rather than forward. They dwell on what they have been, rather than on what they are able to become.

[1] Read before the Friday Evening Club, April 9, 1880.

The grand enterprises that belong to the youth or the vigorous manhood of a nation are foreign to their condition, and they remain from one age to another, if not content with being only what they are, at least without any grand aspirations for the destiny which was once nurtured, and then lost forever. Nothing is more striking than the clinging to antiquated modes of tilling the soil, and of conducting most of the mechanic arts, which has long prevailed in Italy. Nor is the common mode of life materially different from that which existed there long ago. New tastes and foreign fashions have been introduced among the wealthy and the refined, but they have left no traces in the homes of the poor and the lowly, and it is among them that the national characteristics are really found. Nor do the relative proportions which these classes bear to one another appear to be different now from what they were before. Splendor and squalor still flourish side by side, and sustain about the same relations to each other as they did at far earlier periods of history. Northern Italy, it is true, still has its marked social and industrial characteristics, which make it appear almost like a different country from the Italy of the south. Its people are vigorous, industrious, and in many respects progressive; while those of Southern Italy are of feeble organization, indolent, superstitious, and stationary. But, after all, the two are near enough alike to show their common origin, and the common features which so many similar agencies have imparted to their character. The former are more Gothic, the latter are more Latin ; but they are all distinctively Italian. In all this, Italy as a whole appeared to me to have changed but little in the interval between 1852 and 1879, though I suspect that even this little was more than had taken place in a century preceding.

In revisiting the peninsula, the first conspicuous novelty

which struck me was seen in the vastly altered mode of traveling. The mountain ranges which environ Italy have at all periods rendered it difficult of access. Over several of these ranges roads were made in some period of remote antiquity, along which invading hordes of Carthaginians, Gauls, Germans, Lombards, in successive ages, forced their conquering way to the gates of Rome. To the traveler, however, Italy was never readily accessible by land, until Napoleon constructed those wonderful passages over the Alps which were designed to aid him in the conquest of Europe. Of these stupendous roads, one ran along the shore of the Mediterranean, at the base of the Maritime Alps. Others traversed Mont Cenis, the Simplon, the Great and the Little St. Bernard. Thirty years ago these magnificent roads were the admiration of the crowds of travelers who went to Italy by land, though the route by sea was then far more frequented than either of them or perhaps all of them together. For more than half of every year, however, excepting that along the shore of the Mediterranean, they were all more or less obstructed by Alpine snows, and scarcely a winter passed in which travelers were not overtaken with storms or threatened with avalanches that filled Europe with alarm, and called forth those splendid feats of benevolent heroism which we associate with the monks of St. Bernard.

Entering Italy over either of these roads, by short stages or long stages, according to his own pleasure, the traveler with observing eye made himself acquainted with the entire route along which he passed. He obtained views of the scenery which spread itself around him ; he caught the spirit of every historic spot; he saw the people, both peasants and villagers, in their own homes, and at their daily labors both in the field and in the shop ; he alighted, if he chose, at wayside shrines and rural churches, and looked at the pictures, sometimes painted

by great masters, which adorned them. At the end of
each day's travel he was conscious that he had added to
his treasures of knowledge and experience, and that a
new quickening had been imparted to his intellectual and
moral life. This mode of journeying undoubtedly had
its drawbacks, for it certainly consumed much time and
money, yet it was singularly favorable to the best objects
for which one goes to a country like Italy, for he is thus
enabled to make himself in some degree acquainted with
what is most worth visiting and knowing in this historic
land.

How changed is all this to the traveler who now makes
his pilgrimage to that country ! The diligence, the vettu-
rino, and the post chaise of a few years since are all past
and gone. They are as obsolete on all the great routes of
travel as the stage-coach is in New England. Railroads,
which were then (thirty years ago) scarcely known south
of the Alps, have now been built along the most frequented passes; and the Alpine ranges, which from the
creation encircled the peninsula with their ramparts, and
made it so difficult of access, are now pierced by tunnels
and traversed by locomotives and trains, in utter disregard
of the stately grandeur that invests them. The Nicene
Railroad runs from Nice to Geneva along the military
road of Napoleon, though, at nearly every point at which
the views are the finest, it shuts itself up in tunnels
through the Maritime Alps. A railroad was built in zig-
zag sections over Mont Cenis some twenty years ago, but
in 1870 the tunnel through the mountain was completed,
and has ever since formed the great avenue of communication between France and Italy. So recently as the 29th
of February, in this year [1880], the stupendous tunnel
of Mt. St. Gothard was completed for the connection of
Switzerland and Germany with Italy. The former is a
little less than eight miles in length, and its construction

required nine years. The latter is nine and a quarter miles in length, and its construction required a little less than seven years and a half. They are by far the longest tunnels in the world, and their united effect on the commerce of the great nations which have united in their creation must be beyond all present estimate.

It is needless to remark that this introduction of railroads has made the approach to Italy a very different affair from what it was twenty-five or thirty years ago. The common mode of making the journey now is to enter the train at Paris, and to leave it only when the Alps have been penetrated and some great city in Italy has been reached. This is what we call traveling in Europe, and what we cross the ocean to accomplish. Nor is it different when Italy is reached ; for scarcely any one now thinks of traveling there save by the railroad, on which he is borne along with the smallest possible opportunities of seeing either the face of nature or the life of the people, or of gaining any useful impressions of any kind respecting the country. I remember with pleasure that in the spring of 1852 I made the journey from Rome to Florence in a hired carriage, with Mr. Hazard as one of my companions. We were four days on the way, and I think that both he and I received very distinct impressions of natural scenery, of churches and works of art, of famous historic spots, and also of the character and life of the Italian people, which we shall never lose. In my recent visit I made the journey between the same cities four times on a railroad train, being eight hours in accomplishing what then required four days ; and I can only say that I received no impression whatever that I now retain, except of the amazing disadvantage of traveling by railroad. If we go abroad for business, or for any purpose which demands the utmost saving of time, the railroad is, of course, a help above all estimate. But if, as most Americans do, we go in order to become in some degree familiar with the countries in Europe which we visit, the railroad is certainly a very unsatisfactory mode of making our journeys. The experience which it affords is substantially the same in all countries, and it leaves little in the mind of the traveler, whatever part of the world he may traverse, but the confused and useless memory of monotonous locomotion. For all the higher purposes of travel, it is but little better than being at sea in a steamer. The only satisfaction is in having reached the journey's end.

Nor is this all. The old mode of travel was continually diversified by suggestive incidents or exciting adventures, some of which, indeed, may have helped to verify the saying of Dr. Johnson, that "it is not pleasant to travel but to *have* traveled," but of which, after all, we were sure to think, *et haec olim meminisse juvabit.*

The consequence of this new mode of traveling is, that in foreign countries we now see only the great cities, — all that lies between them is to us only a barren waste, — and in cities we live at great hotels, where we meet, not the people of the country, but travelers like ourselves. We thus lose in a great degree the peculiarities of the countries we visit, for great cities are very much alike the world over, and so are railroads and great hotels. Living at the latter is substantially the same thing, whether we are in Paris, in Rome, in Vienna, or in New York. Since railroads have been introduced, travelers, especially from the United States, have multiplied perhaps a hundredfold. They also make the tour of Europe in less than half the time that was formerly required. But, if I am not greatly mistaken, they bring home vastly less information, vastly less of that practical experience of the world which it is the special office of foreign travel to supply, and vastly less intellectual benefit of any kind, than did the same classes of persons five and twenty years ago.

In visiting Italy a second time, I was immediately and forcibly struck with the great political change which had come over the country; and this underlies and accounts for nearly every other change that has taken place. When I was there in 1852, the peninsula was divided into some ten or twelve separate states, more or less independent and sovereign, some of which were called kingdoms, others were called states, and others duchies, while one and perhaps more bore the name of principality, and one also the name of republic. They had each a separate government, a separate army, a separate police force, a separate custom house, and a separate currency, — all forming together a combination of annoyances, extortions, and frauds such as the unwary traveler encountered nowhere else in Europe. The passport system, too, was in full force, and presented an opportunity for the exercise of the petty suspicions and absurd apprehensions which a despotic government is sure everywhere to breed among its ignorant officials. All these, too, had then been intensified by the popular uprisings which followed the French Revolution of 1848. The whole crowd of lilliputian sovereigns had been driven away, and were now just reinstated in their lost authority by the reactionary movement which had taken place. The result was, that the people of the Italian States were the wretched victims of several of the meanest and most contemptible of despotisms. In Naples, the King of the Two Sicilies, as he was styled, had come back to his throne, as Napoleon said of his Bourbon cousins in France, having " learned nothing and forgotten nothing " during his enforced absence. He had wreaked his vengeance on the whole liberal party, and it was said that the prisons of the city, and of the islands that stud the beautiful waters that lie around it, then held not less than twenty thousand of the best young men of the country, — statesmen, scholars, patriots of every calling, who had opposed his government. Mr. Gladstone had just before visited Naples, and had attended the trials and learned the history of several of these state prisoners; and I well remember how his description of their sufferings stirred the indignant sympathy of liberal minds in every land. Nor were things much better in the Papal States, where the Pope, himself at first a reformer and a champion of Italian freedom, had been driven from Rome by the republic of Mazzini. He had now just been restored, and was still guarded in his own capital by the troops of Louis Napoleon. In Tuscany, in Venice, in Lombardy, the hereditary dukes had been reëstablished by Austria, and her troops alone kept the people in subjection. In Sardinia alone was there anything like constitutional government. Here, under the liberal statesmanship of Count Cavour, the king had made generous concessions to the people, and was consolidating a government which was at length to bring redemption to all Italy. With this exception, the governments were despotisms as hateful and repulsive as could be found in the civilized world. Their narrow, suspicious, and mercenary spirit pervaded their humblest officials, and the traveler encountered it constantly in his dealings with the custom-house inspectors, the passport examiners, the local police of every degree with whom the necessities of travel in those days brought him in contact.

Now all this is happily changed, and one sees from his first experience in Italy how radical and beneficent this change has become. Not only is all Italy under one government, but it is immediately evident that this government is constitutional and liberal. There is no longer interference with private rights, no espionage of personal conduct, no extortion, no petty tyranny of officials. Even custom-house inspectors treat you civilly, and make no demands for passing your baggage. You become immedi-

ately impressed with the fact that you are in a country as
free and as well governed as any on the continent of Europe, and this impression abides with you so long as you
remain there. The great social results of this change are
becoming everywhere visible. Education, though still too
much neglected, is awakening greater interest than before.
The condition of the people, it is said, is beginning to improve, especially in the north, where the new order of
things has prevailed the longest. Superstition is still conspicuous everywhere, but religious freedom is the law of
the land, and signs of a higher and better national life are
appearing all over the peninsula.

This unification of Italy, after ages of division and of
strife among its provinces, deserves to rank among the
foremost events of the century to which it belongs. It
was brought about by unexpected agencies singularly
diverse and independent of each other, and often designed
for ends very different from that which they finally accomplished. The central force among them all was always the resolute purpose of the King of Sardinia, whose
constant aim was towards this single result. Among the
foremost, however, of the incidental agencies which
brought it to pass was the twofold ambition of Louis
Napoleon, who on the one hand desired to be considered
the protector of the Papacy, and on the other was determined to humble the Emperor of Austria. This led him,
first of all, to overthrow the Roman republic, and soon to
secure the Pontifical States with French troops; and then
to engage with Victor Emmanuel in the war with Austria,
which resulted in the annexation of Lombardy, Parma,
and Modena to Sardinia in 1860. On this large accession
to his territory Victor Emmanuel was proclaimed King
of Italy, and the Grand Duchy of Tuscany immediately
placed itself under his jurisdiction. Another agency, of
quite an opposite character, now for a time becomes con-

spicuous, and, though with doubtful willingness, contributes
to the same result.   Garibaldi, the military creator of the
fallen republic of Rome, without authority of any kind
fits out an expedition of a thousand men at Genoa, and
invades Sicily and the Neapolitan States.   The people
everywhere receive him with acclamations; the king flees
in terror from his capital; and Garibaldi forms a provi-
sional government, apparently on his own account.   When
the King of Sardinia demands an explanation of this
singular movement, apparently for founding a separate
republic, he answers that his only purpose had been from
the beginning to make the Two Sicilies a part of the
Italian kingdom, which was accomplished without delay by the votes of the people.   His success in Naples
prompted him to attempt a similar enterprise in Venetia,
which was still in possession of Austria; but the Italian
king was obliged to suppress it, which he was able to do
only by the arrest and imprisonment of its daring and
valorous leader.   In 1865 the capital of Italy, hitherto at
Turin, was established at Florence, a city of central position, and more secure alike from Austria and from France.
And in the following year, the contest between Austria
and Prussia led to the abandonment by the latter of the
Venetian States, and their voluntary incorporation with
the Italian kingdom.   Meanwhile the French occupation
of the Papal States had been partially abandoned by the
withdrawal of the troops from several of these states,
and these had immediately added themselves to United
Italy.

In this manner, within six years, was accomplished what
had been the fruitless aspiration of centuries of struggle,
and Italy was now free from her foreign oppressors.
Nothing remained but the absorption of the Pontifical
States to make her union complete.   This the irrepres-
sible Garibaldi and his associates were ready to bring

about by rifle clubs and popular uprisings, and for this
they were willing to drive the Pope from his ancient seat,
and make him a wanderer on the face of the earth. The
king, however, and advisers saw the difficulty and delicacy
of the situation, and he determined to take no step which
he should be obliged to recall. Indeed, had it been possible, there is reason to think that he would have preferred
to leave the Pope with little or no further disturbance.
Excommunicated though he was, he evidently had a
kindly regard for the sovereign pontiff of the Church.
The Pope, however, had denounced him from the beginning. He had denied all right to the title of king of
Italy, and had declared it to be impossible for the Church
to recognize his authority.

But the question was soon to be decided by the unexpected course of events. The war between France and
Germany broke out, and detachment after detachment of
the French troops was recalled by the exigencies of the
time. The last embarked at Civita Vecchia on the 9th of
August, 1870. On the 1st of September Louis Napoleon
surrendered at Sedan, and with that event the French
Empire fell. The country was greatly excited by the
revolutionary ideas which were widely prevalent. They
were propagated by the emissaries of Mazzini and Garibaldi, and were designed to excite the young men of Italy
to strike for what was called the Universal Republic. In
these circumstances, Victor Emmanuel saw that decisive
action could no longer be delayed. It was as necessary
for the safety of the Pope as for that of the kingdom of
Italy. He immediately ordered a division of his army to
enter the papal territory, and at the same time addressed
to the Pope a most respectful letter, remarkable alike for
its practical wisdom and the careful consideration which
it expressed of what was due to the head of the Church. It
assured him that his temporal power was no longer possible,

and implored his assistance in carrying into effect measures for securing and harmonizing the rights of the Roman population, the inviolability of the supreme pontiff,
and the independence of the Holy See. The Pope made
no answer to the letter. He saw that the end was at
hand, but he refused all overtures, and simply protested
against what he denounced as "a great sacrilege and a
most enormous injustice." At the end of eight days the
king sent a flag of truce to Rome, demanding the surrender of the garrison that defended the city. Every
effort was made by the foreign ministers at the papal
court to bring about the surrender without the loss of
life. The papal general, however, had received orders
not to yield till a breach had been made by the Italian
troops. The cannonading lasted four hours, when the
gates were opened, and the king, on the 20th of September, 1870, took possession of Rome, amidst the acclamations of the people for United Italy. Thus fell the temporal sovereignty of the Roman pontiff, — a sovereignty
which dates back from that distant period when the imperial capital was occupied by Alaric the Goth, which
ruled over a wide district of Italy as early as the first
quarter of the eighth century, and which at its overthrow
was by far the oldest sovereignty in Europe. By a strange
coincidence the Vatican Council, which in the preceding
July had sanctioned the dogma of Papal Infallibility,
was still in session at St. Peter's, and illustrious ecclesiastics from every country of Christendom were thus present at Rome to witness the final overthrow of the pontifical power, and the personal humiliation of the head of
the Church, and the union of the entire papal territory
with the kingdom of Italy. To them, the spectacle must
have presented a melancholy contrast with that transcendent arrogance with which the Pope had summoned
a council of the world to give its solemn sanction to his

claim to infallibility. Indeed, had it not been for the promulgation of this dogma, so threatening in its bearings on civil allegiance, the catastrophe which had befallen them might have been alleviated by the sympathy, perhaps even partially averted by the interference, of the Roman Catholic sovereigns of Europe. The alienation, however, which it created in Austria, in Germany, and in Spain, is to be reckoned as another of the agencies which made this catastrophe so complete.

The King and the Parliament of Italy now addressed themselves to the great questions which the course of events had forced upon their consideration; especially, what position should be assigned to the Pope, and what relations should subsist between the Church and the new State. These questions received the most careful attention, and in May, 1871, they were formally settled in what is called the "Law of Papal Guarantees," which, it must be admitted, is exceedingly liberal in its provisions. By this law the person of the Pope is declared to be sacred and inviolable, and any offense against him is to be punished as an offense against the king. He is to be received by the government officials with royal honors, and is always to have the same precedence as is accorded to him in all Catholic countries; to have as many guards as he may desire; to remain in possession of the Vatican, the Lateran, and the Castel Gandolpho, with all their outbuildings, libraries, picture galleries, and furniture, and other contents, which are to be inalienable and exempt from taxation. No official of the government, without permission, can enter them for any purpose whatever. He is to have a post-office and a telegraph service of his own for each of his palaces, and is free to correspond, without interference, with whomever he pleases. The seminaries and places of education in Rome and the suburban dioceses are also to be under his sole control.[1] As for the relations of the Church and the State, the law declares the Church to be entirely independent of the authority of the State. The State abandons all right of nominating for offices in the Church, providing only that Italian subjects alone shall be appointed to them; and claims no right of revision of decrees, or publications of ecclesiastical authorities, and no appeal is to be allowed from any sentence of ecclesiastical courts, but the civil officers are not permitted to assist in executing such sentences. It is to be a free Church in a free State.

This law was offered to the Pope in the most respectful manner by the Italian government as a basis of settlement, but he indignantly refused to take notice of it, or to make any terms whatever. He claimed that his authority and his possession could rest only on divine appointment. He would not accept the annual allowance of $645,000, or allow that the government had any right to guarantee his personal safety, his sovereign rank, or the property that had always belonged to him and his predecessors. In short, he showed himself wholly impracticable, and chose to regard and represent himself as a prisoner shut up in his own palace, and stripped not only of the means of maintaining his state as the supreme head of Christendom, but also of procuring the comforts of life. The postulates which he enjoined on the acceptance of all faithful Catholics in Italy were: 1. That the temporal power must be speedily reëstablished. 2. That all sincere votaries of the Church must abstain from political elections. 3. That it is impossible for the Papacy and the kingdom of Italy to exist together. This was of course a declaration of relentless hostility to the entire new order of things.

[1] He is also to receive an annual allowance of 3,225,000 *lire* ($645,000), free from all taxes.

This hostile and disdainful attitude of the Pope, however, made no difference in the conduct of the government. The removal of the capital to Rome had become a state necessity which the king could not escape, reluctant though he might be to take the step. Accordingly, so soon as arrangements were completed, the government offices were transferred from Florence, and the king arrived in Rome on July 2, 1871, and made his residence at the Quirinal Palace, amidst the loyal demonstrations of the Roman people.

Had it been possible to avoid this removal, I cannot but think that it would have been better to do so. In the first place, Florence is a healthy and cheerful city; sufficiently central for all the interests of the kingdom, and in all respects suitable to be capital of Italy. Rome, on the contrary, apart from the associations that belong to it as the seat of the ancient empire, has no such suitableness. It is not central; it is not healthy; for at least five months of the year the king and the chief officers of state must reside elsewhere, because of the malaria that broods over the city. The population withal is not of a character to be desired in the national capital. The mass of the people are essentially republican; and however loyal for the time, they regard the present order of things only as a prelude to the restoration of the Roman republic. The noble families, on the other hand, very generally sympathize with the Pope. They turn their backs on the king and his court. They never visit the Quirinal, and present themselves only at the receptions of the Vatican. The presence, too, of the king in what has for ages been the papal capital, is sure to be a perpetual grievance to the Pope, and an unfailing reminder of the humiliation to which he has been reduced. It is said the king himself had no desire to establish himself in Rome. At the same time there seemed to be no alternative, and in the judgment of his wisest ministers, it was as essential to the security of the Pope as it was to the satisfaction and quiet of Italy. The only other plan that was suggested was that Rome be made a free city, though a part of the royal domain, and that the Pope be placed at its head, with guarantees similar to those enacted by the Italian Parliament. It is not probable, however, that he would have fared as well with the people as with the king.

When I was in Rome a year ago, it had been for eight years the capital of United Italy. In that time both a new Pope and a new king had come upon the scene, but the Quirinal and the Vatican were still wholly at variance with each other. They were the seats of opposite and hostile jurisdictions. The young king and queen were daily seen in the public drives of the city, on the Pincian Hill, and in the Borghesè Gardens. The Pope, on the contrary, never leaves the Vatican. He acts on the theory of his predecessor, that he has been robbed of his rightful possessions, and that he is now restricted as a prisoner to his palace and its inclosures. And in this view he is encouraged by the sympathies of a very influential portion of Roman society, whom the king finds it impossible to conciliate. So it is likely to be until some future and wiser Pope shall show himself willing to accept what is inevitable, to relinquish all pretensions to temporal sovereignty, and to make the most of that unrestricted spiritual dominion which seems to be spreading more and more widely over the world.

Meanwhile Rome is undergoing changes of the most striking character. The whole machinery of the old despotism has been demolished and destroyed. There is entire freedom of the press, entire freedom of speech, and entire freedom of thought, action, and worship. In these particulars it is no longer the same place that I had visited before. Then suspicion and espionage were in the air, and half the population seemed to be spies on the rest. The government professed to watch over the souls of its subjects. It took Bibles and Protestant books from the trunks of travelers, and allowed no word nor thought of dissent from either the religion or the politics of the Pope. The English church stood, as it stands now, without the gates, because no permission could be had to build it within them, and the little congregation of Americans held their worship in the apartments of Mr. Cass, the minister of the United States, because no room could be rented for the purpose. Now an American Episcopal church stands within the walls, and congregations of worshipers from several Protestant countries meet every Sunday; and more than this, the British and Foreign Bible Society has opened a Depository of Italian Bibles and Testaments, and is scattering them all over Italy, and there are mission schools and chapels of Wesleyan Methodists, of Scottish Presbyterians, of Baptists, of French Protestants, and perhaps of others, all openly maintained in the heart of the city. The same is true of other Italian cities. The Pope has issued a pastoral letter denouncing these schools and chapels, which shows full well how pernicious he thinks them to be, but I doubt if the letter serves any other purpose than to make them more widely known.

During the brief period in which the Italian government has been in possession, a special commission has been appointed for prosecuting antiquarian researches in Rome, in accordance with a definite and carefully considered plan, and very important results have been obtained. Up to this period the work had been carried on sometimes by the papal government and sometimes by foreign governments, especially those of France, Russia, and Germany, but always with too little method and persistency. Now, under the direction of a commission com-

posed of the most enlightened antiquaries, the task of un-
earthing the ruins of the ancient city is making progress
more advantageously than ever before. I was most forcibly impressed with what had been accomplished on and
near the Palatine Hill. On the slopes formerly covered
with convents and villas and gardens are now disclosed,
some thirty feet below them, the ruins of those stupendous structures which bear the name of Palaces of the
Cæsars, which are regarded as among the most interesting and important ruins of the days of the emperors. In
the progress of this work, relics and works of art of every
kind have been found in such numbers that a new museum has been opened for their reception. Of the extent
to which the old Roman soil is filled with this curious
wealth, some idea may be formed from the following list
of what was obtained in the year 1873 alone, viz.: 17
statues, 24 busts, 6 basso-rilievo, 7 sarcophagi, 2,700
fragmentary sculptures, 125 epigraphs on marble, 14,900
coins, 700 stamped bricks, 2,050 stamps on amphoræ,
217 terra-cotta lamps, 8 rings, and 2 collars of gold, besides numerous objects in bronze, all estimated at £8,000
sterling.[1]

But far more noticeable than these, to the traveler who
revisits the city, are the local transformations which certain parts of it have already undergone. The creation of
the new is more striking than the uncovering of the old.
The coming of the government to Rome is said to have
added some 30,000 to its population. The consequence is,
that vast enterprises and local improvements of different
kinds have been undertaken to an extent which had not
been witnessed before in many centuries. Most of these
are in the region of the Quirinal Hill, where the old palace of the popes, now the residence of the king, has been
renovated and enlarged, and where grand buildings for

[1] Hemans, p. 696.

the several departments of the government have been erected.

It is evident that a people thus recently brought together requires the guiding hand of some sagacious statesman and leader, such as Count Cavour was to Sardinia, for there are many serious difficulties to be overcome, and such a statesman, I fear, Italy does not now possess. The national debt is so large as to destroy the public credit. The currency is wholly of paper, and is, of course, immensely depreciated. The government, too, is afflicted with the apprehension of Austrian or other foreign invasion, and, in addition to an expensive fleet, it maintains a peace establishment of 600,000 men taken from the industrial population of the country. In addition to this, the people are still in wretched ignorance, scarcely more than one third of them being able to read and write. But no single problem relating to the condition of Italy is so pregnant with danger or so difficult of solution as the problem of the Papacy. The attitude of the Pope, from the beginning, has cast a blight over the political interests of the new kingdom. He denies its right to exist; he pronounces anathemas on its government, and warns its subjects, if they would be faithful to the Church, to refrain from participating in political affairs. Whether it be in consequence of this or not, it is said to be a fact that not more than a third of the voting population ever take part in elections. The high ecclesiastics and the parish priests everywhere echo the utterances of the Vatican; and the Pope, pauper and prisoner though he claims to be, is yet able to wield a power which the King and Parliament cannot control. To conciliate this hostile agency has thus far proved to be impossible; to annihilate it is deemed equally impossible.

But I will not enter into the possibilities which attend this embarrassing and difficult problem. I need only refer to the methods in which, on the one side or the other, it is hoped that a solution may be found. In the first place, there are those who maintain that the temporal power may yet be restored to the Pope; that, as its overthrow was made possible only by a peculiar juncture in the affairs of Europe, so, in some future juncture, it may be reëstablished. Associations for securing this result exist in several Roman Catholic countries, and even in England. These all cherish the idea that the Almighty will punish the sacrilege which has been committed, and reinstate the Church in her rightful authority. On the other hand, several different methods of settling the relations between the Pope and the Italian government have been suggested on the part of those who are champions of Italian unity, and care nothing for the vested rights of the Papacy.

I. It is proposed that the government repeal the Law of Guarantees, abolish the quasi-sovereign rights of the pontiff over the Vatican and the Lateran palaces, and place him in the same civil condition as every other ecclesiastic in Italy. It is held that the government did not go far enough at the beginning, that it was a mistake to leave him in possession even of the semblance of temporal sovereignty which he now possesses, and that nothing short of the annihilation of this sovereignty can destroy his power to injure the state. It is feared, however, that a proceeding like this would awaken the sympathy of Catholic Christendom, and produce a reaction most harmful to the government.

II. It is proposed that Italy shall invite other Roman Catholic governments to join with her in some plan of guaranteeing the support of the Pope in honorable independence, with a stipulation that he will abandon his antagonism and place the Church in full harmony with the State. The obvious objection to this is that it involves foreign interference and coöperation, and thus perils the independence of Italy.

III. There are those, both in Italy and out of it, who think that the present Pope is possessed of excellent sense, and even of statesmanship, — attributes to which his predecessor possessed no claim whatever. They believe that he fully appreciates the necessity of a final adjustment of some kind. Indeed, he has announced it to be his desire to adapt the Church to the condition and spirit of modern civilization. The advice, therefore, which they give to the government is, to avoid all collision with the Pope, to maintain a conciliatory policy, and wait till an occasion shall arise that shall be favorable to a reciprocal recognition, on the one hand, of the political supremacy of the Italian State, on the other, of the spiritual supremacy of the papal Church, of a temporal kingdom in which the head of Latin Christendom shall be secure and independent, and of a spiritual church which shall be the unfailing moral bulwark of the civil throne. It must be admitted that this would require the Pope always to be an Italian, as indeed he has in fact been for the past three hundred and fifty years ; and, what is of far graver importance, it would give to the Papacy an aspect of local nationality, instead of the universality which is inseparable from its real character. That the relations of the two be established on an amicable basis is of great importance to Italy, and of nearly equal importance to the Papacy. The attitude of irreconcilable hostility is adverse to every interest of both. Nor is the interest in this question confined to Italy, or even to the limits of the Latin Church.

Cardinal Newman has recently called attention to the vastly altered tone of public sentiment towards Roman Catholics in England. He has had ample reason for this in his own personal experience. The same may be said of public sentiment in this country, and probably in every

Protestant country, for every Protestant government reck-
ons them in multitudes among its own subjects. These
altered feelings towards the individuals naturally extend
to the Church itself. Enlightened Protestants no longer
regard it with the hostility which they once cherished.
The Pope thus naturally becomes a subject of interest
throughout Christendom, by more than half of whose inhabitants he is acknowleged as their spiritual ruler. He
is the most conspicuous personage in Christendom, even
to those who have separated themselves most widely from
his sway. While very few Catholics probably desire him
to stand in the way of Italian unity and progress, there
are also very few Protestants who desire to have him subjected to any needless humiliations. His independence is
undoubtedly indispensable to the Roman Catholic Church ;
and after all that has been said about it, no thoughtful
man believes that the destruction of the Roman Catholic
Church would now be other than a disaster alike to
Christianity and civilization.

PUBLIC ADDRESSES.

ADDRESS DELIVERED BEFORE THE RHODE ISLAND HISTORICAL SOCIETY

AT THE OPENING OF THEIR CABINET, NOVEMBER 20, 1844.

GENTLEMEN OF THE HISTORICAL SOCIETY: —

WE have come together to celebrate an event which may well form an era in the history of our Society, — the completion and opening of the chaste and commodious structure which is henceforth to become the permanent depository of our collections for Rhode Island history. The occasion, though far removed from the exciting scenes that ordinarily occupy the attention of men in this bustling and restless age, is yet one which holds high and important connections with the dignity, the prosperity, and the fame of the city and of the State. Let us, then, turn aside, for a brief time, from the engrossing occupations of every-day life to consider the purposes of our association, and at this new altar to kindle afresh our devotion to the objects to which it is to-day to be forever consecrated. They are objects which intimately concern some of the best interests of society, and they earnestly appeal to some of the noblest sympathies of our intellectual and spiritual nature.

The care which preserves the materials for a people's history is characteristic only of advanced stages of civilization, and a high degree of social and intellectual culture. The barbarous passions that crave merely present gratification, and the engrossing spirit of trade that heeds only the prospect of pecuniary gain, are alike unmindful of the connection that subsists between a nation's history and a nation's character. Wealth and power may rear costly monuments to the memories of the great; the bard of a rude age may celebrate in mythic verse the achievements of heroism and courage; but the collection of the scattered memorials of the past, the nice and discriminating research into its obscure recesses, and the writing of history, — such history as may instruct mankind, — these are never accomplished until society has made progress in social and moral culture, until out of the mighty mass of its baser passions and perishable interests there has sprung an intellectual spirit, — a sense that craves a deeper wisdom than the voices of the living world can ever teach. It is then that we study the characters of the past, and reproduce them in the present.

> "We give in charge
> Their names to the sweet lyre. The historic muse,
> Proud of the treasure, marches with it down
> To latest times; and Sculpture, in her turn,
> Gives bond in stone and ever-during brass,
> To guard them and to immortalize her trust."

It is the appropriate object of an historical society to collect and preserve all the relics of the past that may serve as materials for history. This object, when liberally prosecuted, cannot fail to exert the most salutary influences, not only upon those immediately engaged in its accomplishment, but upon the whole spirit of a community. It leads us along the checkered course of human affairs. It conducts us through the successive experiments that have been made in politics and morals; the changes of social condition, of language, and of manners; the controversies that have agitated society, and the enterprises that have resulted in its comfort and improvement; and it brings to our notice all that has affected the interests of humanity within the sphere to which it more especially relates. This object, in all civilized lands, has at all times been regarded as of the highest importance. Not only does its successful accomplishment ensure accuracy and completeness to the labors of the historian, but it also suggests innumerable topics to the philosopher and moralist, and sheds new light upon the mysterious problems of man's social progress and destiny.

But in this country, especially, the objects which associations like ours have in view address themselves with still more commanding interest to the attention of the scholar and the citizen, and ally themselves even more closely with the well-being and improvement of society. I speak not now of the shadowy period which elapsed before the settlement of America began, fraught with curious interest, and fruitful of mighty problems though it be. The researches of the antiquarian traveler are just disclosing the burial-place of its perished races, and lifting the veil of oblivion from the ruins of its wonderful civilization. Without reference, however, to this remote antiquity, so filled with mysteries and marvels, and so overwhelming by its vastness, there are subjects enough of transcendent interest in the origin and progress of our own civilization, which has sprung up and borne its astonishing fruits upon these transatlantic shores. It is indeed of recent origin, but it is of peculiar character. It was engrafted upon this wild continent from the world's best stock. Its earliest eras are comparatively of yesterday; but its growth and development have been marked by great events, and illustrated by deeds and characters of the loftiest heroism. It has given a new continent to the dominion of the Anglo-Saxon race, and has opened here, for the language, the laws, and the religion of our British forefathers, the path to a destiny more glorious and sublime than has ever been recorded in the annals of mankind. The origin and history of this peculiar civilization, the early struggles it maintained with the perils of the wilderness and the hostility of savages, the virtues that adorned its character, and the men who pioneered its progress, — these and all their numerous relationships and results are subjects that demand the careful and reverent study of the American people. That such subjects be thoroughly investigated, and the memorials relating to them be carefully treasured up, may be of unspeakable benefit to the future fortunes of mankind. No toil, whether of hands or of minds; no expenditure, whether of effort or of wealth, that may be required to do this, — will be bestowed in vain.

Nor is the influence which such inquiries exert upon the spirit and character of a people to be lightly estimated. It liberalizes their aims, breaks down their prejudices, elevates and ennobles their interests, and enlarges their sympathy with the changeful fortunes of the common humanity. The English moralist has well remarked, that "whatever withdraws us from the power of the senses, and makes the past, the distant, or the future predominate over the present, advances us in the dignity of thinking beings." Now it is precisely this influence which historic studies, above all other pursuits, are particularly fitted to exert. They serve to multiply the ties which bind a people to an honored ancestry, and to rally with new energy their hopes and affections around the brilliant eras of their history, and the monuments which record the struggles of patriotism or the triumphs of freedom. They call back the buried forms, the forgotten achievements, the vanished scenes, of a departed age, and cause them to move again, in a brilliant and impressive panorama, before the mind of the present generation. They thus mingle the interests and images of other times with the engrossing cares and pursuits that now occupy our attention, and, amid the wrecks of departed ages, they read to us lessons of the truest practical wisdom. By thus opening to the minds of a people the fountains of their early history, may be best secured that unity of national character and that high-toned national spirit which more than armies or navies, more than legislative codes or written constitutions, preserve from decay the institutions of a country. "These noble studies," as Milton has said of kindred pursuits, "are of power to imbreed and cherish in a great people the seeds of virtue and public civility." They interpret the prophetic voices of the past, and by clothing each familiar spot, each ruin and hill-top and river, with the associations of history, they increase and justify the feelings of veneration and pride with which the patriot clings to the institutions of his country.

No sooner does a nation become indifferent to her history than her national spirit begins to decline. The chain of consanguinity which runs through successive generations, and binds them in perpetual union, is broken asunder. The state, no longer venerated as a parent, is subjected to the experiments of wretched empirics, or, it may be, is turned adrift on the wild sea of revolution, with no principles of inherited wisdom to guide her, no lights of the storied past to shine upon her wayward course. Modern times have furnished at least one memorable example of this truth in the frenzied struggles of revolutionary France, and that one example, it may be hoped, is enough for all ages. It seemed as though, to her, her whole previous existence as a nation were utterly useless, and almost as though Time had rolled his course in vain. In her proud self-conceit she heeded none of the lessons of her own or of others' experience. From the ages of her national glory, from the brilliant rallying-points of her history, she turned away in contempt to pursue the glittering phantoms of an upstart, impracticable philosophy. The altars of her ancient religion she threw down,

and from the proudest spots of her soil she removed the
monuments of early patriotism and valor, hallowed by the
associations of centuries, that she might set up there the
blood-stained emblems of her fanatical, atheistical republic. It was said by one of her own statesmen, with almost
literal truth, that "you might alter the whole political
frame of the government in France, with greater ease
than you could introduce the most insignificant change
into the customs or even the fashions of England."

But the labors of an historical society are of more
particular benefit in their specific connection with the
office of the historian. Their object is to provide the materials of which history is to be composed. In this country, especially, this is a work which private associations
must do. The government, whether of the States or the
nation, has hitherto done but little to rescue from oblivion
the minuter materials for our national history. They
must be discovered and brought together, and prepared
for the historian's use, by private efforts alone, or they
will perish forever. It is thus only that the narratives of
American history can be raised to that higher standard
of truth and accuracy which shall make them faithful exponents of the real progress of the nation. Lord Bacon
has remarked, that "nothing is so seldom found among
the writings of men as true and perfect civil history."
And the remark is scarcely less applicable to the writings
of our own age than of that in which it was uttered. A
part, however, of the imperfection which it implies, may
be remedied by a nicer and more discriminating research,
a more careful collection and preservation of all the materials that can illustrate the spirit or the facts of an age
or a nation.

But, after all, what is written history but the exponent
and suggester of that which is not, and which cannot be,
written? The events that no pen records always far out-

number those contained on the historic page; and there are a multitude of characters haunting the mysterious chambers of the past, whom no artist has ever sketched for the picture galleries of history. This fact the historian must keep constantly in view, and he must write in such a manner as to concentrate and preserve the spirit of the whole in the part which he records. For this purpose, he must pursue innumerable investigations whose results he cannot use; he must thread many a labyrinth of controversy which will not yield him a single fact; and he must study the lives and deeds of men whose names even will not appear in the pages of his writings. It is only in accordance with this principle that historical accuracy has ever been secured. Herodotus, the father of this species of composition, spent years in traveling over many lands, in conversing with their various inhabitants, in gathering up their scattered traditions and legends, and in extracting from them all whatever could illustrate the times of which he wrote, ere he delivered his immortal work to his assembled countrymen at the games of Greece. Gibbon devoted the enthusiasm of youth, and the best energies of manhood, to delving in the lore of classic antiquity. He studied the doctrines of every philosophic school, the principles of every art and every science, and " crossed and re-crossed, again and again, the gloomy gulf that separates the ancient from the modern world," and gathered the relics of many a perished race and broken dynasty, ere he was prepared to write the "Decline and Fall of the Roman Empire." And the historian of modern Europe informs us that his recent brilliant work on the French Revolution was the result of fourteen years of traveling and study, and of fourteen more devoted to the labors of composition.

There is also another respect in which the collections of an association like ours are of essential service to the his-

torian. It is not always the most splendid events that
do most in moulding the character of an age, or in shaping the destiny of a people. The mightiest streams of
political or of moral influence often spring from some
humble fountain embosomed in the retreats of private
life, and quite shut out from the notice of the mere general inquirer. To these sequestered places the historian
must penetrate, by the aid of the minutest investigation
and of the most comprehensive generalizations. In doing
this, his first resort is to the collections which others have
made, to the materials which have been provided ready to
his hand. He uses them and makes them tributary to the
lessons he would teach, in accordance with the same high
principle as that on which the philosophic astronomer employs the results of the humble observer who nightly
watches the stars, and chronicles the silent changes
through which they pass. As, in comparative anatomy,
a single disconnected bone reveals to the naturalist the
structure and habits of a race of animals that has been
extinct for ages; so, often, the mutilated record of some
forgotten manuscript, the neglected work of some ancient
chronicler, will open to the historian the whole history of
an age, and enable him to revive its spirit and exhibit
"its very form and pressure." Thucydides has sketched,
in glowing colors, the revolutions of the States of Greece;
but could some Athenian letters, written by the patriots
who lived during the terrific era he describes, now be
rescued from the oblivion to which they have passed, they
might reveal to us the scenes of Corcyra or of Corinth,
the motives of statesmen and the springs of revolution,
far more fully than they can now be gathered even from
the pages of the most graphic of historians. And, to take
a more familiar example, he who would thoroughly understand the social spirit and character of the early settlers of our own Providence Plantations must have re-

course, not to the provisions of the first or the second charter, nor even to the records of the town alone, but to the scattered documents that describe their strifes with the people at Pawtuxet, and their endless disputes about bounds, and about the meaning of the famous words, " up stream without limits," in the sachem's original deed; or to the singular paper which Roger Williams submitted to the town, entitled " Considerations Touching Rates." It is from these, and such as these, the incidental relics of things that have passed away forever, that the historian forms his conception of an age, and spreads it forth upon his pictured page.

But collections like these of which I am speaking are not only of essential service to the historian; they also enable the reader to verify the statements, to enlarge and extend the views, contained in history itself. How many theories have been exploded, how many misrepresentations have been corrected, long after they have been chronicled in history, by the subsequent researches of more diligent or impartial inquirers! Hume was for a long time regarded as the almost perfect embodiment of philosophical impartiality, and his " History of England " was read with universal delight, as the authentic narrative of the proud march of the English people from barbarism to civilization through the checkered fortunes of their career. But the researches of later inquirers, and especially the publication of documentary details, relating to the more important periods of which he treats, have cast a shadow over his historic fame, which is growing deeper and deeper with every succeeding generation. The inimitable qualities of his style, and the charming grace of his manner, will long make his great work the delight of all who read English history; but it is only when its errors have been corrected, its partial representations extended, its cold indifference to the interests of humanity animated with philanthropic sentiment and generous sympathy, that it becomes a safe guide to the true principles of the English Constitution, or the real fortunes of the English nation.

We may recur, for other illustrations, to the history of our own State, at a period within the recollection of some who are present to day. All are familiar with the fact that Rhode Island was the last of the thirteen States to adopt the Federal Constitution, and to join the union which had been formed. But how small a portion of the real history of that event is this single fact! There is here no explanation of the causes of this reluctant assent; no illustration of the influences which were at work to blind the people to the true dignity and happiness of the State. It is only when we leave the historic record, and go back to the scattered chronicles of the day, or converse with the aged men who still live to describe it, that we can form any adequate conception of the conflicting passions which then rent our little republic on this engrossing question. Many a quiet citizen of the present day, who glories in the Constitution of his country, would hear with astonishment of the strifes which agitated this State at the period of its adoption; when town and country were in arms against each other, and military officers, and even legislators and judges, assembled with a rustic mob to prevent by violence the civil rejoicings which the success of the Constitution in other States called forth among the people of Providence!

Other illustrations without number might be adduced to show how much of our knowledge of the spirit and progress of a people depends upon collecting and carefully treasuring up all the materials for composing, illustrating, and explaining their history. But I need not dwell upon these familiar and well-established views respecting the importance of historic studies. In other countries they have created a deep and widespread interest, they have received the fostering care of government, and have resulted in the accumulation of the most magnificent treasures of historic lore. The rich collections of the King's Library at Paris, of the British Museum at London, of the splendid libraries at Copenhagen and Göttingen, at Berlin and Vienna, each containing, on an average nearly 400,000 volumes, show how much has been done to keep the past from being forgotten, and to preserve all its important facts and teachings, and even its evanescent spirit, for the future instruction and guidance of mankind. What event in the history of modern Europe cannot there be illustrated! What age cannot there be revived! The visitor to these stupendous collections of books and manuscripts, as he wanders amazed through their crowded alcoves, sees piled on every side around him all that the diligence of man, aided by princely munificence and imperial power, has been able to rescue from the mighty wrecks of the past; and he feels a generous pride in the thought that so much at least is safe, of all which gifted genius has created, or which the race of man has suffered and achieved, through the long centuries of its existence.

Our own country, though far behind the leading nations of Europe in her collections of books, has, however, begun to cultivate a most worthy and commendable interest in the monuments of her early history. Everything pertaining to the planting and the early growth of the settlements of America has at length acquired a high value, and is becoming a matter of universal demand. It can now no longer be said that the richest collections of materials for American history are in foreign lands, shut up in the libraries of princes or of curious scholars, or sealed away in the Plantation Offices of the British government. They are here in the heart of New England, where they have been gathered by the munificence of private citizens, and the enlightened agency of our literary institutions, and here they must remain forever.

The numerous Historical Societies which have been formed in this country, furnish also another most gratifying proof of the growing interest in all that pertains to American History. The Massachusetts Historical Society was founded in 1790. During the period which has since elapsed, it has published twenty-seven volumes of its Collections. It has accumulated, by its researches, a library of books and manuscripts of immense value, and has set on foot inquiries and historic labors, whose influence has been felt in every part of the land. At later periods, similar societies have been established in the others of the New England States, in New York, Pennsylvania, Ohio, Kentucky, Indiana, and Georgia, each one of which has contributed something for the illustration or the enriching of our local or general history. Of these, the society in New York is by far the most liberal in its resources and aims, and the most active and diligent in its inquiries. It has published six volumes of Collections pertaining to the history of its own State, and is at this moment prosecuting its objects, with a zeal and enterprise which give full assurance that all that has ever been achieved, in earlier or in later days, by the sturdy settlers of the New Netherlands or their persevering successors, will be duly chronicled on the pages of American history.

But the history of no State in the Union, we may safely say, presents claims upon the attention and study of her citizens so strong as does that of Rhode Island. Her origin was peculiar, and her position among the States of New England was marked, for many generations, by the same peculiarity. The three divisions of the State, the Plantations of Providence, the settlement at Aquetneck, and the settlement at Warwick, were first peopled by those who had been driven from the neighboring colonies for opinion's sake. Though differing in almost every other respect, they were entirely agreed in maintaining the one great principle which persecution had taught them, the inalienable freedom of the conscience, the underived, unchartered independence of the human soul. In others of their political and ethical opinions, they partook of the errors of their time, other interests of society they may even have neglected, but in their perception and application of this principle — the basis of all real freedom — they strode far before the age to which they belonged. They seemed to their contemporaries to be pursuing, with reckless zeal, a startling and impracticable paradox; but they felt, themselves, the greatness of the mission they were appointed to accomplish — to found a refuge for "true soul liberty," to hold forth to mankind the first "lively experiment, that a most flourishing civil State may stand, and be best maintained, with a full liberty in religious concernments." This noble purpose they adhered to with a tenacity that never yielded — with a consistency that never was marred, amidst the penury and the privations of the wilderness, amidst the scorn and the persecutions of all their neighbors. The colony, from the first, in the language of the settlers at Newport, was "a birth and breeding of the Most High." Here, "beyond the chartered grasp of civilized men," it was founded' by "an outcast people," who gloried most in "bearing with the several judgments and consciences of each other in all the towns of the colony." In this consisted the peculiarity of Rhode Island. In this, the fundamental principle of her society, she stood forth in the age, single and alone — *nec viget quidquam simile, aut secundum.*

This peculiarity in her early character made her the object of incessant suspicion and distrust, and, at length, arrayed against her the combined legislation and proscription of all the other colonies of New England. They chose to regard her as a heterodox, and almost as an outlaw State, whose interests and happiness they might prey upon at pleasure, and without rebuke. They laid claim to her territory, and extended their jurisdiction over her people, and well-nigh crushed her in her very cradle. Massachusetts passed a law forbidding the inhabitants of Providence from coming to her towns; and when a respected clergyman of Newport, with two companions, went to visit an aged member of his church, resident at Lynn, he was seized by the beadles of the town, while preaching on the Sabbath, at the house of his friend, and was punished, under sentence of the court, by a heavy fine and imprisonment, with the alternative of being publicly whipped! The fine was paid without the good man's knowledge or consent, and he was released from prison. One of his companions, however, was still retained in confinement, and when set at liberty, was whipped with thirty stripes, inflicted with that merciless severity which heresy alone could have provoked. Under the operation of this exclusive policy, which was adopted by the neighboring colonies, the inhabitants of Rhode Island were not only cut off from the trade of the country, but were often obliged to forego the comforts and the common necessaries of life. This hostility, which, from the beginning, had characterized the intercourse of the other settlements with the fathers of Rhode Island, in 1643, was embodied in the confederacy which was established among the colonies of New England. The leading object of this confederacy was the mutual protection of its members against the Indians, whose hostility was threatened on every side, and against the rising settlements of the French and the Dutch, with whom England was then frequently at war. The circumstances of its formation are worthy of a moment's particular consideration. The contracting parties to the league were the colonies of Massachusetts and Plymouth, of New Haven and Connecticut, each of which, by its commissioners, signed the articles at Boston, on the 19th of May, 1643. This union Rhode Island was not invited to join, and subsequently, at her own application to be admitted a member, she was *deliberately refused admission;* an act which, taken in all its circumstances, stands out among the most unchristian and inhuman recorded in Puritan history, in whose strange records are so often blended the direst atrocity and the loftiest virtue. Here was an infant, feeble colony, situated between two powerful races of savages — the Wampanoags on the east and the Narragansetts on the west — and separated by the wide Atlantic from the mother country. Its people were of the same Anglo-Saxon stock, and professed the same Protestant faith with their neighbors. They had come from England in the same ships which bore the colonists of Plymouth and Boston, of New Haven and Hartford. Like them they had lighted the fires of civilization in the wilderness, and by their beneficent influence with the Indians they had, more than once, saved the whole country from the desolations of savage war. Yet it was all in vain. They had adopted the startling heresy, that men are responsible for their opinions to God alone ; that the civil power may not interfere in religious concernments ; and that before the law of the land all should alike be equal, whether Protestants or Papists, whether Jews or Turks. For this opinion, which they had dared to proclaim, and to carry into practice, they were placed beneath the ban of universal proscription, and were deliberately excluded from the alliance and the sympathies of the whole civilization of the country — to perish, it might be, from the wastings of starvation and disease, or amid the terrors of Indian massacre and conflagration.

At a recent celebration of the era of this confederacy,

in a neighboring State, a distinguished and venerable orator discoursed, with more of rhetoric than of truth, concerning what he was pleased to term "the conscientious,
contentious spirit" of the early fathers of Rhode Island.
But to what manner of spirit shall we attribute this act of
the Puritans of New England, by which a Christian colony,
of their own brethren, was deprived of all the benefits of
their neighborhood, and left unprotected in the wilderness, to contend with merciless savages and struggle alone
"against necessity's sharp pinch!" Was it mere indifference to the fate of those whom they deemed heretics
and outcasts? Or was it the vain hope, that by the pressure of want, or the threats of Indian massacre, the colony
would yield to her confederate neighbors, and quietly submit to be partitioned among their several jurisdictions?
Whichever of these may have been the motive, the act
itself bespeaks a dark and malignant bigotry, which cannot be veiled, and for which it is in vain to apologize — a
bigotry which, indeed, need not be dwelt upon, amid the
general blaze of Puritan virtues, but which we may well
be proud to think, has left no traces of its existence in the
history or the character of Rhode Island.

How different from all this is the spirit which characterized *her* legislation, even at the same gloomy periods of
New England history! In turning to consider it we seem
to have advanced a whole age in the progress of civil and
intellectual freedom. Take a single illustration. In
1656, Massachusetts commenced the persecution of the
Quakers, which soon extended through all New England.
Banished from every other colony, they fled to Rhode
Island, where, though they had but few sympathies with
the inhabitants, they were kindly received, and were admitted to all the privileges of citizens and freemen. But
the Commissioners of the United Colonies hunted them
even here. In two several appeals, they urged the author-

ities of this colony, by every motive that could be addressed to the self-interest of a community, to join in the general persecution. But with what dignity does the Legislature reply : " As concerning these Quakers (so called), which are now among us, we have no law whereby to punish any for only declaring, by words, their minds and understandings, concerning the things and ways of God as to salvation and an eternal condition." And, when finding all persuasives vain, the Commissioners, irritated at her inflexible adherence to her noble principles, threaten to suspend all intercourse, and thus dry up the very sources of subsistence to the colony, the Assembly calmly make their appeal to " his Highness and honorable council " in England, and, through their agent, ask that they " may not be compelled to exercise any civil power over men's consciences, so long as human orders, in point of civility, are not corrupted or violated ; which," say they, " our neighbors about us do frequently practice, whereof many of us have *large experience*, and do judge it to be no less than a point of *absolute cruelty.*"

Now, look along the history of mankind, up to the latter half of the seventeenth century, and where else do you find that language like this had ever proceeded from a legislative assembly ? Yet, strange to say, the age was preëminently distinguished for its attention to religious truth and to the rights of conscience. England was rent by civil wars, of which these rights were professed as the sustaining principle. Her people were divided into four great parties, the Roman Catholics, the Episcopalians, the Presbyterians, and the Independents, all of whom were contending for what they called *freedom of conscience ;* and many a noble spirit had been offered up as a sacrifice to the cause, on the scaffold, or on the field of battle. Here, too, upon the barren coasts of New England, were hardy settlements, just springing into vigorous existence, each of which had been planted for the *freedom of the conscience.* Yet on a closer inspection, the freedom which all were pursuing proves to be freedom only for themselves, not for others. It was freedom to rear their own altars and to offer their own worship. Beyond this it did not go. And the student of history turns from them all; from the religious parties then struggling for ascendancy in England, and from the colonies which had sprung up on the shores of America, and finds here alone, in a colony which had been neglected by her mother and despised by all her sisters, the solitary refuge for true soul-liberty — that unlimited intellectual freedom, higher than mere toleration — which makes all opinions equal in the eye of the law, and which forbids the civil power to touch the inviolable sanctuary of the conscience.

Thus peculiar — far more so than has been generally understood — was the spirit of the early fathers of this State. The memorials of their labors, of their legislation, of their sufferings for the maintenance of this principle — which they alone of all the world understood and cherished — are worthy of the minutest inquiry. They cannot be too thoroughly explored, or too carefully treasured up in the depositories of historic lore.

But, in addition to the greatness and value of the principles at issue, there is another consideration, which urges us perhaps, still more strongly, to the careful collection and preservation of the materials, especially for our early history. It is found in the fact that these principles, and the characters of the men who here asserted them, have been singularly misrepresented and misunderstood. The literature of New England, at that day, was confined to Massachusetts and Plymouth, and their early annalists seem never to have dreamed, that a faithful narrative of the planting and growth of this heterodox colony, where all sorts of consciences were tolerated, would ever be of the slightest interest or benefit to mankind. Hence it happened, that our early history became known to the world, mainly through the imperfect sketches of Winthrop or Hubbard, the prejudiced statements of Morton, the controversial sarcasms of Mr. Cotton, and the ridiculous, and sometimes vulgar jibes, of Cotton Mather. Many of these misrepresentations have been corrected by subsequent writers, in the same States from which they emanated ; and the fame of Rhode Island has been brightened by their labors. But she still appeals to her own sons for a fuller vindication ; she claims it for the lessons she has taught them, for the inheritance of freedom she has transmitted to them. From these eminences in her social progress to which she has attained, she points us back to the scattered graves of her original Planters, and demands of us that we build monuments to their memory; that we guard their fame, and transmit their principles, undisguised and unperverted, in the imperishable records of history.

Among these early fathers of the State, I may here mention one, whose fame has been too much neglected, but whose character has descended to us, in the memory of his deeds, embalmed with the purest associations of devoted patriotism and exalted virtue. I refer to Dr. John Clarke, of Newport — the associate of Roger Williams — the procurer of the second Charter — the tried friend of the colony, at a time when friendship for her was the sacrifice of all else that New England had to bestow. His life ought long ago to have been written, and every lineament of his pure and spotless character, on which even enmity and envy have fastened no reproach, should have been held forth to the respect and admiration of those who enjoy the fruits of his labors. A scholar, bred probably at one of England's ancient Universities — a physician, accustomed to the practice of his profession

in the circles of the British Metropolis — a teacher of religion, despised and persecuted by those among whom he
had cast his lot — he came hither, the mild and benignant
advocate of religious freedom, and, next to the exiled
founder of Providence, was the truest friend, and the most
generous benefactor of Rhode Island. For twelve troubled
years he resided in England as the representative of the
colony, supporting himself during all this period by his
own labors, and by the mortgage of his estate in Newport.
He was an intimate associate of many of the eminent men
of the time, and was doubtless a witness of many of the
stirring scenes of the English Revolution. By his unwavering fidelity, by his winning manners, and his diplomatic skill, he maintained the rights of the colony, amid
the changes and tumults of a revolutionary age, and at
length, upon the restoration of the Stuarts, he succeeded
in obtaining from the second Charles that Charter of
civil government which has shaped the institutions of the
State, and identified itself with all her glory. The disinterested benevolence which had animated his life, still
lighted up its closing hours. He died at Newport in
1676, and in his last will bequeathed a handsome estate
"for the relief of the poor, and the bringing up of children unto learning."

> " Peace to the just man's memory — let it grow
>   Greener with years, and blossom through the flight
>   Of ages ; let the mimic canvas show
>   His calm benevolent features ; let the light
>   Stream on his deeds of love that shunned the sight
>   Of all but Heaven ; and in the book of fame,
>   The glorious record of his virtues write,
>   And hold it up to men, and bid them claim
>   A palm like his, and catch from him the hallowed flame."

I have referred more particularly to the early periods
of the history of Rhode Island, in illustrating the peculiarity of her position, and the value of her fame.   But

other periods are equally replete with historic interest, and present scarcely fewer claims upon the attention and the study of her sons. Her participation in the struggles of the Revolution has not yet been fully told. All that may illustrate the services she rendered the cause of national independence, whether by legislation or by arms ; all that embodies the spirit that made her the nursery of heroic commanders and of brave troops ; and all that may explain her reluctant adoption of the Federal Constitution, or the origin and growth of her great social interests, her commerce and her manufactures, her education and her religion — all these should be faithfully explored and carefully garnered up, away from the reach of oblivion.

There is also another period, equally important to the fame of the State, and it may be equally instructive in its lessons for mankind, the memorials of which we, of the present generation, are especially bound to preserve from decay. I refer to the recent civil controversy, whose furious passions have scarcely yet died away. Whatever may be the opinions we entertain respecting it, all will admit the importance of treasuring up everything that can explain its origin and issue, or illustrate its spirit and character. We owe it to the State, whose bosom has been rent, and whose peace has been disturbed — and we owe it scarcely less to the nation, whose interests are involved in the principles at issue, to see to it that its history be faithfully written, not with the pen of partisan passion, or beneath the narrowing influence of political prejudice ; but that it be written in the light of the Constitution, with the spirit of calm philosophy and discriminating research. Let everything pertaining to it be carefully preserved, that when in a future age, after our petty interests shall have perished, and our short-lived passions shall have died away, the historian shall come to trace the causes of these unhappy strifes, he may find here the means of thoroughly

understanding the principles at issue between the contending parties, and the spirit and the acts that have marked
the character of each, as well as the issue that has sprung
from the angry passions that have been so deeply stirred.
Thus let the cause be committed to the tribunals of posterity.   Let there be materials for removing every blot
that may have been cast upon the escutcheon of the State,
of refuting every calumny that has been uttered against
her fair fame, that the truth, the simple unvarnished truth,
may alone be committed to the records of history.

For purposes such as these has the Rhode Island Historical Society been established.   It dates back to the
year 1822, and in the order of time it was the fourth institution of the kind established in the United States.   It
owes its origin to the spirit and activity of a few true-
hearted sons of Rhode Island, who chanced to meet in the
office of a gentleman [1] whose historic zeal, even then distinguished, has since led him onward to the most commendable labors, and the most valuable results.   It was
in the course of their conversation that the suggestion
was first made of a Society, whose aim should be to collect
and preserve, for the use of the historian, the scattered
memorials of the successive periods of our progress as a
Colony and a State.   The suggestion was speedily carried
into effect, and this Society commenced its useful career.
Twenty-two years have since elapsed, and, amidst many
discouragements it has gone steadily forward in the prosecution of its worthy aims.   Though it has never occupied
a conspicuous place in the public estimation, and its active supporters have always been few, yet it has already
done essential service in the illustration of the spirit and
the characters that belong to our early annals.   It has
published five volumes of its collections, and has garnered
up in its archives a large mass of materials, which have

[1] Hon. William R. Staples, author of the *Annals of Providence.*

already rendered valuable aid to writers of American history, and among which the future historian of the State or of the country will find all that now remains of many a forgotten era of the past. Through the agency of a succession of indefatigable secretaries and directors, the Society has maintained an extensive and useful correspondence with similar associations in this country and in foreign lands. Its correspondence has rendered signal aid to the antiquarians of Denmark, in their attempts to decipher those mysterious inscriptions upon the rocky shores of New England, which seem to point back to the visit of some unknown voyagers centuries before the heroic enterprise of Columbus. The aid which was thus received has been acknowledged with grateful applause by this learned association, in the "Antiquitates Americanæ," — the magnificent work in which they have embodied their researches respecting the ante-Columbian periods of American history.

After many efforts and long delays, the Society, aided in part by private munificence, has at length been able to rear the modest structure, whose completion we have to-day come up to celebrate. We have watched its progress, from its commencement to its final consummation. In hope and in joy we now set it apart to the purposes for which it has been erected. We dedicate it to the muse of history — " the muse of saintly aspect and awful form," who ever watches over the fortunes of men, and guards the virtues of humanity. We wish it to be a place of secure and perpetual deposit, where, beyond the reach of accident, or the approach of decay, we may accumulate all the materials for our yet unwritten history. We would gather here all that can illustrate the early planting or the subsequent growth of our State, the lives of its founders and settlers, the manuscripts of its departed worthies, the history of its towns, its glorious proclamations of religious

liberty, and its heroic sacrifices, both in peace and in war.
We would also gather here, the few remaining relics of
the long perished race of Canonicus and Miantonomo, and
keep them as precious memorials of men, who, though un-
taught in the lessons of civilized benevolence, received to
their rude hospitality, the fathers of the State, when Christian pilgrims persecuted and banished them. We would
also deposit here everything that is connected with the interests of society within the limits of the Commonwealth —
the chronicles of every controversy, the organs of every
party, the wretched sheet, that in its day was too worth-
less to be read, if so be it illustrate the morals, the manners, or the deeds of the time, and the most valuable
volume in which genius and wisdom have embodied their
immortal thoughts. We may hope, too, that within its
alcoves, " rich with the spoils of time," may at length be
seen the features and forms of the men, who in peace and
in war have reflected honor on the State, by the wisdom
they have carried to the councils, or the glory they have
added to the name of the country. Thus, distant generations may come up hither, and while they study the memorials of the past, they may gaze upon the lineaments of
the men whose names they have learned to identify with
whatever is heroic in action, or dignified in character.

It is to these objects, and to others such as these, that
we dedicate this edifice, which we have reared in this
friendly neighborhood of learning, as the depository of
historic lore. They are liberal and noble objects, and
worthy to command the respect, and enlist the efforts, of
an enlightened community. They are limited to no local
bounds. They embrace the whole territory of the Commonwealth, and concern as intimately the settlements on
Rhode Island, the Asylum from persecution at Warwick,
the romantic legends of Mount Hope and Narragansett,
as they do the Plantations of Providence. Whether they

are ever fully accomplished, will depend on the efforts which the members of this Society put forth, and upon the sympathy and aid which we receive from our fellow-citizens throughout the State. We invite, therefore, the co-operation of all, in carrying forward the work which we have begun, and of which so much remains to be accomplished. The State is the common parent of us all, and her fame should be dear to us all. That fame, which two hundred years have established, has at length been committed to us, to guard and to perpetuate. Let us be faithful to the trust; and in the temple which literary genius may rear to American History, let us erect an humble shrine, and dedicate it to Rhode Island, and adorn it with her stainless escutcheon of RELIGIOUS FREEDOM.

ADDRESS

AT A PUBLIC MEETING OF THE CITIZENS OF PROVIDENCE
JUNE 7, 1856, CALLED TO CONSIDER THE ASSAULT UPON
THE HONORABLE CHARLES SUMNER, IN THE SENATE-
CHAMBER AT WASHINGTON.

MR. PRESIDENT — Your appearance in the chair of this
meeting, this greeting with which you are welcomed by
your fellow-citizens on your return after a long absence,
again to take your place among us, as well as your own
distinct avowal, proclaim that it is no common and no
party object which has called us together to-night. Had
any such purpose dictated the meeting, neither you nor
I might have participated in its proceedings.

There are those among us to whom our whole heavens
seem to be hung in black, and our whole horizon is low-
ering with portentous clouds. But as you have so clearly
stated, we are now assembled to consider a single occurrence which stands forth most conspicuous among the
occasions of public excitements, and which has filled all
our minds with abhorrence and dismay. The country
has been dishonored in its high places, and its good name
has been injured throughout the civilized world. A Senator of the United States has been struck down by the
hand of brutal violence in his seat in the Senate — a Senator who represents an ancient and illustrious Commonwealth, one of the most honored in the sisterhood of the
States, whose history furnished some of the proudest
chapters in our national annals. The circumstances and
the place too, in which this deed was perpetrated, impart

to it an ominous and fearful import, and make it a matter of national concern. It was done in no moment of excited debate, in no impulse of sudden passion, but it was deliberate and cold-blooded, plotted and consulted beforehand, and meditated for two days and nights. Or rather, as the evidence has fully shown, it was a *conspiracy*, not alone against the safety and life of a single citizen or a single Senator, but against free speech and free legislation in the Capitol of the nation. Look at that single scene in the gate-house of the Capitol grounds, on the morning of the day which witnessed this unparalleled outrage, and see the perpetrator plotting with his accomplice, and consulting how he may best accomplish his cowardly purpose, and strike his victim when most unprepared and defenseless. These men, thus stealthily lurking at the gates of the Capitol, are members of the House of Representatives; but if they were not, how should we characterize them but as a highwayman and his accomplice lying in wait for their prey?

The outrage, too, borrows a still darker atrocity from the place in which it was at length committed. There is a peculiar sanctity attached to the Senate House of this Republic. It was long ago described as the " sanctuary of the Constitution, — the citadel of Order, Liberty, and Law." It is the place where the representatives of sovereign States meet on the basis of perfect equality, where the smallest and weakest members of the Union are raised to the rank of the largest and the most powerful, — where Delaware and Rhode Island take counsel as equals with New York and Pennsylvania, with Ohio and Virginia. It was in that most sacred chamber of the government that the assassin entered and waited his opportunity, and at length dealt his bludgeon blows upon the head of the defenseless Senator, till he fell prostrate and bleeding upon the floor.

This is the dastardly outrage, this the humiliating, shameful spectacle, which we have come together to-night to consider. Those blows fell not alone on the manly brow of the Senator from Massachusetts. They fell on the head of this Republic. They descended on the honor and dignity, the peace and security, of the American people, on you and on me, fellow-citizens. We to-night confess the humiliation and suffering they have inflicted, and demand their redress and the utmost and immediate punishment of their author. We claim it for the dignity and purity of the government under which we live, and with millions around us we claim it for ourselves, our honor and our good name as a people. But, Mr. President, it is asked what redress can be had and what punishment can be inflicted on the perpetrator of a deed that has thus disgraced the American name, and dishonored and outraged the American people. This is a question which certainly claims the thoughtful consideration of every citizen. Let us consider it as its gravity and importance demand. In speaking of it, I have no redress and no punishment to suggest which is at variance with the Constitution and laws of the land, or with the common obligations which rest upon us, whether as citizens or as States. I still believe in and reverence the Constitution of the United States, and still regard it, when administered in its true spirit, as containing or allowing abundant remedy for every national wrong. What, then, ought to be done in the case we are now considering?

First of all then, sir, we can and we do demand that this man and his accomplice be punished by the House of Representatives to which they belong, to the full extent of its power. The question is now pending in that House, and no graver question will receive its consideration while its session lasts. Its committee has reported by its majority and by its minority, and it must choose between the two. Those reports are before the country, and are at this moment receiving the verdict of millions of the people. The former, I think, is all that could be desired to indicate the insulted dignity both of the House and the Senate. It recites, as we all know, the disgusting story of this wrong, and gives the testimony of those who witnessed it. It declares the privileges which the Constitution assigns to the legislators of this Republic to have been shamefully and wantonly violated, and closes with the unqualified resolves that the principal offender in this great outrage be expelled from the House, and that his accessories be censured by solemn vote. Let that be done, and the House may again challenge the respect of the country. The latter of these reports presents an opposite view, very different in its spirit and in the conclusion to which it comes. It declares that no privilege has been violated, that no offense has been committed, and that nothing need be done. It covers the whole transaction with palliations and special pleadings, and thus seeks to hide from public view the intolerable wrong which it involves. It is signed by two names, one of them hitherto a name of distinction and honor; but I trust that no authority which it thus acquires can save it from the reprobation which it deserves. It cites the precedents it employs from the parliamentary history of England, to show that the House has no power in a case like this. But it passes by at least one most conspicuous instance in our own history, in the early and palmy days of the American Senate, which is exceedingly pertinent and appropriate, and which many gentlemen around me will readily recall. In the summer of 1797, a few months after the close of the second administration of President Washington, and while the shadow of his unsullied dignity and his great character still rested upon the government he had so lately left, the Senate, with but one dissenting voice, expelled William Blount, a Senator from Tennessee, then but lately admitted to the Union. He had violated no privilege of either House of Congress; he had committed no crime at the seat of the government; nor had he been condemned, nor even indicted, before any judicial tribunal in the country. As a land speculator and a political adventurer, he had headed a combination, for mere money-making and selfish ends, to transfer the territory beyond the Mississippi from the jurisdiction of Spain to that of England, and had thus violated the treaties and compromised the neutrality of the government. To make the precedent still more striking, the offense had been committed while he was acting as governor of the territory which now, as a sovereign State, he was representing in the Senate. Charges were preferred to that grave and reverend body by the action of the House below, and Blount was expelled from his seat because his conduct in a public position had dishonored the country, and was incompatible with the duties and office of a Senator. Let that precedent be now followed; and if there be no other on record, the perpetrator of this recent outrage will be driven from his seat in the House of Representatives by the indignant vote of every member. Unless this be done, a stain of dishonor will still rest upon the body. A sense of foul and unforgotten wrong will still rankle like iron in the heart of the nation, and ruffianism will be installed at the Capitol.

But, sir, this man has also violated the laws which are provided for the common security of us all. Apart from the privileges of rank and station, I hope it is still a crime in the District of Columbia to waylay and assault, and beat to unconsciousness and almost to death, an American citizen, even the humblest that approaches the seat of government. If it be not, it is a matter which it concerns us all to know. We have a right, then, to expect that this man, whatever he may be in other respects, will be tried and punished as a criminal under the laws which Congress has enacted, and before the tribunals which Congress has established for the District of Columbia. Let that be done and another item is added to the redress which this outrage demands, and all will be done which constituted authorities and law can do.

But, Mr. President, it will be said that even that is but an imperfect redress for a crime like this. I admit it, sir, and I think there yet remains another and a severer punishment than any which courts of law can impose. Their heaviest inflictions are endured and are soon at an end. But there exists in the moral nature of man, and in the tone of civilized society, an instrument of retribution whose agency cannot be escaped, whose power continues while life lasts, or memory and name endure. This instrument is the scorn and abhorrence of high-minded men. Tell me not of prisons and gibbets, as if these were the punishment of final resort. There is a direr and more fearful retribution in the loss of an honorable standing, in the blight of a reputation, in the anathema of a proud name, in desertion, neglect, and contempt from respectable men. We are not without signal examples of punishment like this that may well now be recalled. That traitor general of the Revolution who surrendered West Point to the enemy, and then led an expedition against the inhabitants of the hills and hamlets where his own infancy had been nursed, — look at him as, years afterwards, when the Revolution was ended, and with the price of his treachery in his hands, he is introduced as a private man upon the floor of the British House of Commons, and see him quail and wither before the scorn with which a member then speaking folds his arms and declares, "I will not speak while the air of this House is tainted with the presence of a traitor." Think you he did not then wish that he had fallen in battle, or even been captured and hanged in the place of that youthful officer whom his betrayed commander was obliged to sacrifice in his stead ? Or take another example of a similar retribution. It is now some fifty years since a man who had been honored with his country's favor, inflamed by curious and vengeful passions, challenged and shot in mortal combat the foremost statesman of the age. He was visited with no punishment by the laws of the land. But his deed had outraged the moral sentiments of a great civilized community, and through the thirty years of his remaining life he lived a wretched and blighted man. Forsaken almost of heaven and earth, childless and solitary, he lingered to old age in the midst of a great metropolis, neglected, avoided, hated and despised. This is the heaviest punishment which man can inflict for great wrongs to justice, freedom, and to humanity. So, fellow-citizens, let it be with him who lays the parricidal hand of violence upon the embodied majesty of the Republic. Let all men avoid him and turn away from him, in the halls of the legislature, in the marts of business, and in the circles of society. Let an anathema, like that of the ancient Church, rest upon him so long as he lives, and let his name be coupled only with oblivion or contempt. When all this has been done the redress is complete, and the justice of the earth is satisfied.

I know not, sir, what existing organizations will favor demands like these. It may be that none will do it. I remember to have read a treatise written by an eminent Christian statesman, still living on the continent of Europe, on what he styled " the Church of the Future." Wearied with the divisions and distractions of Christendom, disheartened with its want of union, its want of energy, and its want of action, he meditated in rapturous vision, and wrote with fervid eloquence, upon the future

Church which was yet to arise to embody the spirit of Him who spake as never man spake, to present the lineaments of our holy religion, and to unite the faithful of every land in carrying blessings to all the world. So, sir, it may be, we must wait for some *party of the future* to enshrine in itself the spirit of the Constitution, to unite all "good men and true," from every State, and to hold forth to the world the fair form of American freedom and American civilization. But if the vision should be too long delayed, if violence and barbarism shall continue to encroach unresisted, we, sir, are still to stand fast in the liberty wherewith we have been made free. Dwelling on the soil that was purchased with our fathers' blood, we are never to yield, but still to show that the same blood is not yet exhausted in our veins. Thus, and thus alone, can we, as citizens of the Republic, be true to ourselves, to our country, and to God.

ADDRESS AT THE OPENING OF THE RHODE ISLAND HOSPITAL, OCTOBER 1, 1868.

MR. PRESIDENT, AND LADIES AND GENTLEMEN:

WE have come together to-day to celebrate the opening of the Rhode Island Hospital; to congratulate each other on the completion of this noble structure, and in devout gratitude and humble faith to consecrate it to the benefi-cent work for which it has been erected. It bears the name of the State; it has been aided by personal contri-butions from every part of the State; and in the compre-hensive and catholic spirit of the State, it is designed to be an asylum for all who may need its healing care. We gather to it, therefore, with the liveliest interest and the fondest hope, and hail it as the grandest and most benef-icent work which Rhode Island charity has thus far, achieved. We gaze with delight upon the graceful pro-portions of its well-chosen architecture. We survey with the fullest satisfaction its airy pavilions, its spacious and sun-lighted wards, and their admirable appointments for the convenience and comfort of those who are to be its inmates. We contemplate with pleasure the rare salubrity of its situation, and the ample grounds which environ it, with their capacities for lawn, and garden, and park, yet to be developed. We recall with gratitude the generous spirits who first conceived it, the earnest and self-denying men who solicited its funds, and the faithful and laborious guardians who have given to it their daily care, and who now present it to us as their completed work, — their dele-gated trust, most judiciously and honorably fulfilled. As fellow-laborers and sharers together in the ennobling enterprise, we enter with them into the rare felicities of this occasion; and as citizens of the community which it is designed to bless, we behold with joy and pride these doors thrown open to-day for all who may need the comfort and care, the tender nursing and the skillful healing, which are here to be dispensed in all future time.

A hospital for the treatment of the infirm and the sick may well be selected as the most genuine and appropriate manifestation of the Christian civilization which we have inherited. No other charity is so strictly of Christian origin, or illustrates so conspicuously that new spirit of universal benevolence which Christianity first breathed into the world. The splendid paganisms of antiquity have left their characteristic monuments of genius and skill, of wealth and power. Majestic structures whose ruins now lie along the track of time, proclaim the great ideas and the heroic endeavors of those ages on which Christianity had not dawned. But in all their magnificence they bore no fruit like this. Humane maxims were not wanting in their literature and philosophy, kindly sentiments were not unknown in their domestic or their civil life. But neither India nor Egypt, neither Greece nor Italy, could point to a single spot in their storied soil which was consecrated to the care of the injured and the healing of the sick, — the relief of human suffering and the saving of human life. Their civilizations, it is true, recognized, in some imperfect degree, the value of the human being to society as a producer of happiness to others, as a defender of the state, and a laborer for the common weal. But they were wholly indifferent to his transcendent value to himself as a creature of God, with a probation on earth and an immortal life to come. They called into exercise no sentiments of comprehensive charity, and made no recognition of anything like brotherhood among men. They utterly failed, as every mere material civilization must fail, in developing that larger and higher humanity which overleaps the barriers of country and race, which rises above distinctions of caste and condition, which gathers to its embrace the outcast and forsaken, and bestows its nursing and care, its costly medicines and its healing skill, on the sick and the insane, on the maimed and the injured, who would otherwise perish in penury and neglect. Man learned his true relations to his brother man only from the Divine Redeemer. The grand reciprocities and charities of human life were so constantly reiterated in his teachings, so sublimely generalized and exemplified in his career, that the practice of them became inseparable from Christianity. It was of charity to the sick, the destitute, and the imprisoned, — those from whom others turned away with indifference or contempt, — that He uttered the words which will not cease to be repeated through all the ages of history : "*Inasmuch as ye have done it unto one of the least of these my brethren, ye have done it unto me.*" It is this broader and higher benevolence which was thus taught to men — this feeling that whoever is forsaken or in want, whoever is stricken with injury or disease, is our neighbor and our brother, — it is this that has prompted the great charities of modern civilization and has distinguished this civilization from all which preceded it.

But more than this is true. The peculiar charity which is here illustrated is that which is most conspicuously characteristic of Christianity. The feeding of the hungry had been already recognized both as a virtue and a necessity. It had been made an institution of the State, and in all the great nations of antiquity whole classes of the population received their daily bread either from public or from private bounty. Christianity did not fail to commend a charity which became so necessary amidst the miseries of the world. But its highest sanctions and its divinest benedictions were reserved for that other benevolence which carries relief to the sufferings and healing to the diseases with which man is everywhere so grievously afflicted. It has been well remarked that there were but two occasions on which our Lord exerted his miraculous power to feed the hungry multitudes who so often thronged his path; while the occasions were innumerable on which He stretched forth his hand to restore the maimed and to heal the sick. He wrought no miracle that set aside the law which makes subsistence dependent on industry and prudence. He fed the multitudes only when far from home and in a desert place, and because, having come to hear his teachings, they were apparently dependent on his hospitality and care. Not so, however, with his miraculous healing. The lame walked, the blind saw, the lepers were cleansed, those who were smitten with any disease that visits the human frame were made whole, whenever they sought his marvelous interposition. In city and in village, in the market place and in the temple, in the house and by the wayside, his mysterious power was ever ready to arrest the wasting of disease and to avert the sufferings it produced. And when He separated his chosen apostles and endued them with divine gifts like his own, He bade them go forth on two grand errands of mercy to men; the one to preach the kingdom of God, the other to heal all manner of diseases. To do these two, the latter as truly as the former, became the distinguishing characteristic of the new religion, and wherever it was received among men the practice of an exalted charity was as unfailing among Christians as their belief in the kingdom of God.

The new society which received these grand ideas and enshrined this universal charity was unlike any other that had existed in the world, and from it have sprung the most cherished social institutions of our modern life. It

everywhere wrought a social transformation which no history has described and no imagination has fully conceived.
It extended itself into all countries and among all races;
and yet, even amidst the iron separations of ancient ranks,
to be a Christian, of whatever kindred or clime, in all the
early years of the Church, was a passport to every Christian home in the world. At a later period, in all the
chief centres of the ever-widening Christendom, the hospitality which every believer had extended to all his brethren was intrusted to a few who acted for the others, and
at length it was concentrated at certain well-known places,
and freely dispensed to all who sought it there. The
hospital thus arose as a necessity of the times, to do for
Christians in sickness or in distress, when far from home,
what could no longer be done by private hospitality. It
was at first denounced as a reproach and a proof of declining benevolence, but it met a great and growing want,
and the princes and ecclesiastics of Christendom gave it
their favor and bestowed upon it their munificence. It
became connected with every monastery that was established, and the blessings which it thus dispensed constitute perhaps the humanest service which the monastic
orders of the Middle Age rendered to mankind. And
when in later times the cross, once so humble and despised, became the badge of empire and was blazoned on
the banners of armies, even crusading knighthood did not
forget the care and nursing of the sick, which, more than
all things else, emblemed the religion it sought to propa-
gate.

But an institution for the healing of the sick and the
care of the injured must be an expression of something
more than Christian benevolence alone. It must also be
the embodiment of every device and arrangement which
science has discovered or art has contrived for the alleviation of suffering and the restoration of health. Christian

philanthropy prompts the enterprise, but it is science that presides over its accomplishment and fits it for its high ends. Civilization must lavish upon it its choicest treasures, both of humanity and of knowledge, in making it all that it ought to be. The earliest hospital of Western Europe is said to have been founded by the Empress Helena, — a native of Britain and the mother of Constantine. But in all save the motive that prompted it, how different must it have been from any one of those hospitals which another British lady, in our own time, established for her countrymen at Scutari, with a zeal so enlightened and a success so beneficent that her woman's name shines, above that of any general or any statesman, as the most heroic and famous in the annals of the Crimean War! In the cloistered hall which the Benedictine monks set apart, in every monastery which they built, for the stranger and the invalid who should seek their hospitality and require their care, we recognize the same benevolence which Christianity always inspires in its votaries. They toiled as faithfully, they sacrificed as generously, as philanthropists in any later age. But how often were their pious purposes wholly thwarted and their toilsome philanthropy well nigh wasted for the want of knowledge of the work in which they were engaged! The same is true of those representatives of the Church who accompanied the crusading armies in order to restore the sick and care for the wounded. They bore the spirit of humanity into the scenes of Moslem war, and made care for human suffering a knightly and chivalrous distinction. Beyond this, however, and the services which it involved, they were unable to go; and the armies they accompanied wasted away on the plains of Palestine, as if poisoned by the very air they breathed. Now it is only when we compare the apartment of the sick in some Benedictine monastery with a structure like this in which we are to-day assembled,

or place the kindly services of the knights of St. John in
the Crusades beside the manifold ministries of the United
States Sanitary Commission in our Civil War, that we are
able to appreciate how much the advancement of human
knowledge, and the improvements which have been made
in every science and every art, have enabled Christian
benevolence to achieve for the relief of suffering and the
healing of disease.   Comparisons such as these fully justify the claim we make for a great hospital, as, in our own
day, the truest and most comprehensive exponent that can
be named, alike of the humanity and the piety, the science
and the art, which constitute the glory of Christian civilization.   No other institution that exists proclaims so fully
the progress which society has made, both in knowledge of
Nature and in sympathy for man.

Let it not be thought, however, that a hospital for the
sick and the injured is a mere gratuitous benefaction to
those whom it may receive as patients.   Like every other
judicious social charity, it reacts with manifold blessings
on its authors and on the whole community.   The spirit
in which it has its origin, and in which it must be sustained, is essential to the well-being and progress of society.
Who would wish to live where it does not exist?   All that
makes up the higher life of man springs from the sympathy which he feels for his fellow-man.   It is what we do
for others that ennobles and hallows what we do for ourselves.   Even the wealth for which we strive so earnestly,
and to which we cling so fondly, is made up of something
more than mere material gains.   It is the result of a thousand dependencies and relationships without which it could
not exist.   It grows only under the protection of law.   It
dwells securely only in the midst of intelligence and virtue.   It puts forth its energies and spreads its agencies,
on the right hand and on the left, only where justice and
humanity and religious faith have fixed their abode.   For

the presence of these, the highest attributes of manhood and of society, no greed of gain, no tireless industry, no sagacious forethought, can long be a substitute. They must be secured and maintained, or high prosperity will take its departure. This is a part of that "Moral Law of Accumulation" which a great Teacher among ourselves used so often to expound to us. It underlies all that we call Political Economy, and is as truly a condition of social wealth as is the labor from which it seems to spring. Adam Smith designed his great work on the Wealth of Nations to be a supplement to that which he had already written on the Moral Sentiments; and the liberal science of which he is the founder, in its essential doctrines, is but an expansion of the law, Thou shalt love thy neighbor as thyself.

It is of generous sentiments and comprehensive considerations like these that a charity such as we have here established should be the full and perfect expression. It springs from cultivated Christian humanity, but it gathers to itself, and concentrates upon its construction and appointments, all the fruits both of scientific knowledge and of mechanical and professional skill. Its efficiency and success as a place for the treatment of disease must depend on the careful observance of a multitude of delicate but indispensable laws. Everything that can affect, however remotely, the sources of human health, or the vigor of human life, is to be thought of in the selection of its site, in the planning of its architecture, and in the final construction of its buildings. The exposure to the rays of the sun, the underlying soil, the surrounding air, the adjacent water, the material to be used in the formation of its several parts both within and without, its division into apartments and their dimensions and relations to each other, its capacity for the amplest ventilation, its adaptation for interior salubrity, and all its arrangements for easy, quiet, and most efficient administration, are but specimens and illustrations of the elements that enter into a problem which social philanthropy, after the lapse of many ages, has even now but imperfectly solved. Let errors be made in any of these conditions of success, and a hospital will not fail to disclose glaring defects, such as have rendered perhaps one half of all that now exist comparatively inadequate to the ends for which they were designed. Indeed, it is only within the past thirty or forty years that the healing virtues of sunlight and air have been fully understood, and it is probably a much shorter period since any mechanical arrangements for employing them as curative agents were devised. Since this has been done, sanitary rules have undergone the greatest of revolutions. The idea has been wholly abandoned that any large building that is tolerably accessible will answer the purposes of a hospital. We have bidden farewell to isolated chambers with here and there a curtained window, and in their place have been substituted lofty pavilions, whose sides present an almost unbroken surface of glass to the rays alike of the morning and the evening sun; and long wards or continuous chambers, adjusted to a temperature sufficiently uniform, and ventilated with unfailing currents of atmospheric air that will continually replace all that is consumed by the patients and their attendants within. The languishing victim of injury or disease is thus kept under the immediate influence of Nature's own most potent medicaments, while he also receives all the aid that the highest professional science and the most practiced professional skill are able to render.

Such has been the endeavor in the work whose external completion we celebrate to-day. It is a most important step in the social progress of the State, but it has not been taken until its necessity had long been acknowledged, or until most of the States around us had set us the example. Indeed, our history shows that our works of public beneficence have scarcely kept pace either with our social needs or with our increase in wealth. For three quarters of a century the University stood alone, — the solitary public institution which Rhode Island wealth had mainly endowed. The Butler Hospital for the Insane was not begun till its necessity had been so clearly demonstrated that none presumed to question it. Other charities, more strictly local in their character and influence, have since arisen to illustrate and to promote the growing liberality of the community, until the way was at length prepared for this far greater and more comprehensive undertaking which has now been so liberally accomplished.

The need of a general hospital for the sick and the injured, in the midst of a population so largely employed in the mechanic arts, was first urged upon public attention in this city by the gentlemen of the medical profession, who, better than any others, knew how much suffering was occasioned, and how much life was lost, because there was no such institution here. In October, 1851, the Providence Medical Association appointed a committee of their fraternity to consider the subject, and to report a mode in which it might most effectually be brought to the consideration of the public. This was done at the instance of their President, Dr. Usher Parsons, our venerable friend, who to-day beholds the full accomplishment of all his benevolent plans. With the approval of the Association, they addressed a circular letter to every citizen of Providence who was assessed with a tax of one hundred dollars or more. It bore the well-known names of Usher Parsons, J. Mauran, Lewis L. Miller, Richmond Brownell, George Capron, S. A. Arnold, and C. W. Fabyan. The letter, however, was so far in advance of any general interest in its object, that it met with no effectual response. In the following year the Association, still more deeply impressed with the importance of the enterprise, addressed a petition to the City Council, to which they also obtained the signatures of many leading citizens not connected with the profession. The petition prayed that the Tockwotten estate, then as now the seat of the Reform School, should be appropriated to the uses of a hospital to be supported entirely at private expense, when subscriptions should be obtained to the amount of fifty thousand dollars. The members of the Association also offered their own gratuitous services as physicians and surgeons, in furtherance of the benevolent object they sought to accomplish. The liberal-minded gentleman[1] who then presided over our municipal affairs commended, in his annual address, the need of a hospital to the special consideration of the Council. The proposal received from them a respectful attention, and a committee was appointed to confer with the representatives of the Medical Association. The movement, however, proved to be premature. The fifty thousand dollars were not subscribed; the committee of the Council did not agree in opinion as to the propriety of diverting the Tockwotten estate from the purpose to which it had already been devoted; and the project of a general hospital passed from the consideration of the City Government, though it was still cherished in the thoughts of many a benevolent mind in the community.

The real origin, however, of the institution as it is now established, is associated with the benevolent designs of a late eminent citizen[2] who had already impressed his sound judgment, his large public spirit, and his thoughtful generosity upon nearly every social interest of his native

---

[1] Hon. James Y. Smith, then Mayor of Providence.

[2] Moses Brown Ives, who died August 7, 1857. In his will he constituted his brother, Robert Hale Ives, and his son, Thomas Poynton Ives, trustees of the bequest here mentioned.

State, and who, in the closing days of his useful and honored life, bequeathed to his trustees the sum of fifty thousand dollars, to be devoted to such objects of public beneficence as they should select. A portion of this liberal. bequest had been expended for other charities which claimed its aid, and forty thousand dollars remained for future appropriation. It was in the spring of 1863 that the two gentlemen who had been charged with this benevolent trust, believing that the time had now come for the realization of hopes which had long been cherished, decided to set apart the remainder of this bequest for the purpose with which it is now inseparably identified. It was by them that the enterprise, which had failed before, was now revived on a broader scale and with a more comprehensive design, and it was at their instance that the Rhode Island Hospital was called into existence. The eminent physicians who, twelve years before, had set forth the need of such an institution and made so earnest an appeal for its establishment, were happily all living, and, with five others added to their number, they were now invited to seek a legislative act of incorporation. They readily accepted the invitation, and immediately organized themselves for the purpose. A charter was prepared and enacted by the legislature in March, 1863, and the Rhode Island Hospital became a corporate institution of the State. Its corporators, all of whom were at first physicians, immediately directed their attention to this beautiful and salubrious site, which for three quarters of a century had been used by the people of Providence for hospital purposes. They addressed a memorial to the City Council, praying that so much of this land as was then public property might be conveyed to this corporation, to be used forever for the purposes of the new institution. The land was readily granted on the condition that the corporation should first of all secure a subscription to the amount of at least seventy-five thousand dollars. The two gentlemen, who had given the first impulse to the movement, now, in their capacity as trustees, subscribed the sum of forty thousand dollars, and as individuals they added for themselves, one twenty-five thousand dollars, and the other ten thousand dollars more. The conditions were fulfilled, and the land was immediately conveyed. A grant like this was liberal and honorable, and worthy of the city in whose name it was made; and the act of private munificence which fulfilled its conditions secured at once, as the site of this noble charity, a spot whose salubrity of situation, whose readiness of access, and whose obvious advantages of every kind, all combine to render it the most eligible that could have been chosen.

But even with this auspicious beginning, a vast labor still remained to be performed. The grand idea that animated the movement was to have a hospital of the very highest order. It had also been agreed that, out of the subscriptions, there should be set apart at least one hundred thousand dollars as a fund to aid in maintaining it. Beyond this, the whole enterprise was thus far only a benevolent purpose in a comparatively few minds for meeting a long existing social want. The design was to be elaborated and matured, and wrought into proportions that should insure its practical success. Information was to be obtained and diffused in the community, public interest was to be awakened in its behalf, and, most important of all, a sum of money, larger than had ever before been contributed for any one, I may almost say for all, of the charitable institutions in the State, was to be solicited and obtained from the bounty of our citizens. The time, too, was one of unequaled public peril and alarm. The Civil War was at the height of its grim and desolating fury, and on the day on which the books were opened, and the two earliest and largest of the general subscriptions — of twenty thousand dollars each — were made, the rebel army was entering Pennsylvania, and the bloody tide of battle seemed to be rolling to the very borders of New England. As the result however proved, it was one of those moments in history that are most favorable to every benevolent as well as to every heroic enterprise. Patriotism was kindled to its utmost fervor in behalf of the distracted republic. Our brothers and our sons were struggling and dying in our defense. Every breeze bore to us some wail of suffering from battlefields now nearer than ever before. Anxiety for the absent or sorrow for the lost was in all our homes. It was a time when, if ever, men are inspired with generous sentiments, and are ready to acknowledge the high humanities and duties that bind them to each other and to their race. It was among the compensations of that dreadful period of national suffering, that it opened new fountains of benevolence in all our hearts, and revealed to us resources which we had not thought of before for doing good to others. In the true spirit of such a time, the people of the State generously responded to the appeal which was made to them in behalf of this long delayed and much needed charity. The subscription was commenced early in July, 1863, and at the end of sixty days it had reached an amount of more than two hundred thousand dollars. This amount was soon increased to three hundred thousand dollars, and at the present time it has reached a total of three hundred and eighty thousand dollars, which has been subscribed in the cities of Providence and Newport, and in eighteen of the towns of the State. There is, I believe, no class of our citizens who have not acknowledged its claims, and are not represented in the contributions which have been made for its establishment. They have come not from the rich alone, but from the benevolent in every gradation of wealth; and among them all there are none more suggestive of the real character of this comprehensive charity than those — however small in amount — which were made by the laboring mechanics in several of our industrial establishments, and by ten of the churches of Providence, in the names of their respective ministers, to express their sympathy with this truly Christian enterprise. In addition to the subscription thus nobly carried forward, the site originally conveyed by the wise liberality of the municipal authorities has been greatly enlarged by the benevolent forethought of a few of the earliest friends of the undertaking, and provision has also been made for a still further enlargement, in case the interests of the hospital shall require it.

Nor, as we gather here to-day, can we fail to recall those benefactors who have been numbered with the dead, before its doors are opened or its work is begun. It had its origin, as has been said, in the munificent bequest of one who in his life was a leader in every enterprise of public improvement, and whose benefactions and services to Learning, Philanthropy, and Religion illustrate alike the best uses of wealth and the highest qualities of character. Death came to him while he was yet in the glory and strength of a vigorous manhood, but it did not thwart his generous purposes for the good of the community with which he was identified, and his dying legacy was designed for any great charity that should require its aid. One [1] of the physicians who, seventeen years ago, first set forth the pressing need of a hospital in this city, and who was afterwards one of the earliest members of this corporation, has passed away; and three [2] other physicians

[1] Dr. Richmond Brownell, one of the original committee of the Providence Medical Association.

[2] Dr. Ezekiel Fowler, Dr. Nathaniel Miller, and Dr. J. Davis Jones. The books thus received number about eleven hundred volumes. To these Dr. Usher Parsons has added two hundred and fifty more.

of the State, two of them dying in the prime of their
career, have bequeathed their books to its medical library
as an expression of their faith in its usefulness and its
destiny. We also gratefully reckon among its leading
benefactors another,[1] — himself long a trusted physician
here, — who, from the day when this hospital was first
proposed to the day of his lamented death, devoted to it
an almost unceasing care, and who, as chairman of its
Executive Committee for soliciting funds, brought to that
arduous work a tireless energy and zeal, and performed
in its prosecution an amount of labor which no one, and
not all even of his associates, earnest though they were,
were able to equal or to approach. And there is one
other[2] whose memory now comes back to the thoughts of
us all, radiant with the lustre that belongs to heroic patriotism and pure philanthropy. The worthy son of an
honored sire, he was associated with the earliest begin-
nings of this institution, and as one of the trustees of his
father's will he placed at its foundation the corner-stone
on which it has been built. He added his own generous
gift of ten thousand dollars; and having worn out his life
in the service of his country in her years of peril and trial,
he went abroad to seek for health which he did not find,
and died in a foreign land. But ere he left his Rhode
Island home he wrote in his will, along with other liberal
provisions for the public good, a bequest of fifty thousand
dollars for the noble charity which he had helped to
found, and of which he thus became by far the most
munificent benefactor.

1 will not attempt a delineation of this beautiful building, in whose faultless architecture massive strength and
exquisite grace are so admirably blended in securing every

---

[1] Samuel Boyd Tobey, M. D., who died June 23, 1867.

[2] Thomas Poynton Ives, Volunteer Commander in the United
States Navy, who died at Havre, France, November 17, 1865.

arrangement for convenience, and in fulfilling every requirement of sanitary law.   It will soon be officially
described by one [1] who assisted in forming its plan, and
has watched over its progress from the beginning, and
whose large acquaintance with the leading hospitals of
the world, aided by recent opportunities of inspecting
them, gives authority to his deliberate conclusion that
our own is not surpassed by any other that exists.   It is
built in accordance with the most approved models, and,
so far as is known, nothing has been omitted of all that
skill has thus far devised or experience has suggested in
providing for the best treatment of disease, and in guard-
ing against every peril that may beset a hospital.   There
is no more dangerous fallacy than that which lurks in the
suggestion that all this is not required for those who are
most likely to come here for medical treatment.   Such
a view is sanctioned neither by humanity nor wisdom.
These provisions are not for the gratification of the lan-
guid valetudinarian, but for the comfort and restoration
of the sick and the injured.   A human frame when thus
afflicted, be it that of beggar or of prince, requires substantially the same healing agencies for its cure.   Neither
medical nor surgical practice can vary much with the taste
of the patient.   The same ample air must be provided
for all.   The medicines of one must be as genuine and as
carefully prepared as those of another.   The anæsthetics
and the stimulants which are prescribed must be equally
potent and equally costly, if pain is to be assuaged, if
disease is to be baffled, and if life is to be saved.   A hospital must take the lead in all medical improvements.   Its
essential work should be thoroughly done, or it should not
be attempted.   It has, heretofore, been the aspiration of
this corporation to have a hospital building that is fully
equal to the highest standard of the age, and as nearly

[1] Thomas P. Shepard, M. D.

perfect as can now be built. Other views may hereafter prevail, and other methods may be adopted : but so long as separate wings, connected by open arcades with one central building, shall be favorable to the classification and the isolation of the sick, and to the administration incident to their treatment; so long as the light of the sun and the unadulterated air in ever-fresh supplies shall continue to be Nature's great restorers, these pavilions and wards, and these varied appointments for cleanliness, comfort, and care, can never be other than most suitable for the humane objects to which they are consecrated.

Standing at this entrance of its opening career, we anticipate with delight the blessings which this new charity will scatter along its path. They will develop and expand in ever-growing proportions through all the years of its progress. The first and most immediate recipients of these blessings will be the suffering patients who will repair to it for medical and surgical treatment. They will come from every class of our population, for the benefits of a hospital, in the present condition of society, are not for the poor and the homeless alone. It concentrates in itself medical and surgical skill, and appliances of care and treatment, such as can seldom be combined in any private practice, even at the homes of the most affluent. Many will come from their own comfortable abodes to purchase here a nursing and care, a skillful treatment and a constant watching, which elsewhere they may not be able to secure. The apprentice who has been disabled by injury, or the clerk who has been smitten with disease, will be glad to leave his narrow lodgings in boarding-house or hotel, and seek here the healing aid which would be there beyond his reach. The laborer, stricken down in the midst of his toil by some casualty on the railroad, some accident at the mill or the wharf, will be brought here without delay, to receive, if need be without money and without price, those benefits which perhaps no money or price could elsewhere purchase. This has been the history of every hospital that has truly fulfilled its benevolent design, and it cannot fail to be recorded of our own. For some it will only smooth the bed of death; but with the blessing of Heaven resting upon its agencies, it will restore health in long succession to multitudes of the sick, and send joy and gladness to families in every part of the State, that without its benignant ministry would have been clouded with the shadow of death.

Nor should we overlook the signal advantages which must accrue from this institution to the members of the medical profession, who have already evinced their interest in its founding, and pledged to it their continued cooperation and support. When the Massachusetts General Hospital was first projected, in 1810, it was claimed by those eminent physicians, Dr. James Jackson and Dr. John C. Warren, that such an institution is essential to high professional excellence. And the subsequent careers, so lately closed, of those illustrious practitioners and teachers of medical and surgical science, fully illustrate the advantages they derived from the noble hospital which they helped to found, and of which, for fifty years, they were the ornament and the strength. The hospitals of Philadelphia, New York, and Boston have made those cities centres of medical education for nearly the whole country. And with the aid of the Rhode Island Hospital, why may we not have a Rhode Island Medical School again associated with our own University, as there used to be some forty years ago? Indeed, even without any formal establishment for the purpose, the hospital will be in itself a school of practical medicine of the greatest importance to the profession. It will concentrate a knowledge of every form of disease; it will bring together the results of varied experience; it will stimulate ingenuity, and suggest improvements and discoveries. It was in our oldest New England hospital that a surgical operation was first rendered painless by the inhalation of sulphuric ether, and it was in a hospital in Edinburgh that a similar result was first secured by the use of chloroform. It is in these institutions, in all modern ages, that science and skill have won many of their most splendid triumphs in the service of suffering humanity. Nor are such benefits limited to the profession; for who of us is not the gainer, and that in large proportions, by every advantage that is afforded and every aid that is given towards forming, for the service of the community, the wise and good physician, to be our confidant and counselor, our guide and friend?

And in addition to these, there are blessings innumerable, both social and moral, that will flow to us all, and to those who come after us, from a beneficent charity like this, founded by our efforts, committed to our continual care, and appealing to us through all generations for its support. Its character and spirit are as broad as the sufferings it is designed to relieve. Though planted in Providence, and largely aided by the munificence of the city, it is designed for the people of Rhode Island, and for the wayfarer and the stranger who may seek its asylum. Benevolent citizens in twenty of our cities and towns have contributed to its founding, and to these, and others like them in every town, it must always look for its continued maintenance and efficiency. It rises here in serene beauty, the fairest structure that meets the eye within our borders. It towers above workshop and factory, above every monument of our busy industry, to remind us of that higher humanity and that Christian civilization from which it has sprung, and to which all our industry and our thrift should at last be tributary. It is not possessions but institutions, and the manner in which they are maintained and administered, that proclaim the highest character of a people. Let this hospital, then, be sustained in the spirit of that large liberality in which it has been begun ; let its every necessity be generously supplied as soon as it is known; let it live in the sympathies, the coöperation, and the services of the people of the State. Thus will it honor forever the name which it bears. Thus will it bring upon all its benefactors the grateful benedictions of multitudes ready to perish, whose sufferings have been lightened, whose limbs have been restored, and whose lives have been saved in these halls, which to-day we reverently consecrate to the service of Him who on earth delighted to heal the sick and minister to the wretched.